Goodbye
Liverpool

Anne Baker

headline

First published in 2002
by HEADLINE BOOK PUBLISHING

First published in paperback in 2002
by HEADLINE BOOK PUBLISHING

10 9 8 7

ISBN 0 7472 6778 2

Typeset in Times by Avon Dataset Ltd, Bidford-on-Avon, Warks

Printed and bound in Great Britain by
Mackays of Chatham plc, Chatham, Kent

HEADLINE BOOK PUBLISHING
A division of Hodder Headline
338 Euston Road
London NW1 3BH

www.headline.co.uk
www.hodderheadline.com

Goodbye Liverpool

Chapter One

May 1926

Josie Lunt felt on edge. She was icing the words 'Happy Birthday' on a sponge cake for her daughter's tenth birthday when her hand slipped.

'Bother! I've smudged it.' Usually Josie enjoyed cake decorating but worries were crowding in on her today.

Her daughter, Suzy, looked up from *The Wind in the Willows*, which she was reading for a second time because the library, like almost everything else, was closed.

'It's not smudged much, Mam. I think it looks lovely.' Suzy's brown eyes shone with pleasure. 'I'm hungry. I'd love a slice of it now.'

'You'll have to wait until tomorrow. The stew's ready — we're just waiting for your dad.' Josie's gaze lingered fondly on her daughter.

Suzy was tall for her age, strong and well-built. Josie believed in giving her cod-liver oil and malt regularly, and saw that she always had plenty of good food. She wanted her to have a healthier, happier childhood than she'd had herself.

She was always looking for her own likeness in her child. Nature had given them uncompromisingly straight hair and they both longed for curls. For special occasions, Josie wound Suzy's hair round rags the night before to make ringlets. For ordinary days she liked her daughter to wear her hair taken straight back from her high forehead and tied on the crown

1

with a ribbon, but all too frequently Josie couldn't spare the time to do this, or the ribbon would be lost. Left to dress on her own, Suzy would push a couple of kirby grips in to hold her hair back from her face.

Josie's perm was growing out and her straight locks now ended incongruously in tight waves, but she thought cutting them off would not improve matters. Once her hair had been the same rich nut-brown colour as Suzy's but now, at forty, a few grey hairs were beginning to show and the colour was fading.

Suzy took after her family rather than Ted's. She'd inherited too much of her grandfather's determined chin and forthright gaze to be a pretty child, but Josie hoped she'd blossom as she grew older. She herself had been considered good-looking in her youth, but now her waist was thickening from her own good cooking.

Suzy's eyes met hers. 'With Dad out on strike, will I be able to have candles on my cake?'

'Yes, love.'

For Josie, that touched a nerve. It was the strike that was bothering her. Luckily, she had candles and holders left over from last year.

Where was Ted? She went to the living-room window and looked up the street. There was no sign of him though he'd said he wouldn't be late. It was a grey overcast evening and chilly for the time of the year; the pavements glistened in the rain. She felt a shiver run down her spine.

Ted was happy in his job as a conductor with Liverpool Corporation Tramways. The thought of him being out on strike had scared them both sick. They'd been managing to make ends meet on his wage of two pounds fifteen shillings a week, augmented by Josie's wage, but it didn't give them much leeway.

Before she was married, Josie had worked as a cook in private houses. Once Suzy had started school, she'd begun working part time as a cook in the Imperial Hotel in Lime Street. Josie prided herself on being thrifty and had eighteen pounds saved up in the Liverpool Savings Bank, but with Ted on strike she feared her savings would soon be eroded.

Ted was worried too. 'I've got to strike – no choice in the matter. Everybody else at the depot is coming out.' He'd sounded desperate. 'Most are militant. They say if some of us try to work and take a tram out, they'll turn it over. They're going to block the roads too. It's not only the miners now but all transport workers, trains and buses as well as trams.'

'Dockers and printers and engineers and lots of other trades,' Josie had added. 'There's notices about it in shop windows.'

'Have we got candles? There'll be a run on them if the gas and electricity workers are coming out. It's a general strike against the Government, love. But there'll be strike pay from the trade union. They'll give us what they can.'

Josie had sighed. 'That's not the same as being able to rely on your wages.'

She'd been so sure that she and Ted would be able to pay their way. They'd moved to these comfortable rooms in Upper Parliament Street three years ago. Living here was lovely and so quiet. They'd started their married life in rooms in Sparling Street and had been kept awake by the noise of shunting from Wapping Goods Station that had gone on all through the night. They'd had billowing smoke and smells and smuts there too, and had wanted to find a better place in which to bring up Suzy.

They thought the rent here expensive at six shillings and sixpence a week but reckoned the rooms were worth it. They had the middle floor of a large Georgian terraced house. The landlord and his wife lived on the ground floor and the Rimmers, another couple with a young son, rented the floor above.

Olga Rimmer was ten years younger than Josie, pretty, with curling light brown hair and a plump face dominated by saucer-sized tawny eyes. She was friendly and so was her son, Frankie, who was in Suzy's class at school. The Lunts had made friends here and were happily settled.

They had a living room and a bedroom for her and Ted, both lovely big rooms. Best of all, they had a bathroom to themselves, though the gas stove was in it too. Josie found it strange to be doing her cooking there. The kitchen was big enough to take Suzy's bed, her chest of drawers and a chair as well as her toys. Josie had been able to curtain off Suzy's area, though it had taken yards and yards of pink material and had cost a lot. She'd had to curtain the window into Suzy's cubicle, which shut off the light from the kitchen sink, but you couldn't have everything in this life.

Josie saw this general strike taking away their financial wellbeing. Already they were feeling the pinch and she'd had to spend some of the money she'd saved. She was full of foreboding.

Ted had explained it all to her. Wages were said to have doubled since the beginning of the war, and though prices had increased, the Government was saying they were only seventy-five per cent higher. But employers were having problems making ends meet and the Government wanted to reduce wages and increase hours of work. The workers didn't think this was fair and were not going to put up with it. They meant to bring the country to a standstill.

She and Ted had talked over what they could do. He'd said: 'I'll try and get another job, one with regular hours and no shifts. Even if it doesn't pay much more I could add to my wages by working in the bar at the Imperial too.'

'Better if we weren't both there together,' Josie had replied. 'I'd rather one of us was here with Suzy.'

The school holidays had been difficult when Suzy was younger and so Josie had settled for regular hours on Friday and Saturday evenings. If Ted's shifts didn't allow him to be home, then she'd asked Olga Rimmer upstairs to keep an eye on Suzy and put her to bed.

She said: 'Suzy's nearly ten, old enough to manage on her own now. I'll work more hours. The boss is always asking me if I will.'

'I don't like you working all hours. You never stop when you're at home.'

'We'll have to see how things turn out. If I have to, then I will.'

'I do appreciate all you do for me, Josie.' Ted's eyes had been full of gentle kindliness. 'You never complain, though I don't earn much. You're always ready to help, nothing's too much . . .'

'For you it isn't.' He'd always been so loving. Forgiving, too. Not many men would have accepted a wife like her. Her father had said she was shopsoiled and would never get a decent husband, but she had. She'd had eleven wonderful years with Ted. Never once had he mentioned the affair she'd had with Ray Bissell. They hadn't spoken of it again since the night she'd told him.

Josie had been a nervous wreck at the time. She'd had to tell Ted. She'd wanted to be fair to him and have everything out in the open. She'd wanted him to know before he committed himself, but at the same time she was terrified he'd not want her when he knew. However, her fears had never been realised.

'I love you,' he'd said, 'and I want to marry you. What happened is over and done with. It has been for years, since long before we met. I shall forget it, put it out of my mind, and so should you.'

But giving birth to a son was not something Josie could put out of her mind. She'd been just eighteen. First there was the horror of trying to keep her pregnancy hidden and then the shame and the awfulness of the home for unmarried mothers.

Those memories were fading with the years. She could even find reasons to believe the mistake hadn't been all hers. She'd been sixteen when she'd first met Ray Bissell; he was her first boyfriend and he'd swept her off her feet. He'd been thirty-one, a handsome sailor who'd taken a job on the Mersey ferries so he could stay home and be near her. He'd seemed so caring and attentive. He'd talked of marriage and the home they'd set up together, but as soon as she'd told him a baby was on the way he'd abandoned her and signed up for a two-year voyage on a ship going deep sea.

There was so much from that time she wanted to forget, but it was impossible to forget the baby. She'd nursed him for six weeks and listened to what Nurse Silk and the Reverend Ingleby-Jones had had to say about the adoption process. They were united in their opinion.

'Undoubtedly much the best thing for both mother and baby. You're all young single girls – you won't be able to provide adequately, nor bring up a child properly. By accepting the adoption process, you will be giving your children two parents and a financially secure childhood in a Christian home.'

When the time came for Josie to leave the home, she felt her baby had been ripped from her arms. She'd wanted very much to keep her son, but felt unable to do so.

She'd been put out of the house where she was working as soon as her pregnancy became impossible to hide. After that, she went home to keep house for her father, her mother having died when she was a child, and she also worked in a café. Her father had refused to let her bring the child home.

'I'm not having a bastard in my house. I don't mind supporting you, but I draw the line at your bastard. I'm not bringing him up. Such a disgrace, and who's going to look after him when you're at work? Get him adopted. Get rid of him. Much the best thing.'

Josie hadn't seen any way in which she could support a baby as well as herself. She had nowhere to go, if she didn't go home to Pa. She'd had to let her baby go.

She'd called him Robert, after her father, in the vain hope that he'd relent and let her keep him. Little Robert had had such soft down on his head . . . That would have long since gone, of course. He'd been born on the first of April 1904 and she'd thought of him almost every day since and particularly on his birthday. She'd had to imagine what he was like as a boy. She hoped he was happy and had a good home. He'd be twenty-two now, a grown man.

Josie looked at the clock. It was after six. She hadn't seen Ted since his driver, Luke Palmer, had come to fetch him just after lunch.

Ted hadn't known Luke for very long. They'd been working together on the number 33 electric tramcar that travelled the route between Garston, Dingle and the Pier Head for only the last month or so.

'Luke's larger than life,' Ted had told Josie. 'Plenty of go about him. The sort who always stands up for his rights and persuades all the other workers to do the same.'

The middle classes were turning up at the depots and taking

the trams out on the road. Solicitors and accountants – they all thought they could drive a tram.

'They think it's great fun,' Ted had said, 'and they think they're doing their duty and supporting the Government by keeping the transport system running. And they're unloading ships and delivering mail and everything else.'

Luke Palmer and many of Ted's other colleagues saw that as strikebreaking and wanted to stop it. That was what they'd planned to do this afternoon.

'We'll go down to the depot and see what's going on,' Luke had said.

'Which depot?' Ted had asked. Their tram ran from the Dingle Depot but most of the trouble was in the bigger ones.

'I thought we could go down to Edge Lane. Most of the lads are going there.'

Josie was feeling more uneasy by the moment. Ted had brought home a copy of the *British Gazette*, a newspaper the Government was publishing daily, as all the national newspapers had disappeared because of the strike. She had read that there was increasing violence, that in some places police were clearing the streets of angry workers with baton charges and armoured cars.

She put the birthday cake in the cupboard that served as a larder and laid the cloth on the living-room table.

'We might as well have our tea. I can warm up Daddy's when he comes home.'

'He's coming now, Mam.' Suzy was at the front window.

'Oh good. Just in time. I'll drain the potatoes and then we'll be ready.'

'He's got that man with him, the one who came before, Mr Palmer. They're coming up.'

Josie flung open the door and rushed across the landing to look down. Ted had one hand splayed across the mahogany banister as he hauled himself up. Luke was supporting him on the other side. She could see that Ted's face was white and he was biting his lip as he climbed. At that moment, she felt all her fears explode within her.

'Ted? Are you all right? What's happened?'

He reached the living room and collapsed on his easy chair. 'I'll be all right in a minute.' He sounded out of breath. He smiled at Suzy.

'Daddy? Are you hurt?'

Josie turned on Luke. 'What's happened?'

He was twisting his cap in his hands, looking apologetic. Luke, a big man with big hands who dwarfed Ted, acted as their trade union convener.

'There was a bit of a tussle at the depot, like. Volunteers were taking out the trams. We had to stop them, didn't we? Ted got hurt in the scuffle.'

Josie was horrified. 'You've been fighting, Ted?'

'No, love, you know me.' She did: Ted would be the last person to fight.

'He got caught up in it,' Luke continued. 'He was just a bystander, got a bump on his head. Here, look, on the back. He caught his head on the tram platform as he went down. It isn't much.'

'He fell?'

'I got knocked over,' Ted told her ruefully. 'Somebody sent me flying.'

'So there was a fight?'

Luke was defensive. 'Sort of. I'm sorry but you've got to fight for what you want in this life. I don't just fight for myself, Josie, I do it for the men I work with.'

She couldn't help pursing her lips. Luke was the sort who would enjoy a fight. He had dark, almost swarthy skin; a handsome man who walked tall with his head held high. He looked like a man who was going places – not at all like Ted, who was gentle-eyed and kind.

'Ted didn't do much.'

Josie examined his wound and was reassured. It was just a graze, with a bit of swelling round it.

'Let me put a plaster on,' Suzy begged. 'That'll make you better, Daddy.'

'You can wash it,' Josie told her. 'Better without a plaster. It would stick to his hair.'

'I'll leave you, Ted,' Luke Palmer told him. 'You're in good hands now you're back with your missus. You'll come with me again tomorrow, won't you? We've all got to stick together, to stop these strikebreakers.'

'No,' Suzy burst out. 'No, Daddy, don't you go again. I'm afraid you'll get hurt. Mam's afraid you'll get hurt too.'

Luke said awkwardly: 'I'll come round tomorrow to see how you are. You can make up your mind then.'

Josie listened to his footsteps clattering downstairs.

'A clean face cloth, Suzy, and some warm water and soap. Just make sure that graze is clean.'

'Like you do my knees when I fall down?'

'That's right. Honestly, Ted, I'd have thought Luke could have done that for you. There's a washroom there, isn't there? I'll dish up our tea. The cabbage will be overcooked already. I didn't expect you to be this late.'

'What time is it, Josie? I seem to have lost track. I passed out and they put me to lie down for a while.'

'It's half six. I was worried about where you'd got to.'

'I didn't realise it was that late.'

'Does that make it feel better, Daddy?' Suzy dabbed gingerly at the graze.

'Yes, I'm all right, love.'

'Are you sure?' Josie asked.

'Just a bit of a headache.'

'An aspirin? You'll feel better when you've eaten.'

'Yes,' he agreed, but moments later he said: 'I feel a bit sick. I can't eat any tea. Sorry, love.'

Then he snatched the bowl of water from Suzy and vomited into it.

'Yuck, Dad.'

'Ted!' Josie rushed to empty the bowl in the bathroom. 'Come and lie down on the bed for a bit. You'll be better if you have a little sleep.'

Josie settled him on their bed and found him the aspirins while Suzy filled a tumbler with water. Then she dished up two helpings of the stew with cabbage and mashed potato.

'Will Daddy be all right?' Suzy asked anxiously as they ate.

Josie's own head was reeling with the same worry. She was relieved when an hour later Ted got up and came back to his chair. She warmed his meal up for him and he ate it. 'I feel better now,' he told them.

'Well enough to play cards with me, Daddy?'

Josie said: 'Not tonight, love. Daddy won't feel up to it. You read.'

'I've been reading a lot already today.'

Ted said: 'I'm all right. Get the cards out then; we'll have one game. What's it to be, snap?'

'Rummy, Daddy. That's what we played last night.'

'All right.'

'Just for half an hour,' Josie said, sitting down at the table. 'You still look white.'

'I'll be as right as rain in the morning.'

'You'll have to be, because it's my birthday,' Suzy told him. 'And you promised you'd take me to New Brighton.'

11

'So I did, but we won't be able to go, love. There's this strike on. No trams running, no trains or boats or omnibuses either.'

'I thought you said that volunteers were driving the trams?'

'They are, and the buses, but we couldn't go all the way to New Brighton. We mightn't be able to get back.'

'We'll do something,' Josie told her. 'Even if it's only to go for a walk together.'

They played for the best part of an hour and Ted won. 'I've had enough,' he yawned. 'And it's time you were going to bed, Suzy.'

Josie said: 'Shall I put rags in your hair so you'll have curls tomorrow?'

'Yes, please. Frankie says it's silly to make curls. He says he prefers straight hair like mine rather than his curls. I wish we could swap.'

Suzy didn't know what woke her up. Everything was pitch-black and she was fuzzy with sleep. The hard knots in the rags were uncomfortable when she lay on them. She lifted her head from the pillow and realised there was quite a commotion in the next room. It sounded as though there were a lot of people there, almost as if there was a party. It came again. It was her mother's voice, and she sounded terrified.

'Ted! Ted, talk to me. Wake up, will you?'

Suzy's stomach was filled with cramps as she shot out of bed. There was something very infectious about Mam being frightened.

She blinked in the brightness. Every light seemed to be on in the bedroom, the living room and on the landing. Mrs Maynard, who was married to their landlord and lived downstairs, threw her arms round Suzy and tried to lead her back to her bed in the kitchen.

Suzy fought to free herself. 'Let me go. Let me go. Mam?'

'Come back to bed. Your mam will come and see you in a minute.'

'Ted, oh, Ted!' she heard her mother scream.

Suzy responded to her mother's panic, twisting free and shooting back to the living room. There were ambulance men there, lifting Daddy's lifeless body on to a stretcher.

'Daddy!' Suzy's terror boiled over. It was her mother's face that truly frightened her. Tear-stained and anguished, she was crying noisily like a child. 'Where are they taking him?'

'To hospital, love.'

Mam put her arms round her then. Once the stretcher had gone, Olga Rimmer from upstairs made a pot of tea. Suzy shared Mam's chair at the table. Once the neighbours went, Mam led her back to her bed and got under the bedclothes with her. Suzy could feel her body shaking with sobs.

'Daddy lost consciousness. I thought he was just asleep but I couldn't wake him.'

'Won't he wake up in the morning?' Though Suzy knew before she asked that he wouldn't. She knew everything had changed for them.

'No, love, I don't think so.' She heard the sob in Mam's throat. 'He'd stopped breathing before the ambulance came. Do you understand what I'm saying?'

Suzy felt the tears burning her eyes. 'Daddy's dead?'

Chapter Two

Suzy woke up to find her mother looking down at her with red and swollen eyes. She'd never seen Mam so upset before, and her stomach churned. That Daddy had died in the night came instantly back to her mind.

'Suzy, love ... If only I could wish you a happy birthday . . .'

'It can't be, not this one.' With Daddy gone that was impossible. Impossible to think of anything else today.

'Why did Daddy die? I mean, what made him die? He seemed all right when I was getting ready for bed.'

She heard her mother catch her breath. 'I don't know either, love. Not really. Unless he had a heart attack. I've heard of people dying suddenly with that.'

Mam was making a big effort; taking the rags out of her hair and combing it round her fingers to make ringlets. Suzy watched her in the mirror.

'You look lovely,' Mam assured her. It was the way Suzy looked on the special days in her life, her birthday look.

She felt too sad to have a birthday. Mam could do nothing but cry. Neighbours kept coming and going, all trying to be sympathetic, but they were making Mam worse. It seemed almost an afterthought when, in the late morning, Mam took her by the hand and led her to the bedroom she'd shared with Daddy. She felt in her wardrobe and brought out a parcel.

Suzy knew what it was; she unwrapped it carefully. 'A lovely new dress.' It was of crisp cotton and had blue flowers on a white background.

'For the summer.'

Mam had made it for her. Once the main pieces were tacked together, Suzy had had to try it on to make sure it would fit. It had been all pins and loose threads then. Now it was finished and neatly pressed.

'It's lovely, Mam. Thank you.'

'Daddy made something for you too.' From under the bed Mam brought out a pair of stilts. 'Daddy thought you wouldn't mind that they weren't wrapped. They'd take so much paper.'

Suzy was blinking hard as she ran her hand over the smooth, beautifully varnished wood.

'I didn't see him make them. I didn't know . . .'

'He couldn't make them here and, anyway, he wanted them to be a surprise. He made them round at his friend's house. You've heard him talk of Wally Simpson?'

Suzy tried to swallow the lump in her throat.

'Daddy saw some stilts in Bunney's window last Christmas and thought they'd be just the thing for you. He was sure you'd like them.'

'I do. I love them.' Suzy hugged them to her.

'Something new for you to play with.'

She didn't feel like playing this morning and she'd never dare play with these. She didn't want them to be anything less than perfect because Daddy would never make anything else for her.

'Where is he now?' she asked her mother.

'At the hospital, like I told you. They have to find out why he died so suddenly.'

Nothing could be the same ever again. Despite the new dress and the stilts, Suzy had never felt so low. She'd had a happy childhood. Her father had loved both her and her mother, but all that had gone.

* * *

Josie felt in a total ferment. Normality had gone for good. She hardly knew what to do with herself. Suzy was clinging to her skirt and looking woebegone.

They were dusting the living room when the little girl asked: 'Mam, if you died too, what would happen to me? Who would look after me?'

That brought Josie out in goose pimples. It echoed her own terrible insecurity. She'd flopped down on the couch and pulled Suzy down beside her to give her a hug. If Ted could die so suddenly and silently so might Suzy – so might she. She felt that any minute the same thing could happen again. What was there to stop it? Josie knew she had to take a grip on herself.

She said with as much confidence as she could muster: 'I'm not going to die. I'll be taking care of you until you're grown up.'

'How can you be sure? You didn't know about Daddy. He didn't either, I'm sure he didn't. He'd have told us if he had, wouldn't he? How d'you know it won't happen again?'

Josie didn't know. Cold shivers ran down her spine. 'I just know. Nothing is going to happen to me. The trouble is, there'll be just the two of us. We won't have Daddy.'

Suzy cried then. She hadn't cried in the night and it had bothered Josie that she was bottling up her feelings. Suzy had thought the world of her father. Tears should bring release. For herself, she'd cried so much already, but still felt on the brink of tears all the time.

Ted was proud of having been employed on the Liverpool Corporation Tramways for fifteen years. He got on well with the other conductors and drivers. He'd told Josie about the rest times they had in the canteen at the depot, where they all got to know each other.

She knew several of the conductors. They wouldn't accept a fare from her when she travelled into town to work. If an inspector got on unexpectedly they would come up smiling and give her a ticket, but usually she travelled without. They were a good crowd and looked after each other where they could.

Ted would have liked to have spent more of his precious leisure time with them, but Josie had had to work and, now it was too late, she resented the time she'd spent cooking at the hotel while he was at home looking after Suzy. He hadn't wanted her to do it, but she'd felt she had to add to the family income.

She and Ted had talked it over many times. Now Suzy was getting older Josie had been thinking about trying to get a job in a canteen or café that did lunches only. The long school holidays had stopped her doing that before. That and the fact that she enjoyed cooking dinner at the Imperial Hotel two nights each week. She liked her fellow workers, and the boss let her take leftover food home. She and Ted had often eaten a good supper when she'd got home, and frequently there were bits for lunch the next day.

She heard the front doorbell ring, and a moment or two later Mrs Maynard called: 'Are you there, Josie? It's someone for you.'

She could see Luke Palmer, cheerful and smiling, standing at the open door as she went slowly downstairs.

'How's Ted this morning? Better, I hope, and ready to come and do his bit?'

That brought stinging tears to her eyes again. She was full up and hardly able to speak. 'He's dead.' She swallowed. 'Died in the night.'

Luke's mouth dropped open. The shock and horror on his face made her feel worse.

'What happened?'

'Come up. I'll tell you.'

He took her hand sympathetically. 'How awful. Poor Ted. Poor you too. It must be dreadful for you.'

Josie was weeping openly; she couldn't help it. Luke's arm went round her shoulders in a hug, but she broke free and stumbled upstairs.

In the living room, Suzy was still nursing her new stilts. Her eyes were unwelcoming when she saw Luke.

His tone was authoritarian. 'You're Suzy, aren't you? Your dad told me about you. Make a cup of tea for your mother, will you?'

She scurried off obediently but Josie saw the flare of resentment. Poor Suzy – she was hurting too.

'Make a cup of tea for us all, please, love,' she added.

Josie did her best to explain what had happened, but she wished she knew more. That the reason for Ted's death seemed something of a mystery made it all the more upsetting.

The ambulance man had said: 'He's stopped breathing. I'm afraid he's already dead. We'll take him to the morgue. There'll have to be a post mortem to find the cause.'

Not to know why . . . It took away every last feeling of normality, of safety.

Luke stayed quite a long time. He was clearly upset too.

'A terrible thing to happen. Ted said he wasn't hurt bad. I'd have taken him to hospital if I'd known . . . I hope you don't think it's my fault.'

Josie blamed herself. She wanted to shut herself away in her bedroom where she could have peace to think of Ted. Luke had no sooner gone than Olga Rimmer from upstairs came down with two plates of hotpot on a tray.

'I'm sure you don't feel like cooking, but you must both eat.'

She was looking at Suzy and that made Josie feel guilty. She hadn't given the first thought to making a meal for her daughter. There was a bank of sympathy in Olga's tawny eyes, but Josie felt she couldn't face any more of it.

'Do you still want me to bring Frankie down at tea time? I know you asked us but—'

'Yes,' Josie said quickly. 'Do come.' That it was Suzy's birthday was making things ten times harder. 'Better if we stick to what we planned. Besides, I've made a cake and scones and jelly in paper cases . . . Poor Suzy, she's having a horrible birthday.' And worse, every future birthday would remind them both of this melancholy day. Josie ached inside.

Olga and Frankie came promptly at four o'clock as arranged. Josie saw Suzy smile for the first time that day as Frankie gave her a birthday card and a bar of chocolate. He also brought a new card game down of his own, and they began to play.

Josie had planned this little celebration for the four of them with afternoon tea and cakes. She'd intended them to sing 'Happy Birthday to You' before Suzy blew out her candles. Then, when Ted came home at six they'd have high tea and afterwards she'd relight the candles and they'd have what remained of the birthday cake for afters.

Now she decided against singing at all. It wasn't a happy birthday and nothing could make it so. No candles either. They'd keep until next year.

Luke Palmer was shaking. It had come as such a shock; the last thing he'd expected to hear. Ted Lunt was dead!

Once outside Ted's house, the tea he'd drunk rose in his throat and he had to stand still on the pavement, taking great gulps of air. This on top of everything else. As if he hadn't enough troubles. God, he needed a proper drink; he'd have to find a pub.

It wasn't his fault. Nobody could blame him for what had happened. Yes, he'd had to persuade Ted to go with him to the depot. He'd had to persuade all the lazy good-for-nothings to get off their backsides and do something to help the cause. Ted would have sat back at home if he hadn't fetched him to do his share. He should have known Ted wasn't the sort to look after himself; he couldn't see trouble coming and get out of the way. Truly, he'd been a bit dozy. This was his own fault.

Luke staggered blindly down the street, almost bumping into an old woman in black with a shawl drawn close about her head and shoulders – a Mary Ellen they called them round here.

He could hardly believe Ted was dead! He'd been planning to take him down to the Pier Head this morning. There'd been plenty of action there yesterday. An urchin kicking a tin can ran into his legs, but Luke was so shaken, he couldn't even swear at him.

Here was a pub, the door was standing open – the Flag and Sailor; it would do. He stumbled into the public bar and had to push his way through the crowd to order a double brandy. The talk all round him was of the General Strike. This private landlord was making good money out of it. The voices drummed in Luke's ears. He felt the warmth of the brandy running down his throat, then steadying his head and settling his stomach. What a thing to happen!

He'd always been a little envious of Ted. He'd spoken with such contentment of his little family and his nice home. Luke had liked the look of Josie when they'd first come face to face yesterday. He'd thought her caring and affectionate to Ted. Not a beauty any more, but he bet she had been in her youth.

Today, there'd been a quiet dignity about her, though she was clearly devastated by Ted's death.

Luke ordered another brandy into his glass and a bottle of whisky to take home; he scuffed his boot into the sawdust on the floor while he waited. Everything was going wrong for him. His life was in chaos. Ida, the bitch, had walked out on him last week. She knew how much he dreaded being left by himself, but she no longer cared what happened to him. Women were like that. They used him for their own ends. Women always had. He felt left in the lurch, rejected. He was having to scrape together his own meals and there was nobody to take care of the washing. Nobody to warm his bed either.

He'd needed a drink or two to get through the days that followed, but the boss had called him into the office and given him a warning. He'd accused him of being on duty the worse for drink. It was a gross exaggeration. He'd had one beer, just one beer. Nobody was the worse for drink on one beer. He'd had to have it to help him through the morning. The boss picked on him. He'd sent him home before the end of his shift and docked his pay. The gaffer knew where to put his foot in to hurt him. This strike was a godsend. It was giving him a break. Nobody needed that more.

Damn Ida, she was nothing but an idle trollop anyway. He'd find someone else. Someone better. Someone who'd really appreciate him. He'd break Ida's neck if he could get his hands on her. He'd told her that several times. No doubt, she'd take good care to stay out of his way.

He thought about Josie, bowed with grief at the moment, but yesterday, he'd quite fancied her. He ought to do something to help her. He hoped the crowd at the tram depot weren't going to say Ted's death was his fault. It certainly wasn't – his conscience was quite clear on that – but he usually got the blame for things that went wrong.

Luke felt all the fight had been knocked out of him by Ted's death. He'd go home instead of going to the Pier Head. He bought himself some fish and chips for his dinner on the way. His mouth was watering with the succulent smell but with the whisky under his arm it was impossible to unwrap his newspaper parcel and start eating.

He pushed open his front door and let himself into his fetid living room. The window was jammed. Ida had told him she couldn't get it open, and he'd been meaning to do something about it for some time. It was a miserable dump – he'd never been able to get Ida to do much cleaning. She'd been lazy, and she'd also been a tight-fisted bitch who wouldn't hand over any of the money she'd earned. The place seemed worse than usual after looking at Ted's living room.

He poured himself a whisky, threw himself into his sagging armchair and ate his fish and chips. He was hungry – he'd had no breakfast because there was nothing to eat in the house. It was awful having no woman rushing to put a filled plate on the table in front of him. He didn't think he'd ever get used to living alone.

As a child he'd been hungry: his mother hadn't cared whether she fed him or not. She'd been just as rejecting as Ida. And Leila before her.

It was easily the worst birthday Suzy had ever had, and the next day wasn't any better. She wanted Mam to go out for a walk with her. Mam wasn't keen but she'd almost persuaded her when that Mr Palmer came round again.

There was something about Mr Palmer that gave Suzy the shivers. He had a big, big nose that wasn't completely straight – the sort of nose you noticed before you saw anything else of his face. Suzy didn't like him. It was his fault Daddy had been killed.

Now she was taking a second look, he was taller and broader and stronger than Daddy had been; a huge man, a giant of a man. When she'd described him like that to Mam last night, she'd said: 'He's a gentle giant.'

But that wasn't how Suzy saw him. He seemed anything but gentle. His hair was almost black, his skin swarthy; but it was his eyes that really scared her. Everything else about him was large but his eyes were small and deeply hooded and flashed with dark anger.

They were eyes that could bore into her, they followed her around the room; the sort of eyes that had the power to see her even when she took refuge from them in the kitchen. They seemed to see right into her mind.

Luke Palmer knew how she felt about him – not exactly scared, but apprehensive about the power he had. He had the will and the strength to hurt her and hurt Mam. Suzy was tall for her age but he made her feel weak and puny.

Big Nose had brought several packages with him. Suzy thought at first they were belated birthday presents for her. Mam had told him yesterday that it was her birthday when she'd taken three cups of tea on a tray into the living room for them. But Mr Palmer was giving the packages to Mam. She was opening them up. He'd brought eggs and cheese and butter.

'Thank you, Luke.'

'I was afraid you might be short. With Ted, you know . . .'

'We're going to be very short. It's kind of you.'

Suzy couldn't understand why Mam sat talking to him like this. He stayed until Mrs Rimmer came down from upstairs with a pie for their dinner.

When they'd eaten it and cleared away, Suzy asked Mam to go to the park for a walk, but Mam shook her head. Suzy couldn't remember a time when Mam had refused to do things with her like this.

* * *

Josie felt half paralysed over the next few days and hardly knew what she was doing. Ted's death had ripped her life apart.

And the General Strike, over which the tramway workers had so worried and fought, had collapsed after nine days and had achieved nothing. Only the miners were still out. Everybody said they were glad to see the country functioning again as it should, but Josie blamed the strike for Ted's death and felt very bitter about it.

Anger was beginning to boil up inside her. Why did it have to be her Ted? She couldn't believe that he'd died so silently, so suddenly. He'd been quiet in life and quiet in death too, but a wonderful man – a loving and caring husband and father. They'd been such a happy family. The circumstances in which he'd died made everything worse.

Josie was told she'd have to attend the Coroner's court inquest and answer questions. She was dreading it.

'I'm dreading it too,' Luke told her. 'I've been told to attend as well. I'll call for you and we'll go together.'

Josie sent Suzy to school that day and arranged with Olga Rimmer to keep an eye on her if she was home before her.

Luke came to collect her promptly, and Josie was glad she didn't have to attend by herself. The bosses from the tramway service were seated in the court when they arrived. Luke pointed them out to her. Josie didn't know them except by name. Ted had kept his home life and his work apart as most good husbands did.

She heard then that two other men had been hurt at the same time as Ted. Both were called to the witness stand; both described the fracas that had taken place as 'a running battle'. They said they were volunteers, trying to take a tram out to maintain the service, when a crowd blocked the tramlines.

They'd had to stop, and the crowd, thought to be mainly of militant employees of Liverpool Corporation Tramways, had boarded the tram and attacked them with clubs and stones and broken bottles.

They were hauled bodily off the tram and were hurt. Then one of the managers had sent for an ambulance and they'd been taken to hospital. One had suffered a broken arm, and the other cuts and grazes.

Josie's head swam with grief when she heard that. Why hadn't they taken Ted to hospital too?

Luke was called next. He spoke clearly, with great confidence. He denied there had been much of a fight, describing it as 'just a skirmish'. Ted had accidentally been thrown off balance and had banged his head as he'd fallen. It had knocked him out but Ted had said he was all right and didn't seem much hurt. He'd had a nose bleed but that hadn't lasted long. Ted had said he didn't want to go to hospital, he didn't think it was needed. Luke had taken him home.

Then Josie was called. It was all she could do to keep her tears under control. She agreed that Ted didn't seem badly hurt and described his wound as minor. When questioned, she said he'd seemed much as usual though he'd had a headache and had vomited. Four hours after he came home, when they were getting ready to go to bed, he'd complained of seeing double and having funny shapes before his eyes, and his breathing had seemed irregular. Once in bed, she'd thought he was settling down to sleep and had tried to sleep herself. Suddenly, she'd realised he wasn't breathing at all and when she tried to wake him, she couldn't. Then she'd panicked.

She was in tears when she sat down. It was Luke who pressed a clean handkerchief into her hand and patted her arm to comfort her.

A doctor was called next. Josie tried hard to concentrate on what he was saying. 'The post mortem showed massive internal bleeding into the brain which was commensurate with the injuries as had been described.

'Following a head injury, a patient can have massive internal bleeding without any external bleeding wounds on the head. And bleeding under the skull can begin immediately after the injury is sustained, or it can be delayed for several hours, as would appear to have been the case in this instance. Mr Lunt should have been taken straight to hospital.'

That floored Josie. She gasped at Luke: 'He needn't have died?'

The Coroner asked the same question of the doctor.

'I'm not saying it would have been possible to save Mr Lunt's life. Not every case of head injury can be saved, but he would have stood a chance if he'd received medical attention.'

'If only you'd taken him to hospital,' she whispered to Luke. 'If only . . .'

'I would have done, if I'd known,' Luke mourned. 'I didn't think it was needed. Ted said he was all right. If you'd asked me to take him to hospital I would have done. I didn't know.'

She could see Luke was as shocked as she was.

'You know I'd do my best for Ted. He was a mate.'

She couldn't blame Luke – after all, she hadn't done what was needed either.

'If only . . . I should have called the doctor.'

She'd done nothing when Ted needed help. She blamed herself. She'd let him down. She'd let him die.

A verdict of accidental death was given. Josie felt numb inside as she went out into the sunshine.

'Are you all right?' Luke seemed concerned. He took her home on the tram and saw her inside the front door.

'I'll come and see you tomorrow,' he said, taking her hand in his.

'No need,' she gulped. 'I'll be all right.'

Concerned eyes were studying her. 'That's what Ted said.'

At three o'clock the following afternoon, Josie was just about to take Suzy shopping when Luke called again. This time he had two colleagues of Ted's with him, whom Josie knew by sight. He introduced them as Pat Rankin and Wally Simpson. Ted had talked a lot about his friend Wally.

'If there's anything I can do to help,' he murmured. He had carroty coloured hair and the sort of mouth that always seemed to have a slight smile.

Josie wasn't pleased to see them, but since they were already up on the landing, she felt she had to ask them into the living room. She didn't feel up to coping with more visitors and was impatient when the usual small talk started: How was she? How shocked and sorry they all were at the tram shed to hear about Ted. Everybody sent their condolences . . .

Suzy was already wearing her hat and coat. She sat down with them, swinging her legs and clearly looking as though she wanted them gone. Luke put the large manila envelope he'd brought on the table and pushed it towards Josie.

'We had a whip-round for Ted,' he said awkwardly. 'And there's a contribution from Trade Union funds. Some wanted to buy a wreath or flowers, but I thought you'd find the money more useful. A lass like that,' he nodded towards Suzy, 'is an expensive item.'

Josie was struggling for self-control again. 'You're so kind . . .' She was contrite because she hadn't wanted to ask them in. 'Yes, I'm worried about money. Thank you. Thank everybody for me. I'm very grateful.'

They didn't stay long. As soon as they were clattering downstairs she tipped the contents of the envelope out on the table and Suzy helped her count the coins into piles.

'Fifteen pounds, three shillings and four pence,' Suzy said. 'Such a lot. That'll keep us going for a long time, won't it?'

'Yes, quite a long time.' Josie was relieved as well as grateful. It put the wolf further away from her front door. 'But not for ever.'

The day of the funeral was another terrible day. Luke had arranged to be at the Lunts' flat when the hearse arrived at the front door. He escorted Josie and Suzy in the car following behind for the main mourners. Josie's eyes felt sore and they were permanently red-rimmed and watery. The church was packed with men from the Corporation Tramways. Luke was introducing them but she couldn't concentrate. Suzy was holding her hand in a steel-like grip.

'Mr Hopkins, our boss,' Luke told Josie. A hand was offered, she knew she took too long to see it and respond.

'So sorry, Mrs Lunt. Such a sad accident. Come and see me in the office in a day or two when you're feeling better. We'll be able to help a little – the funeral expenses at least.'

'Thank you.' Josie felt like a zombie but, even so, the promise of money lifted her a little.

Olga Rimmer had helped her prepare sandwiches and tea for those who came back to their rooms: Wally Simpson and his wife, together with Luke Palmer and the neighbours. It wasn't the sort of send-off she wanted to give Ted, but somehow she couldn't get herself moving; couldn't make the effort to do more. Ted's death had knocked the stuffing out of her.

She'd been worried about losing Ted's wages while he was out on strike and now she'd lost them for ever. Lost Ted too, which was much, much worse. She'd had eleven contented years with him and his death left her feeling insecure and helpless. She had no idea how she was going to manage. She'd relied on Ted – depended on him; he'd been her life. But she had Suzy to think of. She must pull herself together for her sake.

By the next day the weather had changed. The brilliant sunshine cheered Josie and made her feel stronger. She had to think about their future. The real problem would be earning enough money for them to live on.

She didn't want to leave Upper Parliament Street, but it was expensive and she wouldn't be able to earn as much alone as they had when Ted was earning too.

When they'd moved here three years ago, she'd saved twenty pounds as a cushion and she'd taken out two pounds to buy curtain material for Suzy's cubicle. Since Ted's death, Suzy had moved into his place in Josie's bed, and the curtains were drawn right back to let the light into the kitchen, but there were plenty of other things they still needed.

Ted had wanted a wireless. He'd been saving up and also reading up on how to build a crystal set. He'd said he could buy the parts for sixteen shillings. Luxuries like that were out of the question now. Over a lunch of scrambled eggs on toast Josie talked to Suzy about the future.

'I shall have to get a full-time job, love, though I don't like leaving you alone.'

'I'm ten, old enough now, Mam.'

'Not every night. Evening work won't do.'

'Auntie Olga says I can go up and play with Frankie any time.'

'Not every night, I'd rather you didn't. Up to now I've paid her.'

'Paid her? I didn't know . . .'

'When Daddy had to do a late shift and we were both out, she gave you your tea and saw you into bed. She has to make ends meet too.'

Suzy looked so fiercely strong. 'There's no need for that now. I can get myself something to eat and put myself to bed. I could get a job too.'

Josie had to smile at that. 'You're too young. You can't leave school until you're fourteen. I wouldn't want you to.'

'I could do shopping for people, or look after other children.'

'Ten is too young. Nobody would want you to look after their children. They'd say you need looking after yourself.'

'There must be something I could do. We'll manage somehow, Mam. We'll be all right together. I'll look after you when I'm bigger.'

'I know you will, love.'

Suzy was a delightful child. Josie was very lucky to have her. Losing her son had made her possessive about Suzy, wanting to hang on to her tightly and keep her extra safe.

She made up her mind that from now on, her aim in life would be to keep a roof over their heads; to keep Suzy happy, well fed and warmly dressed. She couldn't bear to be parted from her, not ever. She'd been parted from Robert so soon after he was born and he probably wasn't even called Robert now. She couldn't have that happen again.

After they'd washed up and cleared away, Josie said: 'Let's go out. I'll buy some liver and onions for tea. We'll call at the newsagent's on the way and stop that monthly magazine that Daddy ordered.'

'The one about wireless? How to build your own crystal set?'

'Yes, and I'll get a newspaper to see if there are any daytime jobs advertised for cooks.'

'And then can we take a tram down to the river and walk along the shore? We could pick up driftwood for the fire.'

'I think it's warm enough to do without a fire tonight.'

'It won't always be.'

'You're right.' Suzy was looking ahead too.

Chapter Three

Suzy was looking out the shopping bags when the doorbell rang. They needed the biggest ones to gather driftwood and two carrier bags too. She heard heavy footsteps cross the landing and her spirits sank.

'It's Uncle Luke, Suzy.' Her mother sounded more cheerful than she had for ages. He was coming so often that Mrs Maynard knew him now and just sent him up.

'Hello, how are you?' Suzy didn't like the way he took her mother's hand in his and held on to it for a long time. 'I've brought some meat for you. I hope you like lamb?' He had a brown-paper carrier bag full of packages.

'Yes, love it.'

With a heavy heart Suzy watched her mother unpack what he'd brought and open up the parcels. Mam was pleased, she could see. Giving her presents of food was his way of getting Mam to like him. It was despicable.

'Look, Suzy, cream cakes. What a treat, a whole box of them. Luke! How can I thank you? Lovely lamb chops and so many of them – far more than we'll be able to eat. Six big ones.'

'I wasn't sure whether Suzy would be able to eat more than one.'

'So generous of you. Suzy eats as much as I do. She can eat two. Luke, you must stay and have your tea with us. There'll be plenty here for us all.'

Suzy froze. She was afraid it was what Luke had intended Mam to say. He was pushing in on them and she didn't like it, didn't like him either.

'Were you going out?'

Suzy fumed. Surely he could see they were? Mam had her hat on – the new black cloche one, pulled down tight so no hair showed. Mam didn't look at all nice in it. She said it was mourning, that she had to wear black to show she was missing Daddy.

When Suzy had first started school, she could see that her mam was not like the other mothers who'd clustered round the school gate when it was time to go home. It took her a long time to decide why. It wasn't that she was less pretty than the others because mothers can be anything from beautiful to plain. Her mam had a faded prettiness, but she was different because she was older than the others.

Suzy hoped Big Nose wasn't going to come with them, spoiling the lovely walk.

'Yes, but I won't need to buy the liver.' Mam was frowning in concentration.

'You wanted to go to the newspaper shop,' Suzy prompted mutinously.

'I'll need to get more vegetables too.'

It was turning out in exactly the way Suzy wanted to avoid. Nosey was taking all Mam's attention for himself. Suzy felt cut out and on her own. She trailed behind them and hated the way he took her mother's arm.

She didn't go inside the newspaper shop with them but stood reading the notices pinned up in the window. Often they had toys for sale, dolls' prams and bikes.

A large card caught her eye and she began to read:

Reliable boys required for daily newspaper deliveries,
mornings and evenings, as well as weekends.
Minimum age twelve.
Good wages.

Suzy wanted to laugh out loud. Why hadn't she thought of being a newspaper girl? It said boys, but girls could do it just as well. She could do it. She was only ten but she was big for her age. She was the biggest in her class at school. She looked twelve, everybody said so. Her heart was pounding at the idea.

Frankie had talked of getting a paper round when he was old enough. Well, she'd beat him to it, if she could. Mam wouldn't need to be pleased with Mr Palmer's presents. She'd be able to help Mam buy food.

She wanted to rush into the shop and ask about the job. How much was good wages? But she couldn't do it in front of Mam. She'd be bound to say: 'You have to be twelve before you can do that. However eager you are, Suzy, you're only ten.'

Suzy made up her mind to come back on her own later. It was only a hundred yards or so from the end of their street. It would be ideal if only they'd take her on.

They took a tram to Otterspool and Suzy trailed behind her mother and Nosey along the shore. The tide was on the ebb and had left a thick line of pebbles encrusted with bottles and tins, bits of wood, old galoshes and smelly seaweed.

There were rich pickings to be had. Suzy filled the bags with anything that would burn. She'd done this often enough on a winter's day with Daddy. There were pieces of solid heavy wood that would keep the fire dancing with flames for ages, and bits of packing cases that made good firelighters. Flotsam, Daddy had called it, thrown overboard from the ships in the river. Once dried out it would make a good fire. Suzy felt buoyed up with the thought of doing a newspaper round and helping Mam, but this outing was turning out just as she'd supposed: Nosey talking to Mam the whole time and neither of them picking up any wood or taking any notice of her. As soon as they reached home, Mr Palmer was taking over.

'How about putting the kettle on, Suzy? Your mam would like a cup of tea and she needs a sit-down after that long walk.'

Suzy bristled as she made a pot of tea. What he really meant was that *he* felt like a cup of tea. When he asked like that, Mam thought he was thinking of her. It was so obvious, but Mam couldn't see what he was like.

When Suzy took the tea to the living room, he said: 'Can you scrape new potatoes, Suzy? Are you clever enough to do that? It would help your mam a lot.' How she resented the smarmy way he spoke to her.

'I often peel our potatoes,' she told him frostily.

'Suzy's a great help to me.' Her mother was smiling up at him. Mam liked him! Suzy couldn't understand how she could.

Suzy stood at the kitchen sink scraping potatoes and listening to the murmur of the voices from the next room. Mam had taken the green beans he'd brought and they were chopping them together on the living-room table. She thumped the pan down on the gas stove in the bathroom and ran downstairs. She was going to the newspaper shop now. Mam would never miss her with Mr Palmer in the house. She was beginning to rely on him. Suzy had to make him unnecessary to her mother.

'We've never had a girl before,' the shopkeeper said, looking doubtful. 'Can you get up early in the mornings?'

'Yes, and I'm very reliable and I live just round the corner in Upper Parliament Street.'

'How old are you?'

'I had my birthday last week. I'm twelve.'

There were delicious sweets all round her in bottles and in

open boxes on the counter. The place smelled lovely, a mixture of chocolate, liquorice, tobacco and fresh newsprint.

She asked: 'How much do you pay?'

'Four shillings to start, if you do night and morning. Four and six after three months if you're reliable. What's your name?'

'Suzy Lunt.'

'You're not . . .?'

'Yes, my dad was killed in the General Strike.'

'We read about it in the paper. He was a customer . . . It must have been terrible for you and your mam.'

'Can I have the job? We need the money, you see.'

'A month's trial to see how you get on. We start everybody that way. You've got to be punctual. People don't like waiting for their papers.'

'Right.'

'And you'll have to get this form signed by your mother. It's to give her permission for you to do it and to confirm your age.'

Suzy's heart sank. Mam wouldn't like saying she was twelve when she wasn't. 'Right.'

'Bring it back as soon as you can, and you can start. Tomorrow if you like.'

Suzy went slowly home feeling deflated. She was afraid Mam wouldn't let her do the job after all. As she came up the stairs to the landing, there was a lovely smell of lamb chops cooking. Both her mother and Luke Palmer were standing at the gas stove in the bathroom.

'Have you been out, Suzy?' Mam asked.

So she had missed her. 'Yes, I can get a job as a newspaper girl, if only you'll sign this form. I can start tomorrow.'

Nosey threw back his head and guffawed with delight.

'She's got a bit of go in her, this one. That's what I call initiative.'

Suzy smiled. Perhaps after all it was not wrong to lie about your age. 'I saw the notice in the window when we went this afternoon, I thought . . . Well, Frankie was talking of getting a newspaper round and—'

'You've got to be twelve.' Mam sounded shocked.

'I told them I was twelve,' Suzy said defensively. 'I can do the job, I know I can. It's delivering in the streets all round here. Why do I need to be twelve to do that?'

'It's a by-law. It says so here.'

'Mam, I want to do it. Who's to know? I look twelve.'

Old Nosey gave another guffaw. 'She does, Josie. I'd let her do it. It could be the making of her.'

'But she's only—'

'If you're working, Mam, wouldn't I be better off working too, instead of playing with Frankie?'

'Course you would,' Nosey agreed. 'Hard work never hurt anyone, Josie.'

Suzy enjoyed her meal. It was the best she'd had for ages, better than anything on her birthday. She was fizzing with triumph and felt that perhaps she'd misjudged Mr Palmer.

Josie wrote a note to Mr Hollis at the Imperial Hotel to let him know she'd be coming in to work as usual on Friday and Saturday. She still felt raw but knew he'd be understanding. He'd sent a wreath and come with some of the staff to Ted's funeral. Josie had missed her two nights' work last week and felt she couldn't afford to miss any more.

She was in the hotel kitchen making mock turtle soup when he came down to see her. Mr Hollis's head was bald and rose dome-like from a thin edging of mouse-brown hair; he was portly and dapper.

'I didn't expect you to rush back like this, Josie.'

'I'm all right,' she sighed. 'Quite capable of working. I need the money.'

He went to a tray of bread rolls that had been made earlier, broke one in half and bit into it. Mr Hollis wore a dinner suit and black bow tie until evening, when he always changed into tails and striped trousers to make the Imperial Hotel seem a sophisticated place to stay while doing business in the city.

'Do you want more hours? You know I'm always looking for cooks.'

'I do, but I don't want to leave Suzy on her own more than I have to. It's wrong, when she's upset about losing her dad.'

'You could work two full days. Do every meal.'

'Not on Saturdays when she's home. And even then . . . well, I'm the only breadwinner now, so that wouldn't be enough. What I'd really like to do is breakfasts and lunches.'

He thought for a moment. 'I think perhaps that could be arranged. Bernard says he's tired of getting up early six days a week.' Bernard was another cook who'd worked there for a long time. 'He wants to do more dinners.'

'I wouldn't mind getting in early. It would suit me, but I couldn't do Saturdays. I'm sorry, only five mornings.'

'Let me talk to him, see what I can set up.'

'You're very kind.'

'I have to keep the staff happy. You've been reliable, Josie. Always turned in when you're expected.'

'Until last week . . .'

He shrugged. 'Understandable.'

By the following week it was all arranged. Josie would do breakfasts and lunches five days a week. She'd have to be at work by seven thirty, as they started serving breakfasts by eight. Lunches were served up to two o'clock, and after she'd seen that the kitchens were cleaned, she could go home. She was to be paid thirty-five shillings a week.

Josie thought it would fit in quite well. She and Suzy got up together at six o'clock. She made a breakfast of porridge or bread and milk before Suzy set off on her paper round.

Then she poured a tumbler of milk and cut a sandwich which she left between two plates for her to eat when she came home from school at dinner time. Olga had offered to give her a meal with Frankie, and though that would have been more pleasant for Suzy, Josie couldn't afford to pay Olga, and to accept would be sponging on her.

Wally Simpson was a conductor on the number 4 route, the tram that took her to Lime Street, and if she got on his tramcar he always came to talk to her in between collecting fares.

'How are you doing, Josie? I'm off next Sunday. Esther thought you might like to bring Suzy round to tea. How about it?'

'Wally, I can't, I'm sorry. I've asked . . . Well, I've asked Luke Palmer round to my place for tea.'

'Luke Palmer?' Wally wrinkled up his nose. 'I didn't realise he was a friend of yours.' His usual smile was absent and he looked perplexed. 'Some other time, then.'

On rainy mornings it wasn't very pleasant to turn out so early, and she worried about Suzy sitting about in wet clothes in the classroom. But they managed, and often there was food Josie could take home so they could have a good hot meal together when Suzy came back from doing her evening deliveries.

Suzy enjoyed running up and down the streets pushing newspapers through letter boxes in the early mornings. It made her feel grown up and that she was doing her bit to help Mam. Particularly, as Mam had admitted, she'd hoped to be earning a little more than she was.

'Mam, we'll be all right,' Suzy told her, 'you and me together. With what I'm earning we'll have almost two pounds a week.'

It seemed a vast sum to her. She turned all her wages over to Mam on a Friday night and received a penny back to buy sweets.

'I'll pull my weight here, keep everything tidy. We'll be fine. And when I'm grown up I'll look after you.'

Mam had laughed at that.

Sometimes on a Friday night, if they had the money, they went to the pictures. They saw Lillian Gish in *Orphans of the Storm*, Gloria Swanson in *Untamed Lady* and Charlie Chaplin in *The Gold Rush*. They specially enjoyed those three. Suzy loved having Mam to herself, holding on to her arm as they walked home. Once back in their rooms, Mam would make two cups of cocoa while Suzy got undressed. Then she'd go to sleep in Mam's big bed.

'You warm it up for me,' Mam had told her, 'and that's nice now the nights are getting cooler.'

They'd got through the summer months and, with Olga's help, through the long school holidays. Even when winter came and she had to get up and out while it was still dark, Suzy enjoyed her job.

What she didn't like was finding Mr Palmer in their living room when she came home from delivering the *Evening Echo*.

'He's here more and more,' she complained to her mother.

'He's generous and kind to us.' Mam looked serious. 'And you know it depends on what shift he's working. He can only come here when he's on earlies.'

That meant, Suzy thought mutinously, he'd be with them most nights this week. And every alternate week the same. He was coming between her and Mam. When Suzy went to bed, she could hear them talking softly, even laughing occasionally. She wanted him to leave so Mam would come to bed and be with her, but he seemed to be staying later and later.

One night, she heard him say: 'Why don't we go out to the pictures, Josie? She's old enough to leave once in a while.'

Suzy strained her ears for Mam's reply. 'No, I can't do that. I don't want to leave Suzy alone.'

'She wouldn't be alone. You said she's friendly with the people upstairs. You could ask them to keep an eye on her.'

'No, Luke.'

'Just for a drink then, after you've put her to bed? She wouldn't know the difference, would she? You need taking out of yourself.'

Suzy could feel herself boiling with resentment against Mr Palmer. That Mam had not fallen in with his wishes brought a flush of triumph. It proved Mam thought more of her than she did of him, but Suzy couldn't understand why Mam kept letting him come for meals. As time went on he was coming more often until now, when she returned from her evening deliveries, he was always there when his shift allowed.

Suzy loved the weekends. She still had to deliver newspapers on Saturdays, but she didn't need to get up quite so early because she didn't have to rush off to school. She jumped straight out of bed, threw on her clothes and ran off.

Mam didn't go to work, so by the time Suzy came back she'd made a proper breakfast of bacon butties. Then Suzy would play with Frankie.

Frankie Rimmer was three months older than she, but he wasn't as tall and robust. Suzy knew Mam didn't really approve of him.

'Why not? Why don't you like him, Mam?'

Josie said primly: 'He's got an extensive vocabulary of swear words which I'd rather he didn't teach you.'

Suzy laughed. 'Too late, I've learned them already at school. Same as him.'

'He should know better than to use them.'

'He's teasing you, Mam, trying to shock you. I can tell by the way he rolls them across his tongue. He knows you don't like it.'

'They are words I don't want you to use.'

'I don't,' she protested. 'I won't. He doesn't swear in front of his mam or dad. They'd give him a clip over the ear if he did.'

'Quite right. Anyway, it's not just the swearing – he fights with you. You were rolling over and over on the hearth rug yesterday.'

'I won, Mam. I'm stronger than he is.'

'You won't be for long. You're a girl. He'll soon get the upper hand. You shouldn't fight like that.'

'If I couldn't win, then I'd stop. But I know I can.'

Her mother had laughed at that.

'Frankie likes to practise with me. They call him a sissy at school and he doesn't like it.'

'A sissy?'

'He likes girlie things, doesn't he? Cooking with his mother and storybooks and that. He thinks he can be a film star when he's grown up. No, the latest is he's going to be a detective like Sherlock Holmes. He thinks he can do anything, but he can't fight and he can't play football or do the things boys do.'

'All the same, I don't approve of him fighting you.'

'His mam doesn't approve of some of the things we do.'

'What things?' Suzy could see her mother was aghast.

'They don't think I should be doing the paper round. They say I'm not old enough, which is silly. I can do it perfectly well.'

She could see the flush running up Mam's cheeks and knew she didn't like that either.

'Mr Palmer said it was all right for me to say I was twelve.'

Mam's lips had straightened into a disapproving line.

Suzy went on, 'They don't think it is, and they don't like him much. They don't think he should come here so often either. It's wrong, they say because it's only six months since Daddy died.'

The pink flush on Mam's cheeks was turning to beetroot. Suzy heard a door slam upstairs and footsteps scampering down. 'Here's Frankie coming to call for me now.'

'Dinner's at one o'clock sharp,' Mam reminded her. 'Don't be late.'

'Right oh.' Suzy grabbed for her coat and went out on the landing.

Frankie came hurtling down. His soft curly hair was much in need of a cut and fell in corkscrews around his thin face. No boy should have hair that long.

His eyes were dreamy and of bright blue, and were fringed with long curling lashes that swept his cheeks. He was small for his age, considerably smaller than Suzy. There was something girlish about his build and the grace with which he moved, but if anyone dared suggest such a thing, his fists would be up and ready to deliver a right hook to the nose. He'd said as much to Suzy.

'Isn't it supposed to be the chin you aim for?'

'Nah. Better results if you hit the nose. Did you see what I did to Ben Briggs yesterday?'

'He had blood everywhere. Down his jersey, even on his shoes.'

'Yeah, and it hurts more.'

Now she asked: 'What are we doing today?'

'Let's go and see my dad.' They often did that. Frankie's father was the local park keeper, in charge of Wavertree Park. Frankie called it 'our park'.

'He keeps it very nice,' Suzy told Frankie, looking at the neat flowerbeds and smoothly shorn grass.

'He has other people to help him do all that sort of work,' Frankie boasted. 'My dad tells them what to do and locks up every night before he comes home for his tea.'

'It's not a very big park,' Suzy said to take him down a peg.

'He looks after the Wavertree Playground too,' Frankie said proudly. 'Here he is now. Da-ad.'

Mr Rimmer, small and lightly built like Frankie, wore a smart navy serge uniform with a peaked cap, and was driving small enamelled notices into the turf which said 'Keep off the grass'.

'Hello, son.' He nodded affably at Suzy. 'Look at these pansies. The rain last night really battered them down. Pity, they were quite a show.'

'Won't they stand up again?' Suzy asked.

He smiled at her. 'Not in time to look good for this afternoon.'

'Why this afternoon?'

'There's a band coming to play. A brass band from the fire station. There's the notice, look. You should bring your mam, Suzy, and you too, Frankie. They'd enjoy it.'

45

'My dad said the Tramways have a band. When are you having them here?'

'I don't know. Perhaps I should ask them.'

'It's a fine bandstand.'

'Yes, and they'll be playing fit to lift the roof off it this afternoon. Here,' he said indulgently, putting his hand in his trouser pocket, 'get yourselves some sweets.'

He pushed a halfpenny into Suzy's palm and did the same to Frankie. It was why, Suzy reflected, they went so often to see him. Frankie said his dad would treat them if he was in a good mood but he always seemed to be in a good enough mood for that.

When Mr Rimmer went to do something else, Frankie looked round carefully to make sure they wouldn't be seen, then moved the board they'd loosened on the side and they went into their special hiding place underneath. It was dark in here and the ground was bare and hard and cold.

He said: 'It would be good in here while the band was playing.'

On wet days, she and Frankie came to shelter here. They flopped down and started to talk of all the things they were going to do when they were grown up. It was Frankie's favourite subject.

'We'll go to London, just you and me. We'll see Buckingham Palace and the Tower.'

'Where are we going to get the money?' Suzy thought he was given to flights of fancy and ignored reality.

'We could hitchhike, if you like. We could even work our way round the world. You could be a cook like your mother.'

'Or work in a shop. I'd love to work in a sweet shop. We could work together then.'

'I'd like to learn to drive a tram like old Nosey.'

'You think you can do anything.'

'I can do anything Nosey can. I think I'll ask my dad if I can learn the trumpet. Then I could play in a band in parks like this.'

Suzy crawled back towards the loose board. 'What are we going to do now?'

'We could go down to the docks and stow away on a ship.'

'I mean *really* do.'

'Make sure the coast is clear before you get out,' Frankie reminded her. 'If my dad finds out about this he'll nail it up.'

They drifted off towards the dogs' home. It drew them like a magnet. They both enjoyed drooling over the dogs. Frankie said he was working on a plan to let them all out when the kennel maids weren't looking.

'Dare we go again?'

'Yes, let's.'

They couldn't go too often because to get in Frankie had to say his dog had gone missing and he was hoping it had been picked up and brought here.

They always asked: 'What kind of a dog is it?'

'He's a sort of mixture. Bit of terrier in him, medium-sized, brown and black and white.'

Frankie had explained they mustn't give too exact a description, or the dog catchers could just say no, they had no such animal in their pound.

'Answers to the name of Monty,' Suzy added.

'Was it wearing a collar with its name on it?'

'Slipped his collar,' Frankie said regretfully.

They got in again and were allowed to look round at all the dogs. They huddled together in front of the cages, stroking those who could be enticed forward and fantasising in whispers about which one they'd take home if only they were allowed to have a pet.

'Is this the dog you were looking for last month?' a red-haired kennel maid asked.

'Yes, he came home but now he's gone missing again,' Frankie told her with assumed innocence.

'Some dogs are like that,' she sympathised. 'Always off on the razzle. Perhaps he'll come home again.'

They left. 'We're going too often.' Frankie clung to Suzy as both tried to control their giggles until they were off the premises.

'But I loved that young Alsatian.'

'Shall we find a sweet shop and spend our halfpennies?'

'If we had twopence each we could go to the pictures this afternoon,' Frankie suggested.

'Or the baths.'

'Nah – too cold. Will your mam give you more money?'

'I thought we were supposed to take them to hear the band in the park.'

'Nah – that would be boring.'

They crossed the road to a sweet shop and spent five minutes looking in the window. 'I'm having liquorice boot laces,' Suzy decided.

'A lollipop for me. A red one.' They drifted back into the park eating their spoils and spent some time admiring the two cannon captured at Sebastopol in 1854.

'I could join the army,' Frankie said, 'and learn to fire guns like these at the enemy.'

'Guns aren't like this any more,' Suzy told him. 'And how d'you know you'd like the army? My mam said the Great War was awful.'

'I'd like to ride a horse and wear a red jacket and a shiny helmet.'

'Frankie! It's not like that any more. That's picturebook stuff from history. Besides,' she looked at his tumbling curls and dreamy eyes, 'you aren't the sort they want in the army.'

'What sort do they want?' His lip was pouting.

'Like old Nosey, tough, you know.'

They'd reached the liver bird fountain. Frankie set his lollipop stick to float on the water. It bobbed up and down for a few moments, then swirled round, caught in the bubbling currents caused by the water pouring down. Suzy found a small stick and threw that in too. Both sticks got caught against the stone plinth in the centre.

'Leave them,' Suzy advised.

But Frankie found a longer stick and, standing on the parapet of the pool, poked through the cascading water, trying to move them on. He overreached and got sprayed by the torrent. The shock made him jerk back but he lost his balance and was forced to put a foot down in the pool.

'It's freezing,' he shrieked, 'absolutely freezing!' Suzy tried to brush the beads of moisture off his coat, but they were soaking in fast. At that moment, a nearby church clock struck the half-hour.

'Is that half twelve? I'm supposed to be home by now.' Frankie panicked and they set off home at a brisk pace.

'Mam will be mad at me,' he said as they climbed the stairs, his boot squelching. 'They're almost new and my sock is wringing.'

'See you this afternoon,' Suzy said as they reached her landing.

'Yep, bring your stilts out. I'd love another go on them. I'll bring my roller skates for you, if you like. That's if Mam'll let me out again.'

Chapter Four

It was a fine morning and Luke Palmer felt cheered by the winter sun. The weather made a lot of difference to him, the Bellamy tramcar he was driving at the moment had no protective glass windscreens. In winter it was freezing cold, and his uniform got wet when it rained. It was all right for the bosses to say the top deck covered the driver. It certainly did overhang a bit, but when the tram was in motion it didn't stop the rain blowing in and soaking him.

Luke disliked wet weather. He found the dark glistening streets depressing. Not only did he get wet but passengers getting on in wet clothing made puddles on the floor and the inside of the tram smelled like a wet dog. The conductors said it meant fewer passengers and therefore less work for them, but that made no difference to Luke. On the whole he enjoyed his work. It was a job that made him feel very much in control. He knew every inch of the track now, and was able to perform all the necessary manoeuvres automatically.

It gave him time to daydream about Josie. What he really wanted was for her to take Ida's place. He thought she might if he went about it the right way. He needed to make himself attractive to her, but of course, he mustn't say a word about Ida or Leila. Josie was the sort who'd be shocked if she knew he'd spent the best years of his life living first with Leila and then Ida without marrying either of them.

He was heading the electric tramcar back into the city when he slowed down along Shaw Street to pull up outside the Women's Hospital.

51

It was a dismal-looking building of smoke-blackened brick, more like a prison than a hospital. He'd read in the newspaper of plans to build a brand-new hospital for women in Catherine Street, after which this would be pulled down.

There were always a few ill-looking women waiting to get on here. Today was no exception. The car was emptying of passengers when an elderly woman caught his eye. She was waving at him as she stepped off the pavement to come into the middle of the road where the tramlines were set.

'Hell,' he said under his breath. It was his mother. He'd not said a word to Josie about her, or about the hate he'd built up for her over his lifetime.

'How are you, Lukey?' she called to him, still waving like a mad thing and drawing everybody's attention to them. He didn't like that. He'd told everybody she was dead.

'I've got to go in here for an operation.' Her finger jabbed towards the hospital.

If there was one thing he didn't like about this route, it was that his mother lived in Dingle, through which it passed. She used his tram occasionally; he sometimes came face to face with her in the street. There were days when he felt she was pursuing him. Was she going to get on his tram now? Probably not, she'd need one outward bound to get home. He'd already gone through the Dingle.

'Come round and see me, Lukey, please. I'd love to have a chat.' The sight of her old lined face, so eager to reach him, tore him apart.

'Come round and have a cup of tea with me. I saw—'

That galvanised him into action, making him set the tram in motion. He had to get away from her.

Immediately the bell clanged furiously for him to stop again but he didn't. He knew he'd done the wrong thing when his new conductor, Tommy Curtis, started yelling at him from the other end of the car that one of the passengers had fallen.

'She's hurt herself. What made you start off like that? Such an unexpected jerk. It threw her.' The stupid fellow was shouting at him as he came closer. 'We weren't ready. We've left half a dozen passengers behind.'

Luke saw red and turned on him. 'You rang for me to start, you know you did.'

'Rubbish,' chorused several passengers. 'You set off like a madman just when passengers were starting to board.'

He felt a surge of fury. 'Oh, it's always my fault. Blame me,' and turned back to the controls.

'I do blame you,' the woman was railing at him in front of a whole carload of passengers. 'You threw me off my feet. You're dangerous. You'll hear more about this.'

Tommy Curtis was fussing over her, signalling to Luke by ringing the bell to stop the car. Telling her what number tram she must change to, to go up to the Infirmary to have her leg seen to.

Luke felt anger twisting in his stomach. He was ready to explode with temper, almost too furious to drive the tram. He'd be in trouble if this woman reported him as she was threatening, and it was all his mother's fault.

Mam wanted to be on friendly terms now he was grown up and earning. She was always saying: 'After all this time, surely we can let bygones be bygones?'

Well, he couldn't. He didn't want anything to do with her after what she'd done to him. Who would? His father had been killed in some minor native uprising while he'd been serving in the army in India. She'd married again quite soon and Luke had never been able to tolerate his stepfather. He'd been a bully and within days they were having terrible rows. His mother had blamed Luke. He always got the blame for everything that went wrong.

He'd told his mam that she had to choose between them and she'd chosen his stepfather. She'd never really cared about him and called him a troublemaker. He'd had to run away from home. He'd been twelve at the time and the police had picked him up one wet night when he was trying to find somewhere dry to sleep in the docks.

He'd spent three nights locked up in the police station. It had taken them that long to get his home address from him. They'd withheld food until he told them, otherwise he never would have. They'd taken Luke back to his mother then, but he wasn't planning to stay and have more trouble from his stepfather, no thank you. He'd had more guts than to put up with that. He'd been off again as soon as he'd had a good sleep, some clean clothes and got plenty of food in him. He'd been careful to take warmer clothes and his mackintosh with him the second time.

He'd been caught again within days, trying to sign on a ship as a cabin boy, and he'd ended up in that awful orphanage. The kids there all said their mothers were dead. Those that had come to the orphanage before they could remember any home were told that to give them a reason for being there. But also, there were a lot like him whose mothers didn't want to be bothered looking after them or weren't capable of it, and they all went round saying their mothers were dead too. If the death of a parent had put them where they were, no blame attached to anybody. If your mother didn't want you, some people might think you weren't a nice person.

Luke blamed his mother's rejection for all the trouble he'd had with women later in his life. She'd always been cold and indifferent to his needs, never given him any love or care. As an adult that had left him permanently anxious and worried that the woman he loved would leave him as she had. And up to now, they all had. He'd been very unlucky with his women.

He'd married Flora Perkins when he was eighteen – much too young for anyone to get married, though she'd been a little older. She'd gone off with another man within three years, taking their two children with her. She'd blamed him for the break-up but it had come as an almighty shock to him that she intended leaving at all. He hadn't wanted her to; he'd done his best to persuade her to stay.

Josie was different, though. She was a caring person. Hadn't Ted said exactly that to him one day when he'd been sounding off about women in general? And the less Josie knew about his mother the better.

The dreadful stepfather was dead now. He'd wished him dead so often, it had probably helped him on his way, but Mam, the miserable sod, still clung to life. He didn't want to visit her and take tea – it would only open up old wounds. It was easier to think of her as he always had; as already dead.

Josie was later than usual returning home on Tuesday afternoon. She rushed home, feeling tense and excited as she set about tidying the room and making preparations for their evening meal.

When Suzy came home from school they had a cup of tea and some bread and jam together before Suzy had to go out to make her evening deliveries. The *Evening Echo*es arrived at the paper shop at about five o'clock.

Josie put the kettle on to make more tea and left the living-room door open. Luke would be here any minute now. Suzy had been gone barely three minutes when she heard his step on the stairs. She leaped up to meet him.

He was smiling as he crossed the landing to give her a carrier bag. He'd brought more bottles of port and lemonade for her, together with a bottle of dandelion and burdock for Suzy. Josie never drank whisky but he brought bottles of it here to drink himself.

'If you won't come out with me, we can have a quiet drink together after Suzy's gone to bed. What do you like to drink?'

She wasn't particularly fond of any drink, but it seemed to turn an ordinary evening into an occasion. Josie had never drunk alcohol with Ted. He might buy a bottle as a Christmas treat but normally they stuck to tea. She already had a bottle of sherry and another of port in her sideboard that Luke had brought at different times. Always there was a bottle of whisky there, which needed to be replaced surprisingly often.

'You're very generous, always bringing us gifts,' she told him.

Usually they were of food, but quite often Josie was given food to bring home from the hotel; enough to make a meal for the three of them. Luke was fond of fancy cheeses and often brought them to finish their meals. He brought cakes too because Suzy preferred them. Josie had two big tins of assorted biscuits in her cupboard, one of savoury to go with his cheese and one of the chocolate biscuits that Suzy loved. He brought fruit too.

'For Suzy,' he'd say. 'Oranges are good for her.'

Josie thought their standard of living was much enhanced because of Luke's generosity.

She looked forward now to the hour or so she and Luke could be alone. It was so much more peaceful when she wasn't distracted by Suzy. She recognised from the beginning that Luke was courting her and didn't quite know what to make of him. She liked the way he held his head high and thought him attractive, though there was something vaguely lop-sided about his face. His large Roman nose wasn't quite straight, but it wasn't wholly that. There were times when she thought he had a slight turn in his eye, but it wasn't always there to see. His features would have been film-star perfect if they'd been straight. The fact that they were ever so slightly lopsided made him seem homely and lovable.

She was flattered that he seemed to like her company and knew he was attracted to her – she could see it in his dark eyes as they followed her round the room. He conveyed to her with great charm that he was interested in her.

'You're like a flower,' he told her. 'So fragile and pretty. I want to take care of you.'

He had much stronger opinions about everything than Ted had had. He was stronger in every way, and more ambitious. He talked a lot about his duties as a trade union convener, and was very wrapped up in that.

'You've got to fight for what you want in this life,' he told her. 'I don't just fight for myself, I do it for the men I work with. We have to fight to get a living wage.'

Josie thought he was the sort who would enjoy almost any confrontation. He looked like a man who was going places.

Suzy came back on time with flushed cheeks. Her straight hair was too short, just level with her ear lobes. Last night Josie had cut and washed it. It had looked a mess with kirby grips jammed in anywhere just to keep it out of her eyes. But her eyes were glowing and she had plenty to say, shattering the quiet peace as Josie dished up their tea.

Tonight, once their meal was eaten and cleared away and Suzy was doing the washing up in the kitchen, Luke helped himself to another whisky and poured drinks for Josie and Suzy.

'Oh lovely, lovely, dandelion and burdock, thank you.' Suzy gulped half of hers down at once.

'Play ludo with me, Mam,' she pleaded. It was what Suzy liked to do in the hour before she went to bed. They usually played some board game if they were alone.

Josie held her breath. She couldn't refuse and she didn't want Suzy to think she was being pushed out because Luke was here with her, but Luke would be excluded if she agreed.

'Set up for the three of us,' Luke said easily. 'We'll all have a game.'

He let Suzy win. Josie hoped Suzy didn't notice that he wasn't moving his own counters on as far as he should. It was a noisy game. They were left in no doubt that Suzy enjoyed it.

Afterwards, privately to Josie, Luke called it 'humouring Suzy'.

It was time then for her to go to bed. She was good about going without fuss, though Josie sensed she didn't like leaving her here with Luke.

'Good night, Mr Palmer,' she said primly before she went.

When Josie came back from tucking Suzy into bed and kissing her good night, Luke had poured another drink for each of them and moved to the couch. Now Suzy was gone, they could sit there side by side again.

'It must be hard for you, looking after a child on your own.' His large hand covered hers in a show of sympathy.

'Very hard. I really miss Ted.'

'I know. I was very lonely when my wife died.'

Josie was surprised. 'I didn't know . . . Ted just said you weren't married. What was her name?'

'Flora.' She heard the gulp of pain in his voice. 'She was only thirty-four when she died.'

Josie was appalled. 'What of?'

'In childbirth.'

That seemed to make it ten times worse. 'So it was sudden too?'

'Yes, she was going to have the baby at home, but then at the last minute I was told to take her to the hospital. She didn't come out. Neither did our son.'

Josie had felt his sympathy from the moment she'd told him Ted was dead. Now she knew why.

'It's a shared experience,' he said. 'It draws me to you. You understand how I feel.'

'How long ago was it?'

'Two years.'

'Does it get easier? Being without her?'

He looked so sad. 'I don't know, sometimes . . . Perhaps, yes it does, in some ways, but for me, life has never been the same since. No welcome when I go home, nobody to cook a meal. That's why I push myself on you so often.'

'You're very welcome,' Josie told him. 'You know that. And you provide us with so many extras.'

He was smiling at her. 'I hope that isn't the only reason I get a welcome.'

She laughed. 'I like having you. A bit of adult company after Suzy's gone to bed.'

He leaned over and his lips brushed her cheek. 'I like coming and it isn't just for your good cooking. I could take to you, Josie.'

She shook her head slowly. Apologetically she whispered: 'I'm not over Ted. I couldn't.'

'I can wait. For someone like you, I can wait.'

She was finding him increasingly attractive. She could feel his passion, his desire. He was getting to her. He could make her tingle. He seemed so genuine, so much in love with her.

She began to think seriously about Luke. Often, this was when she was in bed with Suzy sleeping alongside her. She liked him; he was good company and he cheered her up, but she didn't love him and he couldn't take Ted's place, not ever.

She continued to invite him for meals. He understood her worries and talked them through with her. He was someone to lean on, and, goodness knows she needed that. Nowadays he always kissed her when he arrived and when he left. Often it was a real lovers' kiss; occasionally they did quite a lot of kissing on the couch.

But, of course, not if Suzy was watching. She made it only too obvious she wasn't ready to let Luke take Ted's place in her affections.

Josie was curious about Luke; he intrigued her. She wanted to hear more about his life, really get to know him.

A few days after that first tentative kiss, after Suzy had gone to bed, Luke said: 'You don't know how much I appreciate being able to come into a family home like this.'

'You have a house, Luke, haven't you? A whole house to yourself?'

'Yes, a two up and two down, but it's soulless now Flora isn't there. It's not as though I have any children. I'm just on my own.'

'It would have been very hard for you if your son had survived and your wife had not – a newborn baby to bring up single-handed. Do you have a sister or mother who could have helped?'

'No, I've never had any relatives. That's why I long for a family and a home I can call my own. I was brought up in an orphanage.' He'd told her that in his youth, he'd gone to sea.

'The Seaman's Orphanage?'

'No, worst luck. To get a place there I'd have had to be the son of a sailor lost at sea.' His sigh was full of pain. 'My orphanage was a rough place and I found myself in a tough crowd of boys. There were endless fights there. My nose was broken in one, and they never bothered to do anything about getting it properly set and straightened.'

Josie smiled: 'I see you as a fighter. Ted did too. You could hold your own in any crowd, tough or not.'

'That's where I learned to stand up for myself. I was put on at first – I had to get my fists up to survive. The discipline was iron-handed too, but it was continually flouted. Some of the lads I knew there ended up in Borstal, and probably went on to prison. It wasn't a good place to be brought up.'

'Luke, it sounds dreadful.'

'It did one thing for me: it made me stand on my own feet, look after myself. I can cope very well on my own but I'd rather be with you and look after you and little Suzy too.'

Josie thought there was something endearing about the way he called her 'little Suzy'. She was growing up fast; in truth she was quite a lump now.

'What did you do when you left the orphanage? How old were you?'

'Twelve. I went to sea school – the *Indefatigable* – you've seen her moored in the Mersey?'

'Yes.'

'It's a sea school for orphan boys, to teach them a trade.'

'You all went on there?'

'Many did. Seafaring is in the blood of us Liverpool lads, and it got me out of that orphanage. Otherwise, I'd have had to go on living in that dump for another year or so.'

'But you didn't stay at sea.'

'No.' He lay back in his corner of the couch. His eyes were half closed and his voice low, as slowly he told her of his past.

'After a couple of years on the *Indefatigable* I had a trade, I was a seaman. I signed on a tramp going round the small ports of the Mediterranean. I enjoyed seeing something of the world that I'd never be able to see otherwise, though the ship

I was on usually tied up miles from the centre of the port. And I had to sign on as a stoker to start with, and shovelling coal into the furnace isn't the best job going, I can tell you.

'I wanted a home, Josie, and a family of my own. I tried almost every trade in the book after I decided the sea wasn't for me, but I wanted to be a bus driver. I worked in a garage for a while but the others there had worked apprenticeships in car mechanics. I'd have loved to have had a go at driving a car. I felt I could do it, you know? The nearest I got to any car was filling it with petrol or cleaning it.

'Then I thought of being a tram driver. I had to fight for that too, Josie. I was a conductor for five years, but eventually they trained me to drive. I've had to fight for everything I've ever got in this life. I'm fighting to get you now.'

'Fighting?' She smiled. 'I hope it won't come to that.'

'There are more ways of fighting than putting your fists up. I do love you, Josie.'

How could she not warm to Luke? He had charm. She daydreamed about him as she lay in her bed beside Suzy, and as she lay in the three inches of warm water she allowed herself in her bath. That Luke wanted her in this way lifted her out of her daily rut. She wanted to sing as she cleaned their rooms, or went about her duties at the hotel. She wasn't the dried-up middle-aged widow she'd believed herself to be. Who said life began at forty? She felt she could dance, even walk on air.

Luke really was a very nice person and he certainly knew how to turn a woman's head. She could feel his passion and felt he was forcing the pace, wanting more from her than she was able to give. More than once, he'd opened the bedroom door so she could see Suzy asleep, absolutely flat out in bed. Then he'd suggested they go to the bed where she used to sleep behind the curtains in the kitchen.

The intensity of his appeal was becoming harder to resist. He was so full of life and quite explicit about what he wanted. He wanted sex.

Luke lifted her life, sharpened her senses; made her believe she hadn't lost everything with Ted's death. Made her believe life could be wonderful again. It was as heady as the sherry he kept bringing her, but although she was very tempted, she wasn't going to give in and let him make love to her like that.

'Relax, love, and let it happen,' he'd murmured in her ear. 'You'll enjoy it, I promise you.'

Josie didn't doubt that she would, but she could never forget Ray Bissell and the son she'd borne him out of wedlock. Although she didn't tell Luke the reason, nothing would make her give in and risk having that happen again.

Luke Palmer had had a terrible day. The woman who'd fallen and hurt herself on his tramcar had written a letter of complaint to the office. The dreaded interview with his boss had taken place at three o'clock.

Tommy Curtis had had his say and told the boss that Luke had driven off without warning, before Tommy had rung the bell, which was the signal for him to start.

Luke had also been handed a written warning, the second one. Another of those and he'd get the sack. That had really put the wind up him. He'd had to bite his tongue to stop himself answering back, though he'd wanted to crack his fist into his boss's merciless face. As soon as he was out of the office he'd rushed across the depot to the gents' lavatory. He'd been so incensed, he'd jabbed his fist at the door, splintering the wood and knocking a panel right out. That had put him in such a ferment, he'd torn up the written warning into stamp-sized pieces and flushed them away; he couldn't help himself. It wasn't as though any of it was his fault. He was always blamed for everything that went wrong.

Luke had felt shaky for an hour afterwards. He was going to Josie's for his tea – that usually soothed him and made him feel better – but tonight his fist hurt and he needed more than a hot meal. He'd tried his hardest to charm her but she wouldn't give an inch on having a bit of slap and tickle.

It had taken all his willpower not to blow up at her refusal and slam out of her place. All the same, last time he'd left sooner than he'd intended. Bile had been rising in his throat and he'd wanted to hit out at her because she wouldn't listen to reason. He'd had to go before he lost his temper again.

The way he saw it, when Josie said she was missing Ted, she meant she was missing having sex with Ted. But she was behaving like a seventeen-year-old, churchgoing virgin, not a woman with eleven years of marriage behind her.

Now he was striding home through the darkness in a fever of frustration and anger. Josie was playing hard to get. After all the gifts and the sweet talk, he hadn't softened her up one bit. He'd been so sure that after the three port and lemons he'd poured for her, she'd give something in return. Ted had been getting everything he wanted from her. Why didn't she give it to him?

Luke knew well enough it was marriage she was after. She was a bit prim and proper, but if she wouldn't bed him without being married, it meant she wouldn't go off with the next man who asked her. She'd be more likely to stay, so she might be worth taking the risk for.

Luke hadn't heard from Flora since she'd walked out on him in 1895. He counted up the years: thirty-two. Flora was probably dead by now. His mother had told him years ago that she was in hospital and at death's door. He'd thought of himself as a widower for a long time.

Perhaps he should marry Josie?

Josie knew that Suzy's eleventh birthday could not be a truly happy occasion. It fell too close to the anniversary of Ted's death and he was very much in their minds.

She made a birthday cake for her and took both Suzy and Frankie to the first house at the Empire as a treat. It was a variety show, which they all enjoyed. Luke had suggested it and given her the money, but he was working and couldn't go with them.

It comforted Josie that she and Suzy were coping. She went on telling herself they were managing fine, until the following winter when a measles epidemic raged through Suzy's school. Frankie was one of the first to catch it and had been in bed for the last four days.

Josie was afraid Suzy would catch it too. She'd forbidden her to go upstairs to Frankie, though she knew they'd been together a lot in the days before he was taken ill. On Monday, Suzy had a runny nose and a bit of a cough.

'I'm all right, Mam,' she insisted. 'It's just a cold.'

So Josie let her set out to do her morning deliveries and went to work herself. Suzy seemed no worse that evening, so Josie relaxed, believing it to be just a head cold.

But the next afternoon when she got home at three o'clock, Josie went into her bedroom to take off her hat and coat, and pulled up with a gasp when she saw Suzy curled up in bed asleep.

Full of remorse, she gently laid her hand on Suzy's forehead. The child felt burning hot! She leaped back, feeling guilty that she let her go to school, and now she'd woken her out of a sleep.

In a hoarse voice Suzy told her she'd been sent home because she wasn't well and had been given a note. With shaking fingers, Josie opened it up. It said a large number of their pupils had measles and Suzy must remain off school for at least ten days after the rash appeared.

In another wave of guilt, Josie made her way to the living-room couch. She should never have let her go to school today. There was guilt from another direction too, because she hated to let Mr Hollis down when he'd been so kind to her. She had no way of letting him know she wouldn't be in to cook tomorrow's breakfasts unless she went out to phone. She couldn't think where the nearest phone box might be, and anyway, she'd hardly ever used one and was nervous of doing so. She decided it would be almost as quick to go down to the hotel, and in that case she might as well leave it until morning and go in and cook the breakfasts.

She could ask for time off and be back home by eleven. She rushed up to see Olga, to ask her to look in on Suzy the next morning.

'I'll take her a bit of breakfast about nine. It's no bother.' Olga Rimmer pushed her brown curly hair back from her face. 'The doctor's calling to see our Frankie tomorrow morning. Shall I take him down to see Suzy when he comes?'

'Yes,' Josie gulped. She was relieved when she found she was home the next morning in time to speak to him herself.

'Measles,' the doctor said, looking in Suzy's mouth.

'But she hasn't got a rash.'

'She will have by tomorrow. Starts behind her ears and along her hairline here on her forehead. Keep her in bed until her temperature settles. I'll come back in five days to see how she is.'

When he'd gone, Josie made them some tea, and drank

hers sitting on the bed, but Suzy was soon dozing again, and she crept to the living-room couch. She felt down in the dumps: all her arrangements fell apart when Suzy was sick. She wouldn't be able to go to work and she'd have to draw on her savings to pay the doctor and to provide living expenses for the next fortnight.

Josie had to remind herself that it would only be for a fortnight. A rest at home would do her good; there was no point in worrying about it. She had enough saved up to cover what was needed.

It was mid-afternoon before she thought of Suzy's job and ran round to the newsagent to tell them she wouldn't be able to come for the next fortnight.

At tea-time she prepared scrambled eggs, and wished Luke was coming round, but he'd be working until nearly midnight this week. It made her realise that she'd come to rely on him. He was a help and support to her.

Suzy was quite poorly. Josie leaned on Olga, who was going through the same problems with Frankie. At least they could all mix since they had the same infection.

The following week, Luke was able to come round in the evenings again. Josie was glad to see him. Suzy was getting up now, but spending quite a lot of time lying on the couch with a rug over her. He brought her a bottle of orange squash, a bar of chocolate and some comics.

When later in the evening Josie sent her to bed and settled down on the couch with Luke, he said: 'Another thing my orphanage upbringing gave me was a hankering for a family and a home of my own.'

'At least it hasn't scarred you for life.'

'You don't know how lucky you are to have Suzy.'

'I do, Luke. I cling to her.'

He said earnestly: 'Would you consider taking pity on me? Taking me into your family? We should get married, Josie. It would make things easier for you. You'd know you and Suzy wouldn't starve even if you had to stay off work. Think about it.'

Josie felt a flush run up her cheeks. She had thought about it, particularly this last week. She said softly: 'I don't think . . . I'm not in love with you. I'm not really over Ted yet. I don't feel as much for you as I did for him.'

'But you feel something?'

'Yes, you know I'm fond—'

Luke shrugged his broad shoulders. 'You might love me in time.'

She shook her head, unable to admit the possibility.

'I could settle for being second best for you, if that's the way it is.'

She shook her head again.

'Ted's gone, Josie. The question now is whether second best would be better than being on your own.'

Josie closed her eyes. She'd thought that way too. Oh God, how many times had she thought about that?

'I want you to understand that you wouldn't be second best for me. I've had longer to get over my loss. I do understand how it knocks you back, and how hard it is to pick yourself up and get going again.'

Josie closed her eyes. 'I'm not ready to get married again, Luke.' He couldn't take Ted's place. She didn't love him, not enough for that.

'I'm falling in love with you. I want to look after you, and Suzy too. She's a girl with real guts.'

Josie knew Suzy didn't welcome his visits. She'd said when they were eating tea together last week: 'Nosey's on lates this week. He won't be able to come. Good-oh.'

Josie said: 'She isn't ready to accept you as her father yet, Luke. She hasn't got over Ted either.'

'She will,' he said gravely. 'In time. You must both take all the time you need. I'll not rush you but I hope you'll not push me away. If I keep coming, Suzy will get used to me. I'll win her over, you'll see.'

Josie thought about Luke a good deal. Of course it was a comfort having him say he loved her and wanted to marry her. It did wonders for her ego, but . . .

She wanted to remember Ted. It seemed disloyal to think of marrying someone else when only eighteen months had passed. She couldn't do that.

Chapter Five

It seemed to Josie that no sooner was Suzy over the measles and back at school than chickenpox was rife in the neighbourhood.

'Surely they won't catch this too,' she said to Olga. For another month Suzy and Frankie remained well, and then one night Suzy was scratching her back in bed and in the morning Josie could see a rash. This time she didn't let her do her deliveries, though Suzy said she didn't feel too ill and was quite capable of it.

Josie went to work and cooked the hotel's breakfast. On the way home she called in at the doctor's surgery. He told her to keep Suzy in bed on a light diet for a day or two.

'How long will she need to be kept off school?' That was the important thing to her.

'Until the last scab has fallen off the last pustule.'

That sounded as though it could stretch to infinity; Josie needed to know the number of days. 'How long will that take?'

The doctor shrugged. 'It varies, but Suzy will be deemed infectious until they've all gone.'

'They won't leave scars, will they? On her face?'

'Don't let her pick at them.'

Josie wondered how she was supposed to stop her.

'I'll give you some carbolised oil. If you apply this to them, it will help the scabs to come off without leaving a mark, and it will also speed up the separation. Very gently, mind – use a feather.'

When he heard she was a cook at the Imperial Hotel, and that she'd come straight from cooking breakfast there, he told her she must stay off work.

'Chickenpox is extremely infectious and can be carried on your hands after you've attended to your daughter. No library books – the disease can be passed on that way. You must be careful to disinfect everything. Use plenty of carbolic.'

Josie walked home with a heavy heart. Suzy's rash was more marked and had spread to other parts of her body.

At four o'clock there was a tap at their living-room door and Olga put her head round.

'Our Frankie's come out in a rash. Is this the chickenpox that's going round?'

They lined him up alongside Suzy, who by now had a heavy disfiguring rash all over her.

'She's even got pustules in her hair. That's what the doctor called them, pustules.'

'Frankie's are the same,' Olga sighed. 'It's chickenpox all right.'

'The good thing is that I don't feel ill,' Suzy smiled.

Frankie pulled a face. 'I feel funny.'

'You feel a bit off colour, don't you, Frankie? That's all.'

'You'll be all right by tomorrow,' Suzy told him.

Josie tried to look on the bright side. At least she needn't worry about her as she had over the measles.

'There's no keeping her in bed,' she said to Olga.

'I'm glad you've caught it too, Frankie. Now I'll have somebody to play with.'

'A holiday from school,' Frankie said with satisfaction.

'All right for you, and your mam,' Josie sighed. 'But I have to stay off work too.' She tried to smile at Olga. 'At times like this I really miss Ted. Having a husband makes life so much easier.'

72

'Josie love, you aren't over it yet. Give yourself time.'

'I don't think I'll ever get over Ted. What I meant was that any husband in work would make it less desperate. The loss of my wages . . .'

'If I can help?'

'No, Olga, you do enough for me. You're always our first backstop when things go wrong.' She knew her friend had a struggle to make ends meet on her husband's wage.

To pull her weight where she could, Josie took both children for long walks. The weather was cold and damp, and during school hours there were few people about. She walked them down to the river and along the shore, where they picked up driftwood along the tidemark. They had the place to themselves and it allowed the youngsters to get some fresh air and run off some of their energy.

It seemed a long way home with their load, but once there, Josie could treat herself to a fire that blazed halfway up the chimney. She was enjoying the break in her routine, though Suzy's scabs seemed to cling to her for ever.

For Josie, the worst part was that her savings were going down again. Every time she had to stay off work she had to dip into them to tide them over. Quite apart from the loss of her wages, these breaks were robbing her of her sense of security. She felt pulled in both directions. She hated telling Mr Hollis she couldn't come to work. She felt she was letting him down, as it meant he had to find someone else to take her place.

She tried to console herself with the thought that summer was coming, but with it would come the long school holidays. Josie would be due for one week's paid holiday, which she'd take when Suzy was off. She'd dreamed about taking her away to the Isle of Man for a real holiday, but a dream was what it had become now. She daren't risk spending her savings in case she had to fall back on them again and needed the money for necessities. They'd have days out if the weather was good – trips to New Brighton on the ferry.

'I'll be all right on my own,' Suzy insisted. 'You worry too much. I'll have Frankie to play with.'

Josie told herself that once Suzy was thirteen she'd be old enough. She was a sensible and responsible girl. And anyway, she herself would be home just after three every afternoon. They could do a lot on a fine summer's evening.

All the same, Josie was coming round to the idea that marriage to Luke made sense. He understood about it being second best. He'd get the home and family he wanted and she'd not worry herself sick every time Suzy went down with some childhood illness and had to stay off school.

When she'd been abandoned by Ray Bissell she'd longed for a husband who would have made a comfortable life possible for her and the baby. A husband hadn't been forth-coming when she'd really needed one. She'd have jumped at the chance of marrying anyone then.

She'd been twenty-nine when she'd married Ted and he'd given her eleven golden years. To Josie, another husband seemed the best answer, the only practical answer. Suzy needed a father too and they both needed a breadwinner. Life was incredibly difficult on what Josie could earn. Because marriage had worked last time, Josie was quite sure it would again.

At the weekend, she knew Luke Palmer's shift would change and that he'd come round to see her. She'd missed his company. She knew she could expect him on Sunday and had bought bloaters for their tea. She was missing not only her wages but the food she was often given to bring home.

When she heard his footsteps coming upstairs she leaped up to open the door. She was so pleased to see him. It made her realise how much she'd come to rely on him.

'I hope you've had chickenpox,' she told him before he came in. 'Suzy's got it. She's infectious.'

'Don't know whether I've had it or not, but I don't care.' He kissed her cheek. 'Where is she?'

'Upstairs, playing with her friend Frankie.'

'Poor Josie, you're worried, aren't you?'

'Not about Suzy, she's all right.'

He understood exactly what it meant for her. 'You'll let me help?' He patted the breast pocket of his Harris tweed jacket. 'I'd like to.'

Josie shook her head. She couldn't accept money from him, not while she still had a little left of her own. She made the usual cup of tea and they sat down side by side on the couch. He leaned across and kissed her cheek. It made the heat run through her body.

'I've decided,' Josie said slowly. 'I will marry you, if you still want—'

'Of course I do.' His arms went round her and hugged her tight. 'I'm so pleased . . . Delighted, thrilled, over the moon. You won't be sorry, I promise you. Much the best thing for us both.'

'Don't say anything to Suzy just yet. I'll have to choose the right moment.'

'It'll be a good thing for her too, Josie. I'll do my best to be a good father.'

Saturday had come round again. Suzy went with Frankie down to the Pier Head. They took a trip across the river without getting off at the other side and so didn't have to pay their fare. The Mersey was full of ships. Frankie could point out which ones belonged to the Cunard Shipping Company and which were Blue Funnel, White Star, Elder Dempster or Brocklebank. There was a blustery breeze and the seagulls screamed over their heads. Suzy had a lovely morning.

When they came home, Suzy could smell her dinner cooking. They had their main meal at dinner time at the weekend. She bounded into her living room, only to pull up short. She hadn't expected to find old Nosey here. He was sitting with Mam on the couch and Suzy distinctly saw them move apart and his hand fall away from Mam's shoulder. He'd been kissing her!

'You're back early, Suzy.'

Mam's voice sounded strange. She must have known he was coming but she hadn't said. Suzy knew he'd been working the afternoon shift all this week because she hadn't seen much of him. He wouldn't be staying all that long today because he'd have to start work at two o'clock, but next week he'd be here every evening. Mam loved him, she must do to kiss him like that. Suzy felt aggrieved and let down. Mam was turning to Nosey and rejecting her.

'Luke has brought you some apples.' They were on the table in a dish. His fearsome eyes were on her.

'Thank you, very generous of you, Mr Palmer.'

Mam had drilled into her how she must respond. She was strict about Suzy showing good manners. Mam would say that was little enough to say for such nice rosy apples. She added: 'They smell lovely.'

'We might as well eat since you're home.'

Mam was on her feet, bounding towards the cooker in the bathroom. The table was set for three. They had stew and dumplings and there were blackcurrant tarts to follow.

'Luke bought them at Taskers. They're your favourite, aren't they, Suzy?'

They were. 'Absolutely marvellous,' she said. The pastry melted on the tongue. She risked a glance at him. 'You're very generous, Mr Palmer.'

Mam beamed at her. Suzy had done what she was told she must.

'Perhaps, Suzy, you should call me Uncle Luke? Mr Palmer sounds very formal.'

Suzy felt the blood rush to her cheeks on a wave of resentment. It was the last thing she wanted to do. He was clawing his way in between her and Mam, pushing her out. Mam was giving her a bleeding hearts look; she'd probably told him to say that.

'Perhaps.' She leaped to her feet. 'I'll make a pot of tea.'

Mam wouldn't want the table cleared and the washing up started until Mr Palmer had gone, but he wouldn't be able to stay much longer.

Suzy had to go back and hear him being invited for meals next week. He was casting a blight on the life she and Mam had together, spoiling everything. She was glad when he stood up to go. Suzy collected the plates together and ran the kitchen tap hard so she wouldn't hear Mam saying goodbye to him.

That took a long time but at last Mam came in with the rest of the dishes and slid them into the washing-up water.

'I've something I want to tell you, Suzy.'

She knew it was something important by Mam's tone of voice. It made her freeze. 'What?'

'Luke and I are going to be married.'

Suzy gasped. It was worse than she'd thought. Mam's gentle eyes smiled into hers.

'He's been asking me to marry him for months. He says he wants to look after us both.'

'No! Mam, no! We're all right on our own. We can manage.'

'We aren't managing very well.'

'Well enough.'

'No, love, we have money troubles when I can't go to work. Luke wants to take care of us. It will make things better for us all.'

'You're taking care of him, Mam. You're cooking meals for him, and didn't I see you sewing buttons on his coat the other day? You do a lot for him and you'll be doing more if you marry him, not less. Don't do it. I don't like him.'

'He's very fond of you.'

'He isn't.'

'He says you've got real guts.'

'That's not the same as liking me. Oh, Mam, don't marry him!'

'You don't understand, love.'

Josie was shocked at the vehemence of Suzy's reaction. She'd thought she was coming round to accept Luke. He was always very kind to her.

The next time he came round, she said doubtfully: 'Perhaps we should leave it for a while. There's really no hurry—'

'Oh no, Josie. I want us to be married as soon as we can. We're both getting on in life, so why waste time?' He was fifty-three, considerably older than her forty-one.

'Suzy will come round,' he said several times. 'I'll make her like me. I want us to go ahead and be married.'

Josie was persuaded. 'D'you know, I haven't even seen your house yet?' She thought it strange that he'd never suggested she might like to see it. He rarely spoke of it either. 'Where are we going to live?'

'I think you'd prefer to stay here. You keep telling me you like this place and feel settled.'

'But you've got a whole house to yourself, haven't you?'

'Yes, but . . . You'd better come and see it, so you can decide for yourself.'

He took her the following evening, while Suzy was doing her newspaper deliveries. It wasn't very far – ten minutes' walk, he'd said. It took them a little longer, though Josie walked briskly in order to be sure of getting back before Suzy.

She didn't like Stockton Street. Luke had known she wouldn't. It was down near the docks and the houses were old and mean-looking. Number fifteen, which Luke rented, was in a bad state of repair. As he pushed against the front door, which opened straight into the living room, balls of dust skittered across the lino in the draught. There was a scullery behind, its one cold tap dripping into a stone sink. The rooms were poky and she felt an urge to throw open the windows – if they were still capable of being opened. It looked as though no woman had ever tidied it up. There was thick dust on the furniture, though he'd just told her he'd spent two hours cleaning before she came.

'It's nearer the Imperial Hotel,' he said. 'And the rent's less. Only four and six a week.'

Josie couldn't see herself settling happily here. It seemed a retrograde step. She thought it a slum, as bad if not worse than the place they'd rented behind the railway goods station down near the docks.

'We're in the best house in Upper Parliament Street. I much prefer that.'

'So do I,' he said. 'It's settled then. I'll move in with you. Is there anything here you'd like me to bring?'

Josie looked round. She hadn't much space left in her rooms. 'Is there anything you really want?'

'No.'

She'd expected him to have a better house. He'd kept on telling her how much he'd longed for a place he could call his own. This poor home was somehow out of character. He was fussy about his clothes and clean about his person. He went to a good barber and bought expensive food. Why didn't his home reflect that? She and Suzy were settled in Upper Parliament Street; it was better that they should stay where they were.

Going to work one morning on the tram, Josie said to Wally Simpson: 'I suppose you've heard from Luke that we're going to get married?'

'No!' His freckled face was twisting with concern. 'He doesn't tell us much, not about personal matters. You are sure, Josie? I mean . . . Well, he's not at all like Ted. Very different.'

'I'm sure. I've been thinking about it for the past year.'

When Luke came round later that evening, he said: 'We'll have a quiet wedding – no point in making a big fuss at our age. Not for the second time round.' He gave a gusty sigh. 'It's not as though either of us has relatives to invite. We'll have the minimum to make it legal then? The register office?'

'We've got friends,' Josie said in surprise, 'and we'll need witnesses. What about Wally Simpson and his wife? We both know them, they were Ted's—'

Luke sniffed indignantly. 'Not him!' Josie got the idea that he and Wally disliked each other.

'Who then?'

'You've got friends here, your neighbours.'

'And at work.'

'That'll be more than enough. We don't want a big do. A honeymoon would be nice, though. We might as well make a bit of a holiday of it.'

'Suzy will—'

'It's a big occasion for us and a reason to celebrate. Couldn't you leave her with Frankie and his mother for a few days?'

'No, Suzy must come too. She'd never forgive me if I left her behind.'

'Hardly a honeymoon if she comes.'

Josie found that a little hurtful. She'd made it clear to Luke that she had to consider Suzy's wellbeing. 'Better then if we don't have one.'

Josie had seen how the news that she and Luke were going to marry had wiped the smile off Suzy's face. She didn't want that to happen again. Suzy was trying to understand how she felt. If she was ever to accept Luke, nothing must upset her now.

'If that's the way you want it,' he gave in.

'Your mam's going to marry old Nosey?' Frankie let out a wild scream when Suzy told him the news. 'Surely not?'

They were in the kitchen looking for biscuits, and it so happened that Mam was in the living room with her intended groom.

'Shush, they'll hear you. Mam doesn't like me calling him that.'

'She knows I do it too,' Frankie whispered, laughing.

'It's not a laughing matter,' Suzy was saying when she saw her mother come to the door.

'What did you call Luke? You mustn't, Suzy dear, you'll upset him.'

But he was behind her at that moment. Suzy thought his nose looked more red and shiny, but he was smiling.

'They aren't the first, Josie. They call me that at the tram depot. I'm flattered really. I believe the Duke of Wellington had a nose like mine, and he was called Old Nosey by his men. I'm in good company.'

'Here,' Suzy pushed a couple of chocolate biscuits into Frankie's hand and helped herself to more. 'He brought me this box of biscuits.'

'Perhaps he's not too bad,' Frankie whispered. 'Not as bad as you think.'

Suzy was very wary of Luke Palmer. He was scary – his eyes were mean and watchful and hard – she couldn't take to him and she couldn't understand why Mam had. She felt quite sure it was wrong for her to marry him. She couldn't see him taking Daddy's place. But Mam was equally certain it was the right thing for her to do.

'He's a very kind person, Suzy. I won't have to worry about my money running out. He earns more than Daddy did. We'll be much better off. He'll give us security.'

Suzy couldn't see that. She didn't want him here all the time in her house, but she couldn't stop Mam making preparations for her wedding.

'I shall buy us each a smart outfit,' Josie told her. 'I can use some of my savings. Once I have a husband, it won't be so desperate to keep a few pounds between us and the wolf at the door. You'd like that, wouldn't you?'

Suzy agreed. She'd love to have a whole new outfit. 'Can I choose it?'

'We'll have to see. We'll go to Blacklers. I won't have time to make new dresses.'

'When is the wedding to be?'

'We've decided to leave it until your school holidays have started.'

Suzy thought they were not far off.

'Because we're all going away for a little holiday afterwards. Luke has booked us into a boarding house in Rhyl for a week. That will be lovely, won't it?'

Suzy had to agree it was exciting. Mam was full of regrets

that Rita and Millie, who worked with her at the Imperial, wouldn't be able to come because they had to work as usual. They clubbed together to buy her a smart leather handbag since she already had an equipped home.

'It's beautiful, isn't it?' Mam stroked it. 'I shall use it on my wedding day. We'll not have many guests, though. Nobody at all from the Corporation Tramways.'

'That's the way you said you wanted it,' Luke said. 'A quiet wedding. No fuss.'

Suzy had a heavy weight in her stomach when she put on her new blue dress and straw hat with blue flowers round the rim. Mam had done her hair up in rags the night before and she had lovely nut-brown ringlets round her face. She thought they looked a bit like Frankie's curls.

The marriage took place at eleven o'clock on a sunny morning at the end of July. Mam was in deeper blue and had more flowers and lots of veiling on her hat. Suzy thought she'd never seen her look so eager and excited, or so pretty. She'd had a new Eugene perm for the occasion. Old Nosey wore a smart striped suit and a new trilby.

Mr and Mrs Maynard from downstairs were there, and Olga and Eric Rimmer from upstairs. Frankie looked angelic in his best clothes. To Suzy, the ceremony seemed over and the deed accomplished almost before it had begun.

Old Nosey paid for two taxis to take them back to Upper Parliament Street where Suzy had helped lay out cakes and sandwiches on their living-room table.

Josie felt she'd had two difficult years since Ted had died. On the day of her wedding she felt relieved that she was shedding some of her responsibilities. In future she'd be able to relax and enjoy life.

She was looking forward to the week's holiday in Rhyl. She felt she needed a break from her busy routine of working at the Imperial and looking after Suzy.

At what Luke called rather grandly their wedding reception, she drank too much port and lemon, and by the time they were on the train to Rhyl that afternoon, it had given her a headache. Josie was surprised at how much whisky Luke managed to drink and told him so.

'It's our wedding day. I've got something to celebrate. My annual holiday from driving the trams too, that's another reason. I don't get the chance to drink much when I have to work.'

Josie had to leave Olga to wash up and clear away because they had to catch a tram down to the Central Station, then the low-level train over to Birkenhead Woodside to catch the four fifteen steam train to Rhyl. Suzy was excited and couldn't keep still.

Rhyl looked a magnificent place when they arrived, with late afternoon sun sparkling on the blue sea. The swimmers and sunbathers were beginning to leave the yellow sand.

Josie felt rather shy that first night going to bed with Luke, but his touch sent long anticipatory shivers down her spine. He was a good lover. Rather better than Ted had been. He needed it often too – before going to sleep as well as on wakening.

Josie told herself she'd held him at arm's length for two years, so no wonder he was hungry for it. When they woke up the first morning in Rhyl to find the sun streaming through the curtains, Luke sighed with pleasure.

'This beats going to work, doesn't it?'

Josie stretched luxuriously in the comfortable bed. 'Certainly does. I've told Mr Hollis I won't need to do so many hours now.'

She saw her future life more as it had been with Ted. She'd work perhaps two evenings a week to pay for a few extras.

Luke kissed her and held her tight.

'You've got the job now, Josie, and you say you enjoy it. Not much point in throwing it over. We could come on holiday like this every summer.'

Josie frowned. 'It's Suzy having such long school holidays. I don't like to think of her at home alone.'

'She won't be, love. I'll be there many times when you are not, and Suzy's twelve now. She doesn't need continual supervision. She's out with that Frankie a lot of the time, anyway. I'm sure his mother would give her the odd meal if we were both working.'

'She's done that before today, but I have to pay her something. I can't sponge. She and Eric aren't all that well off.'

It wasn't what Josie had expected, but she told herself there was a lot of sense in what he said. She'd try it.

'At least I won't be worried if I have to take time off when Suzy's sick.'

'No, we'll be quids in. After all, I won't have the rent to pay on Stockton Street. It is true that two can live as cheaply as one.'

'In this case, it's three as cheaply as two,' Josie retorted.

She felt just a little bit let down. All was not going to be quite as she'd hoped.

Suzy liked the boarding house but she was given a room to herself. It was at the back and a long way down the corridor from the room Mam was sharing with old Nosey. To Suzy, it was like being on her own in the boarding house, especially as old Nosey didn't like her going to their room.

They had breakfast and high tea at the boarding house but

spent the rest of the day outside. Suzy felt that a good deal of the time she was walking the promenade two paces behind her mother and stepfather. She liked it better when they sat in deck chairs on the beach and she was allowed to paddle or swim or trawl up and down the high-water mark as she pleased. Old Nosey very generously bought each of them a swimming costume; they were all of the same material, in broad black, white and red stripes. Mam's and Nosey's each had a vest-shaped top, but Suzy's was in a different style. She thought hers much more fashionable.

'We look like a real family now,' he said to Mam when they all changed into them.

Suzy loved splashing about in the waves. Nosey and Mam sunbathed in deck chairs and hardly got theirs wet.

He took them all to the pictures to see Rudolph Valentino in *The Son of the Sheikh*, one of the last films he made. It was Mam's choice; she'd been wanting to see it since he'd died in 1926. Suzy thought it was lovely.

She was beginning to think she'd been mistaken about Mr Palmer. He wasn't all that bad. She must be imagining the malevolence in those slits of eyes when they settled on her. If Mam wanted to be married to him and he made her happy Suzy had to go along with it. Mam had been right when she said he'd make their lives better.

Suzy felt low when they returned home to Liverpool. Once the excitement of the holiday was over everything seemed so much worse. She felt she had no time with Mam any more. Mr Palmer was always there between them, taking all her attention.

'Luke is your stepfather now, dear. It upsets him when you insist on calling him Mr Palmer.'

'It's polite, Mam. Better than old Nosey.'

'Look, I know it would be hard for you to call him Father or Dad—'

'He isn't!'

Mam sighed. 'I know, but couldn't you call him Uncle Luke? It sounds more friendly.'

'I'll try,' she mumbled. If Mam wanted it, she'd try, but she didn't feel that friendly towards him. He'd put her out of her mother's bed. There had been no apology or explanation from him or from Mam. Her narrow bed in the kitchen was made ready and Suzy was expected to sleep there from now on. She felt he was ousting her from Mam's affections. Mam preferred him. This was what she'd wanted.

For Mam and old Nosey, their one annual week of paid holiday was over, but for Suzy, another four weeks off school stretched ahead. This week, she and Mam would have to get up and go out early in the morning. He would be working during the afternoon and evening.

Suzy had always looked forward to the weeks when he worked that shift because it meant she saw little of him. But now when she came back from doing her deliveries, he would be here and they'd be alone together. She hated the thought of being alone with him.

'Bring me back a *Daily Mail* and twenty Woodbines in the morning, Suzy,' he said as she was drying the dishes after tea. He put the money for them on the end of the draining board.

When she came home from her delivery round the first morning back, old Nosey was in the bathroom. She'd never seen him with his shirtsleeves rolled up and his braces so much in evidence. He'd knocked in a nail by the window and tied a leather strap to it on which he was sharpening his cut-throat razor. His hand was flying back and forth, rhythmically stropping. The open steel blade gleamed in the dull light.

'Got to get it sharp, Suzy,' he said when he saw her

watching him. 'Sharp enough to carve you into slices if you're a naughty girl.'

He lathered his chin with his shaving brush and then deftly scraped off his beard with long clean movements. She shuddered as she took in the chipped shaving mug and tin of Brilliantine, so much masculine equipment spread out along the windowsill.

'How about some breakfast, then? Egg and bacon would be nice, eh?'

'We haven't any.' The shops had been on the point of closing when they'd got home last night.

'Here,' he rattled the change in his trouser pockets and gave her some. 'Bring a fresh loaf as well, and some sausage. I fancy a pork sausage.'

Suzy went out again and met Frankie on the stairs. He was swinging a shopping bag too. 'I'm going to the shops for me ma. Come with me?'

'Got to. I've been sent by old Nosey.'

The newsagent she worked for was in a small parade of shops with a grocer's, a greengrocer's and a butcher's.

'If only he'd asked me last night, I could have got it after I'd done my newspapers.'

'But you'd have come back with me anyway, wouldn't you? We'll go to the park afterwards.'

When Suzy took the pork sausages in, the living room smelled of smoke from Nosey's cigarettes. He was lying on the couch with his newspaper.

'I've brought everything you wanted,' she told him, putting the bag on the table.

'Good. Two sausages, and I like my bacon crisp. Two eggs, Suzy, and I like the yolks soft.'

'You'll have to do your own cooking,' she said. 'I'm going out.'

'No you're not. Your mother doesn't want you roaming the streets.'

'She lets me go out to play with Frankie. We're going to the park.'

'She wants me to look after you, you know that. You'll stay here with me. Now get that coat off and those sausages on to cook. You'll have a decent breakfast. Your mam's worried about you not having proper meals.'

'I had my breakfast with her. It was bread and milk.'

'You can call this your dinner then.'

He pushed her into the bathroom and blocked her escape by standing in the doorway with his hands pressing against the frame.

Suzy wanted to yell at him but his huge hands scared her. She was afraid he wouldn't hesitate to use them on her and they'd pack a real wallop. Silently, she reached for the frying pan.

Chapter Six

At the end of his shift, Luke Palmer handed over his Bellamy car to another crew to run the number 33 route and headed towards the cloakroom. He took off his navy serge jacket with the stand-up collar, brushed the dandruff off the braid with which it was decorated and put on his tie and pullover. One of the things Josie said she liked about him was that he always wore a tie.

He exchanged his peaked cap for his trilby and tossed his mackintosh over his arm. It was Friday and he'd been paid; he wanted to go into town today before going home. Now he was a married man again he had to keep himself decent. He needed another pair of pyjamas. Before his wedding, he'd needed so many things he'd been able to get only one new pair.

He was heading back to the tram shed for a lift when he changed his mind and went to the canteen instead. He bought himself a cup of tea and an Eccles cake from the counter, and sat down at a table by himself.

Luke felt he had good reason to congratulate himself. He'd accomplished what he'd set out to do. He had Josie as his wife and a comfortable home. Upper Parliament Street was a terrace of gracious Georgian townhouses, a bit run down, of course, and not in a smart part of the city, but his house was in a good state of repair and had been newly painted. He was well pleased with what he'd got, except for the brat Suzy. He could have done without her.

She was always there between him and Josie, trying to draw her mother's attention to herself, giving them no privacy.

He'd seen hostility and resentment in her eyes from the very beginning. Suzy was treating him as an enemy.

Luke was finding it an effort to hide from Josie that he reciprocated all Suzy's malice. He bought sweets and fizzy pop for her but what he really wanted to do was to give the spoiled child a kick up the backside.

He wondered what she said about him when he wasn't with them. He could imagine outpourings of hate.

Tommy Curtis came in. The conductors had to take their bags containing the fares they'd taken and their remaining tickets to the office at the end of their shifts. They were always a few minutes later knocking off.

'You're looking well pleased with yourself,' Tommy taunted as he passed to another table.

'Yes,' Luke agreed, but he couldn't tell him why. The less everyone knew of his business the better. Anyway, Tommy Curtis got him down. He was always saying things like: 'Hadn't we better go if we're going to get the tram out on time?'

Luke resented anything like that. It was his job to keep to time, not his conductor's.

But he drained his cup and got to his feet. The number 33 was due to leave. It was much better sitting as a passenger than being at the controls. His legs ached with all the standing.

He bought his pyjamas in Bunney's. He liked to have high-quality clothes; they made him feel good. He wanted to buy a present for Josie. When they'd been in Rhyl and had their photograph taken on the promenade, he'd half promised to buy her a camera. She'd seen that as an enormous luxury.

He'd heard the lads at work saying it was possible to buy a box camera in Woolworths for one shilling and sixpence. Although nothing there cost more than sixpence they broke cameras down into separate parts and priced each one separately. He wasn't sure whether this was the famous Box

Brownie or just a cheaper copy. Either way, Josie would be impressed. The lads had thought it a bargain. Luke couldn't remember whether the thing had two parts and the film was the third, or whether he'd have to pay extra for a film.

Woolworths was full of customers. He had to push his way past the counter selling sweets and chocolate. They had such an array and they smelled delicious. Perhaps he should buy some of those chocolate eclairs for Josie too? Where were the cameras? He felt someone touch his arm and jerked it away.

'Mam?' Oh God! Not again! And she was still wearing that awful knitted hat like a tea cosy. She must have had it for at least a decade.

'Lukey, why don't you come and see me? I've been in hospital, had half my inside removed. I've been right poorly.'

He was trying to edge away from her, but her gnarled old fingers were plucking at his mac. 'If you're ill, what are you doing down here in this crush?'

'I'm feeling a bit better. Listen, Flora came round and brought—'

'Who?' Luke went cold and then hot.

'Flora, your wife. Don't pretend you don't know her. You always act very strange.'

'What are you trying to do? Drive me bananas?'

'Flora wants—'

'You told me she was dead!'

'Don't be silly!'

'You said she was, years ago.'

Luke couldn't listen to any more. He put his head down and bulldozed through the customers to the shop door and out into the street.

Flora! Surely she couldn't be still alive? No, his mother had heard he'd married again and was deliberately baiting

him. She was that sort, out to get even with him, give him
something to worry about, wear him down.

But what if she wasn't? He could be in big trouble, and
that would be Josie's fault. She wouldn't let him near her
unless he married her. Oh God, he needed a drink, and the
pubs were shut at this time of day. He hadn't bought anything
for Josie either, but what did that matter?

No, his mother was up to her tricks again; he must put her
and Flora out of his mind.

Suzy didn't like her stepfather being on the late shift. This
morning it was raining. After she'd done her newspaper round
and cooked breakfast for him, he stretched himself out on the
couch as usual to smoke. His deeply hooded eyes watched
her over the top of his newspaper.

'You can't go out and play in this rain. Your mam wouldn't
like it,' he told her. 'There's plenty you can do here. Get the
fire set, for a start.'

She'd done that when there was a tap on the living room
door and Frankie's curly head came round.

'Suzy? I've got a new card game. Look, it's called Lexicon.
How about giving it a try?'

'She's got jobs to do yet,' Nosey said. 'There's clothes that
need ironing, and shoes to clean.'

'I'll give you a hand then,' Frankie said. 'Where are the
shoes?' Nosey took them into the kitchen.

'These are all his shoes and shirts,' he whispered to Suzy
while they worked.

Afterwards, they sat down at the living-room table and
played a few games of Lexicon. They were shouting and
squabbling a bit, but all in fun. After twenty minutes, Nosey
roused himself.

'Stop that racket, you kids.' His swarthy cheeks were

flushed with irritation. 'Suzy, little girls should be seen and not heard.'

Frankie gasped. 'It's your home, Suzy,' he said under his breath.

'And I'd like it better if little boys were not seen or heard here at all.'

Suzy said: 'Mam doesn't mind us playing like this. She says it must be turn and turn about or Frankie's mam will get fed up with me being there all the time.'

'I'm fed up with it already,' he snarled. 'Get going, go somewhere else. I've had as much as I can stand of you.'

'Come on, Suzy.' Frankie's bright blue eyes were angry and he was on his feet. 'Let's go up to my place.'

'Thank God for that.' Nosey rattled his newspaper.

Suzy said: 'Wait till I tell Mam—'

His fist shot out and caught at her skirt as she passed him. She was swung almost off her feet. His other fist was screwing her bodice so tight at the neck that it threatened to throttle her. She let out a strangled scream.

The next moment, Frankie was laying into him with both fists. 'Get off her!'

Luke had to let go of Suzy to defend himself. She felt Frankie haul her out of Nosey's reach.

'Wait till I tell Mam!' she yelled, but he was on his feet and his fist clipped her ear, knocking her against the table.

'You'll be asking for more of that if you do,' he shouted after them. 'I'll knock hell out of the pair of you. Little brats.'

Frankie's mother had heard the commotion and wanted to know what had happened. When she heard that Suzy was scared of Luke, she invited her to have a bowl of soup with them at dinner time so she was able to stay out of his way. Suzy stayed upstairs until she heard Mam come home.

The fire was burning up in the grate, he'd swept the hearth and brought up another bucket of coal. He'd been out shopping too and bought two sorts of cheese, some good strawberry jam and a fruit cake.

Mam was loud in his praise. 'Isn't he kind?' she asked Suzy.

Suzy couldn't believe it. 'He's horrible to me,' she said. It was as though Mam saw a different person.

The next day was worse. When she came home with his newspaper and cigarettes, he said: 'Don't you disappear today. I'm not having that.'

His big nose was red and shiny, and his eyes seemed malevolent. 'From now on you'll do as you're told. Your mam's afraid you're running wild when there's nobody here to look after you.'

He kept her busy: 'Sweep the floor, take the hearth rug down to the back yard and give it a shake.'

When she'd done that it was: 'Bring up a bucket of coal for your mam. She'll be tired when she comes in from work.'

He spent the whole time lying on the couch with his newspaper and his bottle of whisky. When he suggested she clean the bath and washbowl with Vim, she retorted: 'Why don't you do something to help? You haven't lifted a finger. Why leave it all to Mam and me?'

'It's woman's work, isn't it?' he said. 'By jove, you've a lot to learn.'

When Frankie knocked on the living-room door, wanting her to come and play, Nosey said: 'She's not going out today. I'm teaching her how to help about the house.'

To Suzy he said: 'Your mam will be pleased when she comes home and sees what you've done for her.' The rooms were spotless, the table was set for two and the kettle would be on the boil.

'Now don't go crying to her about me. It won't do you any good.' His huge hand took a grip on the neck of her dress and gave it a twist. 'She's asked me to take on a father's responsibilities. She wants me to take care of you, civilise you, show you what's what. I've promised her I'll do my best to knock you into shape.'

Nosey went off to work half an hour before Mam came home. Suzy sat down for the first time that day, tired and full of burning anger at him.

She wanted to scream at the way he'd taken over. He'd not allowed her a minute to herself all morning. She didn't believe her mother had asked him to keep on at her as he had, but when Mam came in she looked round and said: 'Everywhere looks lovely, Suzy. You must have worked hard this morning.'

'I have. Nosey kept me at it. One job after the other.'

'Thank you, love, you've done wonders.' Mam looked weary and there was more grey in her hair than there had been last year. 'Isn't it just like Luke? He doesn't like to see me doing housework when I've been at the Imperial all morning.'

Suzy didn't know how Mam could love such a horrible person as Nosey, but she said she did, and she'd married him so she could have him here always. Mam had told her she felt happy and secure now. She wouldn't hear a word against him. Suzy thought Mam didn't love her as much as she used to, but she didn't want to complain and let her know how much she hated and feared Nosey. Mam would love her even less if she knew that.

'What about the housekeeping?' Josie asked Luke a week after they returned from their honeymoon. 'How much are you going to give me?'

She'd tried to discuss it with him while they were away, and she was afraid he didn't want to commit himself to any set sum. He even looked a little hurt now that she'd asked again.

'How would it be if I go on buying food for us, just as I do now?' he asked. He bought luxury food and a good deal of meat. 'You must tell me if there's anything you'd like me to get.'

Josie said: 'The money would go further if you handed it over to me and let me buy what's needed.'

'You're too careful, Josie. We wouldn't eat nearly so well. How about if I paid the rent as well? And saved up to take us all away again on holiday? You bring a lot of food home and you've got your own money anyway.'

Josie protested: 'Luke, I'd find it easier to budget if—'

'I'll pay the coalman too. That'll only leave the basic foodstuffs for you to buy.'

'There's the electric and the gas as well, and Suzy's growing so fast, she's always needing new clothes.'

'Yes, well, Suzy . . .'

The inference wasn't lost on Josie. If Suzy needed clothes it wasn't his responsibility.

'I'm not being unfair, am I?' Luke beamed his charm down at her. 'I expect to pay my whack.'

Josie thought Luke wanted to be boss in what he now considered to be his own home. He'd always ordered Suzy about, assuming an authority over her. Now he was beginning to use the same tone to Josie herself. He was testing her, setting up a power base.

She stood her ground. 'Luke, I need to know exactly what you're going to provide by way of food.'

'Right, I'll guarantee to bring steak or chops for our dinner on Mondays, Wednesdays and Fridays. How about that?'

'But I might be able to bring something home from the hotel.'

'We can use that up for snacks, can't we? We ought to provide one decent meal a day for Suzy. She's a growing girl.'

Josie realised she wasn't going to win. Luke wanted to control the way the household was managed. She told herself that perhaps, with his wage, it would work out all right.

When he put himself out to charm her, life was absolutely wonderful. Luke told her he needed a lot of love, he was a passionate man. He had only to touch her to make her tingle, and his lovemaking could thrill her. But over the first month or so, she found marriage less satisfying than she'd expected. There were times when he was irritable and the Thursday she'd dished up goose pudding for his tea, he'd flown into a frenzy.

'What's this?' He was frowning heavily as he tasted it.

'It's a bake. A stopgap . . .' It was a recipe for days when she'd run out of money.

'That's obvious. What's in it?'

'You've had it before. I made it after Ted died . . .'

He bellowed: 'What's in it, woman?'

'Dripping left over from Sunday's beef, some stale bread and a little sage and—'

'It's disgusting, and you call yourself a cook?'

'I've got nothing to cook. It's something from nothing.'

He crashed his knife and fork down on his plate. 'I can't eat it. What else is there?'

Suzy was tucking in. 'I like goose pudding. It's hot and crunchy on top. I'll finish yours if you don't want it.'

That ignited Luke; he flew into such a rage that he hurled his plate on the floor rather than let Suzy eat his helping.

'Are you trying to poison me? I suppose you want me dead?'

Josie's heart was thudding, her mouth was dry; she was

scared of him when he was like this. She could see Suzy cringing back in her chair too. She had to keep calm.

'It's pay day tomorrow, Luke. I've run out of money. I can't provide steak if I've no money.'

'Run out? Why can't you manage? It isn't that difficult, for God's sake!'

'I could manage perfectly well if you bought what you promised; if you paid your share.'

'Are you saying I don't?' His face, twisting with fury, came within six inches of hers. He looked evil.

'Luke, you said you'd provide us with meat on Wednesdays and this week you didn't. I had to send Suzy to fetch some liver.'

'So it's my fault we have to eat this rubbish? You're trying to blame me?'

Josie never knew what mood he'd be in. He could change in an instant from being kind and loving to raging like a wild bull.

She was more careful after that not to say or do anything to upset him.

She had to get up very early, and when she came home from work between three and half-past, there was housework to do and an evening meal to cook for her family.

It irked her to find him home before her sometimes, reading his newspaper and lolling back on the couch. It made her complain.

'You might have lit the fire for me. I need it to burn up to get hot water for the washing.'

Luke produced a lot of extra washing for her to do. It wasn't easy when she couldn't start it until late afternoon. It was a long way down to the garden to hang it out, and with so little of the day left it rarely dried adequately. There was a pulley controlling rails over the bath where it could continue to drip overnight but she had no airing cupboard. All her washing had to be aired on the maiden round the living-room fire.

'Sorry, love, didn't think. I've only just come in.' He did get up then, and raked out the ashes and relit the fire.

Josie was tired more often than she used to be. She told herself there was a lot she should have sorted out before she'd agreed to marriage. It was harder now to say she wanted to work fewer hours or tell him he'd have to give her more help about the house. Luke's expectations of her were high and it seemed to Josie that her expectations of him were not being met.

Suzy was stiff with fear. She hadn't realised that Mam was scared of Nosey too, not until she'd seen her swallow back her terror when he'd gone mad over the goose pudding. There'd been nothing the matter with it. Daddy had liked goose pudding. Nosey had had a terrible tantrum over nothing. He wasn't acting like a reasonable person.

Mam couldn't cope with him any more than she could, and that was the most frightening thing of all. Mam was like putty in his hands too.

Yet Mam said she loved him and that he loved them both. Clearly, love meant something different to Nosey. Suzy was beginning to think he was a madman.

'There are times when he needs a strait-jacket,' she railed at Frankie the next day. 'I told Mam she shouldn't marry him. I never liked him.'

'But she's done it.'

'I know. I wish we could get rid of him. What are we going to do?'

'Kill him.'

'Yes, Frankie, and how am I going to do that?'

'Poison him. My dad's got all sorts of things to poison plants.'

'He's more than a plant.'

'Weedkiller, you know. I've heard that can kill people.'

'You're in cloud-cuckoo-land too. I want to get rid of him, not get hanged for murder. What's the matter with all you fellows?'

With Suzy back at school, Josie settled into a new routine. The run-up to Christmas was always a busy time for her, and just a fortnight before, Rita, the other cook at the Imperial, went off sick with tonsillitis and Josie had more to do than usual. She was late getting home and, because Luke was out working, she'd changed the sheets on their bed and then washed them so that he wouldn't see her working.

She'd hung them out on the line and left them there until after she'd cooked some fish for her and Suzy. With the cooker in the bathroom, cooking smells could cling to the washing.

She'd had to rush down to get the sheets in the middle of her meal because rain began to patter against the windows. Suzy was full of energy as usual and had borrowed Frankie's Lexicon cards and persuaded her to play. After Suzy had gone to bed, Josie settled down to rest but Olga had come down for a chat.

Josie was yawning and looking forward to bed when Luke came home at ten thirty.

'I'm hungry,' he said as he bent to kiss her. 'Starving, in fact. What have you got for my supper? I just fancy a bit of steak or a pork chop.'

'I've kept a piece of cod for you.'

'I'm not mad about fish, you know that.' The note of complaint in his voice was faint but it was there.

102

'Suzy and I had it for tea. It was very nice.' Josie felt defensive. 'Will you have it?'

'I'm empty. Had nothing but a cheese sandwich in the canteen at tea-time. Yes, I've got to eat something.'

Josie put the frying pan on the stove, and said cheerfully: 'Fried cod with bread and butter?'

'Don't frill it up, Josie, you know it's bread and marge.'

She stifled another yawn. When it was ready to dish up, she poured two cups of tea. Luke didn't like eating alone; he always wanted her to sit at the table to keep him company. She got to her feet as soon as he put his knife and fork down.

'I'm shattered. I'll have to go to bed.'

He was never in a hurry to do that when he was working late. 'I need to unwind first,' he told her, and poured himself a whisky.

Josie left the bedroom light on for him but she could feel herself fading away the moment she pulled the bedclothes up round her neck. She half woke up twenty minutes later and was vaguely aware of Luke moving about the bedroom. She heard the light click off, turned on to her side and expected to be away again in moments. Cold hands went round her body, pulling her over into the middle of the bed.

'Josie? You can't be asleep yet. I came almost straight away.' Forceful lips pressed down on hers.

'I am,' she gasped. 'Good night.'

She could feel herself relaxing, her breathing was slow and even. Then his lips were pressing on hers again and staying there. She could feel the passion behind them. His cold hand moved under her nightdress.

'Luke, not tonight, please. I'm half asleep.'

He half lifted her to drag her closer. 'Ah, come on, Josie. Don't be mean.'

103

'I'm exhausted. Let's put it off till morning.'

'You've got to get up to go to work. You're always telling me that when I want to make love in the mornings.'

'Set the alarm half an hour earlier.'

'I want it now. I do love you, Josie. You know that.' His voice was cajoling, his breath hot against her cheek. 'You're awake now. We'll sleep so much better if you let me tonight.' His lips were forcing down hard enough to bruise hers.

'No, Luke. I'm three parts asleep, half dead.' She tried to pull herself from his arms.

He jerked away from her to his side of the bed. 'No you're not.' His voice was sharp. 'What have I done to deserve this? You don't care about my feelings, it's always what you want.'

That took Josie's breath away. How many times had she allowed it without so much as a word to dissuade him?

'You're my wife. I want my marital rights.'

'What about my rights?'

'It's a wife's duty.'

'I don't see why . . .'

'You're a selfish bitch. You're turning your back on me.'

Josie was shocked into wakefulness. She knew he was gripped with terrible fury at her refusal. 'No, Luke, I'm just tired. Surely I have some—'

'You're rejecting me.'

'No! Nothing was further from my—'

He was so angry he leaped out of bed and stumbled round in the dark. She could hear him swearing at her and calling her dreadful names. She cringed back, pulling the bedclothes more tightly round her. Then something crashed violently against the wardrobe mirror and glass tinkled as it shattered. She could feel shards landing on top of the bed.

It made her yelp. Her heart was pounding away like an

engine. Luke was acting like a madman. That he was just a black shadow in the dark made everything more frightening.

'What's the matter? What have I done?'

'You know what you've done. Where else can I go for sex, goddamnit! You're my wife and I'm supposed to get it from you.' His voice was loud and thick with fury.

Josie quaked. He'd wake Olga upstairs if he carried on like this. Probably had already.

'Don't make so much noise,' she urged. 'You'll wake everybody up.'

'You don't love me at all. If you did you wouldn't treat me like this.'

'What if somebody comes to see what's going on?' Josie was so scared she could hardly speak. 'Put the light on, Luke,' she hissed. One of the glass splinters she'd felt shower down on her had caught her arm and it hurt. She was afraid to get up in the dark with nothing on her feet. She had to ask him to do it a second time before the light came on. She wanted to cry when she saw the damage.

'Oh my goodness! Luke!'

It was worse than she'd feared. The full-length mirror on the front of her wardrobe was in bits, mostly on the lino, but there were shards all over the room. He'd hurled the alarm clock at it in a fit of uncontrollable rage. The glass in that had shattered too. Luke's eyes were wild. He couldn't keep still, he was still pacing round the room.

'Don't be such a fool,' she spat at him. 'Calm down, put your slippers on, or you'll get glass in your feet.'

She shook shards out of her own slippers and put them on. She'd been so proud of her bedroom suite, which had cost twelve pounds. She and Ted had saved up for it for ages.

'Mam?' The door opened and a sleepy-looking Suzy stood in the doorway. 'Has something happened?' The shock was apparent on her face when she saw the damage. 'Good Lord!' Her eyes went to Luke. 'What have you done?'

'Go back to bed,' he shouted. 'It's none of your business but your mother's broken her mirror.'

'Mam?'

'Better if you go, love.' Josie put an arm round her daughter's shoulders and led her back.

'Did you do it, Mam, or was it him?'

'It's all right, love. Nothing to worry about.'

It took great effort for Josie to keep her voice calm, but she had to soothe Suzy and keep her away from Luke. She didn't want any harm to come to her.

'But he's spoiled your lovely mirror. It's the only one we've got.'

'We'll have to get another.'

'It's seven years' bad luck for the person who did it, isn't it?'

'So they say.' Josie had her tucked up in her bed again. 'Go back to sleep, there's a good girl.' She kissed her, picked up her broom and the dustpan and brush, put out Suzy's light and shut the door firmly.

'I suppose you're going to say you've already had seven years' bad luck,' Luke growled when she started sweeping up the broken glass. 'Breaking a mirror can't make things any worse for you.'

Josie's self-control snapped. For the first time ever, she let him see that she was losing patience with him. 'Don't be ridiculous, Luke. You know I didn't break the mirror. Don't try to pretend I did.'

'It was your fault, you refused me. You rejected me.'

'I didn't. I was really tired and I wanted to go to sleep. Surely, I have some say in whether we make love or not? Why should it always be what you want?'

'I've told you, marital rights.'

'What about my rights? Half the time it should be what I want, that's only fair.'

He sank back on the bed in a sulk.

'Don't do that!' she screamed at him. 'Not until I've got the glass off. You'll get cut if you lie on it. For heaven's sake, Luke, help me clear up this mess.'

He opened the window wider, then lifted off the eiderdown and shook it over the sill.

'The glass will be all over the pavement.'

'Better there than in our bed.'

'The alarm clock's broken. It isn't just the glass, it's stopped going. How are we going to get up in the morning to go to work?'

'I'm always awake. I'll get you up in time.'

'You aren't, not always.'

'You're wide awake now.'

'I'm exhausted and it's gone midnight. This time you've gone too far.' Josie's own anger was growing. 'I've always given in and done exactly what you want up to now. I've done it with good grace because I want you to love me, but I expect some give and take on your part. I'm not putting up with you flying into a rage like this for practically nothing.'

'Don't say things like that.' Luke's face was crumbling, his earlier arrogance gone. 'I'm sorry.' He threw himself on the bed. 'So sorry, Josie. I'll get another mirror put in your wardrobe, and I'll buy us another alarm clock tomorrow.'

She put the light out and got back into bed beside him. She could feel it shaking and he was making little gulping noises. It took her a moment or two to realise he was sobbing. His face was wet with tears when he put it against hers. That shocked her, drove home how upset he was too. For Luke to cry seemed very alien to his nature – the last thing she'd ever expected him to do. He'd always seemed so strong, so much in control of his feelings.

'I'll change, I promise you. I know I'm moody and very much up and down, I always have been, but I'll change. It's because of the pressure at work – all the trade union work as well as the job itself. I'm sorry. I love you more than any other woman in the world, truly I do.'

Josie put her arm round him to comfort him.

'I hate to upset you, Josie. I've had a difficult day. It's a great responsibility, driving a tram. I shouldn't take it out on you, I know that, and I'm truly sorry.'

'It's all right.'

'You know I love you, I really do. Don't leave me, I couldn't stand it if you left. I need you.'

Josie reflected that she needed him too. That was why she'd married him. And . . . 'I love you too,' she told him.

They ended up making love. Slowly and passionately. When they were finally settling down to go to sleep, Josie heard a nearby church clock striking three. It seemed that Luke had got what he wanted after all. She would have been better off if she'd have let him get on with it when he'd first suggested it. This way she'd been scared out of her wits, had her mirror and clock broken, and been kept awake for several more hours. She felt in an emotional turmoil. Such an outburst of red-hot rage for so little reason seemed incredible. Now, listening to Luke's deep and steady breathing, she was afraid she'd not wake up in the morning.

It was Suzy who woke her, and it was a real rush to get to work on time. Luke had stirred, then turned over and gone straight back to sleep. His shift didn't start until the afternoon.

Josie didn't understand Luke. On the one hand he was lazy and contributed little to the running of the house, but there were times when he could make her feel like a queen.

He told her often that he loved her. He wanted to make love frequently and he didn't care whether she wanted to or not. She felt he didn't consider her feelings in that respect at all. She knew better now than to refuse him.

He was happy to provide them with lovely treats. When he was in the mood to charm her, nothing was too expensive for him to buy. Sometimes she thought him too generous. A little more thought before he spent his money might result in it meeting more of their needs.

He was never content with anything. He often seemed full of anger that could boil over for no reason. Life with Ted had been more peaceful. This was a very different sort of marriage.

Josie and Ted had spent hours talking over everything that concerned them. They'd shared everything. Ted had been as transparent as glass and she'd trusted him completely. She wanted the same sort of relationship with Luke. She'd thought a relationship with any husband would be similar.

With Luke, she had an uncomfortable feeling that he kept a lot of what he did and thought hidden from her. She wasn't sure she completely trusted him.

Chapter Seven

Christmas 1928 came and went. Luke provided a turkey and took Josie and Suzy to the Empire to see *Aladdin*. He also provided a Christmas tree and crackers and bought new frocks for both his wife and stepdaughter. Suzy enjoyed the celebrations, but when all the fun was over, she had two more weeks off school. She was beginning to dread the school holidays. She didn't like being home alone with her stepfather. She felt he was baiting her.

'I won't let him hurt you,' Frankie said.

'Only this week to get through.'

'We're off next week too.'

'Nosey's on earlies then. Mam will be home all the time he's off. It's just the rest of this week.'

'I'll stay with you, help you do all these chores he gives you. Then we'll play afterwards.'

But it didn't happen like that. As soon as Nosey caught sight of Frankie, he'd say, 'Out, go on. Scram, vamoose, I can't put up with both of you here. Too noisy.'

After Suzy had endured his attentions for several mornings on the run, she made up her mind she'd stay right out of his way. When she came back from her paper round on Friday, she could hear Nosey running the taps in the bathroom. The door was shut.

She crept into the living room and put his *Daily Mail* and cigarettes on the table. If she stayed, he'd expect her to light the fire for him now and cook his breakfast.

It was another wet morning so she crept straight upstairs to

Frankie's place and they played in his bedroom for hours, while his mother pottered about cleaning and cooking.

At one o'clock, Olga started putting a meal on the table. She was setting out three places.

'Your dad will be home for his dinner today, Frankie. Afterwards, I want you to change into your best trousers. We're all going over to see Auntie Maisie. It's her birthday.'

Olga's Auntie Maisie lived in Rock Ferry, and the Rimmers went over quite often to see her. Suzy knew it was time to go home and crept quietly down the stairs to the floor below. All was silent. All the rooms opened directly off the landing and all were closed except the one to the kitchen. She thought of going to the park for an hour or so until it was time for Mam to come home, but she was hungry. She crept into the kitchen to get something to eat and started to cut herself a slice of bread.

She heard the living-room door open and looked up to find her stepfather's slit-like eyes scorching into hers.

'Where've you been till now, you little devil?'

'Upstairs with Frankie.'

'I wish I'd known, I'd have fetched you back. You've no business to take yourself off like that when I'm supposed to be looking after you. You've got to tell me where you're going.'

'Mam always lets me play with him. I've come home to get something to eat.'

He sneered at her. 'Your friends not being generous today?'

'Frankie's dad's come home. They're going out this afternoon and they're having a proper dinner first.'

'I was worried stiff about where you'd got to.'

'I bet,' she said.

The next second, his hand came down against her shoulder. It felt like an iron spade and sent her spinning across the room. She fell against the brass rails of her bed.

'Don't answer me back like that. I won't have it.'

Suzy pulled herself back to her feet. She hurt all down one side and her heart was racing.

'Why didn't you come home at the usual time?' he spat at her. He had the most fearsome eyes.

She swallowed. 'I did. I brought your fags and paper for you.'

'Then you went sneaking off without so much as a word. Oh, I know why.'

Suzy stared at him but said nothing.

'You're a lazy good-for-nothing. Not prepared to do a hand's turn in the house. You know how hard your mother has to work. I'd have thought you'd want to help her.'

'I'll help her this afternoon, when she comes home.'

'That's too late. You left me with a sink full of your breakfast dishes.'

'You haven't done them,' she retorted. 'They're still waiting for me.'

His hand came down again with even more weight behind it. Once more it threw her against her bed. She banged the back of her head against the bottom rail this time. Suzy was ravaged with pain and shock and burst into tears.

'I had to cook my own breakfast,' he stormed. 'And light the fire.'

Suzy pulled herself up again, full of resentment. 'Hard bun. I'm not your skivvy.'

This time she saw his hand descending and rolled out of the way so he hit the bed rail instead. It made him yelp with pain and kick out at her with his feet. She rolled further out of his way.

His gaze was corrosive. She didn't dare meet his eyes now. His hand shot out to box her ears, and her head sang with the force he used. He was as fast as a snake unfurling its tongue to stab venom into its victim.

'I'll tell Mam about this when she comes home. I'll tell her you kicked and punched me. You'll not get away with this. You're a bully.'

His great hand grabbed at the front of her blouse and took up a handful of cloth, twisting it round until it tightened at her throat. Suzy screamed. She was afraid he'd choke her.

'Shut up this minute and listen to me. If you so much as breathe an inkling of this to your mam I'll give you a real walloping tomorrow. You'll get what for. Do you understand? This has been just a taster.'

His slit-like eyes were only inches from her face. His nose was red and shiny. Suzy wanted to spit at him, but she didn't dare. When she and Frankie had a fight she stood some chance of winning. With Nosey she didn't. She never would.

He left her then, and she climbed up on her bed and hugged her knees until the sharpness of the pain faded.

Suzy woke from a light doze and lay on her bed listening. All was silent. She wondered what the time was, and whether Nosey had gone to work. If he had, Mam would be home soon and she mustn't be found like this. Mam would want to know what had happened and he'd promised a greater beating if she breathed a word to her. Besides, Mam couldn't do anything. She was as much in Luke Palmer's power as she was.

Suzy turned over and felt the pain shoot up her leg. She'd always known Nosey disliked her. When his scary eyes came to rest on her, she'd realised she could expect trouble. She'd tried never to draw his attention, to behave as he'd want her to, but when he'd provoked her she'd forgotten all this and stood up for herself. She couldn't just lie there and let him kick her about. She'd had to answer him back. But she understood he'd have hurt her less if she'd kept her mouth shut.

The violence she'd provoked was far worse than anything she'd anticipated. Her face felt stiff where her tears had dried on it. She rolled off the bed and stood up. She could walk but it hurt. Her shoulder hurt where she'd fallen against the bed rail.

She limped to the living room to look at the clock. Mam would be home soon. She mustn't limp! But it was just stiffness and it was wearing off. She washed her face in the bathroom and combed her hair and was surprised to see her usual face. Nothing of what Luke Palmer had done to her showed. She looked normal. She filled the kettle and put it on the gas. Mam would want tea when she came in.

She felt better after her little sleep, but she was still shaky inside. She'd had nothing to eat since her porridge at seven o'clock this morning. The loaf she'd been cutting in the kitchen had gone, which meant Nosey had eaten lunch. She found it on the living-room table much reduced, together with the remains of a pork pie. She finished that off and felt more her usual self.

She didn't understand how Mam could have been so mistaken about Luke Palmer. Suzy had been able to see what he was like from the moment he started coming for meals, so why hadn't she? Adults were supposed to know more than children, but Mam hadn't. She'd never hear a word against him.

Would Mam listen now? Had she changed her mind about Luke? Would she believe that he'd knocked her about? There was a bit of a bruise on Suzy's shoulder. It felt much worse than it looked. Mam might say it was an accident, that he hadn't meant to hurt her. Suzy could hear her saying it now in soothing tones, as though she was making a fuss about nothing.

Besides, he'd promised her the walloping of her life if she said anything. Mam couldn't stand having rows with him – she went to pieces. Perhaps she understood better than Suzy that it was no use standing up to him – that only made him more vicious. Suzy decided it would be safer all round if she didn't tell Mam. It might make more trouble.

Nosey had been gunning for her; saying she must stay in with him, do exactly what he wanted. The only good thing was that he'd be working the early shift next week, and Mam would be here with him when he was at home.

Mam was coming now. Suzy could hear her footfall on the stairs.

'Hello, love.' She was easing her black cloche off as she put her head round the door.

'I'll make the tea,' Suzy said. 'The kettle's just boiled.'

Mam had taken her coat off in her bedroom and was behind her again in seconds.

'I've got fried egg and bacon for you. There was a mix-up with the orders and I cooked one helping too many at breakfast. It's cold but it would make a good sandwich. Would you like that?'

Suzy was no longer hungry but she never refused food. She watched her mother cutting bread for her and saw her in a different light. She'd always thought of Mam as being a strong person who had her own way about everything, but she wasn't like that any longer. Somehow, Nosey was having the same effect on Mam as he had on her. He was in control here.

Perhaps she should tell Mam he was knocking her about? She ought to know what he was doing to her.

'Mam?' Suzy felt daring. 'It's all right if I go out while you're at work? To play with Frankie?'

'Yes, of course. It's what you do anyway, isn't it?'

'Yes, but Mr Palmer wants me to stay in with him all the time. He says he needs to keep an eye on me, but I'm perfectly all right on my own. I have to be, to deliver the papers and fetch his tobacco and stuff. Will you tell him?'

'Why don't you tell him?'

'I have, but he thinks you want me to stay at home with him.'

'Well, isn't it nice that he wants your company?'

Suzy wanted to shout 'No!' at her. 'No, no, no!' Instead she said: 'I'd rather be playing with Frankie. This is my holiday, after all. Frankie wants my company too. Will you tell Nosey?' She kicked off her shoes. This wasn't how she'd meant this conversation to go. 'Mam, he—'

'Suzy? What are those marks on your socks? It was raining when you went out this morning. Are your shoes letting in water?'

The moment when Suzy might have told her was gone. 'They are a bit.'

'Where are they? Let me see.' Suzy lifted them and handed them over.

'This one's still damp inside. Oh dear, it's badly worn. There's almost a hole here. You need new shoes. Wear your Wellingtons tonight.'

'They leak too.'

Suzy didn't see leaking shoes as being important. She was far more concerned about what Nosey was doing to both of them.

'Didn't Luke glue a rubber patch over the hole? He said he would.'

'No, Mam.'

'Bring them here, I'll do it now. They'll last a bit longer with a patch.'

'I think my sandals are all right.'

'You've been wearing them as slippers. Didn't we cut the toes out because they were too small?'

'Yes.'

'Not much good in the rain then, are they? Perhaps if I put an inner sole inside this shoe, just for the time being . . . I'll get you another pair soon.'

It was a bitterly cold afternoon in late February. Josie was later than usual leaving the Imperial Hotel and the tram she'd set out to catch had just gone. She'd been just in time to see it turn the corner at the top of the road.

She stood alone, stamping at the tram stop. The wind felt icy and seemed to cut right through her coat. After working in the tropical heat of the kitchen all morning, the difference in temperature was very noticeable.

The restaurant had been unusually busy this lunch-time, and today the steak and kidney pudding and the baked ham had all been served up. Even the last of the finnan haddock had gone. There was nothing left over for her to bring home.

Expecting to have food to bring home had become a habit. Usually she prepared more meals than were needed and even the staff couldn't finish them. Josie was not fussy about what she brought; these days she was grateful even for bits. She'd cooked it and she knew it was all good.

Luke would be home before her today and he liked a snack of some sort straight away. She'd eaten a good lunch and was never hungry at this time. She closed her eyes for a moment and leaned back against the wall. She was tired; today had been hard work.

They'd been out quite late last night, which was another reason she was tired. Luke had been in a very good mood and had taken her and Suzy to see Al Jolson in *The Jazz Singer*.

He'd even bought a box of chocolates for them. They'd all loved the picture and had a good time. It had been one of her better days.

Luke would have to make do with a snack of bread and jam for the time being. There was syrup too if he preferred that, as well as those lovely biscuits he'd brought home yesterday.

She'd have a cup of tea and a biscuit and put her feet up for half an hour before walking down to the shops. She needed meat for the dinner she would make ready by the time Suzy came back from her evening deliveries. Some chops perhaps? Luke was fond of lamb chops but they were expensive. She'd see what the butcher had. Stewing meat was more economical and there'd be time to make a hotpot.

At last her tram was coming. There was only one other person waiting to get on and he had his hand out. Josie pushed herself off the wall and got on.

'Hello.' The conductor was Wally Simpson. He was standing on the platform at the bottom of the stairs. 'How are you keeping, Josie?' The tram was almost empty in mid-afternoon.

'Fine,' she told him, sitting down on the end seat facing forward, so she could talk to him. He went to take the fare from the passenger who'd got on with her and came back smiling. Red-haired and freckle-faced, somehow he reminded her of happier times.

'Luke's a lucky fellow. I think he was always envious of what Ted had. He's been much better since he married you.'

'How d'you mean, "better"?'

'It's as though he's turned over a new leaf. He's not drinking as much, is he?'

Josie shivered. Not drinking as much? As far as she was concerned he was drinking a lot, a good deal more than he used to. Bitter or mild could be bought by the jugful from the pub, but Luke preferred to buy his beer by the bottle, and he liked what he called a whisky chaser. By the end of the evening, he'd drink only whisky and seemed to be getting through at least two bottles a week.

'Did he drink a lot?'

'You bet. Got several warnings for turning up to work still the worse for wear. You're a good influence, Josie. Must be.'

Josie could feel her teeth chattering. How could she not have realised? She hadn't seen what was in front of her eyes the whole time. He did drink too much. Much too much. For the first time she wondered where he got the money from to drink so regularly.

She'd asked him how much he earned and he'd not said exactly. He'd fobbed her off and changed the subject. She'd thought that unfair since she'd told him exactly how much she was earning.

Josie understood now why he wanted her to keep on working. She was providing most of the food they ate and paying for the gas and electricity. Luke helped, of course he did. He paid the rent and for the coal and he indulged them very generously. Too generously she feared. She'd talk to him about this – try and instil more thrift in him.

She walked up Upper Parliament Street feeling in a turmoil. She told herself she didn't have such a bad life with him. He was a help with Suzy. Suzy was quieter than she used to be but she seemed to have accepted Luke into the family and to have settled down.

Josie turned her key in the lock and stepped inside. As she opened the lobby door Mr Maynard was crossing the hall. He came over to her.

'Have you got a moment, Mrs Palmer?' He seemed almost embarrassed. 'I'd like a word.'

'Of course, what is it? Not Suzy playing with her stilts in the kitchen again? I told her not to; that to you underneath, it made a terrible noise.'

'No. No, she hasn't done that since. It's about the rent. It hasn't been paid for five weeks.'

The hall began to eddy round Josie. The stairs seemed to be floating. She had to hold on to the newel post as he turned to take a ledger from a drawer in his hall stand. He opened it at the page where he entered the rent when she paid it, and held it in front of her. She couldn't see properly, the figures were dancing before her eyes, blurred by angry tears.

'It's the first time this has ever happened,' he said apologetically. 'I'm sorry I have to bring it to your notice. I thought perhaps you didn't know.'

'I didn't. My husband . . . Luke said he'd take care of the rent. He must have forgotten. I'll see to it now,' she said, and with her back very straight she shot upstairs.

It roused her ire another notch to find Luke stretched out on the couch with a tankard of beer in his hand and his usual whisky chaser beside him on the floor.

She closed the door carefully before hissing at him: 'What do you think you're playing at, Luke? You haven't paid the rent.' She felt disillusioned. Luke had let her down. 'What's happened to all that money? We're five weeks in arrears!'

Luke's face had dropped. His feet swung down to the floor, and he sat up.

'I'm sorry.' He was all charm, trying to smile. 'I must have forgotten.'

'Forgotten? D'you think I'm daft enough to believe that? I've believed far too much of what you've told me. You've been pulling the wool over my eyes all along, haven't you?'

'No, Josie, I love you. We've been happy . . .'

'I didn't realise you were a drunkard.'

'I'm not. When have you seen me drunk?'

'You should be, the amount you put down. You didn't tell me you'd been ticked off at work for being under the influence . . .'

He was twitching with suspicion. 'Who told you that? You've been talking to someone.'

'What if I have? It's the truth. It's not just the odd drink you have. You're on the bottle. You didn't tell me that, did you?' Josie was so agitated she couldn't keep still. 'The rent's gone on booze, hasn't it? You're going to drink yourself into an early grave.'

'You enjoy a drink too.'

'Oh God! It would poison me after this. I'd much rather you paid the rent. It's what you said you'd do. What I can't take is that you let me go on thinking you had. You're not playing fair.' Josie saw the tide of crimson flood into his cheeks.

'I don't like you going for me like this.' He was speaking slowly through his teeth, the way he did when he was angry. 'All these accusations about me not paying the rent—'

'But you haven't!' Josie's own rage bubbled over. She strode to the cupboard and flung open the door.

'You buy me port and sherry. You buy everlasting beer and whisky and cigarettes for yourself, but you don't pay the rent. Where's the sense in that?'

'If you loved me you wouldn't treat me like this. You don't understand, Josie. I know men who spend much more and who go home drunk, but their wives don't stop loving them.'

'You put me into debt and didn't even tell me.'

'It's your own fault. You wanted to go to the pictures last night. You and Suzy talked me into going, and buying those chocolates.'

Luke was agitated too and pacing up and down the room. He stopped in front of the mantelpiece, looking at a vase that had belonged to her mother. Josie held her breath, afraid he'd grab it and hurl it into the grate. It was a habit he had when he wanted to relieve his temper. She watched his hand go out to take it. She leaped at him.

'Don't you dare touch any of my precious ornaments! You break one more thing and I'll finish with you, so help me. I can't take any more of this.'

Luke let her take the ornament from him. He seemed to fold up before her eyes. He was no longer bombastic and straight-shouldered.

'I'm sorry. The last thing I want to do is upset you.'

'Upset me? You know you do.'

His narrow eyes squinted up at her. 'You enjoyed the pictures last night, you said so. It all costs money. You expect chocolates—'

'I'd have choked on them if I'd known about this. Did you think I'd never find out? I've never ever failed to pay the rent. How are we going to make up five weeks of arrears? We'll get turned out if we're not careful.'

The colour had left his face. 'I'm sorry, but there are other rooms to rent. We won't have to live on the streets.'

'I like this place, and I thought you did. I like the Maynards. I want to play fair by them.'

'Landlords. They won't miss a few weeks' rent.'

'Of course they will. They bought this big house to provide an income for themselves when Mr Maynard retired. He was a jobbing builder who worked for himself, that's why the place is kept in such good condition. He hasn't a pension. They live on the rent we pay. We've got to give him something on account.'

Luke was deflating under the barrage Josie was putting up. 'How much can you pay now?'

Reluctantly, he put his fist in his pocket and threw a handful of small change on the table. 'That's all I've got until pay day.'

'We'll owe six weeks by then.'

'I'm sorry—'

'Luke!' Josie felt desperate. 'Where's your wallet? The rent has got to be paid. I won't let us be turned out of here.'

'No, I love you, Josie. Really love you.'

He looked so honest when he said that. She wanted to believe it but he no longer set her flesh tingling.

'There's no need to go off the deep end—'

'There is.' His jacket was thrown over a chair. Josie yanked it across the table and pulled his wallet from the inside pocket. There was still a pound note in it.

'I'm taking this.' From the change he'd flung on the table she tried to pick up some silver but he was scooping it back.

'I've got to have something to keep me going. It's four days to pay day.'

Josie snatched up the rent book and ran downstairs. Whatever happened she had to pay off some of the arrears.

'I'll pay off three weeks now,' she told Mrs Maynard, who answered when she knocked on her living-room door. Josie slid the sixpence change into her pocket, feeling ashamed. 'I'm sorry this has happened. Luke overlooked it. I hope we'll be able to pay off the other three weeks at the weekend.'

She was fuming as she strode back to the living room, burning up with anger. She saw for the first time that Luke had made no attempt to light the fire. He'd been waiting for her to come home and do that too.

Josie wanted to cry. She'd been a fool to marry him. She was far worse off than she'd been as Ted's widow.

'It's all a front, isn't it? A trick. You tell me you love me over and over. You made me believe that. A middle-aged woman like me – I should have had more sense. You don't love anybody but yourself. You bring home luxuries and hand them to me like Father Christmas. It makes you look generous, really bountiful, when really you're as mean as muck. What do I see of your wages? You won't even tell me how much you earn. You don't pay your way here, you batten on me. I was a real fool to agree to this.'

He caught at her hand as she flounced past. She shook him off, and turned on him again.

'I've made your life a bed of roses, haven't I? I've put a roof over your head. I do your washing and cook hot meals for you. Oh, and you push me into having sex whenever you want it. I'm not allowed to say no to that. There's no saying no. Life is wonderful for you now. And what do I get in return? Gifts of steak to cook for you. A glass or two of sherry. Well, I can do without both of those.'

'Josie, forgive me. I wouldn't upset you for the world. We've been happy together, haven't we? I do love you, I want to make you happy, I do try. I can't help it.'

He was beseeching her now, pleading with her. Josie stopped. He had his head in his hands and looked like a lost soul. She was stricken. She had cared for him . . .

There was the sound of two sets of footsteps on the stairs coming up at a run, childish whoops and shrieks of laughter. School was out for the day.

'Here's Suzy. We won't say anything to her.' Josie didn't want to carry on this row in front of her daughter. It was shattering her own peace, tearing at the very fabric of her life. She wanted to protect Suzy from the onslaught of doubt and insecurity that was steamrollering over her. She had to have time to think. The door flew open.

Josie said: 'Hello, love.' It took a superhuman effort to pull herself together. She had to pretend nothing untoward had happened. She couldn't look at Luke. 'How was school today?'

'All right. I got ten out of ten for my sums.'

'Good girl.'

'Frankie got eight. He's mad because I got more. Can I have a chocolate biscuit?'

'You can have two, but you'd better have some bread and jam first, Suzy. If you start on the biscuits you'll finish the lot. Put the kettle on, there's a love. We could all do with a cup of tea.'

When Suzy left the room, Josie hissed at her husband: 'No need to upset her too.' She shivered. 'It's freezing in here, why don't you get the fire going?' She had a thumping headache. She hardly knew what she was doing.

It was Suzy who cut the bread. She was like quicksilver, bringing crockery to the table and bounding back to the bathroom to make the tea.

'You're a good girl,' Luke told her, as he brought up the full coal scuttle, 'helping me and your mam like this.'

Suzy opened the biscuit tin and surveyed the contents. 'Mam, next week the school's closed for three days.' Josie could see she wasn't looking forward to it.

'Teacher's rest again?' Luke asked.

'Half-term.' Suzy turned to him. 'You'll be on earlies next week, won't you?'

'Yes, I won't be here to look after you.'

Josie pushed her hair wearily back from her forehead. 'At least, Suzy, you're old enough now that I don't have to worry about you being on your own.'

'I'll be fine, you know that.'

To Josie, the atmosphere felt leaden. She and Luke were both speaking to Suzy but not to each other.

When her daughter went out to deliver evening papers, Josie said to him: 'What are we going to do?'

She'd calmed down a little now. Her first thought had been to ask Luke to go. She didn't want him here any longer. She felt he'd betrayed her trust.

'Do? What d'you mean?'

'I've had enough, Luke. You spend your money on drink and lie there on my couch consuming it. My money goes on running this house and you let me run round waiting on you. It's only fair that you hand over money for housekeeping. In future, I want three pounds a week from you.'

'For God's sake, Josie! That'll only leave me thirty shillings.'

'How much a week do you think I have to spend on myself? Three pounds isn't asking a lot. You've got to stop spending it on booze. We can't afford it. We can't afford luxury steak or the cream cakes you buy. Suzy needs new shoes. Is that agreed?'

Luke's swaggering manner had gone. He looked like a dog with his tail between his legs. 'I suppose so.'

'Is it, or isn't it? I'm not going on like this. I've never been in debt in my life and I'm not going to start now.'

Josie didn't know where her strength came from. She'd been giving in to Luke's every whim for months. Now she felt he'd been taking advantage of her. 'If you don't agree you can get out. I won't have you here.'

'Steady on, we're married. We've been happy, haven't we? We can put this behind us and be happy again. I love you. We can't let the first row we have break us up.'

'I don't think I've been happy, Luke. Nor is this our first row. I want things to change.'

'You can't put me out.'

'I can stop feeding you and washing your clothes. And I'm definitely not having you in my bed.'

'All right, I'll do it. I love you, Josie. I don't want anything to change.'

127

'Three pounds every week on pay day.'

'I've said all right, haven't I?'

'Dammit, you're still getting this on the cheap. Ted handed over his pay packet.'

Luke blew his nose noisily, glaring at her over his handkerchief. 'He didn't earn that much. Conductors don't.'

She went on, 'I was going to buy some meat for our tea but we can't afford that now. We're neither of us going to buy anything that isn't essential until these rent arrears are paid off.'

To Josie, the days that followed were awful. She felt jittery and on edge. Luke looked depressed and appeared to be sulking. He didn't speak to her and said little to Suzy. He lay on the couch from the time he came home from work until it was time to go to bed. When a meal was put on the table he got up and joined them to eat in silence. Once he got up and went out without saying a word to Josie. He came back with beer and whisky but made no effort to pour her a glass of port as he used to.

When they went to the bed they shared, they each clung to their own side of the mattress and maintained the gulf between them. Josie told herself she was glad, that she needed a rest from his frequent lovemaking. She was afraid their relationship would never be the same again.

She put a huge effort into making things seem normal to Suzy, but she wasn't managing it. Suzy would have to have been blind not to have noticed the long heavy silences between her mother and Luke.

On Thursday, Luke drank the sherry and the port they'd had in the cupboard. Usually he didn't touch it. Josie was feeling jittery, Luke's long sulk was wearing her down. She brought kedgeree and pancakes home, left over from the hotel breakfast. Suzy said it was a nice tea. Luke, Josie knew, didn't care for fish, especially not smoked haddock mixed into a kedgeree, but there was nothing else.

On Friday afternoon, she went home with enough cold shoulder of mutton for Suzy and Luke. There were three pound notes on the table waiting for her.

'Thank you, Luke,' she said. She'd been worried all the time they were behind with the rent. She went straight downstairs to pay off their arrears, and felt she could look the Maynards in the face again once she'd done that.

On Saturday, when the coalman delivered their weekly hundredweight of coal, Josie was furious when she found he hadn't been paid for the last three weeks, and she had to spend another pound to square him.

She raced straight back upstairs and shouted at Luke: 'We've got to have coal. Why didn't you tell me we were running up a bill with the coalman too? Thank goodness I haven't relied on you to pay for anything else.'

He lifted his head from the couch cushion and said: 'Don't fly off the handle again, Josie. I couldn't stand it.'

'But you let me believe you're paying for things when you're not.'

'This week you've had my money, you can spend it how you like.'

'I've spent most of it paying off the debts you've run up.'

'I can't give you any more. You've had practically every penny I've got.'

'You've just been paid.' Josie didn't believe him.

He flared at her. 'I had to pay back what I borrowed last week.'

Josie couldn't help but notice he'd bought himself more beer and whisky and was smoking Woodbines. He was moody and on edge, and spoke only when asked a direct question or when he wanted something. Otherwise he maintained a brooding silence. She thought the atmosphere was like a black pall, weighted with lead.

It had knocked all the confidence out of her to find she had debts she didn't know about. It made her take Suzy to the Co-op that afternoon to buy her the shoes she needed. She hadn't been able to wear her old ones with an inner sole inside – they were too small for that. And Josie also bought her a pair of Wellingtons in a larger size. Suzy was shooting up at such a rate. It was another expense she was able to get out of the way.

Josie also stocked up on basic foods like tea, condensed milk, sugar, flour, potatoes and matches. They had to have them. If she spent her money on food, Luke couldn't persuade her to part with it later in the week for whisky.

Luke had a day off on Sunday. He set great store by his Sunday dinner but Josie had bought liver. That was cheaper than doing a roast, even though there wouldn't be anything left for Monday. She was determined to manage somehow, and if Luke wouldn't help she'd do it alone.

Chapter Eight

On Sunday morning it surprised Josie to hear the alarm go off. Luke grunted and turned over.

Josie said: 'Are you going to work?'

A much less frequent tram service ran on Sundays and he only worked one Sunday in three. It wasn't his turn.

'Of course I'm going to work. Would I have set the alarm otherwise?' He heaved himself off the mattress and started to dress.

'I thought it was your Sunday off.'

'It was, but it's been changed.'

He hadn't told her. 'What about next week?'

'What about it?' He was pulling on his uniform trousers.

'Are you still on earlies?'

'Nope. There's a lot off sick. Like I said, my shift's been changed. I'm on lates again.' He sounded irritable.

'I thought you liked lates better.'

'Not if I can't have a drink,' he said heatedly.

Josie flared up. 'Why are you so bad-tempered?'

'Because you're being so damn difficult. I'm getting all keyed up. I'm out of fags and in need of a drink.'

He slammed out. In the past, he'd always brought her a cup of tea in bed on Saturdays and Sundays if he was getting up early. She heard him fill the kettle in the bathroom. He shaved and ate. She could hear him banging plates.

Josie decided she'd get up as soon as she heard him go downstairs. It surprised her when he came back to her bedroom door, but he wasn't bringing tea.

'I'm spent up, Josie. I've got to have half a crown. I can't drive all day without something from the canteen.'

'You don't spend that much in the canteen.'

'I've got to have some fags too. I'm a nervous wreck. I'm getting the shakes. Where's your handbag?'

Josie's eyes went to it on the end of the dressing table. She shot out of bed to grab it before he did.

She said: 'A shilling. That should be plenty.'

'Don't be mean. I can't go all day with nothing in my pocket.'

'You'll have nothing in your pocket when you come home however much I give you.'

'I've got to get some beer. Another shilling.'

'No.' Josie leaped back into bed, taking her bag with her.

He paused for a moment at the foot of the bed and said deliberately: 'You mean b—'

She didn't actually hear him say the word 'bitch' but she could almost see it form on his lips. Suddenly he leaped at her, ripping the bedclothes away and snatching her handbag. He had her purse out in an instant, coins clattered to the floor and rolled along the lino. He flung her empty purse at her before slamming out of the room.

Josie wept bitter tears as she heard his footsteps rushing downstairs. Then, doubling up with rage, she pulled the sheets over her head. She was shocked that Luke had taken what he wanted by force. She couldn't stand up to him, she hadn't the physical strength. He was making it impossible for her to stretch their money to cover their needs, and he'd still expect her to put his meals on the table. He was going to drag her and Suzy down with him.

It was ten minutes before she got up to look for the money that had fallen on the floor. She found one half-crown on the bedside mat and retrieved another from under the bed. There were a few coppers too. Definitely not enough to exist on until next pay day. Josie wished she'd given him the half-crown he'd asked for; he'd taken at least six shillings.

Half an hour later, Suzy woke and came pushing into the bed beside her. It took another half-hour before Josie felt calm enough to get up. She lit the fire, made more tea and pushed Luke's dirty dishes into the kitchen sink. He'd cut himself some sandwiches to take with him and opened a pot of meat paste to put on them.

Suzy's face screwed as she scraped the pot clean and spread it on her breakfast bread and marge. 'What's the matter, Mam?'

'Nothing, love.'

'There is. Have you had a row with Nosey? I heard him banging around early on. He sounded as grumpy as an old bear.'

'We're running out of money.' Josie tried hard not to sound as anguished as she felt.

'He spends too much on fags and newspapers.'

Josie added mentally: And whisky. 'We're both getting a bit edgy because we don't know how we'll manage until pay day.'

She'd told herself she didn't care as long as she had no debts. She could take ten shillings out of her Post Office Savings account if she had to.

'Don't worry, love. We won't starve.' She had to put on a brave face for Suzy.

On Sunday afternoon when Luke came home after working his shift, he seemed more relaxed.

He smiled and said: 'For heaven's sake, Josie, what are we doing to each other? I can't stand much more of this. Can't we make it up?'

Josie had been expecting him to make more trouble; she breathed a sigh of relief. It had been a six-day sulk on his part, and she didn't want any more of it.

He said: 'Why can't we be happy like we were? I do love you.'

Josie didn't feel very loving but she did her best. Luke kissed her a few times. It took an effort on her part not to draw back.

'I want to make love to you,' he whispered. Josie knew it wouldn't put everything right for her. She didn't tingle to his touch any more. He couldn't rouse her. She felt alienated, off all that, but for the sake of peace with Luke and a return to his good humour, she let him.

On Monday morning Josie had to get up for work; Suzy always got up with her to do her paper round. They left half an hour before Luke. Josie took him a cup of tea in bed to prove all was forgiven.

That Monday morning, Suzy was up in the kitchen before Mam.

'Bread and milk for breakfast today,' Mam called to her. 'It's stale and there isn't much left.'

Suzy cut the bread into squares and put it in two basins, sprinkled sugar on top and then poured half a cup of hot water from the kettle into each to soften the bread. Mam said it made the milk go further, though that was delivered and they weren't running out of it. Lots of creamy milk then, and more sugar to make it delicious.

'There's only the crust left,' Suzy told her mother.

'You'd better get a loaf while you're out.' Mam pressed a shilling into her hand. 'And see if they've got a bit of boiling bacon at Smith's. Don't pay more than six- or sevenpence for the bacon, though.'

They were almost ready to leave when Suzy heard her stepfather calling from his bedroom, 'Suzy?'

She would have ignored it except Mam said: 'Luke's calling you, love. He wants to be friends with us again. You'd better see what he wants.'

Suzy got to her feet reluctantly, but he came into the living room, tucking his shirt into his uniform trousers.

'Did you want Suzy for something?' Josie asked.

'I was afraid you'd already gone. Let me have a few pence more, Josie. I'm skint. Please, I've got to have a fag and a cup of tea when I'm at work.'

Suzy could see the reluctance on her mother's face. 'Sixpence.'

'Make it a bob. Go on.'

'Ninepence then. That leaves me only four and six to last the rest of the week and it won't be enough to buy food.'

'You can bring something from work,' he said easily. But for Josie it wasn't as simple as that. She could only bring what Mr Hollis felt couldn't be used up in the hotel.

Luke turned to Suzy. 'Here's twopence. Get me ten Woodbines, there's a good girl.'

'All right.'

The route Suzy took when delivering papers went past a row of shops. They weren't open yet, but she slowed down to look in the windows. The baker's smelled lovely, and her mouth watered as she surveyed the serried rows of blackcurrant tarts, Eccles cakes and Sally Lunns being set out in the window. She'd buy a large crusty loaf there on her way back.

Next door was the butcher's shop. The window was filled with bare enamel trays but a notice advertised boiling bacon joints at half-price. Mam could do marvellous things with boiling bacon.

Suzy finished her paper round and went back to the parade of shops. She deliberated for a long time over the bacon joints. They were all quite big and the cheapest ones were eightpence. She was going to buy one even though Mam said pay only six- or sevenpence. These would be big enough to provide meals for three or even four days. Lovely and lean too. She'd buy two pennyworth of pot herbs to make broth. Suzy realised she wouldn't be able to get Nosey's fags if she did that, because she had to buy a loaf. But it was all Mam's money anyway. She'd given him ninepence. Why should he always have so much money to spend on himself?

Surely he'd prefer to have food to fags? No, she knew that wasn't true, but Mam was worried about not having food. But he wouldn't be at home until about three, so it would be all right. Mam would be there shortly after him, and Suzy could stay out of the way until she was back. She'd offer to get Nosey's fags for him then.

She went into the shop and bought the bacon before going home. The house was quiet when she got back. Suzy decided to make the broth straight away. She knew how; she'd watched Mam do it.

She got out their largest pan, put in the bacon joint with plenty of cold water and brought it to the boil to draw out the salt. She emptied that water away and tipped the bag of pot herbs on top of the joint, then filled up the pan with fresh water to make the broth and set it on a low heat.

By this evening it would be lovely with the fresh bread. Mam would be pleased with her for getting such good value for the money she'd spent.

Suzy tidied up the living room and relaid the fire just as Nosey had taught her. Then she cut the crust off the new loaf, smeared it with plum jam and ate it before going up to see Frankie.

* * *

Josie had told herself she felt better now Luke was talking to her again but in truth she was very tense. She thought she must have been blind not to have seen that Luke was drinking to excess.

Last night, she'd tried to talk to him about his drinking, but he'd shouted and refused to listen, and she was afraid that he wouldn't or couldn't cut down on the amount he drank, not without help. The future seemed suddenly hopeless.

She wished she'd never married him. She wouldn't have done, if she'd known what she knew now. She and Suzy would have been better off on their own. She felt trapped. After all the thought she'd given to getting married, she'd made the wrong choice.

At work, Josie was busy. There was nothing left over from breakfast except cold toast. She ate a piece of bacon that had been pushed aside uneaten on a guest's plate. She found two sausages on another. They'd make a snack for Suzy or Luke. What they didn't see wouldn't worry them.

The kitchens at the Imperial ran with a staff of two cooks and two kitchen maids on each shift. There were pork chops on the menu for lunch. Rita, the other cook, was setting them out on oven trays at the end of the long table.

She said: 'Josie, what d'you think of these chops? They smell a bit iffy to me.'

Josie went over and sniffed deeply; she almost gagged. 'Oh! They smell awful!'

'What are we going to do?'

'They're definitely off. We can't use them, we don't want to poison people.'

'What shall I put on in their place?'

'I'll go up to the office and phone the butcher, ask him to bring some fresh ones. That'll be the easiest.'

Josie brought Mr Hollis down to smell the chops. He condemned them too, and the bad meat all served to put them behind with their preparations and wind Josie up another notch.

She didn't know quite how it happened, but when she was tipping vegetable water into the soup pan she let some splash on her arm. She let out a little scream and jumped back in surprise, spilling the cauldron of boiling soup down her leg and on to her foot. She felt the kitchen swim round her.

Then Rita's strong arms were guiding her backwards into a chair.

'You've scalded yourself, Josie.' She felt a hand on her head pushing it down between her legs. She certainly felt the torrent of cold water splashing over her scald. Millie, one of the kitchen maids, had emptied a bowlful over her leg.

In a few moments her head cleared, but Josie cringed with pain as Rita helped her ease off her shoe and stocking. There were angry red marks on her foot.

'I'll be all right,' she said, but tears of pain were blurring her vision.

'You nearly fainted, Josie. Would have done if I hadn't sat you down.' Rita was trying to dry her soaking shoe on a towel. 'You ought to go to the hospital with that. Millie, will you fetch Mr Hollis down again?'

Millie wanted to be a cook and was keen to help with the cooking. She was usually pressed into service if one of them went off sick.

Josie was trying to swallow back the pain when Mr Hollis came down. She said: 'I think Millie saved me from worse by dousing me with cold water.'

'All the same, I'll get a taxi to run you to the infirmary to have the burns dressed. If they say you're all right, take the tram straight home. Millie did the right thing. It could have been a lot worse.'

'I'm not too bad. I'll be in tomorrow morning.'

Mr Hollis helped her out to the taxi and paid the fare. 'See how you are, Josie,' he said.

As the taxi pulled away she looked up at the hotel with the big clock on top that lit up in neon lights at night, advertising Guinness. Josie felt grateful. They were a good crowd, always kind. At the hospital too they praised Millie's prompt action, and said Josie's scald was superficial and should heal quite quickly.

Josie tried not to limp as she went out to the tram stop. She knew the accident was her own fault. She was all keyed up and her mind hadn't been on what she was doing. She'd be home early today, and she'd have a rest this afternoon, try to relax. She wanted to be well enough to work tomorrow.

She walked slowly up Upper Parliament Street and let herself into the house. As soon as she started to climb the stairs she heard a cry of pain and a stifled sob.

It sounded like Suzy. Josie went up the remaining stairs as quickly as she could. The living-room door was wide open – she could see there was nobody in there. She threw open the door to the kitchen.

Suzy had rolled herself up in a ball on the floor and Luke's boots were kicking at her. Josie let out a scream. Horror was washing over her.

'What are you doing?' She ran forward to scoop Suzy up in her arms. She knew exactly what he was doing.

Suzy clung to her, sobbing against her shoulder. Josie was in a ferment.

'Get out, Luke! This is the end. I'm not having you here with us any longer. Kicking Suzy like that. What d'you think you're doing?'

Luke's eyes glowered down at her. 'She needs a bit of discipline. I asked her to buy me some fags and what does she do? She spends my money on sweets or something and comes back without them.'

'On a bacon joint,' Suzy wailed. 'It was on cheap offer.'

He was fastening his leather belt round his waist and it was only then Josie realised he'd been thrashing Suzy with that too.

'Get out!' she screamed at him. 'You've no business to lay a finger on her.'

'I thought he was on earlies,' Suzy sobbed. 'I didn't think he'd be back until this afternoon. I thought I could run back for his fags later.'

'Why the hell would I ask you to buy fags if I was going to work?'

'I thought you were. You were on lates last week. You always want the *Mail* if you're staying home in the morning.'

'I can't afford a newspaper. Your mother keeps me short.'

'Get out.' Josie was more controlled now. She couldn't stomach any more of Luke Palmer. She was determined to make him go.

'That child's a pest. She taunts me, she asks for all she gets.'

An awful suspicion assailed Josie. 'Suzy, has he done this before?'

'Yes!' she screamed. 'Yes, he's kicked me before, I had bruises on my shoulder. He's tried to throttle me too.'

Josie couldn't get her breath. This was a nightmare. 'Why didn't you tell me?'

'You like him, you want him here.' Suzy was drying her eyes. 'And he said he'd half kill me if I breathed a word to you. I hate him, I hate him, I hate him.'

Josie was suffused with guilt.

Luke said: 'I've never really hurt her. It was nothing much. She needs a firm hand; you let her run wild.'

Josie was so angry she could hardly get the words out. 'She's a good girl. She runs a lot of errands for you. How dare you hurt her like this? I'll not put up with this.' She was sobbing too.

Suzy swallowed hard. 'He pretends to like me just to keep you buttered up, but really he hates me. Won't listen to reason. I bought bread and a bacon joint and pot herbs to make a nice tea. I know the bacon cost more than you said, but it was a big piece and a bargain. It'll do us lots of meals. He eats more than we do anyway.'

Josie was struggling again with guilt. She'd asked Suzy to buy a bacon joint and she hadn't given her enough money.

Suzy gulped. 'I thought you'd be pleased with what I'd bought.'

'I am.' Josie hugged her. 'I am.' Thank God she'd found out before this went any further. 'Get out, Luke,' she snarled. 'This ends it for us.'

'Don't let's be hasty, Josie. I don't want to leave. I want to stay here with you. You and Suzy are my family now. I want to look after you both. I love you.'

Josie felt nothing but contempt. 'Don't start that again. The only person you love is yourself. I wish I'd never set eyes on you.'

'I thought you loved me. You said you did.'

'I didn't know what you were like.'

'You must have, we've known each other for two years.'

'There's none so blind as those who don't want to see. You're drinking more, you drink too much. You're only happy if you've got a bottle of whisky.'

'I need a drink to live with that kid of yours. But I do love you.'

She wasn't going to be soft-soaped again. 'It makes you violent. You're a bully. I saw you kicking Suzy. I'm not risking that happening again. You've got to go.'

She watched his expression change. He could see entreaties would get him nowhere. Luke pulled himself up to his full six foot one inch.

'Don't be stupid, Josie,' he spat. 'This is my home and you're my wife. That little brat is my stepdaughter. I'm allowed to use reasonable force to discipline both of you. I'm not going anywhere. If you don't like it, you can get out.'

His effrontery made Josie gasp. 'But this is my place; my furniture, my pots and pans, everything.'

'You married me and asked me to share it. I'm staying. And since you've cooked that bacon joint, I'll have some now before I go to work.'

'No you won't!' Suzy screamed. 'You belted me for buying it and now you want to eat it.'

But he was already filling a bowl with hot broth, then lifting the joint out on to a plate and getting ready to hack a thick slice off.

'No!' Suzy yelled.

He turned to the fresh loaf and prepared to have a slice of that too.

Josie was afraid Suzy was going to pummel him with her small fists and that she'd receive another swipe from him. She took Suzy to the bedroom, closed the door and turned the key in the lock.

'We'll stay here until he goes,' she told her daughter grimly. 'Are you all right? Let me see if there are marks where he kicked you.'

Josie hadn't thought of her foot since she'd arrived home but now it was throbbing. She knew she'd brought this on them herself, and that made her feel even worse. She lay down with Suzy on the bed and hugged her close; they sobbed together.

Josie heard Luke slam the living-room door and clatter downstairs, presumably on his way to work. Beside her, Suzy stirred.

'What are we going to do, Mam?'

'He'll not be sleeping in here again.' Josie slid off the bed and started pulling Luke's clothes out of the wardrobe.

'You and I will sleep in here in future. Oh, Suzy, I'm going to look after you better than I have. This is all my fault.'

'We'll push all his things out on the landing,' Suzy chortled. 'Then he'll take them and go away.'

'No.' Josie was brought up short. 'Olga will see them. Everybody will know how things are . . .'

Suzy's face was a picture. 'They'll know anyway. Frankie will have heard us – his mam too.'

Josie shuddered. She was afraid Suzy was right. 'When Luke's shift is finished, he'll want to sleep. I don't want him knocking us up and waking the whole house. He can sleep in your bed until we sort this out. We'll put his things there. There's the Maynards to think of too.'

'Mam, they'll be on our side. You're the one who pays the rent.'

'They won't want trouble in the house. All that shouting . . . I don't want them to turn us out.'

The pan of broth was still simmering on the stove, and Josie dished up a bowl of it for Suzy. She hadn't eaten her usual lunch at the hotel, but she couldn't face food herself, not after that.

Suzy was right. Olga and Frankie had heard the row. Frankie came creeping down to see if Luke had gone, and then Olga came down to commiserate and insisted they go up to her place for a cup of tea.

Josie tried to pull herself together. 'I can't leave Suzy here on her own – not after that – and she's got two more days' holiday.'

Olga's brown eyes were full of sympathy. 'She can come and play with Frankie while you're at work. I'll give her a bite to eat at lunch-time.'

'Thank you. Once school reopens, I feel she's safely out of Luke's reach.'

'Frankie said he was belting her, but I thought it might be just an occasional slap when she was naughty. I didn't hear anything until today, but I was on the point of coming down when you came home. Suzy, you come up to me tomorrow. We don't want to risk him going for you again.'

Josie had thought it was bad when Luke had silently sulked and caused such an atmosphere, but in the following weeks she became as concerned as Suzy about which shift he was on.

If Luke came straight home from his early shift they'd have an hour alone before Suzy returned from school.

'Come on . . .' He'd take her by the arm, push her on to Suzy's narrow bed and then start clawing her clothes off her. 'You know you want to.'

'I don't! Leave me alone. I don't,' Josie had to hiss when she wanted to scream and fight him off. She was afraid of making a noise and having Olga or, worse still, Mr Maynard rushing in to help her. She'd be so ashamed to be caught like that.

'Of course you do. If you shut me out of your bed we'll have to do it now before your brat comes home. I want my marital rights. It's your duty.'

The only good thing as far as Josie was concerned was that he didn't take long. He made no pretence now of showing any affection for her. He did what he wanted, then buttoned up his flies and went back to lie on the couch. Josie hated to be alone with him; he was treating her as an object for his sexual relief.

He didn't lift a finger to give any help in the house. To retaliate, Josie left his bed unmade and his clothes unwashed. He never again stumped up three pounds from his wages, though she asked him for it on the first Friday.

'No, this is my money and I'm hanging on to it. I'm not going down on bended knee for every sixpence I need.'

If he was at home, Luke spent the time lying on the couch smoking Woodbines and drinking. He returned to his old ways of buying beer and whisky chasers for himself, but he no longer brought bottles of port and lemonade for Josie. He continued to buy fancy cheeses for himself and took to eating cream cakes and chocolate in front of them without offering them any.

He ate his share of every meal Josie made. She was acutely short of money, and couldn't make her wages cover the rent, the coal, the gas and their food. It had been difficult when she'd been providing only for herself and Suzy, but now she was having to feed him too. When she put her foot down and said she wasn't catering for him unless he paid something towards the housekeeping costs, Luke roused himself and felt in his pocket for some coins.

'Suzy,' he ordered, 'go out and get me a twopenny fish and a pennyworth of chips.'

'No,' she refused.

'Do as I say. Get some fish and chips for me.' He lit another Woodbine, Suzy didn't stir.

'If you don't,' Luke said through straightened lips, 'I'll give you what for and your mother won't be able to stop me.'

Josie was quaking, fearful that he'd hurt Suzy again. She didn't want another audible row either.

'Josie, tell her to do what I ask. It's not unreasonable – only what any stepfather should be able to expect.'

Josie had to do it. She nodded. 'Go on, Suzy.'

Suzy leaped to her feet. 'I hate him, I hate him. I know I'm a pest. I can't help being naughty to him. He's horrible.' She snatched at the coins he'd put on the table and shot off downstairs.

Luke felt low. Josie's voice rang in his ears above the noise of the motor on his tram. 'This is the end. We're finished.' He couldn't believe she'd actually asked him to move out. Suddenly, she'd turned nasty, and for no reason he could see.

He was desperately disappointed at the way his marriage had turned out. Ted had spoken of Josie with such affection, he'd said he had a very happy home life. When he'd died so suddenly, Luke had thought Josie would be perfect for him.

He'd gone out of his way to be the perfect husband, always telling her how much he loved her and taking her endless gifts. He'd taken a risk for her sake, but he'd wanted her to be happy.

Women! They were all the same: they didn't know how to treat a man decently. After all he'd done for Josie and Suzy, he'd expected better than this.

'I've found a room for you,' she'd said yesterday. Smiling as though she couldn't wait to see the last of him. 'It's big and it's furnished, and it's only four shillings a week. I'll take you to see it now.'

'I'm not going.'

'It's just round the corner from here. It's clean and ready to move in to. I'm sure you'll like it.'

'Can't you get it through your thick skull that I'm not going anywhere?'

'I want you to go, Luke.' Josie had a way of looking at him as though she expected he would.

'You go, if you don't like it here. How many times do I have to tell you before it sinks in? I'm not going to be pushed out on my own.'

Everything was spoiled, though. All the happiness had gone out of the place. She'd worn him down till he felt like crying. The lazy bitch wouldn't even wash his socks. He'd have to buy some more on the way home this afternoon.

After he'd got his socks, he stopped off at the Flag and Sailor for a quick one. There was a jolly crowd inside, a better atmosphere than he could hope for at home. He stayed longer than he'd intended.

Chapter Nine

Josie was scared stiff. Luke had come home roaring drunk yesterday. He'd been horrible, shouting and thrashing out at her. She had no way of controlling him and she'd been afraid he'd go for Suzy. She'd had to grab Suzy's arm and run upstairs to Olga's, where they'd drunk tea and listened to the noise he was making below. It all went quiet eventually, and when she crept down to look, Luke had gone to sleep on the couch.

Josie knew she couldn't go on like this. She was on tenterhooks the whole time and her savings were being used up. She knew she wouldn't be happy until she'd moved Luke Palmer out of her life.

If he wouldn't leave them, then she and Suzy would have to leave him. There was no other way she could have a normal life. Josie didn't want to leave their rooms in Upper Parliament Street but there seemed no other way to cut herself free. She understood now why Luke had wanted to marry her: she'd given him a comfortable home, and there was now no way she could persuade him to go.

The more she thought about it, the more difficult it seemed. Luke knew where she worked. If she found lodgings elsewhere for herself and Suzy, he could find her at the Imperial Hotel any time he wanted to. He knew where Suzy went to school – he could follow her home to her new lodgings and find her that way. If Josie was really to escape from him, she'd have to find herself another job and get right away from here.

The problem seemed insurmountable. She was happy in her job but, like her home, she'd have to turn her back on it.

To find both a new job and a new home at the same time, and take all her furniture and possessions out without Luke knowing what she was doing, seemed next to impossible. If she wasn't quick enough, he'd only have to follow the cart with her furniture to find her again. She didn't doubt he'd push his way in, and then all her efforts would have been in vain.

Josie felt he was wearing her down. The longer she left it, the harder it would be. There had to be some way she could leave him.

She got into the habit of picking a copy of the *Liverpool Echo* out of the collection of papers the porters cleared from the hotel lounge every morning. When she had a spare moment, she spread it out at the 'Positions Vacant' page. There were fewer vacancies than there used to be – times were hard – but there were usually one or two for cooks.

Hotels and boarding houses often wanted live-in cooks. Several of the staff lived in here at the Imperial, but none had a dependent living in with them. Josie had considered asking Mr Hollis if she might live in and bring Suzy, but Luke might come down and make trouble.

He wanted her at home where she could light the fires and cook his meals. She would have to get right away. She didn't want to risk him seeing Suzy in the street. Josie knew she'd fear the approach of any tram if there was a chance Luke might be driving it.

Today an advertisement for a live-in domestic cook caught her eye. There were fewer and fewer of those jobs since the Great War. It was for a household on the other side of the river, and it seemed far enough away for her to feel safe.

Josie had started her working life as a kitchen maid in a private house. She'd worked herself up until she'd been employed as a cook, but there was still the problem of whether she'd be allowed to have Suzy there with her. Not everybody would want to give a home to a twelve-year-old child. Not only was she likely to be thought noisy, but she'd inevitably take some of Josie's attention off the cooking.

Before the war, she most certainly would not have been allowed such a privilege. Josie remembered her employers being very strict. Staff had had to be in by nine thirty on their rare evenings off, and no followers were allowed anywhere near the house. Times had changed, though, and there were fewer workers willing to accept jobs like that. Nowadays, there were factories where wages were higher and there were no restrictions on what you did in your time off.

Josie thought about it all morning; she had to do something, she was becoming a nervous wreck. She liked the idea of crossing the Mersey. Before she went home she wrote applying for the job, giving her address as the Imperial Hotel and explaining that she'd have to bring Suzy. She described her as a quiet responsible girl.

This was the first job Josie had seen that might solve her problem. When she slipped her letter into the pillar box, she was quite hopeful.

After a few days, she began to anticipate an answer but none came. She answered other adverts for jobs, but found in most cases that, although she'd be a little better off financially, she would still need to find herself a room. She confided in Mr Hollis, who was sympathetic and agreed that she had no alternative but to find another job. He said he'd be sorry to lose her and promised a good reference. He also gave her a rise of half a crown, but it couldn't solve her long-term problem and only served to make her less satisfied with the jobs she applied for.

She went for an interview at a hotel in Crosby and received a definite offer. Crosby was at the other end of the city and she almost decided to accept it, although they wouldn't allow Suzy to live in with her. Then, in the *Echo*, her eye caught an advertisement for a room in the same district. She decided to go and see it that afternoon.

It was a full four weeks since she'd applied for the job on the other side of the river. She'd given up hope of that but this morning she had a reply. A Mrs Smallwood invited her to call and see her. Josie telephoned and went that same afternoon. It seemed a better bet than the Crosby vacancy. She found the big house on the outskirts of Birkenhead in a wide, tree-lined road. It looked very different from Upper Parliament Street, and it seemed a long, long way away. Luke would never find her here.

Josie knew better than to knock on the massive front door. She went up a long drive round the back where she found a gate set into a high wall. Inside was an enclosed garden. Washing lines were strung across half of it, and the rest was given over to rows of runner beans and lettuces. She could see the kitchen door now, and knocked on it. A parlourmaid in a black dress with a starched and pleated muslin pinafore and cap was setting a tea tray.

'Hello, you must be Mrs Lunt?'

Josie had decided to drop the name Palmer. For her to be a widow and in need of a live-in job for herself and Suzy was understandable. She couldn't say she was running away from a husband she feared – that would make her less acceptable to a new employer. It would also make it harder for Luke to find her if he should try to seek her out.

'I'm Gertie. You're expected.'

Gertie had reached late middle age. She had mild blue eyes and a permanent half-smile, and wore her frilled cap low on her forehead. Not so much as a strand of grey hair showed round her plain face. Her manner was friendly, and Josie thought she could get along with her.

'How many other staff are kept here?' she asked. It was easier to find out from Gertie than when she was facing the mistress of the house.

'There's me and Edna, she's the tweeny. The cook left without giving notice nearly a month ago,' she whispered. 'They hired another but she lasted only ten days. It's been terrible.'

'Who's done the cooking then?'

'Either Mrs Smallwood tells me to do it, or she comes down and does it herself. Either way, it's desperate. I hope they start you right away.'

'I'll have to give notice,' Josie gulped.

'Oh dear! I'm sure the job's yours if you want it. I'll go up and tell Mrs Smallwood you've arrived.'

Josie looked nervously round the vast kitchen. She could see into a scullery and there seemed to be a warren of other small rooms going off in all directions.

A few minutes later she was being led through a large polished hall to what appeared to be a study. An enormous woman was sitting at a small desk.

'This is Mrs Lunt, ma'am.'

Josie felt almost transfixed by her large dark eyes. She wasn't offered a seat. Questions were fired at her. Was she healthy? What work was she doing at the moment? Why did she want to leave it?

Josie had already told her in her letter that she was a widow and how difficult it was to look after Suzy while she was employed full time. She went through it all again. She was afraid Suzy would be thought a big liability. Who would want a child about the house? She pointed out that at nearly thirteen

153

Suzy needed little attention from her. After all, she'd be looking for her first job on her fourteenth birthday. She even said Suzy would make herself useful about the kitchen.

The questions started again before Josie knew whether Mrs Smallwood was willing to provide bed and board for Suzy or not, though she'd made it clear she couldn't come unless Suzy came too.

'Have you ever worked in a private house before? How old are you? Is the child healthy? I have an invalid daughter, Louise, who's thirteen. She needs a light nourishing diet and generally something different from the rest of the family. Can you cook for an invalid?'

'Yes, ma'am.' Josie was confident she could cook anything.

'Apart from Louise, there are my elderly parents and Christobel, another of my daughters still living at home. In this house meals have to be on time and food has to be hot.'

'Yes, ma'am.'

'You'll have Edna to help you. She divides her time between the kitchen and the cleaning up here.'

There was a lot more before Mrs Smallwood got round to mentioning her wages. She was offered £50 per annum with all found, including uniform. Food and board offered to her daughter too, provided she was quiet and kept out of everybody's way.

'She's very quiet,' Josie assured her, 'a good girl, and she'll be at school a lot of the time. Is there one close?' That was something else she'd have to arrange.

'Age thirteen? A council school? I wouldn't know. Ask Edna in the kitchen.'

'Thank you. I'll see she isn't any trouble to you.'

Josie's throat felt tight. Dare she come here? Mrs Smallwood sounded a hard taskmistress, but Gertie had said she'd worked here for seven years and her employer wasn't too bad. Josie had to accept. She arranged to start a week hence.

'A month's trial then, to see how we get on?'

Josie almost changed her mind at that. Where could she possibly go if she didn't survive the month's trial?

Josie was shaking as she sat on top of a slowly moving bus, looking out at the rain. Gertie had shown her round the kitchen quarters: there were laundry rooms, storerooms, an ironing room, and a butler's pantry. She'd also seen the bedroom she and Suzy would occupy. It was a big one up in the attic, light and airy with two windows. There was only one single bed in it, but Gertie said another would be moved in before Josie and Suzy came. There was a hard knot of dread in Josie's stomach; she had one week to get ready and was now feeling overwhelmed at the thought of all the things she had to do.

She was very late getting home. Suzy had already gone out to do her newspaper round. Josie was relieved when Luke hardly looked up from his newspaper. She'd been dreading questions from him. What if he asked: 'Where've you been till now?'

She'd made up her mind to lie and tell him she'd been working late – she'd have to – but she was afraid she'd look guilty, and surely he'd guess?

Luke mustn't know she was making plans to leave, and when they'd gone he must have no idea where they were. They must get away without leaving any trace. If he ever came looking for her and Suzy . . . Her stomach turned over at the thought. She was afraid he'd go berserk when he found they'd gone, and goodness knew what he'd do. Josie started preparations for their evening meal. As she peeled potatoes she laid her plans.

Tomorrow she'd tell Mr Hollis she was leaving, and that meant the kitchen staff at the Imperial would have to know too. They'd all want to know where she was going, but she mustn't drop the slightest hint. Luke didn't know them anyway, but she couldn't be too careful over this.

It went against the grain to leave behind all the furniture she and Ted had so carefully collected for their home. She knew Millie, the kitchen maid, was planning to get married soon. She'd ask her if she wanted to buy some of it. The answer would probably be yes, but Millie would want to see it first. She'd have to find some way of bringing her here to see it when Luke wasn't about.

She could hear Suzy stampeding up the stairs. 'Where did you go this afternoon, Mam?' she demanded in a loud voice from halfway across the landing. She was bursting with energy and life.

Josie pulled her into the bathroom, closed the door and took her to the washbowl at the far end. Really it would be safer not to tell Suzy, but she'd have to trust her, if only to stop her doing things like that.

Later in the week, she and Millie left work half an hour early. They met her boyfriend, a milkman, at the bottom of the road, so he could see the furniture too. Josie's heart was in her mouth as she took them upstairs. Luke shouldn't be home yet, but there was such a thing as sod's law. The whole time they were there, she dreaded to hear his footsteps on the stairs. They wanted most of what she had; she was letting it go cheap. She had them in and out within fifteen minutes, and collapsed drained on to the couch as soon as the coast was clear again.

She needed to arrange a new school for Suzy. She'd had the forethought to ask about that when she'd been having the interview. Edna, the tweeny, had told her there was a big secondary school in Conway Street. She'd given her the name of the headmistress and found the telephone number for her in the book.

Josie knew she couldn't possibly go and see it if she was to work out her week's notice. She telephoned from the kiosk in the hotel lobby and asked for a place for Suzy. She decided not to give notice at her present school until the last moment, and not say which school Suzy would move to. She mustn't make it possible for Luke to find them.

She wanted to start packing the things they'd need to take but she daren't make it obvious to him that they were going. Nothing must be moved in the living room until the last moment.

There were two suitcases on top of her wardrobe, as well as a large cabin trunk she was now using as a blanket chest at the bottom of her bed. They belonged to Luke; he'd brought his belongings round in them.

Josie had been locking her bedroom door for the past few weeks to keep him out. She couldn't leave everything until the last minute. She hoped he wouldn't notice that she was packing their clothes.

On the morning they were due to move, Luke would be out at work. She and Suzy would be able to pack up and get away without him knowing. She twitched at the thought of his shift being changed. It would be a calamity if he were at home that morning.

Josie told herself not to be silly, it needn't be a calamity. She'd just have to ring Mrs Smallwood and tell her they'd be there late in the afternoon. They'd move out after he'd gone to work. They'd be able to get away unseen just the same. She had to keep calm and keep her wits about her.

She mustn't tell Olga or Frankie in case they gave the game away. And what about Mr Maynard, the landlord? She needn't give notice there, Luke would be staying.

The day before, Josie composed a note to leave behind. She made three drafts before she was satisfied.

Luke,

It was a mistake for us to marry. I wish I'd never set eyes on you. I've put up with a great deal these last few months, but I can't forgive the way you kicked Suzy.

I hoped you'd do the decent thing and get out of my home, but since you won't, we have to go. You must know I've wanted to leave you for a long time. I've got to protect Suzy, and this is the only way I feel she'll be safe. Don't try to find us. We're never coming back.

Josie signed it and sealed it into the envelope she'd brought from the Imperial Hotel for the purpose.

Suzy was scared of moving out but she was scared of staying here in Upper Parliament Street too.

Mam said: 'We're going to have a better life, Suzy, a new home, and for you there's a nice school not far from where we'll live. It takes boys and girls between the ages of eleven and fourteen.'

'But I won't know anybody. And it'll soon be the summer holidays. It's hardly worth—'

'It is, Suzy. It's more than three months, and next term you won't feel like a new girl.'

'But couldn't I wait until—'

'You'll have to go, I'm afraid,' Mam said. 'I have to work, you see. You'll soon make friends, you always do. We'll both love it once we settle down.' But her lips were tight set and there was an air of desperate tension about her. Suzy thought she was jumpy and likely to flare up at things that normally wouldn't upset her.

'You mustn't say a word to anybody about us going. Promise me you won't, Suzy? Nobody here must know until the last minute. We must keep it from Luke or he'll try and stop us.'

'Just Frankie—'

'No, love, especially not Frankie. We've got to get away before Luke realises what we're doing. Nothing must be disturbed about the house to give him a clue that we're about to move.'

Suzy thought there were clues enough in Mam's nerves: they were raw. She'd never seen her so strung up before. In their bedroom, which was now kept locked all the time, Mam was packing their clothes into two suitcases and a large trunk.

'I know they belong to Luke, but we'll have to take them. I've nothing else to pack our things in. *With all my worldly goods I thee endow.*' She tried to smile at Suzy. 'He's said that often enough to me, meaning my things are now his.'

'He'll be getting a bed and a wardrobe and other things in exchange,' Suzy reminded her.

'I've paid for his luggage many times over,' Mam said grimly, pushing spare sheets and blankets into his cabin trunk. 'We've got to take everything we can with us. We never know when we might need them again.'

'Aren't we going to stay in this new place for long?' Suzy was aghast at the thought of yet another move.

'Yes, yes, love. We'll be staying. We're sort of burning our boats by leaving so much of our stuff here.'

'What about my toys and things?' Suzy wanted to know. 'Will I be able to take my stilts?'

'They're so big. Couldn't you give them to Frankie?'

'No, I want them. Daddy made them.'

Suzy had a big dolls' pram that had been bought second-
or third-hand for her sixth birthday. She rarely played with
dolls now and Mam had said she must abandon it, but by
Saturday she'd changed her mind. Mam's spare shoes and
some of their clothes were now carefully stowed at the bottom
of it. It was packed really tight with books and jigsaw puzzles
and everything else that remained of Suzy's childhood that
she wanted to take.

She knew she was going to school for the last time on
Friday.

'Say nothing to anybody about leaving,' Mam commanded
for the umpteenth time. 'They mustn't know where you're
going in case Luke goes there and asks them. He knows how
to put pressure on people and make them tell him what he
wants to know.'

Suzy found all the silent goodbyes very painful. It seemed
she was turning her back on everything and everybody who'd
been part of her life. She wanted to keep all the familiar
things and just get rid of Nosey.

'You know that isn't possible,' Mam said impatiently. 'I
can't get him to leave.'

On the Monday morning they were due to move, Mam's
alarm went off earlier than ever.

She whispered: 'We must be dressed and ready to start the
minute Luke leaves the house.'

They dressed silently, listening to Nosey moving between
the bathroom and the kitchen. Suzy put on her best clothes;
Mam wore hers too. She thought they should look their
best when they arrived at the new place. Pinafores were
tied over them to keep them clean while they packed up.

Two minutes after Luke had clattered downstairs and the
front door had slammed behind him, Mam was in the living

room. She collected the mantel clock and wrapped a towel round her favourite china ornament, a lady wearing a pink crinoline that Dad had given her the last Christmas he'd been with them. Suzy called it Mam's doll, and she was fond of it too. Then the two vases that had belonged to Mam's mother were pushed between the blankets in the cabin trunk, together with a recently bought frying pan and an old chocolate box full of photographs. Then Mam propped the note she'd written to Luke on the bare mantelpiece.

Breakfast was bread and marmalade eaten as they collected together the other things they wanted to take.

At nine o'clock, Millie came round with both her boyfriend and her brother, each of whom had brought a hand cart. They began carrying chairs and tables down the stairs.

Suzy followed Mam when she went down to pay the rent up to date, and to tell the landlord that in future only Luke would be living in the rooms. Mr Maynard pursed his lips at the news, but Mrs Maynard was more sympathetic to Mam and gave Suzy a bag of boiled fruit sweets.

Back upstairs, their living room was looking bare. Mam rolled up her hearth rug and gave that to Millie too.

'I'd rather you had it than Luke,' she told her. 'I don't care if I leave him without any home comforts.'

Suzy helped gather up Mam's best plates and take them up to Olga, who had always admired them.

'Why didn't you tell me you were leaving?' Her round plump face was aghast when she heard how soon they'd be gone. 'I'd have helped you pack everything up.'

'I couldn't.' Mam's voice was thick with unshed tears.

'You know where we are if you need us,' Olga told her. 'Or if there's anything we can do.' She kissed them both 'I hope everything turns out well for you, Josie.'

A tear rolled down Mam's cheek then. 'Oh God! So do I.'

161

Frankie wailed, 'Suzy, I don't want you to go. You might have told me. I wouldn't have let on to old Nosey.'

'My mam said I mustn't in case Nosey wants to live with us again. We're only moving to get away from him.'

'He won't stay here,' Frankie said contemptuously. 'Without your mam cooking and cleaning for him, he'll go into lodgings or something. I heard me dad say so. And once he's gone we'll never see him again. He hates me anyway.'

'You'll see him driving his tram from time to time.'

'I don't go on the number 33 much. I won't let on I know him if I do.'

'It's all right for you,' Suzy sighed. She wished Mam had Frankie's relaxed attitude.

'I don't want you to go. I thought we'd be going to the pictures next Saturday. You said you'd come and see Charlie Chaplin with me. *The Circus* is on.'

Suzy was full of guilt. She'd had to say she would, or go against Mam's orders. 'I'm sorry.'

'I've got the fourpence to go. I sold my Sopwith Camel model so we could.'

'I know.'

Somebody was calling from down in the hall. It was Rita's son, Joe, who had brought his home-made cart on pram wheels to help move the heavy cabin trunk and bulging suitcases.

Olga and Frankie went down with them to help. 'I'd have done this for you, Auntie Josie,' Frankie told her earnestly. 'I could have moved your luggage.'

Suzy could see Mam was put out. 'I know you would have, dear. It's very sweet of you, but . . .'

'I'll find you wherever you go,' Frankie muttered to Suzy. 'I've got to find you if we're ever to get to London together. We agreed, didn't we, that when we're bigger, we'd go?'

Suzy had thought that was all fantasy – a way of escaping from the present when they got bored.

He said, sullen now: 'You could find me any time. You know where I am.'

He helped Joe load the cabin trunk on the pram wheels and tie the suitcases on top. Frankie wanted to walk to the tram stop with them, but his mother held him back.

'Josie would rather you didn't, love.'

He refused to say goodbye to Suzy, or wish her well. She thought he looked really fed up as she set off, pushing her old dolls' pram with her stilts tied to it, behind Joe's cart.

At the tram stop, Joe dismantled his load so it could be manhandled under the stairs on the tram. He wasn't much more than Frankie's age.

'Frankie's got pram wheels on that cart his dad built for him,' Suzy told her mother. 'It's bigger and would have carried more.'

'Luke would have forced him to say where we'd gone.'

'Frankie wouldn't say if he knew. He knows how to keep his mouth shut.'

'Luke doesn't know where Joe lives, or Millie either. He can't pressurise them. It's safer this way.'

Suzy could see her mother shaking. Her cheeks looked quite grey. They'd got away from Upper Parliament Street without Luke being any the wiser, but Suzy knew she was now filled with dread that the tram when it arrived would be driven by Luke. This wasn't his route, but if other drivers failed to turn up for work it was always possible that he could be changed. It didn't often happen but that hadn't stopped Mam having nightmares about it.

As it was, she gave a little whinny of dismay when she recognised the conductor. It was Wally Simpson, Dad's old pal.

163

'Doing a flit, Josie?' he asked cheerfully as he helped stow their baggage. 'You can't be going on holiday, not with all this?'

They sat in a row on the seat facing inwards. 'Don't tell Luke you've seen us,' she pleaded, her voice shaking with nerves. 'Don't tell him we went to the Pier Head.'

'Lots of trams go to the Pier Head, love. He'll not know where you're heading.'

'Unless he sees us.' Suzy thought Mam's eyes looked wet with tears.

'No, you're all right.' Wally looked at his watch. 'His tram should have pulled out five minutes before we get there.'

'Thank goodness for that.' Mam's relief was obvious. 'I thought of getting a taxi but they're so expensive.'

Suzy knew Mam didn't know how to go about getting a taxi. She'd worried about it over and over all week.

'You won't say you've seen us?'

'Don't worry, I won't let on.'

Mam was scared stiff. They could all see that. Suzy was scared of going to live in a place she'd never even seen, but Mam had seen it. She'd chosen to go.

'You'll like it,' she kept telling her. 'A big house with lots of trees round it and in a broad road with trees in that too. The houses there have lovely gardens, but you must be careful not to play where you can be seen from the windows. Nowhere near the house, and you must never make a noise.'

It didn't sound all that good. But they were getting away from Nosey.

They were crossing the Mersey to their new life. Suzy could feel Mam's shoulder leaning heavily against hers as they sat side by side. Joe had wheeled their luggage on to the ferry and was leaning over the rail, watching the tidal currents in the muddy water and the seagulls circling the boat.

Suzy felt her world was changing too quickly. She couldn't keep up with it. She'd been part of a normal happy family until Daddy had died. His death had made her cling to Mam but at the same time Mam had clung to her. The need for comfort had drawn them together, wound them round each other. For a long time, everything Mam did was for her. Suzy knew she was the focus of all her love and care.

That had lasted until Nosey had wormed his way into Mam's heart. Abruptly then, Suzy had felt pushed out on her own. Of course, she knew Mam still cared about her but all her attention and energy had gone on Luke. He'd dazzled her. Suzy thought he'd pushed her out and taken her place in Mam's affections.

Once Mam found out what Nosey was really like, Suzy had expected all her love to be centred on her again. But Mam was different now. He'd turned her into a bag of nerves and she needed Suzy's reassurance.

'I wish Wally hadn't seen us getting on the tram with all this luggage,' Mam worried.

'He won't say anything to Nosey. He promised he wouldn't. I don't think he likes him, anyway.'

'I'd feel safer if he hadn't seen us.'

'Still, we didn't have to pay on the tram.'

'That would have been a small price for peace of mind.'

'We'll be all right, Mam.'

There was another longer ride then on a bus, through unfamiliar roads. Suzy was sure Frankie would never find her here. At last they were walking down Grosvenor Road. Joe whistled through his teeth.

'It's awful posh in these parts. Wouldn't my mam love it here?'

'This is the place.' Mam had come to a halt beside tall wrought-iron gates. Engraved in white letters on the gateposts was the name of the house: 'The Lawns'.

'It's huge,' Suzy gulped. Built of grey stone under a blue slate roof, it had two rows of large windows made up of little panes and a wide front door that was painted red. Above it, set into a stone was the date 1851.

'Not that way,' Mam said, as Suzy went to push the gate open. 'We don't go to the front door. That's for family and their visitors. You and me, we go round the back. Always round the back, Suzy.'

They walked on and were just turning in through another gate to a drive, when they heard footsteps pelting after them and turned round.

'Frankie!'

'Hang on a sec,' he puffed.

Suzy could see Mam's mouth had opened in horror. She knew this was exactly what Mam had hoped to avoid.

'You've followed us,' she accused, a scarlet tide flooding up her cheeks. 'I suppose you think this is clever? You fool . . .' She covered her face with her hands and leaned against the gate post for support.

'Mam?'

Josie sighed. 'Frankie, what did you have to do this for?'

'You know I want to be a detective, don't you? I told Suzy I'd find her. The easiest way was to follow you.'

'But you didn't get on the tram at the Flag and Sailor. I remember looking round and thinking we were safe.'

For once, Frankie's dreamy eyes looked sharp. He was defensive. 'I knew you'd see me if I did. I hung back but I saw you get on. I knew you were heading towards the Pier Head, and I had the feeling you were going all the way. A bus came along just after, and I got on that. Sometimes you were ahead and sometimes I was. I could see you sitting there with your backs to the window. Quite a laugh really.'

Josie didn't think it was a laughing matter. In fact there were tears of distress rolling down her cheeks.

'Suzy, you put him up to this.' It wasn't like Mam to be so harsh and accusing. 'You asked him—'

'No, Mam! No! Don't fly off the handle.'

'She didn't, Auntie Josie. I got on the same ferry but I didn't let you see me. Got on the same bus at Woodside too, but I went upstairs while you sat down below. I had to get off the stop after you, but with that cart you were slow and easy to follow.'

'You shouldn't have, you little silly—'

'Suzy and me, well, we've always been friends. I didn't want to lose touch. When we're grown up we're going to go to London . . .'

'I didn't want you to know; didn't want anybody to know where we were going.'

'No harm in me knowing. I won't tell anybody.'

'Luke will make you tell. I know he will. He won't leave you alone until you do.'

'Who?'

'Luke Palmer. He won't leave you alone and he won't leave us alone.' Mam was crying. It put them all out. Suzy stared at her horrified.

'Maybe he won't, Mam.'

'I won't tell him anyway,' Frankie said stoutly. 'I promise I won't.'

Mam was blowing her nose, dabbing at her tears. 'It can't be helped now, anyway. I must look awful.'

She looked harassed and her eyes were red and wet.

'You look fine,' Suzy told her.

'I wish you hadn't let Mam see you,' she said to Frankie. 'It would have been better if she didn't know. Less for her to worry about.'

'I had to.' He was apologetic now. 'I had fourpence but even paying half fare it cost me threepence to get this far. I need to borrow twopence to get home.'

'Oh God!' Mam said. 'I could do without this too. I'll do it for your mother. She'd be worried about you.'

'I knew you would. I'll pay you back next time I come.'

'Frankie, don't come again. *Please*, don't come again.'

Chapter Ten

Suzy followed her mother as she turned in through the gate. She was looking about her with great curiosity as they walked up the drive which led past some outbuildings, one of which was now being used as a garage. A dog began to bark, deep and throaty, the sound reverberating like that of a big drum.

Much of the rear of the house was behind a high brick wall with a door set into it. Josie pushed it open; inside was an enclosed vegetable garden, with peach trees growing against the south wall. An enormous dog lolloped up the path of stone flags towards them, still barking. He was about the size of a small donkey and looked ferocious, with sagging jowls that continually dripped saliva.

Suzy came to a full stop until she noticed he was wagging his tail and his gait was lethargic. He sniffed at Mam's feet, and then turned back to her. He seemed quiet and gentle, and she bent to stroke the huge fawn head. The back door flew open and a girl came out on the step.

'He's all right, he won't hurt you,' she called. 'Won't hurt anybody. Brutus! Come on, in your kennel.'

There was a wooden edifice about the size of a garden shed beside the back door. The dog obediently went inside, turned round and collapsed on the floor to rest his dripping jowls on his feet. Big soft eyes watched Suzy climb the steps to the scullery.

Once inside, she found herself clinging to Mam. She was the one in need of support. New faces were peering at her –

kindly faces. They told her their names: one was Gertie and the young one who'd come to the door was Edna.

The kitchen seemed huge and there were lots of other rooms off it, sculleries and larders. Lots of narrow stone-flagged passages too. Suzy could see what looked like a laundry just opposite.

The smell of a recently cooked meal was heavy in the air, making her feel hungry, but the scullery was full of dirty dishes and she was afraid they'd come too late for it. Or was the kitchen table set for a meal for three?

Edna was leading the way up to their bedroom. Joe carried their luggage up. After Mam had paid him, he went back down the stairs whistling. Suzy was sorry to see him go. She'd met him for the first time this morning but he seemed the last link with the old life – their real life.

'It's a nice bedroom, isn't it, Suzy?'

It was nicer than the old one – bigger and brighter, but it was all so strange. There were two iron bedsteads with fresh white candlewick counterpanes. As soon as they were alone, Mam was inspecting the sheets and counting the blankets. She seemed satisfied.

'We should be warm enough. You unpack our night things, I'll have to go back to the kitchen.'

'Don't leave me, Mam.' Suzy could hear the panic in her own voice and it made her even more frightened.

'You'll be all right. Just do as I say. We'll soon get used to it. You can find your way back to the kitchen by yourself, can't you?'

Suzy did as she was told and unpacked. Their clothes and ornaments were like old friends. Then she crept down the steep back stairs to the kitchen.

Another lady had joined them. Suzy knew this was the mistress of the house. She wore neither cap nor apron, and was very fat. Cupboards were being opened and uniform dresses and aprons shaken out and held against her mother. Mrs Smallwood hadn't adopted the latest fashion for short skirts. She wore hers below mid-calf and said she expected her staff to do the same. Her hairstyle was right up to the minute, though, an Eton crop of unusual severity.

'Your hair is to be worn inside your cap, Josephine. All of it. I do hope you understand the rules of kitchen hygiene?'

'Yes, Mrs Smallwood.'

Suzy watched, feeling jittery. This woman was making her mam look small; treating her like a schoolmistress treats her pupils. Both Gertie and Edna had assumed a respectful stance. The lady seemed to ooze authority and power. She swung round and caught sight of Suzy.

'So this is your little girl?'

'Yes, Mrs Smallwood, this is Suzy.'

Suzy did a slow deep curtsy. The Countess of Derby had paid a recent visit to her old school and the girls had been taught to curtsy and the boys to bow. There was something queenly about Mrs Smallwood's bearing. Suzy felt instinctively that this lady held the same high opinion of her own status in society.

Knowing how worried Mam had been about whether she'd be allowed to come with her, Suzy said: 'Thank you for letting me come to live here, Mrs Smallwood.'

Her face cracked into a patronising smile. 'I don't expect you to disturb us in any way, Suzy. I don't want to see or hear you about the house at any time. You do understand that?'

'Yes, Mrs Smallwood.'

Josie watched the regal eyes switch back from Suzy to herself.

171

'A nicely mannered child, Josephine. Now then, for dinner tonight – it's pork chops, isn't it, Gertrude? That's what the butcher delivered today?'

'Yes, ma'am.'

Gertie was pushing a dish on the table in front of her. Eight pork chops were laid out on it. Josie's throat felt tight. She was being given her orders and would be expected to cook dinner tonight. She hadn't realised . . . She hadn't been able to think any further than getting herself and Suzy here. She hadn't got her bearings yet and felt totally on edge. She had to calm down.

She sniffed at the chops, remembering those at the Imperial that had been going off. These smelled fresh and in prime condition.

She asked: 'Do you like your pork chops well done, ma'am?'

'All pork should be well done, Josephine. I'm sure you know that.'

Josie swallowed hard. 'Yes, ma'am. Shall I do them in the oven or would you like them grilled?'

'In the oven.'

Josie had to find out what was expected of her. She took a deep breath. 'What is your preference for potatoes, roast or boiled?'

'We always expect to have both, and two other vegetables. Soup to start with and my father is very fond of puddings. Louise will have just the soup.'

The instructions were coming so fast Josie felt she wasn't taking them all in. You'll be all right, she told herself. You're used to cooking for eighty or ninety – this should be easy. But at the hotel there had been two cooks and Rita had done most of the puddings.

Mrs Smallwood was holding forth. Josie had to

concentrate. 'Louise is a delicate child and can't digest heavy meals. She has an early supper. The rest of the family like to sit down at a quarter to seven sharp. My father dislikes being kept waiting for a meal, says there's nothing worse.'

Josie felt a nervous wreck and was glad when Mrs Smallwood swept to the kitchen door. There, she turned round. 'Josephine, I've come to the kitchen to see you today, but in future you are to come up to the dining room to see me. Nine fifteen sharp, and bring a pad and pencil to write down your orders.'

'Yes, ma'am.'

As soon as she'd disappeared, Edna hissed: 'She's going on about dinner and we haven't had our lunch yet.' She was getting out more knives and forks. 'I expect you're hungry.'

Josie felt sick with nerves and her head was spinning. She had until quarter to seven tonight to get this first dinner organised and served up.

Gertie was looking at her. 'I'm afraid our lunch is mostly what's left over from the dining room, but we've got plenty of bread and cheese if you don't fancy it.'

Edna asked: 'Shall I give Harold a shout? Tell him we're ready?'

'Yes. Harold is the gardener-cum-chauffeur. He lives out, but he eats with us at lunch-time – sometimes in the evening too, if he's driving the colonel somewhere. He keeps himself to himself mostly.'

Harold appeared and washed at the kitchen sink, before shaking hands with Josie and Suzy.

'Hope you'll settle and be happy here,' he said. 'It's not a bad place really.'

'There's enough rabbit stew for one, left from last night.'

173

Gertie was putting out a bowl of salad and a piece of cold cod. 'Cold rice pudding and prunes too.'

The staff sat round the kitchen table to eat. Josie felt better once she had something inside her. Compared with what they'd have had at home, this was eating royally. Suzy cleared everything put before her with obvious gusto.

Edna said: 'The missus is awfully fussy. Everything has to be just so or she complains.'

Suzy asked: 'What does Mr Smallwood do?' It must be something very important to afford a house and staff like this.

'There is no Mr Smallwood, but he was a solicitor and had his own practice. A big one.'

'Mrs Smallwood brought her family here to live with her parents when he died,' Edna told them.

Gertie added: 'They're very rich. Colonel and Mrs Ingram wanted them here; they're getting old now.' Gertie had worked for the colonel and his wife before his daughter and her family came.

Josie wanted to fix the family in her mind. 'And there's two daughters, Christobel and the delicate one, Louise?'

'There's two more, older ones, Georgina and Penelope, but they're married and don't live here any more. Christobel is nineteen.'

'Just about my age,' Edna sighed, 'and she has the life of Riley.'

'What does she do?'

'Helps Mummy with the flowers and plays tennis.'

Edna was rather plump, with a round, girlish face. She looked younger than her twenty years, like an overgrown child. There was nothing of the young lady about her.

'Christobel doesn't work?'

'Doesn't need to. Mummy gives her a dress allowance.

She's got some lovely clothes and she goes to the hairdresser every week.'

Gertie said: 'She's very nice really. Into games and all that. Not at all like her mother. She'll talk to anyone.'

'Christobel's given me a dress. She said she didn't like it but it's lovely. A loose bodice with the waist round the hips marked with a line of braid of little rosebuds, the very latest fashion, and it fits me. I was afraid it wouldn't – she's got such a stylish boyish figure and mine's anything but.'

Edna had round childlike eyes; large red hands too, because they were often in water doing the washing up and preparing vegetables. She was a jolly person with a loud laugh.

'Christobel's got a boyfriend; he's so handsome,' Edna sighed, 'and he takes her out driving in a lovely sports car. She's so lucky. Got everything.'

'What about the youngest?' Suzy wanted to know. 'What's she like?'

'Poor little thing,' Gertie said. 'She's thirteen and delicate.'

Suzy was interested in her because she was about her own age. 'Does she go to the school that I'll be going to?'

'No, lovey.' Gertie laughed. 'The likes of them don't send their children to that sort of school.'

Edna began putting their plates together.

'Christobel went to boarding school but Louise has a governess who comes here to teach her. She isn't strong enough to go to school; she lies on her bed for a lot of the time.'

'What's the matter with her?'

'She's a cripple, got some bone disease they can't cure.'

'Poor little thing,' Gertie said. 'Even with all their money... Money's not much use if you haven't got your health. Don't forget that, Edna.'

* * *

Suzy wanted to stay in the kitchen near Mam. Today she couldn't bear to be parted from her. There was a coal range with a rag rug pulled up against it and a shabby armchair in one corner. Suzy curled up in that and felt safer; it was so big she felt half hidden, and they seemed to forget she was there. She could hear Mam talking to the other two and knew exactly what was going on.

Today Mam was at the end of her tether, Suzy could see that. She needed to sit down for an hour and rest after the journey and the shock of seeing Frankie, but she couldn't here. It was taking a great effort for her to start cooking. Mam looked tired, worn out with worry and the emotional upset of leaving the home she'd loved and set up with Daddy.

When Suzy peeped round the back of the chair, she could see her drooping shoulders, and her hand, which rested on the table for a moment, had a slight tremor. But she cooked dinner both for the dining room and for them, and was dishing up spot on time.

Afterwards, when the staff sat round the kitchen table and finished off the chops, Gertie said hers melted in her mouth. Suzy said hers was very nice too, but she knew Mam was disappointed that there was no comment from the dining room.

She saw Mam take two aspirins when Gertie and Edna were up in the dining room.

'I've got a thumping headache,' she whispered. 'But I've done all right. I just wish Frankie hadn't followed us. It adds to the stress. He swore he wouldn't tell Luke . . .'

'He meant it, Mam. He won't.'

'I'd feel safer if he didn't know where we were.' She yawned. 'I'll be glad to get to bed tonight.'

Suzy knew Mam felt overstretched and worried. But when

they did go to bed, it was a long time before either of them went to sleep.

Luke Palmer's shift had gone without incident today. The tramcar he'd been told to take out had just had a refit. It was a car to be proud of. It had been newly painted in crimson lake and looked very smart. There were all manner of improvements; the best by far was that a glass windscreen had been fitted in front of the controls. He'd been looking forward to having this for a long time.

He'd heard that vestibules were going to be added at each end of the tramcars, and there were even rumours of seats being provided for drivers, but it seemed he'd have to wait longer for comforts like that. For the moment, he still had to stand hour after hour at the controls. It made his legs ache. Even the conductors were better off because they could walk about.

Luke felt he'd given Josie long enough to calm down. It was over a month since the big clash when she'd accused him of abusing Suzy. The girl was a handful. Josie had told him she wanted her kept in check but when he did it, she'd gone berserk. He'd done his best to be a father to Suzy and he'd trusted Josie to treat him right, but she always took the little bitch's part against him.

He didn't like his lonely little bed and he wanted some hot meals at home and his clothes washed and ironed. He'd had more than enough of this.

It was mid-afternoon when his shift finished. He felt he needed a drink, but the Flag and Sailor had closed its doors. He had to walk back to a grocer's that sold booze to buy himself a bottle of whisky.

He wanted to get back on good terms with Josie. They couldn't go on like this, it was ridiculous. He'd promise never to touch Suzy again however much she goaded him. She'd asked for all she got, anyway, the cheeky little devil. It had all been her fault – she'd even raised her own fists first at him. No father, step or natural, was going to put up with that from a kid like her.

He'd offer to take them both to the pictures tonight, and see if he could get back into Josie's bed. Damn it, he'd gone out on a limb for her, she shouldn't send him to Coventry like this. The shop had bars of chocolate set out on the counter and he bought two. As an afterthought, he bought a bottle of port for Josie and another of sarsaparilla for the little witch. He really had to get things back to normal.

When he let himself into the house in Upper Parliament Street, the scent of the cooked lunch the Maynards had enjoyed still hung in the air. There was a heavy silence and a feeling of mid-afternoon torpor about the place. He thought the Maynards must be having a siesta on their bed. Upstairs, every door on their landing was closed, which was unusual when Josie was home.

'Josie?'

He threw open the living-room door and stopped dead in his tracks. Most of the furniture had gone!

'Josie?' he roared. It could only mean one thing! She'd flitted. The gorge ran hot up into his throat.

'Josie, you bloody traitor. After all I've done for you. Letting me down like this.'

Everything went black before his eyes. Before he could stop himself Luke had hurled the bottle of whisky he carried at the cold, ash-filled grate. It shattered against the tiled hearth with a crunch loud enough to launch a liner. The smell of spirit inflamed him further. He'd wasted his whisky! The port and sarsaparilla were still whole but he felt so enraged he tossed them one after the other at the grate. The sound of shattering glass and the growing pool of brown fluid spreading out across the lino brought him no relief. He screamed and raved and stamped from room to room.

Josie's bed had gone too, and her dressing table! Only the wardrobe, still lacking a mirror, remained. He was in such a frenzy he didn't hear Mr Maynard come up.

'I don't want you here on your own, Mr Palmer,' he told him. 'I'd like you to go.'

This was another bolt from the blue. Luke's fury was spent; he felt cold. 'It'll take me time to find somewhere else.'

Mr Maynard surveyed the broken glass in the hearth and the ever-spreading pool of alcohol on the lino.

'What are you making a mess like this for? That will soak through to the ceiling below. Get it wiped up immediately, or you'll have to pay for the damage.'

Luke stared back at him insolently. 'I'm not to blame for this.'

'Ghosts, was it? You're the only one here. If you don't get it wiped up I'll send for the police and have you put out straight away.' Reluctantly, Luke fetched a towel from the bathroom and threw it on to the pool. It half did the job.

When he'd gone, Luke lay down on Suzy's narrow bed and wept. Josie had set everybody against him and now she'd gone and abandoned him just as Flora had before her, and as Ida and Leila had.

He'd bent over backwards to help Josie – done all he could for her and her little chit and this was the thanks he got. Josie was going to pay for this. He'd get even with her, he'd see she got her deserts.

After a couple of hours, he felt desperate for a drink. He deemed that the Flag and Sailor would have opened its doors. He got up, washed his face and went.

* * *

On Tuesday, Suzy was to go to her new school. She wasn't looking forward to it. She didn't want to leave Mam.

'I've got to cook breakfast,' Mam told her. 'I can't take you, but Edna will. She used to go to that school herself.'

Suzy asked Edna: 'What's it like?'

'It's good, you'll like it when you get used to it.'

'Take her to the headmistress's office,' Mam said. 'I've spoken to her on the telephone. She's expecting you, Suzy.'

For once Suzy had to struggle to get the boiled egg inside her. Everything was so different. She wished she could run off with Frankie to her old familiar school.

'She needs to take a sandwich with her,' Edna said. 'It's quite a long way to come back at dinner-time.'

Suzy watched her mother cut it for her. It seemed her first day was going to be a long one. All the way there, Edna pointed out landmarks so she could find her way back and Suzy tried to remember them.

'I hope I'm not going to get lost.'

'Shall I come to the gate and meet you?' Edna asked quickly. 'Four o'clock is a quiet time. Gertie won't mind. Once you've walked it in both directions you'll be all right.'

Josie, too, was afraid she was in for another hard day. She'd never found the first days at a new job easy; she had no idea what this family liked to eat or how they liked their food cooked. Gertie was being very kind, showing her over again where things were kept; showing no sign of impatience when Josie had to ask the same thing twice.

After breakfast, Gertie led her through the door that cut off the kitchen quarters from the rest of the house. The hall floor was of highly polished parquet, and the scent of beeswax filled the air.

'That's the dining room.' She indicated a closed door and left her.

Josie tried to get a grip on her nerves. She felt she hardly knew what she was doing. She knocked; there was no response though she could hear voices inside. She knocked again, opened the door and put her head round. The dining table looked vast. Four pairs of eyes swung round to assess her.

'Good morning, Mrs Smallwood.' Up till now, Josie had seen only the mistress of the house. 'Is it convenient to see me now?'

'Come in, Josephine.'

She went to stand beside her. Josie wasn't introduced to the rest of the family, but she studied them from under her lashes. The elderly couple would be Mrs Smallwood's parents and the young girl would be Christobel, the daughter Edna so much admired. She was very pretty, slim, with long blonde hair and a tanned complexion.

'Now then, my parents will be out for lunch today.' Two white heads were nodding in agreement. 'I think perhaps steak—'

'Not for me,' Christobel said in so abrupt a tone it told Josie she was not on good terms with her mother. 'I'll have something light, just a salad. You know I can't eat two big meals a day, Mother.'

There was no mistaking the irritation in Mrs Smallwood's voice. 'You're always slimming, you'll ruin your health.'

'You'd feed me up like a pig for slaughter if I let you.'

'Christobel, please! Steak for me. I'll order a piece of rump—'

'We could all have that for dinner tonight,' her father put in. 'I enjoy a good steak.'

'Too heavy on your stomach in the evening, Father. What about a lamb casserole tonight?'

181

Josie wrote 'lamb casserole' on her pad.

The old lady looked timid and bent. She spoke in a near whisper.

'My husband is fond of steamed puddings, treacle and that sort of thing. Jam roly-poly is his favourite.'

'What was that, Alma? I wish you'd speak up. Yes, indeed . . .' The old man beamed at her.

Josie said: 'Jam roly-poly tonight then?'

'Yes, please, with plenty of custard.'

'You could make me a small bread-and-butter pudding for lunch,' Mrs Smallwood took over again. 'Now then, you said you could cook for an invalid. Louise doesn't get up for breakfast.'

So Josie had discovered. She'd made bread and milk for her and Edna had taken it up to her room on a tray.

'What do you suggest for a light lunch?'

'A little steamed fish, perhaps, with mashed potato? If fish is available?'

'I'll order it. Plaice, I think. And for pudding?'

'Would she not enjoy a little of your bread-and-butter pudding?'

'You'll put dried fruit in it?'

'Sultanas, yes, and a little candied peel.'

'That wouldn't suit Louise. Can you make arrowroot mould?'

'I can make anything from a recipe, ma'am. There are cookery books in the kitchen. I'll look it up. What will she have for her dinner?'

'She has a light supper at six and goes to bed before dinner time. Milk toast, I think. She likes that.'

When she returned to the kitchen, Josie got the books on invalid cookery down from the shelf and looked up milk toast. She read:

Toast a slice of bread until golden brown, butter it, then cut it into squares on a plate. Pour a cup of hot milk over it and grate a little nutmeg on top.

That would be easy enough to make but sounded a bit bland. And surely it would provide much the same nourishment as the bread and milk she'd made for Louise's breakfast?

The arrowroot mould was to be made with arrowroot, milk and sugar, an egg might be added for the convalescent. Josie decided to put the egg in; without it there'd be little nourishment in that either.

If Mrs Smallwood was building up Christobel she certainly didn't intend to overface Louise. Her ideas of invalid cookery went far beyond anything Josie would have suggested. Milk toast for supper!

Gertie came in with a tray of dirty dishes.

'Is Louise overweight?' Josie asked.

'No, nothing but skin and bone. The poor child needs building up.'

For the first few days, Suzy crept about the kitchens, her bedroom and the back stairs.

'You must be like a mouse,' Mam kept saying with a little smile to remind her. If she did forget and speak in a loud voice, then Mam's finger would be set against her lips as a signal that she was to hush up. She felt they were talking in whispers most of the time.

The family were not quiet at all. The house rang with voices, none of which Suzy could recognise. It felt strange to have all these people round her who were strangers. There was a man here, the timbre of whose voice echoed against the high ceilings.

It was several days before she caught sight of Colonel Ingram. He came ambling through the kitchen one evening just before dinner. Mam was making a sauce for the ham, and Suzy was chopping parsley to go in it.

'Hello,' he said to her. 'I see your mother keeps you busy. How d'you like my dog?'

Brutus's back was level with the height of the table. His enormous head moved towards the board of chopped parsley and turned away without interest.

'He's nice.'

'What's Edna got for you then? Any tasty bits for Brutus tonight?'

Edna had saved the rind off the ham, and bones from the lamb chops they'd had for lunch. A sack of dog food was kept in the scullery and the colonel was filling a great bowl with it.

'Dinner then. Come on, you brute. Let's put you to bed.'

'He's nice and friendly,' Suzy said, when he'd gone.

'Stay out of his way,' Mam ordered, but since neither of them ventured into the part of the house the family used, they weren't likely to get in his way.

Mam said she'd had enough of men and was going to have nothing more to do with any of them.

'Women are easier to cope with,' she said. 'You know where you are with women.'

Suzy was in full agreement.

During the following days Josie was able to take a closer look at the family she was cooking for. Although over eighty now, Colonel Theodore Ingram was still slim and straight and stood with his shoulders well back. His eyes were somewhat bleary and moist with age, though they seemed to miss little. He had a head of thick white hair and a bushy white moustache; his complexion was dark and yellowish, the old man having spent much of his life in India with the army, and he was a trifle deaf. He kept his new valve wireless blaring out fortissimo from his study, and as he was particularly interested in politics, it kept everybody in the house up to date with the news.

When meals were being served, Gertie had to carry heavy trays into the dining room. To make it easier for herself, she propped open the doors to the kitchen and dining room.

While the colonel's wife, Alma, seemed to murmur and whisper, he had a voice that reverberated round the house and his opinion was the one Josie was most likely to hear from the kitchen quarters.

One night she clearly heard him say: 'What's this mush, Hebe?' Hebe was Mrs Smallwood's given name.

'Fricassee of chicken. It's light on your stomach before you go to bed.'

'It's tasteless.'

'It's quite nice, Father,' Hebe retorted.

'I wish you wouldn't mumble, Alma . . .'

'We both like it, Gramps,' Christobel told him.

The old man grunted. 'I'd like a good curry. Something with a bit of bite to it. Can this new cook do curries?'

'I haven't asked her. Curry would give you indigestion, you know that. You'd be the first to complain. Besides, Christobel wouldn't eat it, and I dare not offer it to Louise. She'd be awake all night after that.'

'Dammit. Couldn't the cook make something to please me once in a while?'

Later Josie heard his deep gruff voice say: 'Makes a good treacle pudding, I'll say that for her. I'll have a little more, Hebe.'

While life for her employers seemed less than harmonious, Josie found the atmosphere in the kitchen friendly, the three of them working together and seeming to get on well.

'Things can get very acid in the drawing room,' Edna giggled, when they sat down to eat their own meal.

Gertie tried to explain it. 'It's Mrs Smallwood who causes most of the trouble. There's a power struggle going on between her and her father. She's inherited his bossy ways. They both want to run this household.'

'Along army lines,' Edna added.

'What about the old lady, Mrs Ingram?' Josie asked.

Gertie smiled. 'She's polite and gentle and never gives any trouble. She's forever being talked down and just accepts it.'

'Not like Christobel,' Edna laughed. 'Her mother is always laying down what she can or can't do but she's having none of it. She fights back like a tiger.'

'It's a family trait, like her mother and grandfather: she's determined to have her own way with everything.'

Harold had walked Josie round the walled garden and greenhouse, and pointed out the vegetables which were ready for use. The next day she was pulling a lettuce and some spring onions to make a salad when she heard Christobel arguing with her mother.

Josie had taken a quick look round the ground floor of the house one morning, while Gertie was taking morning tea up to the bedrooms. She'd seen the drawing room with the grand piano, and the French windows opening on to a terrace just the other side of the wall.

Mrs Smallwood sounded belligerent. 'I wish you wouldn't interfere, Christobel. We have to be very careful with Louise.'

'Far too careful. You won't let her move.'

'Dr Howarth agrees, Louise—'

'He's totally out of date with his treatment. Should have been pensioned off a decade ago.'

'I have great faith in him. You've no business to get Louise off her bed and walk her round the garden. You'll tire her out.'

'Mother, she enjoyed it. She'll lose the use of her legs if she doesn't get off that bed. She's wasting away just lying there. Getting weaker, not better.'

'You don't understand, Christobel. You're healthy, Louise is delicate. She needs to be looked after.'

'You fuss her too much. You stop her doing anything. What she really needs is to be taken to a swimming pool where she can use all her muscles. Alec is planning one which he'll open to the public.'

'Not one of those new open-air, cold water baths? Don't be so ridiculous. Louise would catch her death of cold. You have some very strange ideas.'

'Modern ideas. Exercise and fresh air – it's the latest thing. It'll build up her strength. If you keep her wrapped in cotton wool, she'll be a permanent invalid.'

'I suppose you think you can turn her into a healthy child, when the best doctors in town have failed?'

'It's you who have failed, Mother. You don't listen to anybody, only Nurse Silk and old Dr Howarth. They've both lost touch, can't have opened a book since they qualified.'

Josie was glad she couldn't hear Mrs Smallwood's reply.

Chapter Eleven

During the first week, Suzy had gone no further on the Ingrams' property than the walled garden, where she'd helped Mam gather vegetables. Then Harold had asked her if she'd like to help with the weeding and he'd taken her to the building where he kept his lawn mowers and other implements, and she'd seen the two limousines he drove.

Then, growing more confident, she'd explored all the grounds, keeping to the side hedges and as far from the house as she could. There was a hard tennis court, a rose garden, and a summerhouse hidden by trees. There were several smooth lawns separated by shrubs and flowerbeds.

Mam too was getting used to being at The Lawns. She was allowed two hours off between lunch and dinner. She'd taken a trip into town and had found the library, and she'd taken Suzy there to choose a book. Sometimes Mam would come down for a walk and Suzy would find her waiting at the school gates when it was time to go home.

But Suzy was missing Frankie, who'd always been on hand ready to play games or go on excursions. She felt lonely, particularly at weekends. Mam sent her out of the kitchen if she noticed her snuggling down in the chair with her library book.

'You need fresh air,' she kept telling her. 'It's not good for you to spend all your time in here.' But without Frankie, Suzy felt at a loose end. To please Mam, she took her book to the summerhouse and pulled out one of the garden chairs stored there. There was a table too, and a sort of day bed. She tried lying straight on the wooden slats of that, but it wasn't comfortable.

Suzy had seen Christobel from a distance several times. One Sunday morning when Suzy was there, she came to the kitchen to ask Mam to make a packed lunch for her and her boyfriend.

'We're having a day out in Chester,' she laughed, excited at the prospect. 'He's going to take me rowing on the river.'

Edna stopped washing up abruptly and came to the scullery door. She couldn't take her eyes from Christobel when she was close. Suzy, too, listened to Mam discussing what she should put in the picnic basket.

They were amazed, because barely ten minutes earlier, they'd all heard Mrs Smallwood expressly forbidding any expedition alone with 'that man'.

She'd barked: 'He is not a suitable person for you to know. I thoroughly disapprove of him.'

Christobel had retorted: 'I like him, Mother. I like him a lot. You'd like him too, if you knew him. We should ask him to dinner. He's good company, he'd amuse Gramps.'

'Absolutely not! We don't mix with people like that. I don't want him anywhere near this house.'

'You mix with some absolute rogues, Mother. At least Alec is honest, which is more than you can say about some of your friends.'

'That's outrageous! What do you mean?'

'You know well enough I'm talking about the Reverend Haydn Ingleby-Jones.'

'Christobel!' her mother exploded. 'How dare you defame a man of the cloth? He's given his life to the Church. He does all he can to help people.'

'But more to help himself. He's on the make.'

'I wish I were more like her,' Edna sighed when Christobel had gone.

'Go on,' Gertie teased. 'You wish you had what she has.'

'That too. Christobel doesn't realise how lucky she is.'

On the following Saturday, Suzy saw Christobel and her boyfriend get out of a sports car which they left by the garage. They headed towards the tennis court in the garden with racquets tucked under their arms. When she told Edna, they both crept up the garden until they could peep through the hedge and watch them play.

'Special clothes just to play a game in,' Edna marvelled. 'Can you believe that?'

Christobel was wearing a short white pleated dress. Vitality shone out of her. She was small and dainty and moved about the court with lithe grace.

'Those are his cricket flannels,' Suzy whispered. 'I heard her ask him.'

'His name's Alec. Isn't he handsome?' Alec was as dark as Christobel was fair.

'He's awfully old. Almost old enough to be her father.'

Edna giggled. 'That's what Mrs Smallwood said, but I think he's rich. I don't know why they're against him.'

'Are they against everything Christobel wants?'

Edna giggled again. 'She bought herself a pair of white shorts that shocked her mother. I heard them arguing last Sunday when I was serving supper. Her mother forbade her to wear them.'

'She's good at this,' Suzy breathed. 'You can see that.'

Christobel's hair bounced and shone like spun gold; her laugh carried across the garden.

Although Suzy kept an eye out for Louise, the youngest daughter, she'd never caught so much as a glimpse of her.

One day, she was engrossed in a new library book called *The Wide, Wide World* when Mam sent her out of the kitchen.

'It's a sunny day – you shouldn't stay in here with us all the time.'

So Suzy took her book to read in the summerhouse, but as she drew near she heard voices, and pulled up short behind a hedge. Then, in a minute or two, she crept forward until she could see that the day bed had been pulled to the front of the summerhouse where it would get the sun. A mattress had been brought out and there was a girl lying on it. Suzy craned further forward, but all she could see were the pillows and the blankets which muffled the figure. She knew it must be Louise.

Mrs Smallwood and another woman were with her; both had chairs pulled up, one each side of the bed. Louise's voice sounded querulous, and the adults were trying to soothe. Suzy crept away to find somewhere else to read her book.

There was plenty of cover in the garden. She'd already explored a small shrubbery where she could get out of sight, but it was dark inside where the sun didn't reach, and the branches tore at her hair when she moved. She read there for a while but the ground she was lying on struck cold and damp through her clothes.

She crawled out into the sun and straightened up. She much preferred being in the summerhouse, where it was more comfortable. She approached cautiously. The two chairs had been vacated. The day bed was still there with its pillows and bedclothes, but all was still and quiet. Suzy thought everybody had gone. She was about to climb the two steps at the front when she realised the girl was still wrapped up on the day bed.

'Hello.' Large violet eyes were watching her. 'Who are you?'

'Suzy Lunt.'

Suzy went to the foot of the bed to look closely at the girl. She had flaxen hair that hung in long curling tendrils over thin shoulders. Her face was small and pretty, but was marred by her wan complexion and disconsolate expression.

The girl asked: 'What are you doing here?'

'I live here.'

'No you don't!'

Suzy grinned at her. 'My mother's your new cook. You're Louise, aren't you?'

'Oh! Nobody told me the new cook had brought a daughter with her.'

'What are you doing?'

'Writing an essay on friendship.' Louise flung down her fountain pen. 'I can't do it. I've nothing to write about. I haven't got any friends.'

They stared at each other. Louise asked: 'Do you go to school?'

'Yes.' Suzy wasn't used to it yet. Her fellow pupils all knew each other; they'd made their friends and were taking little interest in her. She missed her old school.

'I wish I did. It's very dull having lessons by myself.'

'Why don't you go to school?'

'Mummy says I'm not strong enough. I have Miss Greenall, but for only two hours a day in case I get overtired. She leaves me sums to do or an essay to write.'

'That doesn't sound too bad.'

'It's boring. I'm always on my own. Nothing ever happens here. You're lucky to go to school.'

'I don't feel lucky. I'm new there, can't even find my way round the building. I'm still an outsider.'

'You'll get to know everybody. You'll soon have friends.'

'You sound like my mother.'

193

'I suppose all mothers are like that – try to jolly you along. Don't you like living here?'

'Not much. I had to leave all my friends behind to come here. What's the matter with you?'

'I'm a cripple.'

'There was a boy at my last school who was a cripple. John something, he had irons on his leg.' Suzy looked at the rug that covered her legs. 'Have you?'

Louise flung it back to show the iron supports going through the heel of her boot up to wide leather straps above and below her knee. 'Isn't it horrible?'

Suzy felt a rush of sympathy. 'Have you always been like this?'

'I caught a dreadful bone disease called TB when I was four. It left me like this.'

'Can't the doctors cure you?'

'No. I think they've given up.'

'John could walk on his irons, can't you?'

'Sort of, not properly.'

'He couldn't properly. He dragged his foot, but that didn't stop him.'

'Mummy doesn't like me to do too much. She thinks I need more rest. Tell me about your school.'

'This new one isn't very interesting.'

'Tell me about your old one then. You liked it there, didn't you?'

'Yes, but I try not to think about it. I can't go back.'

Because she felt sorry for Louise, she said: 'I had a friend called Frankie. I'll see him again one day. He says we'll go to London together when we're grown up. I'll tell you about him. He's full of wonderful ideas about things we can do. My mam says he's a daydreamer who lives in his own imagination. He could think up a world specially for you.'

'What sort of a world?' The wan face puckered in thought.

'A place where girls can be cured of even the most dreadful diseases; where miracles happen, and where cripples get up and learn to dance on slim shapely legs like your sister Christobel's.'

Suzy smiled. Although she'd met Louise for the first time, it was as though she'd known her all her life. They seemed to be on the same wavelength. They understood each other and laughed at the same things. Suzy liked her enormously, and thought Louise liked her too.

Josie was keeping an eye on the kitchen clock. It was almost time to dish up the lunch of escalope of veal. The sun had climbed high in the cloudless sky. It was hot now, and the windows were all open.

Gertie was setting the dining-room table and had propped the doors open. Josie carried in the tray of cold hors-d'oeuvres and set it on the sideboard.

'Listen,' Gertie mouthed.

Josie heard girlish giggles and then a peal of laughter. Was that Suzy? Suddenly jumpy, Josie went to the open window in the butler's pantry. She was afraid Mrs Smallwood was going to hear this too, and complain.

'It's Louise,' Gertie whispered, following her in.

The family were gathering in the drawing room. The older members were in the habit of taking a glass of sherry at this time of day.

Mrs Smallwood's voice boomed: 'Is that Louise?'

'She's laughing!' Christobel laughed with her. 'What's she doing?'

'Miss Greenall set her an essay to write in the summerhouse.'

'It can't be that,' Christobel retorted. 'There's nothing amusing about Miss Greenall.'

The two French windows were open and it was hot in the sun outside on the terrace.

'I'm amazed,' the colonel said loudly. 'It's the first time I've heard her laugh like that.'

'Here she is.'

Josie heard everyone troop outside on the terrace and stepped back where she couldn't be seen. Now she could see Louise limping across the lawn, supported, almost appearing to be held upright, by Suzy. She groaned; this could mean trouble. Mrs Smallwood wouldn't like it. She was right.

Josie heard her voice boom again: 'What is that girl doing?' The voice was thick with condemnation. 'Louise will suffer after this. I was just going to get her in the wheelchair.'

'Don't be ridiculous, Hebe. The child doesn't need a wheelchair to cross the garden. You fuss too much.'

'Gramps is right, Mother. Haven't I been telling you Louise would be better if she had more exercise? She's enjoying herself for once. She wouldn't be laughing like that if she wasn't. You give her a miserable existence, Miss Greenall is the only person she sees.'

'Who's the girl she's with?' Mrs Ingram wanted to know.

'The new cook's daughter.'

'Not at all suitable as a companion . . .'

'She's doing wonders, Mother. For heaven's sake, you keep Lou caged up alone; no wonder she's miserable and lonely. And you're always trying to get one of us to amuse her or read to her or something. Let this Suzy be. We should all be grateful if Lou's found a friend.'

The following morning was Sunday. Suzy was peeling potatoes to help Edna when Christobel came into the kitchen, her blonde hair held back from her face with an Alice band.

'Suzy, Louise is asking for you. She wants you to go up to her room now. You're not too busy?'

Suzy was pleased, and dropped the potato into the water. 'No, I'm not busy.'

'What for?' Josie asked nervously: 'Will it be all right? Your mother won't mind if she does?'

'No, Louise needs a companion. She's on her own far too much. She was much brighter yesterday, even Mother had to admit she was. Gramps says she isn't getting enough stimulation. He thinks Suzy would be good for her, and so do I. Come on, I'll take you up now.'

Suzy dried her hands and followed her. She thought the house amazing. It was the first time she'd been in the part where the family lived. Christobel was going too fast – she wanted to see it all. It was huge and had such a grand staircase.

'Louise needs exercise. Don't listen to Mother when she says she needs rest. I want you to get her off that bed and doing something. Out in the garden if possible.'

'Right.' Suzy's heart was in her mouth. Whatever Christobel said, she wouldn't dare do anything that would upset Mrs Smallwood. She could make Mam and Gertie jump to her orders.

'And don't pay too much attention to Nurse Silk either. She's one of Mother's cronies and wants to keep Louise in bed permanently. She does it so she can come here to stroke her forehead and have coffee with Mother.'

'She has a nurse? I didn't know that.'

Christobel stopped abruptly at the top of the stairs. 'The nurse comes a couple of mornings a week. Louise doesn't need her. She can dress herself perfectly well. Nurse Silk gives advice to Mother, but it's all wrong. It's what people did in Queen Victoria's time. Did you know Florence Nightingale stayed in bed for over thirty years?'

197

Suzy swallowed. It seemed Christobel expected her to change Louise's whole routine against medical advice.

'Are you sure? I mean . . . A nurse should know . . .'

'She doesn't. Take no notice of her, just do what you did yesterday, all right?'

'All right.'

Christobel was whisking off across the landing and down a corridor. Suzy would have thought her a golden girl except that she knew her moods could be as changeable as the weather. The sparkle in her eyes could turn to fire in an instant, the fun become vitriolic argument. Mam and Gertie agreed that Christobel was always ready for a fight, her mind as quick and lithe in argument as her body was in sport. Energy pulsated out of her.

She threw open a door and ushered Suzy inside. Louise was dressed but lying on a couch even here. She was but a wan copy of her sister, her energy levels nil.

'Hello.' Louise seemed a little shy this morning.

'What a lovely room you have.' Suzy thought it delightful. 'Is this all for you? All these lovely things.' She stopped in front of a large, beautifully furnished dolls' house. 'This is wonderful. I've never seen anything like it.'

'Louise sees nothing else,' Christobel said. 'She needs something different.'

'Of course. What's that you're doing?'

'I'm still writing this essay on friendship. It's to be done by tomorrow morning. I want you to help me.'

Suzy sat on the edge of her couch.

'Don't sit there,' an authoritative voice barked.

Suzy leaped to her feet. An elderly woman in a nurse's blue uniform had come through the open door.

'You depress the springs, upset the level of the bed. It's less comfortable for the patient.'

198

'It isn't uncomfortable,' Louise protested. 'It feels friendly to have someone close.'

Christobel smiled at Suzy and said: 'This is Nurse Silk.'

She had a ferocious expression and her massive chest bulged against a dress that was too tight. She wore a flapping muslin headdress with a tiny puff of white hair showing at each temple.

Christobel turned to go. 'Don't forget what I told you, Suzy. So long, Lou.'

Louise patted the side of her bed. 'Come back.'

'Would you be better sitting at the table?' Suzy asked. 'It would be easier to write there.'

'No, Louise doesn't sit out of her bed until after lunch,' the nurse said. 'It strengthens her back to lie on it.' She put a hard chair beside the couch.

'Right . . .' Suzy sat down gingerly on the edge of it.

Louise's eyes looked up innocently at her nurse. 'Isn't it time you went, Nurse Silk? I'm sure Mother will be wanting her coffee. I don't want to keep you. I'll be all right now.'

The violet eyes flashed mischievously at Suzy. 'I want you to tell me, what makes a person into a friend.'

Suzy screwed up her forehead in thought. 'It's the way you feel about them. You can be at ease with them. They're fun.'

Nurse Silk was going. 'Goodbye, Louise. Take care now. Don't overtire yourself.' The door closed firmly, and Louise grabbed at Suzy in glee.

At lunch-time, Christobel came back to take her sister downstairs. 'Had a good morning?'

Louise smiled. 'Better than usual. I'm glad Suzy found me yesterday. Fancy her being here in the house for four weeks and I didn't know.'

'I've helped Lou write her essay, so it hasn't been all play.'

'Bathroom first,' Christobel said. 'To wash her hands, that's the routine.'

'Suzy took me before. I've been walking round a lot, haven't I?'

'That's the way to build up your strength.'

Christobel said to Suzy: 'Lou's not allowed on the stairs without help. Not yet.'

'Harold used to come to carry me down and then up again before he went home.'

'But you're getting better, you can manage the stairs as long as there's somebody with you.'

'Somebody strong, like you or Gramps.'

'Would I be strong enough?' Suzy asked, going down a step at a time behind them.

'Yes, probably. Mother's faint-hearted and doesn't want to believe Lou can do it.'

'She says she's afraid I'll fall.'

'You won't if you're careful. You're doing great, Lou.'

It seemed painfully slow to Suzy, and she knew it was taking a lot of effort on Louise's part.

Her sister explained to Suzy, 'Lou needs to hold the stair rail on one side, and with somebody on the other, she's perfectly all right. Here, take my place and let's see how she gets on with you. That's right, Lou, another step down. Nothing to it, is there?'

'The steps, they aren't easy. But I'm going to keep at it until I can do it by myself.'

'You have to.'

Christobel said: 'I want her to be able to come down for breakfast and get herself up after supper at night.'

'Mummy says Harold must carry me up and down, but she doesn't allow me down before lunch, and he's gone at six. Earlier sometimes in the winter when it's dark.'

Suzy said: 'It can't be much fun being put to bed with milk toast at six o'clock.'

'I think I could manage the stairs on my own now.' Louise was breathless.

'Don't let Mother see you just yet. We'll have to work her up to it. But tell her you're having no more of Harold. I'll see you down in the mornings and if I'm out with Alec, Suzy can help you up at night.'

When they reached the dining-room door, the two sisters went in and Suzy ran into the kitchen. She was delighted to have found a companion in Louise.

Dishing up a meal was a stressful time for Josie. That was the moment when she could see whether her cooking had been successful or otherwise, and whatever their shortcomings the dishes then had to be put before Mrs Smallwood and her family. Josie wanted her cooking to please them. They were all busy in the kitchen when Suzy came in.

'How did you get on with Louise?' Josie asked.

'Fine. We played happy families and did a jigsaw. The house, Mam – you wouldn't believe . . . And she has so many toys.'

Gertie picked up the hot plates to take to the dining room. 'But she hasn't got good health, Suzy, and that's worth more than anything money can buy.'

'Did you know she had a nurse, Mam?'

'Drain that cauliflower for me, Suzy, and put it in this dish.'

Josie stirred the cheese sauce vigorously. It seemed a bit lumpy, not the best she'd ever made. Perhaps she should strain it?

'A nurse?'

'Well, Christobel says she's not really employed to look after Louise. She's one of Mrs Smallwood's friends.'

'That'll be Nurse Silk,' Edna said, running hot water into the scullery sink ready to start washing up the pans. 'She's always here.'

The strength seemed to go from Josie's legs. They were like jelly. Nurse Silk! That name brought back painful memories.

She asked cautiously: 'What's she like?'

'Old,' Suzy said. 'Louise doesn't like her.'

Josie's tongue seemed suddenly too large for her mouth. It couldn't be the same person, surely not? It was silly even to think it might. There'd been a Nurse Silk in charge of that awful mother-and-baby home her father had sent her to all those years ago. Just to think of her brought anger rising in her throat and the most terrible feelings of guilt.

Edna giggled. 'Old and stout, and she thinks herself very much my superior.'

'Christobel says she takes an interest in Louise. Medical advice and all that. Often takes coffee or tea with Mrs Smallwood and sometimes she's asked to dinner.'

'Mam?' The urgency in Suzy's voice brought Josie's mind back. 'Is something burning?'

'Oh God!' She'd stopped stirring the cheese sauce. She'd let it burn while she was standing over it! No! she told herself. Don't stir it now. It will be burned black on the bottom. She grabbed the pan off the stove and tasted it. 'Thank goodness, Suzy. I think I've caught it in time. Does it taste of burn to you?'

'No, but there's specks of burn in it.'

Josie reached for the sieve. She'd stirred that bit of black up in the first unguarded moment. She skimmed off what she could of the specks and then poured the sauce over the cauliflower. There was still the odd black speck to be seen. She reached for the paprika and sprinkled a little on top.

'That's made it look pretty,' Suzy smiled at her.

Gertie had it on her tray and was taking it to the table within seconds.

Josie sank down wearily on a chair. She'd never stopped thinking about her baby son, though he'd be grown up now. This Nurse Silk was probably not the same person. It was just the name that had brought this avalanche of memories down on her. She'd told herself they were fading with the years, but she'd been wrong. Anything like this could bring them flooding back, as sharp and as painful as ever.

Josie had thought it was all over and done with years ago. She added up the years: twenty-five now, since Robert had been adopted. The decision had been forced on her by circumstances and by Nurse Silk, but it had been irrevocable. Robert was no longer part of her life, not her responsibility, but Suzy was. Josie had to keep this job come what may. She knew she must focus her mind on what she was doing and not get herself churned up about things like this.

Over the days that followed, however, the memories stayed in her mind, growing sharper. Henrietta Silk had been the matron's name. Josie remembered a buxom figure and an irritable voice but could no longer picture her face. She felt torn between wanting to see her when she came again and hiding away where Nurse Silk wouldn't see her. As cook, she saw very little of what went on at the front of the house.

One day, Gertie came back to the kitchen after answering the front doorbell, and happened to mention that she'd shown Nurse Silk to the drawing room, and Mrs Smallwood had asked for coffee to be brought.

As Josie ground the coffee beans, she thought of asking Gertie to let her take the tray up herself. As it happened, she'd put on a clean uniform dress that morning and looked smart enough. She watched the biscuits being put out as though mesmerised, but at the last minute her nerve gave way. She couldn't bring herself to say anything and Gertie took the tray away.

It left Josie feeling deflated and cowardly, but Gertie came hurrying back.

'They're out on the terrace and they're talking about Christobel.'

Edna rushed out into the walled garden and sat herself down on the bench placed against the wall; she couldn't hear enough about Christobel. Gertie took out the cake tin and Josie the three cups of coffee she'd made for them. Nurse Silk was sitting just the other side of the eight-foot wall, receiving Mrs Smallwood's confidences.

'I'm at my wits' end over Christobel. She's such a headstrong girl, won't listen to reason. She's keeping company with a very unsavoury man – twice married already, and twice her age, and I'm sure he's taking advantage of her. His father was a bookie, you know, and he has a string of public houses. Christobel admits that he's taken her inside more than one of them. I really don't know what to do for the best.'

'Why don't you get Haydn to talk to her? I'm sure he'd point out the danger she's putting herself in and get her to change her ways.'

Edna was having difficulty suppressing her giggles. 'I'm sure Christobel would listen to him,' she mouthed. She opened the cake tin, which made a characteristic ping. Gertie put her finger across her lips.

Josie felt a little uncomfortable at listening so obviously to a very private conversation. She started to collect some early carrots for lunch.

'I've done my very best for her,' Mrs Smallwood went on, baring her soul to them all. 'I've tried to introduce her to decent young men of our own class. She won't meet Haydn or his son.'

'Such a shame. Claude's a lovely boy...'

'So suitable, but she's not interested in him. She's besotted with this rotter and she's meeting him alone without a chaperone.'

'My dear,' there was deep sympathy in Nurse Silk's voice, 'I find it hard to believe Christobel would get herself involved with somebody like that. Not after the firm Christian upbringing she's had.'

'I don't know where I've gone wrong, I really don't. I'm beside myself. I never expected any child of mine to have morals like this.'

'It could ruin her life.'

'Certainly her reputation. Decent people won't want to know her.'

'My dear Hebe, I do sympathise. I saw too much of it in my life's work. I'm so afraid of what'll happen next, but the girls were usually from the gutters, not at all like your daughter.'

Josie shivered. This woman sounded very much like the Nurse Silk she'd known.

'I'm so ashamed of her behaviour. I think it must be because she's grown up without a father's firm hand.'

'The colonel, surely...?'

'Oh no, he won't. He says: "They're your brood. It's up to you to discipline them. If I try to correct Christobel, she says: 'Lay off me, I'm not in your army, Gramps. You're my grandfather, not my colonel.' " '

'You must talk to Haydn about her, my dear. He's been a great support and comfort to me over the years. I'm sure he'd be glad to help you and your daughter.'

'I'm ashamed to admit to such bad behaviour in my family.'

Mrs Smallwood gave a gulp of distress. 'It might – turn him away from the rest of us. Would you talk to her?'

Edna was smiling at Josie from the other side of the bean poles.

'He wouldn't see it that way, my dear. He's seen the ways of the world and finds it in him to forgive everybody. You can rest assured, nothing your daughter does will put Haydn off. I've heard him speak so highly of you. He certainly wouldn't turn against you.'

Chapter Twelve

The words Nurse Silk had used stayed in Josie's mind: 'I saw too much of it in my life's work . . . the girls were usually from the gutters.'

That's how she'd treated them all, like girls from the gutters, but until then, Josie had seen herself as respectable. Very respectable.

Another wave of shame flooded over her. She'd been overwhelmed by it when she'd given birth to Robert, and had never dared to talk to anyone about it. Suzy knew nothing of him. That he'd been born was past history and better kept so. But making up her mind not to think along certain lines didn't actually stop her doing it.

It was more a matter of deliberately banishing Nurse Silk and Luke Palmer from her mind when she realised she was mulling over them yet again. She'd been at The Lawns for only five weeks when one morning she went to the dining room to receive Mrs Smallwood's instructions for the day, and she said: 'Josephine, I want you to make some cakes for a bring-and-buy sale at my church tomorrow afternoon.'

'Small cakes, you mean? What sort would you like?'

'Fairy cakes. I want you to ice them, and make them look attractive. Assorted styles. Say six dozen.'

The number rather took Josie's breath away. Making six dozen would take up a lot of time.

'And perhaps a good rich fruit cake too. Put in plenty of sultanas and raisins, but only three currants. Have you got that? It's important. Only three currants, Josephine. I'll run a

207

competition to guess the number of currants in it. Entrants pay three pence and the nearest guess wins the cake.'

'Yes, ma'am.'

'I'll come down to the kitchen later to look through the cupboards to see if there are any jars of jam or chutney I could take.'

'Hold on, Hebe.' The colonel looked up from his toast. 'Don't give away any of that green tomato chutney our last cook made.'

'Or the crab apple jelly,' Alma added. 'I like that with cold meat.'

'Or the raspberry jam,' Louise put in.

Hebe shook her head with impatience. 'Josephine can make more. Chocolate fingers sold very well at the spring fair, and gingerbread men. Perhaps, Josephine, a few dozen—'

'What about our meals?' demanded the colonel. 'It doesn't sound as though Josephine will have any time to cook for us.'

'We'll have something simple, fish perhaps. Father, it wouldn't hurt you to find a few things to put in the sale. Your study's overflowing with books.'

'It's only a week or so since you last did this – that spring fair you were talking about. You cleared me out. I've nothing I want to get rid of.'

'There's a load of rubbish in your room. It's for a good cause, Father. It's to raise money for the church building fund.'

'Not St Saviour's? That other place isn't a real church, Hebe.'

'St Buddolph's is as real as any other. You've done nothing to help, Father, and I think you should. Mother has embroidered some tray cloths . . .'

'Hebe dear, I thought you said for St Saviour's fête.'

'St Buddolph's, Mother. And Louise has been very good knitting a tea cosy. Father, the least you can do is to come and buy something.'

'So you can take it back next month and put it in another church bazaar.'

'There'll be other attractions . . .'

'I don't want my fortune told, and I don't want to roll pennies on to squares.'

'Just come, Father. Two o'clock tomorrow. It's the least you can do.'

Christobel's fresh young face grinned at him from across the table. 'You'll have to go, Gramps.'

Her mother turned on her. 'Why don't you look through your wardrobe, Christobel? You're always buying new clothes; you need to make space for them.'

'No, Mother! No fear. I'm not parting—'

'Fashions for the young, in good condition, sell well.'

'No, you took my blue dinner dress, one of my favourites, for your spring fair. And a new dressing gown I hadn't even worn. Leave my things alone, I've got to have something to wear myself.'

Josie sighed as she returned to the kitchen. She felt even less enthusiasm for the bring-and-buy sale than Mrs Smallwood's family. It was going to give her a lot of extra work.

Colonel Ingram stamped out of the dining room and took his hat from the hall stand. Would he need his coat? Better take it. It had been raining overnight and there could be more to come.

He didn't like what was happening under his own roof, his daughter and granddaughter bickering at every meal. He was trapped between them with no peace.

Christobel was wilful, but Hebe was worse. He didn't know what had got into her since she'd taken up with that dreadful Silk woman and the Reverend Haydn Ingleby-Jones.

She tried to order all the family about, including him. There was an aggressive side to Hebe. She always wanted her own way. Christobel had inherited the trait from her, though Hebe couldn't see that. They were both argumentative and pushy, and Christobel was determined not to be bossed about by her mother. It looked as though they were heading for an out-and-out fight.

He went through the kitchen and let himself out of the scullery door. The dog was still asleep in his kennel and the colonel kicked the side to bring him out.

'Walk, Brutus. Come on.' The dog came slowly, stretching himself.

Once Brutus had belonged to his granddaughter Georgina. She'd got him from an ex-boyfriend who was being sent abroad by his firm.

'The poor thing needs a home, Mummy,' she'd pleaded. 'His kennel can come too. Do let's have him. He's lovely and he'll make a good guard dog.'

But Gina had been wrong about the latter. Brutus was too lethargic, preferring to doze the day away. He didn't care who came and went.

'His name's Rin-Tin-Tin.'

Hebe had taken an instant dislike to the dog and said: 'What a ridiculous name.'

'He was called after that Alsatian in the films.'

'He's to stay outside then. I'll not have him in the house. He's a mongrel, just a great slobbering brute.'

Gina let it be known that his name was to be Brutus henceforth. He didn't always answer to it, but Theo had tried him with Rin-Tin-Tin and he responded no better to that.

Brutus had taken over the mat in front of the kitchen range during his first week, but Hebe had seen him there and banned him from the kitchen on the grounds of hygiene. That had made him move in to share Theo's study.

He was an affectionate dog, the sort that looked up with adoring eyes at any human who stopped to stroke him; who licked at his owners with a rough and smelly tongue. When Gina married and moved to live in a London flat, Theo had taken him over. They walked together through the park every day, to the paper shop near the railway station to buy *The Times*. The walk kept them both going.

Nobody knew how old Brutus was exactly. Theo thought him very old and rather doddery. Gina said her friend had had him fully grown from someone else, who had believed him to be mostly Labrador when he was a puppy, but time had proved there must be a bit of Great Dane in him. He was enormous by the time he came to The Lawns.

Theo fed him every night. Nowadays, he didn't seem as ravenously hungry as he used to. Like his master, Brutus was losing his appetite with age. Or perhaps the maids were to blame. They liked him too, and the old man had seen Gertie feed Brutus titbits during the day, which could be blunting his appetite.

Theo went in through the kitchen because Brutus had got himself wet and dirty in the park, and he wanted Edna to clean him up a bit before Hebe saw him.

There was a heavenly scent of baking and already there were trays of little cakes in paper cases cooling on the table. He helped himself to one as he passed. The new cook looked a bit pressurised.

Theo thought it a longish walk for one of his age, and was glad to return to his study and slump into his favourite armchair. Brutus covered the hearth rug, which made it impossible for Theo to get anywhere near the fire. Fortunately, today it was warm enough not to need the beastly gas fire that Hebe had insisted must replace his open fire. He opened his newspaper as usual, but today he couldn't lose himself in the worsening economic situation.

He was a bit concerned about what Hebe was getting herself in to. She was turning their kitchen into a commercial bakery. Was she going over the top in her support of St Buddolph's church? Perhaps he should go to this bazaar, even to a service to see for himself? It all sounded a bit odd to him.

On Saturday, the day of the church bazaar, Hebe announced at breakfast: 'I've agreed to give a recital on the harmonium while the bazaar is on. The church will provide a place of tranquillity and rest for those who need it. Harold can run me down to St Buddolph's straight after lunch and come back for the rest of you.'

'Count me out,' Christobel said defiantly. 'I'm not going. Got better things to do.'

Hebe pursed her lips in disgust.

'I'll come,' Theo said, 'with your mother.' That pleased her.

'Don't forget Louise. Bring her with you.'

'I want Suzy to come too,' Louise piped up.

'All right, it's somebody for you to lean on. Harold can wait outside.'

Now in the limousine, looking at the two young girls sitting facing him on the foldaway seats, Theo thought they looked so unlike, it was hard to believe they could be friends.

Louise had delicate features, lovely fair skin and long blonde hair hanging in loose curls. But nobody would ever think of her as a beauty because she had a withered leg on which she had to wear a heavy boot and leg irons. Suzy was taller and her robust body moved with a grace Louise would never have. Her brown hair and pink cheeks shone with health, but her face had nothing of Louise's beauty.

There was no mistaking their close friendship. They were chattering away together and Suzy seemed to know instinctively when Louise needed help and when she'd prefer to manage without. Christobel said Suzy was exactly what Louise needed and he was inclined to agree.

Theo had heard a good deal about St Buddolph's. It was in one of the poorer districts of the town. Harold set them down at the gate. Stalls had been set up in the forecourt and all round the hall. The bazaar was attracting a lot of people.

There was a large glass-enclosed veranda on the front and inside was a cake stall manned by two middle-aged, middle-class housewives.

'I helped decorate those fairy cakes,' Suzy beamed at Theo, and waved her hand towards another tray. 'And I turned all these into butterfly buns.'

'Perhaps we should buy some,' Alma suggested. Theo thought she was being too keen to get something bought and get back home.

'No,' Suzy gave her what he'd call a strange look, 'my mother and me . . . we can make you plenty of those any time you want them.'

She was ushering them towards a stall selling clothes. Theo left them to it. He could hear Hebe playing and went into the hall beyond. It was a good harmonium with a rich tone. Hebe was pedalling hard; she played well, letting rip with Bach's Toccata and Fugue in D Minor, which would have sounded better on an organ. It was strange that she should have involved herself to this extent.

He wanted to sit down and listen, but the string seats of the rickety chairs were mostly in need of repair. He found one he could trust with his weight and sank back, asking himself why the place was now called St Buddolph's. Was there a saint of that name? He supposed there must have been once. He wasn't much interested in saints.

He could remember that once this building had been a school, and during the Great War soldiers had been billeted here. He fancied the place might have been a roller-skating rink at one time. An odd building to turn into a church.

A table served as an altar, plain deal legs showing below a black cloth finely embroidered with gold thread, and there were some ecclesiastical ornaments arranged on top. What was Hebe thinking of? The building was in a ramshackle state: there were stains on the ceiling where the rain came in, and two of the windows were cracked.

Theo didn't count himself a religious man. He'd give up going to church altogether if it weren't for Alma; she was still keen, and now he was getting on in years it might be wise to continue, just in case the clergy were right and there was an afterlife. He really found it hard to believe in that, though Alma was convinced of it.

While in the army he'd gone to church regularly because a colonel had to set an example. He enjoyed the hymn singing and the timeless traditions, and it provided something of a social life.

Until recently, he'd have said Hebe felt the same. She'd always appeared to take more interest in the fashions worn by the other ladies in the congregation, than she did in the sermons preached. She'd been approached to be the church organist at St Saviour's. They had a decent organ there and she could play very competently – occasionally she had on special occasions – but she'd said: 'I don't want to be tied down to do it every Sunday. That would be too much. I've got responsibilities here, looking after my children and running the house.'

But all that had changed when she'd been taken up by the Reverend Haydn Ingleby-Jones and Nurse Silk. She said she'd met them at St Saviour's and possibly she had, but Theo had been often enough to know Mr Jones had never been appointed to the clergy at that church.

Hebe had deserted for St Buddolph's when she found he was what she termed 'the leader' there.

Theo had asked: 'He's the vicar, you mean?'

'Yes, but he calls himself our leader. St Buddolph's is different. It's independent, the congregation run it, there are no bishops or archbishops in authority over us.'

'It's Congregationalist then?'

'No, C of E.'

'Nonsense, Hebe. If the fellow's shut himself off from the Archbishop of Canterbury, it can't be. It sounds like some new sect he's started.'

'Father, you don't understand.'

Theo didn't. 'It sounds suspicious to me.'

Particularly so, when he saw Hebe throw herself heart and soul into the new religion. For the past eighteen months, she'd been playing the harmonium here every Sunday, and it seemed she had a say in other Church business; she spoke of disagreements with the ladies in charge of the flowers, and the Mothers' Union and the numerous fund-raising events.

Theo realised another heavy body was bending over him.

'Colonel Ingram, I'm so very pleased to see you here today. Delighted you could spare the time for our little fund-raising event. Your daughter does so much for our cause.'

The Reverend Haydn Ingleby-Jones was lowering his bulk in its large cassock on to the next chair. He had a bald head, a drooping straw-coloured moustache and a waxy complexion.

Theo felt cornered. 'I came to listen . . .' He realised suddenly that the hall had gone silent, but obligingly Hebe launched herself into another piece by Bach.

'Ah. *Jesu, Joy of Man's Desiring.*' Haydn Ingleby-Jones raised his hands as though about to conduct. 'Hebe provides such bliss for the senses. A wonderful performer.'

Theo's heart sank; he hadn't realised they were on first-name terms. Hebe had invited him to meals at the house more than once, but Haydn had always addressed her as 'dear lady'.

Now he said: 'You hold quite a lot of these fund-raising events.' Far too many, the fellow was overdoing it.

'In aid of our Building Fund. God's work, you know.' His voice was thick with piety. 'Allow me to show you our plans.'

Theo was relieved to see him up on his feet and leading the way over to a table by the door where building plans were laid out. He studied them carefully.

'It's going to be a big church.' From the measurements given, it seemed almost the size of Westminster Abbey.

'Our congregation is growing. Very gratifying to be able to say that. Our hall here is too small already.'

The place was filling up, Theo couldn't doubt it. It seemed there were plenty more like Hebe. He found it unbelievable.

'Allow me to show you the progress we're making.' A hand on his arm steered him towards a cardboard graph pinned to the wall. 'We've collected two and a half thousand, but we need thousands more, of course. And once we have the sort of church we may proudly call a House of God, we'll need a church hall for social occasions and we'll need bells and an organ – so many things.'

His hand came down in a graceful arc to indicate the outsize collecting box underneath. He moved it slightly to make the coins within rattle a reminder that more were needed.

Theo ignored it. He could see Henrietta Silk advancing to join them, and felt he had to get away.

'The Lord go with you.' Haydn Ingleby-Jones clasped the colonel's hand between his own.

Theo had had more than enough and what he'd seen had increased his suspicion rather than diminished it. Why should Hebe desert St Saviour's for this? It made no sense to him.

Once outside he felt he could breathe again. He noticed that immediately opposite, one of the semi-detached houses had a sign on the gate announcing it was St Buddolph's vicarage. It had been freshly painted, the net curtains were the whitest in the road, and the garden looked well cared for. He found his car, sent Harold to see if the rest of his family were ready to leave and relaxed thankfully on to the back seat.

In the past, Hebe had persuaded Alma and the girls to attend services at St Buddolph's. Christobel had condemned the place outright and even Alma had said once was enough, but Hebe was still taking Louise with her. She was too young and too timid to stand up to her mother.

Hebe was always praising Haydn Ingleby-Jones's sermons; describing them as uplifting and inspirational. Theo felt it was his duty to see for himself and decided he'd come to morning service tomorrow. He was concerned about what Hebe was getting herself and Louise into. He was afraid she was being brainwashed.

There were things about Haydn Ingleby-Jones that he disliked; his way of addressing Hebe as 'dear lady' in soft pious tones, and his fat white fingers that looked as though they'd never done more than lift a teacup in his life. He was inviting trust so obviously, that Theo felt put off, and he'd pressed too hard to get him to contribute to his building fund.

When he went to the service the next morning, he found the sermon dire – too long by far and exceedingly dull.

The following week, after breakfast had been served, Josie presented herself to Mrs Smallwood in the dining room to get her instructions. She'd forced her worries about Henrietta Silk to the back of her mind and felt reasonably calm. The family were all still at the table.

Mrs Smallwood said: 'I've invited three guests for dinner tonight, Josephine. We'll have a leg of lamb, I think.'

'Who's coming?' the colonel wanted to know. He'd been late rising, and was still eating his egg and bacon.

'Haydn Ingleby-Jones is bringing his son and—'

'Not that Henrietta Silk?'

Josie went rigid as she tried to write on her pad. So it was them! No doubt about it now, there couldn't possibly be another Haydn Ingleby-Jones.

'His sister, yes.'

Josie couldn't get her breath. His sister! She hadn't realised they were related!

'Silly woman, I don't know why you ask her.'

'She's kind to Louise and a great support to me. Anyway, you like Haydn.'

'I don't, he's a pompous ass. I don't know why you keep inviting them here.'

'He's very nice, Father. On Saturday, you said you liked him.'

'I most certainly did not. His Sunday sermon was drivel. I think he's preying on your generosity and that of the rest of his congregation. You're all working like beavers to raise money for him.'

'For his church, Father.'

'Dammit, there's a perfectly good church even nearer. Why go to all this trouble? What's the attraction?'

Josie felt uncomfortable. She asked: 'With thyme and parsley stuffing and roast potatoes?'

Mrs Smallwood ignored her. 'His son is a lovely young man, just the sort of person Christobel would—'

Christobel crashed her cup down on its saucer. 'I won't be here. I'm going out, Mother.'

'Not tonight, dear. Claude Ingleby-Jones was very taken with you when you met at the Christmas—'

'He's a pain, Mother.'

'But I've asked him specially because of you. You need to meet men of your own class. You do realise the family has an aristocratic background? Haydn's grandfather is a hereditary baronet. He's very old now; I don't think it will be long before Haydn—'

Christobel laughed. 'Don't believe everything Mr Ingleby-Jones tells you, Mother. He's no aristocrat.'

'Don't be silly, of course he is. Whatever makes you say such things?'

Christobel pushed her chair back. 'I'm going out tonight. They're your friends, not mine.'

'You'll enjoy their company. They're delightful people.'

'Gramps doesn't like them and neither do I.'

'Father,' Mrs Smallwood turned on the colonel in exasperation, 'you're an irritable old man who sees no good in anybody.'

'Rubbish!'

'I do wish you'd keep your silly opinions to yourself. Now you've turned Christobel against them.'

'They're on the make, Mother. Selling babies for adoption. I don't know why you take such a high moral tone about Alec's businesses when Reverend Ingleby-Jones is adding to his stipend by placing babies for cash.'

'Stipend?' boomed the colonel. 'I'm not sure he's getting a stipend. I think he's probably been unfrocked by the Church and he's trying to run a separate sect.'

Hebe Smallwood's large chest was heaving with indignation. 'You talk such nonsense, both of you. Haydn places the babies in the best possible homes for their own sake. A middle-class upbringing with a Christian family – what better start could a baby have? You're talking nonsense.'

'Do you know how much he charges for a baby?' Christobel continued to goad her.

'Nothing. He does it to help the children.'

'That's not what I've heard. He doesn't do it out of the goodness of his heart. Prospective parents have to pay.'

'That's an outrageous thing to say—'

'Let me put it another way: he charges them, Mother.'

'Well . . . Possibly there are expenses to defray. Where have you heard such things?'

'Alec has a cousin who's a journalist and works on the *Liverpool Mercury.*'

'Alec Landis? That man! I wouldn't believe anything he said. He's an out-and-out bounder.'

'Anyway, I'm going out tonight. You don't like my friends and I can't stand yours.'

'Stop this silly squabbling,' the colonel barked. 'I can't be doing with it in my own home.' He pushed his chair back and stood up. 'I'm going to take Brutus for his morning walk and get my paper. Hebe, I know you're fond of Haydn Ingleby-Jones, but that's no reason to invite him here and inflict him on the rest of us at dinner-time.'

Josie was sweating when she returned to the kitchen. Mrs Smallwood had had some difficulty in settling the menu for tonight, and Josie had been unable to suggest anything. Her mind had been in a whirl.

Selling babies for adoption? Was that why Nurse Silk had pressed her to sign Robert away? She could never forget how forceful the woman had been. She had pressed her to part with him and, at the time, Josie had not asked herself why.

She'd been too young and too deeply immersed in her own problems to imagine Nurse Silk might have a personal motive. It gave Josie a nasty taste in her mouth to think the woman had been taking advantage of her and the other girls in her situation. She hoped for Robert's sake that he'd been found the good home she'd been promised. As she cooked special dishes for the evening, she wondered if there was any way of finding out what had become of her son, and where he had been placed.

All day, Josie's mind was filled with visions of what had happened twenty-five years ago. She tried to imagine what Robert would be like now. Tall and strong and healthy, she hoped, but the image of his father was imprinted on her idea of his appearance. Ray Bissell had been another rotter who had let her down. It reinforced her determination to have nothing more to do with men.

Josie prepared the dinner slowly and carefully; she mustn't make any mistakes, mustn't let Edna or Gertie see how much on edge she was. She kept quiet when they discussed the Reverend Haydn Ingleby-Jones.

'I think Mrs Smallwood fancies him,' Edna said. 'His wife died last year and since then he's been coming here regularly, and I think I've heard her tell Harold to take her to St Buddolph's vicarage. I heard her telling the colonel that the vicar was the son of an hereditary baronet and the old man's now well into his nineties. It would suit her down to the ground to be Lady Ingleby-Jones, wouldn't it?'

'A big lift up from being Mrs Smallwood,' Josie managed.

'She'll feel very equal to it,' Edna sighed. 'Just think of it, rich as Croesus and a title.'

'I don't think he's rich,' Gertie frowned.

'He must be, the son of a baronet.'

'Apparently he has a lot of unmarried sisters that have to be kept in the proper style. He runs a private adoption agency. Miss Christobel says he earns his money that way.'

Edna said: 'Nurse Silk is his sister and she's earned her living all her life. Why shouldn't the others do the same?'

Josie heard the guests arrive. She expected to stay in the kitchen all evening, but it was not to be. Gertie took the meat up on a great silver platter. She'd roasted two small legs of lamb as she didn't think one would be adequate for six of them, not with Louise coming down for dinner too.

Gertie came quickly back to the kitchen. 'The colonel wants you to carve. His wrist is painful.'

Josie swallowed hard. Her legs felt like jelly again, and her heart was pounding away as she went to the dining room. The meat platter had been placed in front of the colonel.

'Sorry,' he said. 'Can't . . . My hands . . . Rheumatics playing up.'

Josie wanted to take it to the sideboard, but there was no space. Gertie had set out too many plates and things there already. With seven people sitting down to eat at the table, there was a space left.

'Do it here.' The colonel pushed the platter across.

Josie had always carved the enormous joints she'd cooked at the Imperial. Carving had been considered one of her duties, she was expert at it, and these legs of lamb were slicing well.

As she worked, she stole surreptitious glances at the guests. The young man looked languid and rather nondescript. Nurse Silk, as she remembered her, had been stout but now she'd grown really fat, even fatter than Mrs Smallwood. Josie knew she wouldn't have recognised her had they met in the street; and as for the Reverend Haydn Ingleby-Jones, only the dog collar was familiar; without that, no, she wouldn't have known him. They wouldn't recognise her. She'd been eighteen years old and just a slip of a thing. She needn't worry about that.

After dinner, Theo took refuge in his study. He was worried about what Haydn Ingleby-Jones wanted from Hebe. He thought him a charlatan and suspected it was money. Hadn't Christobel said he made money from placing babies for adoption? He deliberated on that for an hour. Hebe seemed infatuated with him, but if it could be proved that he wasn't honest, perhaps she would see him in a different light.

He was sitting back in his armchair, enjoying a whisky and soda and listening to the ten o'clock news, when suddenly his study door was flung back and Hebe strode in, her plump face twisting with irritation. She turned the volume down to a whisper.

'Father, you're driving us all mad with the noise.'

Theo pulled himself upright. 'That's a bit high-handed. I can't hear my own wireless now.'

'You're deaf, and you'll make the rest of us so if you have that racket blaring out all the time.'

He couldn't believe the change in her from early evening. 'Has something upset you?'

'You have, Father. You walk away from the dinner table and ignore my guests. Now we can hardly hear ourselves talk.'

'It's about time your friends went home. Turn it up again, Hebe. I always listen to the news.'

With a rasp of impatience, she flounced out, leaving the door open.

Theo sighed as he got up. He'd never have dared to speak to his father like that. Hebe was getting too big for her boots.

He saw the *Evening Echo* on the hall stand; nobody had had time to read it yet. He took it, shut the study door, and turned up his wireless again. There was no point in having it on if he couldn't hear it. He poured himself some more whisky and opened the paper. He'd picked up St Buddolph's parish magazine too, which must have been delivered at the same time. Or perhaps Hebe's guests had brought it with them. He'd never looked at it before, but now he opened it up, wondering if Haydn Ingleby-Jones would be pushing his adoption society in this. There were a few words about the support the Church would give to adoptive parents; a listening ear and, of course, prayers, but no more than one should expect from any Church.

It was when he opened up the evening paper that he saw the advertisement for the Church Adoption Society. Readers were invited to get in touch with Nurse H. Silk, who would advise on all aspects of adoption and baby care.

The Church Adoption Society? Surely, they weren't allowed to call it that? It had nothing to do with the real Church.

Theo stayed up late, waiting for Christobel to come home. The guests had long since departed and the ladies of the house had gone to bed. Brutus snored on his hearth rug and the gas fire hummed and spluttered. The colonel opened his study door wide so he wouldn't miss her as she crossed the hall.

He needed to bring Hebe to her senses. She was besotted with that silly man, though if he was merely silly there was nothing he could do about it, as clearly silliness didn't bother her.

From the advertisement in the paper, it appeared that Christobel was right. Ingleby-Jones and his sister could be making money by selling babies for adoption. He didn't approve of that, not for a Church 'leader' – not for anyone, really – and didn't think Hebe would. It might be something Haydn Ingleby-Jones had done in the past and had given up now. Nurse Silk had certainly retired as matron of the mother-and-baby home, but it seemed she was still involved with adoptions. He needed to know what proof Christobel had for making the statements she had.

She came at last. The colonel saw Brutus cock his ears, then stand up and go slowly to the front door, though she made no sound that he could hear, nor did she put on the lights. He blinked at his clock. It was almost two in the morning.

He knew she was surprised to see the dog still indoors. She was making soothing noises to him, and she'd seen his door open and the light on. Although she had her shoes in her hand she realised there was no way she could reach the stairs without him knowing.

'Hello, Gramps. You still up?'

'Waiting up,' he stifled a yawn, 'to see you.'

The excuses for being so late began. He held up his hand. He didn't approve of her staying out until this hour, but that wasn't what he wanted to discuss.

'I want you to tell me all you know about Reverend Haydn Ingleby-Jones. I've had a rough evening with him and his family.'

'He's all sanctity and holiness, Gramps. Full of sayings like "God Bless", "the Lord go with you", "the Lord keep you", but he doesn't seem sincere. He's a wily bird.'

'In what way? I don't like him any more than you do.'

Christobel's face screwed in concentration. 'I feel he's projecting an image – of being a man of God, a servant of the Church – but it rings false. I think it's just an act.'

'Why do you think that?'

'He's been buttering Mother up . . .'

'I can see that, but what for?'

'She paid for the harmonium in his church.'

'What? She didn't tell me that. Silly woman!'

'She didn't tell me either. I knew she'd chosen it; she had brochures of different makes here in the house, but then I heard him thanking her for it. He said she was giving money for God's work and she'd get her reward in heaven.'

'Good gracious! Has she given any other money?'

'Don't know.'

'We've got to open her eyes. Let her see what he's really like.'

'I can't believe she's so much against Alec and yet so involved with those two.'

'You said they're running an adoption agency.' Theo passed over the newspaper and pointed out the advertisement to her. 'How did you find out about it? Who told you?'

'Alec . . .'

Theo almost gave up. He wasn't sure he shared her faith in Alec.

'We've got to have proof, Christobel. I agree with everything you've said, but if your mother is to see Ingleby-Jones as we do, we'll have to show him up as an unsavoury character. Now, is he that? Or are we just prejudiced?'

'It's like this, Gramps. Alec has a cousin called Monica – well, a distant cousin, second cousin or something like that. She's a journalist on the *Liverpool Mercury*, unmarried and very interested in any scandal she can write about. When she found out that I'd been to St Buddolph's, she asked me about Haydn Ingleby-Jones.'

'So what did you tell her?'

'That I didn't like him. What else could I say?'

'You've made accusations, but . . . can you ask this cousin if she has proof? Proof of specific wrongdoing on his part? Something we could put before your mother?'

Christobel yawned. 'I'll try, Gramps.'

'Right. Let's go to bed, it's been a long day. I'll just put Brutus out of the back door. But don't forget – I'm relying on you.'

Chapter Thirteen

Luke Palmer felt as tense as a drum. He'd come close to having an accident in Castle Street and it had shaken him up. He'd come round a corner almost on to two women crossing the track in front of him; shopping baskets on their arms and chatting away, showing no sense of self-preservation. He'd missed them by a whisker. Women were like that. Sometimes he thought they did it just to upset him.

There was always some problem to wind him up. Breakdowns were frequent. It was awful when it was his tram and full of passengers all desperate to reach their destinations, all blaming him because the damn thing wouldn't go. It was just as bad when the tram ahead of him broke down because they all used the same track. That meant going back to find a way round it.

Always on his back were the inspectors and the problem of keeping to time. If he was running late to the timetable there was nothing they could do about it. He just told them they'd had lots of passengers getting on and off, or heavy traffic had blocked his line. But heaven help any driver caught running early. Even a minute or two ahead meant big trouble. Either he'd get bawled at there and then, in front of everybody, or he'd be summoned to the office later so the boss could tell him off.

As darkness fell, rain had set in for the night. Driving wasn't easy; the streetlamps and glistening roads dazzled him and the rain blew into his face. He was driving a car that was waiting to be reconditioned, another of the old Bellamys, which as yet had no windscreen. He'd really missed that this evening.

He was tired, wet and cold, when at twenty-five minutes to eleven, he drove the last tram for the night on the number 33 route into the Dingle Depot. As he'd slowed down to turn in, Tommy Curtis, the conductor, had dropped off outside the office and Luke had noticed two people waiting there, a man and a woman.

He took the car through the loop siding and parked, feeling stiff with standing so long in front of the controls. He was hungry too but the canteen would have long since closed. Neither would he find a fish-and-chip shop open at this time, not when the weather was so bad.

Most of the staff had gone for the night. The depot was in semidarkness, a vast expanse of blackness. It could hold up to sixty-nine tramcars and they looked ghostly, ranged in still and silent lines. He switched off the lights on his car, both outside and in, and took off his peaked cap to shake it. It was rare to see a woman in this part of the depot, but he could see one coming out of the gloom towards him. She came closer and there was something vaguely familiar about the way she walked.

Luke thought it was the woman he'd seen outside and wondered why she was coming to speak to him; he thought she must want to ask directions or something. He was trying to ease his new leather gloves off his icy hands, and was cross to find them sodden with moisture. He was afraid the rain had spoiled them.

The woman stepped straight on to his tram. 'Hello, Luke,' she said.

He took a closer look and felt the strength ebb from his legs. It couldn't be . . .?

'You must know who I am? Flora.'

'No!' His numb fingers felt for the brass grab rail. 'No!'
Oh God, not Flora!

'Your mother said I'd find you here. "Better wait till he's
finished for the day," she said. "Otherwise his tram will streak
off like a greyhound leaving the starting gate." '

Luke swallowed hard. He could hardly speak.

'Flora?'

She was unbuttoning her mackintosh. It was her, he could
see that now. He strained his eyes to see more in the gloom. A
much older and more wizened Flora; her figure gone and her
hair grey and straggly, but Flora all the same.

His tongue was as dry as the Sahara. 'I thought you were
dead.'

He remembered her laugh – it was a great guffaw. 'Not
yet. Still got a bit of mileage in me.'

'But Mam said years ago . . . You were in the fever hospital
and very ill. Fading fast, she said.'

'Typhoid – a bad do, that – snuffed out a few of our
neighbours but not me.'

Strewth! What had he done? Josie was his wife now. Luke
was sweating. 'What have you come here for?'

'Your mam doesn't know where you live. Not these days,
she'd like to, but—'

'For the love of—'

'Look, it's about Peter . . .'

'Who?'

'Your son, Peter. The younger one. What's the matter with
you? You can't have forgotten your own children?'

'I haven't thought of them for years.'

'Well, you could try to now. He wants to be a tram driver,
a real chip off the old block. He even looks a bit like you. He
thinks you'd want to help him . . .'

'No,' Luke said through parched lips.

231

'Look, I know you and I came to the parting of the ways—'

'You walked out on me, Flora.'

'Yes, well, I don't know why you're giving your mam the cold shoulder, and you can't have any gripes against your kids.'

'You took them away. I don't know them.'

'Peter wants to know you. Look, it's not asking a lot. You could put in a word for him, couldn't you? A senior driver like you, after all these years' service?'

'No,' Luke said. 'It wouldn't do any good.' He'd had his own ambitions; he'd wanted to be an inspector, but there'd be no chance of promotion for him now. Not after what his mother had done outside the hospital.

'Why not?'

'Because . . .' Luke was finding it difficult to think straight. Aspiring tram drivers were taught at the Edge Lane Depot. The opportunity to learn was much sought after amongst conductors. 'Because so many want to do it. I was kept waiting for years. Peter would have to get some other job with the Corporation Tramways first.'

'He has.'

'What?'

That really shook him. His heart was pounding. His old family here all round him and he hadn't known, but they knew about him. They'd been watching him. Did they know about Josie? It was enough to make his blood run cold.

'Where's he working?'

Surely he wasn't one of those young conductors? Dingle Depot was full of cheeky young conductors who had no respect for their elders. He wouldn't know Peter if he stood in front of him now. He'd been a babe in arms last time he'd set eyes on him.

'He started in the ticket printing basement at Hatton Garden. Been there eight months.'

'Well, he's got all the bosses upstairs. Why doesn't he lobby them?'

'He's applied in writing. It's what they told him to do.'

'Then he'll get it, sooner or later.'

'Put in a word for him, write – or, better still, have a word with the instructor at Edge Lane. You know him, don't you?'

Luke did, but he hadn't been popular there either. It wouldn't do any good.

'No,' he said.

'Come on, Luke, don't be so bloody-minded. He's your son too. Nobody's asked you to do much for him all these years. This wouldn't hurt you.'

'For God's sake, woman! I've said no, haven't I? It won't do any good.'

Luke couldn't get over the shock of seeing her again. He was shaking with nerves. He really had believed she'd be dead by now. He wished – how he wished she was.

'Come and say hello to Peter.' Her wheedling voice started again. 'You ought to know your own son. He's a good man, thirty-four now.'

Luke didn't want to know his first wife or his children. He'd thought he was free of them for ever.

'Come on, any normal man would want to see his son.'

'Shut up!'

He didn't like the suggestion that he wasn't normal. Luke felt something explode within him. He couldn't cope with this. He grabbed the bow at the neck of her blouse and twisted it.

Flora pushed him off, coughing and choking. 'Leave me alone. Peter's here with me.'

'Why did you leave me, you silly bitch? You spoiled everything I was building up.'

'You never built up anything.' Her voice was full of scorn. 'Unless it was your thirst. Still drinking hard, are you?'

Luke could feel his temper fizzing up. 'If you'd stayed, we'd have been all right.'

'I couldn't stand any more. You were impossible. A bully and a cheat. We've had a better life without you.'

Her false teeth and white blouse were swinging eerily round in the gloom. He couldn't keep his hands off her. He was twisting the big white bow at her neck again. Harder and tighter. She was fighting to free herself but she didn't stand a chance against him. He'd give her what she deserved. Get even for all he'd suffered when she'd walked out on him.

Flora and his mother – women were all the same. They let him down every time. He felt the fight go out of Flora, her body relaxing against him. He'd got her!

The next second a fist sent him hurtling against the iron stairs. His jaw sang; he banged his head and hurt his back. It took a moment for his head to clear.

Flora was a pale heap against the oak lagging of the floor. His assailant was bending over her, trying to lift her head, trying to rub some life into her hands.

'Oh my God! Mam?'

Flora looked dead! He couldn't have killed her, surely?

'Wake up, Mam.'

The younger man turned to look at Luke. 'You bloody maniac. What have you done?'

Luke pulled himself up and stood staring down at them for a moment. 'Why the hell did you have to come here?'

Then panic overtook him. He knew he had to get away. He jumped off the tram and took to his heels. He was almost out in the street when his mind started to work again.

At this time of night he always went to the cloakroom and changed out of his uniform before leaving. There was a tram over the other side of the shed that would start its last trip into the city in a minute or two. He always took it, as did most of the crews. If he didn't, he'd have a long walk.

There were others in the cloakroom. Luke turned his back on them so they couldn't see how shaken up he was. He couldn't get his gloves off. At last, thank God, but his gilt uniform buttons had never seemed so hard to undo. He left his jacket tossed over the radiator. Others were hanging theirs neatly on coat hangers but they were all leaving and he must go with them. He grabbed his trilby and his mac, and made it to the tram a second before it set off.

He turned to look through the gloom towards the Bellamy that had run on the number 33 route today. A lonely figure was running towards the office, looking as panic-stricken as he felt himself.

Luke shuddered. That must be his son, Peter. He'd not have known him, of course. Flora had said he was like him to look at but he'd hardly noticed what he looked like. He had given him a right biff on the jaw; his chin still ached.

Oh God, what had he done? Cautiously he looked round the car he was on as it turned out of the depot: just a few of the late crew chatting together, full of bonhomie. The rain was still hurtling down but as a passenger Luke was protected by the glass. Nobody talked to him, they never did. He was glad. He wasn't up to small talk; he felt absolutely awful.

He had to walk up Upper Parliament Street. He'd go to the Flag and Sailor for a brandy. He had to have something. What had he done?

The pub was emptying when he reached it. Last orders had already been called, and the landlord wouldn't serve him. He kicked viciously at the bar and within seconds found himself being manhandled out to the pavement again. The door slammed behind him. Luke had never needed a brandy more than he did at that moment.

There was nowhere else to go but home. The house was in darkness, everybody else was already in bed. He was glad he wouldn't have to see the landlord; old Maynard kept asking him when he'd be leaving, letting him know he'd outstayed his welcome here by several weeks. Luke couldn't be bothered looking for somewhere else. He doubted Maynard would ever screw up the courage to evict him forcibly.

His rooms felt cold and cheerless. The living room still smelled of whisky after he'd dropped that bottle on the hearth, but there was nothing he could drink in the house. He'd never craved it more.

He put the kettle on to make some tea. He had to have something. Oh God, what a mess! He wouldn't be able to go back to work ever again. After that fracas on the tram he'd get the sack. He'd already had two warnings, hadn't he? This would certainly cause a third. Thank goodness he had a day off tomorrow. He'd have time to think about what he should do.

But worse, he was worried about Flora. Had he killed her? She'd certainly looked lifeless, and Peter had tried to rouse her and failed. But he'd done so little to harm her, he couldn't believe he could kill with such ease. That hadn't been his intention at all. He wished now he'd stayed; he should have gone to the office and phoned for an ambulance. It had been a terrible accident.

Luke desperately wanted to sleep. He was exhausted and aching, but his mind kept going over and over what had happened in the depot. It was beginning to get light when he finally slept.

He dreamed he was in prison, and woke up feeling uncertain where the dream ended and reality began. He was worried. What if Flora was dead? He could be accused of murder, though it hadn't been his fault. She should never have come hunting for him at the depot. He stayed in Suzy's narrow bed for another hour or so, too drowsy to make a start on the day.

It was the craving for a drink that drove him to dress and it came as a shock to find it had gone two o'clock in the afternoon. The pubs would be shutting before he could get there.

He put the kettle on and looked round for something to eat; he had to put something in his belly. He found a couple of eggs and some stale bread, but there was a bit of lard too. He made himself fried eggs on fried bread, filling the bathroom with succulent scents. When he'd eaten, he took his mug of tea and went to lie on the bed again. There was nowhere else. Josie, damn her, had taken the couch. Between them, women had really knotted up his life . . .

It was five o'clock when he woke up again. He felt bleary-eyed and heavy, and he was right out of Woodbines. He wanted a drink even more, but the pubs didn't open until six.

He made more tea and toasted his last slice of stale bread, and then, because he was bored at home by himself, he crept downstairs and let himself out. He was going to the pub, but to fill the time he'd go to the paper shop first and get himself some smokes. Not to the Flag and Sailor this time – the landlord there had turned nasty last night. Luke had been one of his regular customers over recent months and thought he should have been treated with more respect. He wouldn't be putting any trade that way in future.

He walked on towards the Pier Head. There was a miserable little boozer the dockers used down this way, which would do. Nobody would know him there. It brought another rush of irritation when he found it was not yet open.

The weather was kinder than last night and the clock on the Liver Building told him he had ten minutes to wait. He didn't feel like walking further, so he leaned against the wall near the door and opened the *Evening Echo* that he'd bought with his Woodbines.

He read the sports page first and then turned back to read the news. Within seconds he was sweating and gasping for breath. He felt as though he was suffocating, as though somebody had dropped a ton weight on his chest.

He was staring at a photograph of the Bellamy he'd been driving last night, with a man he still didn't recognise standing on the platform. Large headlines read:

VICIOUS ATTACK IN DINGLE TRAM SHEDS

Late last night Mrs Flora Maud Palmer, 57, was viciously attacked inside the number 33 electric tramcar owned by Liverpool Corporation Tramways. Fortunately, her son, Peter, 34, was with her and able to fight off her attacker and summon help.

The attack came at the end of a nine-hour shift during which Mrs Palmer's husband had been driving the tramcar on the route between Garston and Pier Head.

Mrs Palmer, who is recovering in the Southern Hospital, said she was estranged from her husband and, until last night, had not seen him for over thirty years.

The police want to question Luke Edmund Palmer, aged 55, but after the attack he disappeared. He has not been seen for almost a year at the address he gave his employers.

The door was opening behind him. Luke crumpled his newspaper together and staggered across the sawdust-covered floor
of the public bar. There were no seats here but drinks were a
penny cheaper than they were in the cramped lounge. He
needed to lean against the bar; he felt it was the only thing
keeping him upright.

'Double brandy twice.'

His mouth was sand-dry and his tongue felt twice its usual
size. He was lucky to be the first served. He tossed the
contents of the first glass straight down.

Flora was alive, wasn't she? What would the police want
to question him about? He'd been lucky again because he'd
never got round to letting the office know he'd married Josie
and moved in with her. The police wouldn't be able to find
him. He'd be safe . . .

No, he wouldn't. Not if old Maynard happened to read
tonight's *Echo*. He knew exactly who he was. So did Frankie
upstairs, and both of them would love to drop him into more
trouble. They were that sort.

Oh God! Luke could feel a huge chasm opening up at his
feet. Wally Simpson knew he was married. What if he told
them? It seemed he hadn't yet but if he happened to read
this . . .

Luke could feel himself shaking; he knew he could be
charged with bigamy as well. If he was questioned about
Josie, he'd have to deny marrying her. He'd say, he'd let it be
known they were married to spare her embarrassment and
protect her reputation; that Josie was really his mistress.
They'd understand that.

Luke was sipping his second glass of brandy slowly when
he realised he couldn't stay in Upper Parliament Street. He
was afraid he'd be picked up there. Josie's friends at the
Imperial would know where he was too. He opened the *Echo*

again, this time at the adverts for rooms to let, spreading the paper across the bar in front of him.

The edge of it flicked up against a tankard of ale. Its owner, who was standing beside him, lifted it away.

'You looking for a room or something?'

'Yes,' Luke said.

'A friend of mine's got one to rent.'

Luke was interested. At this time of the evening, it mightn't be easy to get a room advertised in the paper. Landlords expected to show likely tenants round in the daytime.

'How much?'

'Four and sixpence. It's in Picton Street.'

Luke knew Picton Street. It wasn't a place he'd normally choose to live, but he might be able to fix this up straight away. He had to get out of Upper Parliament Street as soon as he could.

'Can we go and see it now?'

'When I've finished my drink.'

Luke managed to attract the barman's attention and get another brandy in his glass. He bought half a bottle of whisky to take with him and felt he could congratulate himself. He'd take the room however awful it was. It would be the safest thing to do.

The room really was awful: filthy dirty, with thin curtains threaded on a sagging string; but it had electric light, a bed, a table and a couple of chairs. He could cook in a shared kitchen on a stove thick with grime and grease, and use a lavatory, which was absolutely disgusting, out in the yard. He didn't like the look of the landlord – he was dirty too – but Luke managed to drive down the amount of rent the man was asking by a shilling.

'I'll take it,' Luke told him, and handed over a week's rent for the key. He'd look for something better as soon as his bit of trouble blew over. A dog-eared rent book was produced with three-quarters of its pages cut out. The landlord removed another one that had been used by a previous tenant.

'What's your name?'

He hesitated. 'Bill Smith.'

A stub of pencil was pushed across to him. 'Write it in for me.'

Luke did so, congratulating himself on his quick thinking. No point in making it easy for the police to find him. He felt safer now he had somewhere different to spend the night, though he'd have to go back to Upper Parliament Street. He wanted to get his clothes and bedding. All he had here was a bare mattress.

'I'll be back,' he told the landlord, who it seemed lived in the rooms upstairs. 'I need to fetch my belongings.'

He strode through the dark streets with a purposeful step now. He was doing the right thing. He was nervous, though, about going back to Josie's rooms. The police could be waiting there for him. Somebody could have told them by now.

From the outside, the house seemed just the same as usual. There were lights on both in the Maynards' and the Rimmers' rooms. His floor was in darkness. He let himself in as quietly as he could. He didn't want to meet Maynard now. He'd complain that he owed rent and expect to be paid.

Silently he closed the front door. The stairs were dark but he wasn't going to risk putting the light on. Up he went. The third step from the top always gave a creak loud enough to sound like a ship breaking its back. He stood carefully close against the wall to keep it quiet, then tiptoed across the landing and only put the light on when he could close his kitchen door behind him.

Some of his clothes still hung on hangers on an open rail. He'd tossed a few pairs of trousers over it and there was a sizeable heap that needed washing on the floor. He crept back across the landing to get his suitcases from the bedroom he'd shared with Josie. The door was no longer locked now she'd gone. The bed had gone too, and the dressing table. What a selfish bitch she was!

He expected to find his cases on top of the wardrobe, but it was bare except for an empty cardboard box. He remembered sliding his two suitcases up there. Suddenly the bile was rising in his throat and he was running with sweat as he raged against Josie. The bitch had taken his cases! He couldn't believe it. He looked round then for his cabin trunk and found that was missing too. How was he going to move his stuff if he had nothing to pack his things in? He pulled down the cardboard box, but decided it was useless.

He'd seen some clean bolster cases in a drawer in Suzy's room. They would be easier to carry than a box. He found two and started to stuff his best suit inside.

Damn Josie! He wanted to wring her neck as he'd wrung Flora's. Nobody deserved it more.

Bolster cases were not much use when it came to moving pillows and the eiderdown. He tied them together with string and left a loop he could put over his shoulder.

As he packed, Luke had time to think. He had to find out where Josie had gone. Frankie was his best bet. He'd know. He'd try and grab hold of him while he was here. If he didn't do it now he'd have to come back again. How could he get him away from his mother? He could hear her voice up there.

Luke was moving his baggage out to the landing when he heard a door slam upstairs, a light came on and footsteps came skidding down. This must be Frankie; his footfall was lighter and faster than either of his parents'.

Luke had one second to position himself against the bathroom wall where Frankie wouldn't see him until he was down on the landing. He felt poised like a tiger ready to leap, and grabbed at the slight figure, swinging him through the open door into the kitchen.

A heavy bucket clanged against the banisters as Frankie dropped it. 'Hey, mister, what are you doing . . .?'

'Shut up.' Luke landed a blow against the side of the child's curly head. 'Be quiet or I'll give you another like that.'

Frankie's big dreamy eyes stared up at him like a frightened gazelle. Luke closed the door quietly behind them, leaning against it.

'Right. I want to know where Suzy's gone. Tell me and I'll let you go.'

'No!' Frankie's face screwed in thought. 'I don't know.'

'Yes you do.'

Luke was almost caught off guard by the sudden pummelling of small fists against his chest, but Frankie was easy to pin down. It was like playing with a puppy. He landed another blow and the lad backed off, breathing hard.

'Where has Suzy's mother taken her? You're not leaving here until you tell me.'

'I don't know.'

Luke was sure he did. The boy was staying over by the bed, out of his reach.

'Let me go. My mam's upstairs. She's sent me to get some coal and she'll come looking for me if I don't go back.'

'You could be back upstairs with the coal before your mam misses you. It won't take you a moment to tell me.'

'I don't know.'

'Is she still going to the same school?'

'I don't know.'

Luke saw that as proof he was lying. 'You must know. Either you see her in the class or you don't.'

'I don't.'

'What about her mother? Is she still working at—'

'I don't know, I tell you.'

Luke could hear increasing anxiety in Frankie's voice. His eyes seemed larger with fear.

Luke started to cross the room. The lad needed another swipe to jog his memory. Frankie dodged past him. He snatched the door open and was leaping back upstairs before he could stop him. Luke had forgotten how quickly he could move.

He wasn't going to leave things there. Olga was upstairs alone with the lad, the voices had told him that much. They knew exactly where Josie was, and Josie knew better than to think she could get away with stealing his suitcases. He started to creep up the stairs and fell over the coal bucket Frankie had dropped. The clang reverberated through the stairwell as it fell off the stairs to the landing, radiating coal dust everywhere, all over the clean bolster cases into which he'd packed his things.

Damn, that would warn them he was coming up. He'd wanted to take them by surprise. Luke listened: all was silent upstairs. He imagined them listening for him, anticipating trouble, growing more nervous by the minute. He'd let them stew for a bit – finish his packing and get everything ready, so he could leave as soon as he'd got Josie's new address.

By the time he was creeping upstairs, he could hear them moving around again and he could see light shining under their living-room door. Up here, there were attic rooms with low ceilings, but the layout was exactly like his flat below. Silently he crossed the landing, narrower and meaner than his own. Then he threw open the door.

Olga let out a little scream of surprise and brandished the flat iron she'd been using on one of Eric's shirts.

'What's the matter, Luke? Why d'you come bursting in here?' She was pulling Frankie behind her buxom frame.

Luke could see she was scared. He took a deep breath, tried to appear calmer than he was.

'I'm not going to hurt you, Olga. I just want to know Josie's new address.'

He crept nearer, causing her to back away from the dining table where she'd been ironing. He sniffed appreciatively. The room smelled of clean warm laundry. It was a long time since a woman had ironed his clothes.

'I don't know where she went. Josie was careful not to tell anybody. She doesn't want you to know.'

'The lad knows,' Luke said. 'Suzy told him. Come on, I'm not going until you tell me. Is Josie still working at the Imperial?'

'Why don't you ask them?' Olga's plump face was defiant. 'I don't know. It's none of my business.'

Luke made a grab for the boy, got him out from behind his mother's skirts; had him half stretched backwards across the old sheets on which Olga had been ironing.

'Now then, tell me.'

'No,' Frankie said, and tried to push him off.

'God, you haven't even got Suzy's strength,' Luke mocked. 'You're puny, nothing but a sissy. Come on, Olga, you tell me or I'll persuade Frankie here to do it.'

He slapped Frankie's face, not hard, just enough to encourage him to talk, but in retaliation, the lad jerked his knee up hard against Luke's groin, making him yelp with pain and causing him to land another harder blow on his curly head.

'Don't do that!' Olga screamed. 'Don't hurt him!'

'Come on then, tell me.' He gave the boy's arm a savage twist, making him cry out.

Olga shouted: 'They're in Birkenhead. Josie got a live-in job as a cook in some big house.'

'Where?' he barked. 'What road?'

'It's on Waterford Road, in Oxton,' Frankie panted.

'What number?'

'No number.'

He lifted the curly head and cracked it down hard on the table. The lad wailed in pain. Luke had to shout above the noise. 'There must be something, a name or a number. Come on, I want it.'

Olga screamed and threw her weight against him. She was trying to claw Frankie away from him. 'Leave him alone! You're hurting him!'

He sent Olga reeling across the room. They were both screaming and crying and he knew he'd have to get out before the Maynards heard the racket and came up.

He'd so nearly got what he wanted, he wasn't going until . . . He turned back to Frankie.

'Come on,' he threatened. 'Come on, where in Waterford Road or I'll kill your mother?' Luke heard the door fly open behind him.

'It's called Oakhurst,' Frankie screamed. 'Oakhurst.'

Luke felt a man's weight hurtle against him. The table scraped six inches along the lino under their combined weight. He turned to see who it was and recognised Frankie's father. Seconds later he felt his fist crash into his face.

Luke wasn't scared of him. He was puny too, like father, like son. He could feel the blood streaming from his nose as he groped for the flat iron that was still on the table. He could hardly see but sensed Eric was coming for him again. He lifted the iron and crashed it against his assailant's head.

He took to his heels then. If he hung about any longer, half Liverpool could come to thump their fists in his face. He grabbed at his bundles as he crossed the landing below, and was racing down the last flight when he met old Maynard coming up.

'What's going on up here?' was all he had time to say. The bundles Luke carried effectively swept the old man against the wall as he passed, and he escaped into the street with Maynard's abuse ringing in his ears.

He set off at a fast pace then, congratulating himself on achieving what he'd wanted. He had Josie's address. He repeated it under his breath as he jogged along. He'd write it down as soon as he reached his hidey-hole.

Nobody knew him there. He'd lie low for a few days, take it easy. Let the police beaver about looking for him first. He wasn't going to prison for teaching Flora a lesson, not if he could help it. She'd asked for all she'd got.

He let himself into his new room. The place stank. He forced the window open to let in some fresh air. He was about to spread the bedding he'd brought on the bed when he noticed a dark stain on the mattress. He put his nose down to smell it and rebounded with a jerk of disgust. It stank of urine and it was still damp.

He flipped the mattress over before making up his bed; poured himself a stiff whisky and lay down. The drink calmed him enough to take another look round his new home. It wasn't up to much but he felt safe here. He could beat the police if he kept his wits about him. No reason why he should be in trouble over what was all Flora's fault.

Chapter Fourteen

Luke found his new mattress lumpy, but he was so exhausted by events and the shock he'd had, that he slid into sleep very quickly.

The next morning, he was up before nine o'clock but, unusually for him, he was feeling the emotional strain. He sighed. It was a big thing for him to turn his back on the job he'd done for six years, and at the same time leave his home. He felt proud of the way he'd managed it, though, quickly and thoroughly.

He opened his curtains; the window looked out across a back yard to a brick wall. He would have liked some breakfast but he couldn't even make himself a cup of tea. He'd have to go out to get some food. He'd felt the lack of many things in Josie's rooms, but here he had virtually nothing. He felt a bit apprehensive about walking the streets in daylight. He had to keep telling himself that nobody knew who he was around here. There were crowds thronging the pavements and shops. Liverpool was a big city. He'd be unlucky to be recognised.

It was a bright fine morning. He set off rather nervously, knowing he'd have to find himself another job too. The money he had wasn't going to last for long and the sooner he started looking, the better. He'd use the name of Smith.

Luke reckoned he was a good tram driver. The clatter and jangle of points and the overhead webs of crisscrossing wires no longer distracted him, but there were few who employed them. He'd have to stay well clear of Liverpool Corporation Tramways. There were trams in Birkenhead – a good idea to go there. He'd not meet any chance acquaintance and it would put him closer to Josie. But if he applied to Birkenhead Corporation for a similar job, they'd ask about his previous experience. He daren't give that or mention the name of Palmer. Liverpool was too close. Any new boss could pick up the phone and ask for references. The same went for Wallasey.

Now he stopped to think about it, it was only too obvious he couldn't get another job of the sort he was used to. He mustn't even attempt it: it would provide a trail for the police to follow.

A seaman then? He still had his book but it was years since he'd been to sea. He must look for something quite different. A barman perhaps?

It was better to saunter along the pavements deep in thought. It prevented him looking anyone in the face. He went into the first newsagent he came to to buy his usual paper and some fags.

Lighting up, he looked for a grocer's shop. He bought enough to feed himself for two or three days. Better if he didn't make a habit of going regularly into the same shops. He'd spend most of his time in his room. He went back, cooked himself a meal and contemplated further how he might get a job.

He'd try and get one the other side of the water, but he wasn't going near the Labour Exchange. He'd get an *Echo* tonight and see if anything suitable was advertised there.

Luke lay on his bed all afternoon. He had his whisky, his Woodbines and a newspaper, but he didn't feel his usual contentment. Seeing Flora alive and well had shaken him to the core. He didn't want to talk to the police about what had happened. They might mention bigamy. Flora shouldn't have hidden herself from him for all these years. He'd been so sure she was dead. He was left in a state of restless anxiety and was glad when six o'clock came round and the pubs were opening. He'd find a different one, but he needed to get out and see a bit of life.

There was a dingy pub on almost every corner. Luke chose one with plenty of dockers already drinking in the public bar and had his glass of bitter and whisky chaser lined up in front of him when he opened his *Evening Echo*. He was turning to the situations vacant when his eye was caught by a photograph of himself. Above it, in large black letters was the word 'WANTED'.

He gasped audibly, hurriedly flicked over to another page, and looked round, feeling sick lest somebody should have noticed. He'd thought the story of his brush with Flora would have run its course and be over. He'd not expected to see more of it in tonight's paper. It was quite three minutes before he could feel for his glass.

He recognised the photograph: it had been taken on the day he'd married Josie! He'd been the loving bridegroom smiling fondly sideways and down, to where Josie had been holding on to his arm. Except that here in the newspaper, she'd been cut off. Old Maynard had a camera and had insisted on taking a few snaps. It had made him nervous at the time but Josie had wanted it. Now his hands were shaking and his insides felt in a turmoil. The police must surely know he'd married for a second time! He hadn't read the article and he didn't dare open the paper again. Somebody might just look down at that picture and then up at him.

It could only mean one thing. Either the Maynards or the Rimmers or both had contacted the police. He was sweating but he counted himself fortunate to have moved out of his room in time. He gulped down his drink. The bar was swinging round and every nerve in his body was dancing with fear. He'd go somewhere else to read what it said about him in the paragraphs below the picture.

He felt better out in the street but it wasn't yet dark. Anyone who'd read the *Echo* might recognise him. Things had got much more dangerous for him now. Surreptitiously he folded his paper to the right page, then folded it again, making it small. There weren't many people about now the shops had closed. He paused, pretending to look in a shop window. It should be safe enough to read the paper here. He was unfolding it when he realised the shop was selling ladies' underwear, stockings and petticoats. Hurriedly, he moved to the shop next door, a newsagent. He positioned himself by the notices displayed in the door, took a deep breath and scanned the article.

Last night, a thirteen-year-old boy, Francis Rimmer of Upper Parliament Street, was attacked on the stairs of his home. When his father, Eric Rimmer, thirty-seven, went to his assistance, he was struck a vicious blow with a flat iron and has since died of his injuries in Walton Hospital. Francis, his son, is recovering in Myrtle Street Children's Hospital.

The police are seeking Luke Edmund Palmer, who has lived in a neighbouring flat for the past year but who disappeared following this attack. They also believe Mr Palmer can help with their enquiries into an attack on his wife Mrs Flora Maud Palmer in a tramcar in Dingle Depot the previous night.

Inspector Cosgrove of the Liverpool Police says this man is dangerous and should not be approached by the public.

Luke went cold. Eric Rimmer had died of his injuries? He'd only hit him once, a glancing blow to get him out of the way. He couldn't have killed him! The police had got it all wrong. None of this was his fault. He was caught up in terrible events, none of which were of his making. Eric Rimmer should never have attacked him. He remembered the weight of him on his back, a slight and puny opponent. He'd not have lifted a finger against him if he hadn't drawn first blood. Luke felt vomit rushing up to his throat. He was always the unlucky one who got the blame for everything.

But if the police had been looking for him after the fracas in the tram, they'd certainly be hunting him down after this. He had to be more careful, had to get out of Liverpool as soon as he could.

He felt half paralysed but he had to move on. A loitering figure attracted more attention than one with purpose in his step. Luke's mouth was dry, his heart was racing and he couldn't get his breath. For the first time he admitted to himself he was scared. He'd stop at the next pub and have a brandy to pull himself together, and buy a couple of bottles of something to take home and stay there out of sight.

Christobel had only to think of Alec to feel a warm glow. Within a week of their meeting he'd told her she'd swept him off his feet and he loved her. A week after that and he'd asked her to marry him. She'd only to look in his eyes to see the adoration he felt for her. She couldn't help but respond, and knew she was very much in love.

Alec wanted her by his side, and wanted her to share in every part of his life.

It was mid-morning when Harold dropped her at the gates to Alec's house, and she found him in his office, working on his accounts. Ten minutes later he was showing them to her and doing his best to explain how his system worked.

After lunch, she'd gone with him to see some of his smart public houses. She'd watched him talk to his staff at each one and sort out the problems they had. Then together they'd checked their books to see how much profit they were making.

At four o'clock, Christobel felt her brain could stand no more, and that she'd been cooped up all day without exercise.

Alec seemed to know instinctively how she felt. As they walked back to his car, he said: 'That's more than enough work for one day. Do you feel like a game of golf?'

He was teaching her to play golf and also to sail. He'd mastered so many things at which she was a novice, she felt she had occasionally to do something at which she could shine.

'I'd rather play tennis.' They'd met at the tennis club. Christobel loved tennis and played a better game than he did. 'I have to be able to beat you at something,' she laughed.

'We haven't booked a court.' In the early evening it was often quite difficult to get one unless it was booked ahead.

She knew Alec wasn't keen to play in the garden at The Lawns. He said he felt uncomfortable there because her mother wouldn't speak to him, but nobody else played on that court now her older sisters were married.

'Come on,' she persuaded. 'My tennis kit's at your place and we'll go back there afterwards.'

Sometimes Christobel could beat him, but not this afternoon. He could whack the ball harder, although she could move faster and was more agile. They had a hard-fought game and Christobel felt she'd been stretched to her capacity. Alec was lowering the net when Edna appeared outside the wire fence.

'A message for you,' she called. Christobel went over. 'Your mother says would you both please come indoors and take a cup of tea in the drawing room?'

Christobel felt a spurt of pleasure. 'Tell her we're on our way, Edna.'

She couldn't really understand why her mother disapproved of Alec. Her sister Penny said it was sheer snobbery. Christobel knew Alec found it hurtful and it was holding up their marriage plans.

'Alec, Mother wants to meet you! At last! Come on, we're to go in and have a cup of tea.'

He smiled: 'I'm to be inspected? I'd better be on my best behaviour.'

'Yes. I've been on at her to let me invite you to luncheon or something. Funny it's not the dining room – we always have tea sitting up at the table. Gramps says it gives him indigestion to eat in an armchair.'

'But at least I'm asked in.'

'Only for a cup of tea, but I'm so pleased! It's a start, isn't it?'

'I hope I'll pass muster.'

'Mother will like you, Alec. I know she will.'

He tossed his racquet into his car. 'I feel all hot and sticky. Do I look all right?'

'Of course. She knows we've been playing tennis. Must have seen you from the window.'

Christobel hurried him inside, took him to the downstairs cloakroom, lent him her comb. He needed to look neat and smart if he was to impress Mother. Then she led the way to the drawing room.

The Reverend Haydn Ingleby-Jones stood up as they went in. He'd been occupying her grandfather's favourite armchair beside the fireplace. Her mother stood up too.

'Come in, my dear. Bring your friend.'

Christobel's heart plummeted as she made the introductions. This wasn't what she'd expected.

'This is Alec Landis. My mother, Alec, and, er – the vicar.'

Alec offered his hand. Her mother pointedly ignored it.

'Tea?' She was busy pouring it for them. 'Do sit down, Mr Landis.' She indicated the chair she'd been occupying. 'Bring up a chair for yourself, Christobel.'

She kicked a footstool towards Alec's chair. 'What's all this about, Mother?' She was beginning to see it as entrapment.

'Reverend Ingleby-Jones has been good enough to say he'll have a word with you on my behalf.'

'Mother!'

'Please listen to what he has to say, and I hope you'll be more polite to him than you are to me. I'll leave you then, Haydn.'

Christobel could feel the heat running up her cheeks. She was angry. When the door closed behind her mother, she said: 'This isn't necessary. Mother shouldn't have asked you.'

Haydn Ingleby-Jones twisted his white hands in his lap over and over. She'd seen him do it countless times before.

'Your mother is very worried about you, Christobel. She's afraid you're going to ruin your life and end up in the gutter.'

'How ridiculous!'

'I do feel sorry for your mother. I would like to put her mind at rest by saying you'll end this liaison with Mr Landis.'

'Look, this is none of your business.'

'My dear child, I feel I have to make it my business because your mother has sought my help. She has discussed your affairs with me.'

Christobel stood up. 'Come on, Alec, we're going.'

'Dear, dear girl, my life's work has been with fallen women. You're likely to end up in trouble unless you take great care. I do hope your life isn't ruined, but conduct like this ... You're on the primrose path to hell. Repent ye of your ways—'

'Hold on!' Christobel was furious. 'I'm not a fallen woman and I don't need your help.'

'Mrs Smallwood particularly asked me to have a word with you, Mr Landis. She feels you're leading Christobel astray, creating trouble both for her and her family.'

'No,' Christobel said vehemently. 'He is not. I'm old enough to make up my own mind about this.'

'But Mr Landis, you're so much older. If you were an upstanding man with any moral sense, you wouldn't want to harm Christobel like this. You're ruining her reputation and might do much worse. Mrs Smallwood is most upset, I can assure you.'

Alec's face flushed with an anger he was trying to control. He said: 'She need not be. I have Christobel's welfare very much at heart. We would be married now if she'd give her consent.'

'She doesn't think you're a suitable person. Your behaviour in this matter—'

'Because of her, we're having to wait until I'm twenty-one and won't need her permission. It's all quite straightforward and above board.'

'But, Christobel, it isn't, not while you do such risky things as visit Mr Landis's house without a chaperone. And, I believe, visit public houses with him?'

She was at him like a tiger. 'Don't be so damn silly. Queen Victoria's been dead for nearly thirty years. Nobody but my mother thinks a chaperone necessary any more.'

'My child, I have to tell you that I do too. Your mother

feels you're being very wilful, ignoring all her advice to keep yourself pure.'

'Pure! How damned pompous!'

'Please don't swear, Mr Landis.' Mr Ingleby-Jones continued to wring his hands.

'You've got it all wrong. The problem as I see it,' Christobel stood up, 'is that Mother wishes to choose a husband for me. I'm not allowed any say in the matter. She won't even talk to Alec. Today is the first time I've been allowed to bring them face to face, and that was to trap us into coming here so you could preach at us. I can assure you that Alec is honest and upstanding, and there's nothing either she or you can do about changing my mind. We're going to be married whether she likes it or not, and nothing you say will alter that. Come on, Alec. I've had enough of this nonsense. I'm sure you have too.'

Christobel took Alec by the arm and led him out to his car at a furious pace.

'How could she? She thinks she has the power of life and death over everybody.'

'Damned insulting,' Alec muttered. 'I can't believe it! That man finding fault with our morals while he—'

'I can't stand it. I'm going to get Louise out of her clutches too if it's the last thing I do. She's doing her positive harm. It's as though Mother's mind has been turned . . . That she's in his power. His and his sister's.

'Silly old fool. How dare he? I think he's the biggest twister . . . I'm going to shame him if it's the last thing I do. You'll have to help me. I want us to show him up so Mother knows exactly what a rogue he is.'

Alec took her arm and laughed. 'Darling Chrissie, I've never seen you so angry.'

'Oh! I'm boiling over. The nerve of him. I could . . .'

* * *

Josie told herself she was settling down in her new job, and that she'd done the right thing by coming here. Suzy too seemed more at ease. She was spending a lot of her time with Louise. But Josie had to keep reassuring herself that they were safe here, because in truth her nerves were still raw. Leaving Luke had left its mark on her.

While she was rolling out pastry for an apple tart, Gertie took Mrs Smallwood's used tea tray through the kitchen to the scullery.

Josie said: 'I see she's eaten two of my Eccles cakes.'

The third had come back on the tray. Gertie picked it up and bit into it. 'There's been a murder in Liverpool, have you heard?'

'No . . .' Josie lifted the pastry carefully on to a plate and used a knife to skim off the edges.

'On the colonel's wireless, just now. A man attacked his wife a couple of nights ago and put her in hospital. Last night, he attacked a young boy, and when his father went to his aid, he killed him with a flat iron. Police are saying the man's dangerous and nobody must approach him.'

'I should think not.' Josie was arranging neat slices of apple on top of her pastry. She thought no more of it.

The following morning started like all the others. She made Suzy some breakfast and sent her off to school. Edna was kept busy lighting fires and cleaning upstairs. Josie was dishing up the breakfast bacon when Gertie tossed last night's *Liverpool Echo* on to the kitchen table.

'The murder I told you about yesterday, it's got all about it in here. Horrible.'

Even then, Josie arranged the dishes to go to the dining room, and Gertie had taken them, before she glanced at it. When she saw Luke's photograph filling so much of the page she couldn't move. She was so shocked, it was a few moments before she could start to read:

Last night, a thirteen-year-old boy, Francis Rimmer . . .

The print was swimming before Josie's eyes. She understood that Luke had attacked Frankie. It was what she'd feared might happen, but he'd killed Eric? Oh God! Surely not killed Eric? Bile was rising in her throat, she felt sick. She had to force herself to read on:

They also believe Mr Palmer can help with their enquiries into an attack on his wife Mrs Flora Maud Palmer in a tramcar in Dingle Depot the previous night.

His wife, Mrs Flora Maud Palmer? She had to read that bit through three times to get the meaning. Did that mean he'd been married to someone else when . . .? That she wasn't his wife?

Everything was going black, she could feel herself swaying and knew she was falling.

'Josie! What's happened?'

She was coming round when Gertie came back and found her on the floor. She was being helped to her feet, half lifted – Gertie was a strong woman.

'You must have fainted. What caused that? You seemed all right before.'

'I felt a bit dizzy. A dizzy spell, that's all.' Josie ached where she'd fallen on the stone floor. She must give no hint of the cause! Not to anybody. She was being lowered into the old armchair by the range. 'I'll be all right in a minute.'

'Are you sure? Perhaps you should see a doctor? Mrs Smallwood—'

'Don't tell her, Gertie. I'm all right, really. Just let me sit here for a minute.'

'The colonel's asking for another fried egg. Don't worry, I'll do it.'

Gertie pulled the hot frying pan back on the range and broke an egg into it. She was standing over it, busying herself, warming a plate for it. The *Echo* was on the floor. Josie closed her eyes. She had a thumping headache but she had to pull herself together.

'Go and lie on your bed for an hour,' Gertie advised.

'No, I'll be all right. I'll have to see Mrs Smallwood for the menus when she's finished her breakfast.'

When Gertie bustled back to the dining room with the colonel's egg, Josie picked up the newspaper and read it again. She couldn't believe that she wasn't Luke's wife.

Gertie was bustling back with a tray of dirty dishes. When she was alone again, Josie pulled herself to her feet and went to look for the *Echo* from the night before amongst the pile of papers collecting in the butler's pantry.

She found what she was looking for. Luke had a wife called Flora Maud, whom he'd said had died in childbirth years ago, which Josie hadn't doubted for one second. She'd even felt sorry for him; she knew what it was to lose a spouse. What had he said? 'It's a bond between us,' or something like that. 'We both understand what it is to lose a loved one.'

But his wife Flora hadn't died! It seemed he must be a bigamist and that meant . . . she was not his wife and never had been. Josie felt gall rising in her throat. Luke had used her. He'd used her to a much greater degree than she'd realised.

That was sickeningly awful, but worse was the fact that he'd killed Eric Rimmer. Such a gentle and kind person. Luke was capable of killing – hadn't she feared for her own life the night he'd broken her wardrobe mirror? But Eric . . .? Luke had no grudge against Eric.

Josie knew what Olga must be feeling. Olga had supported her when Ted had died, but from here there was nothing she could do to help her. Josie felt responsible for what had happened. If she hadn't married Luke and allowed him to come and live in her rooms, then Eric Rimmer would be alive now.

Damn, damn, she hadn't married Luke at all! He'd tricked her into believing it was all legal and above board. Waves of horror were passing through her. She couldn't believe it had really happened. It was too awful. She tore the page out and stuffed it in a pocket beneath her apron.

It was only when she read both articles through that she realised Luke was on the run from the police. They couldn't find him. That put her into a tizzy. She was all of a flutter and couldn't think straight. He was hiding somewhere and he'd be after her, he was that sort. She felt really vulnerable. Frankie had promised not to tell him where they'd gone, but perhaps he had. If Luke had put him in hospital, he'd been violent towards him. Josie felt responsible for that too, and if he'd done that to Frankie he'd be even more violent towards Suzy and herself.

She felt barely in control when she made her way to the dining room to receive Mrs Smallwood's orders for the day.

That night Josie knew she was screaming. She could feel it building in her throat, hear it shattering the silence of the night. She could see Luke standing over her, the mantel clock poised above his head, ready to crash it down on her face. He'd found her. She was getting what he'd promised, what he said she deserved for running away from him. Terror was running through her. She opened her mouth to scream again. Someone was shaking her.

'What's the matter? Wake up.' A shocked face was six inches above her own. It was Suzy. 'Mam! Mam! Whatever's the matter?'

Josie raised herself on her arm. The room was in darkness. She was in a lather of sweat.

'Where is he?'

'Who?'

'Oh God! I've been dreaming.'

'A nightmare, more like.'

'Yes, a terrible nightmare.' She pulled on Suzy's arm. 'Get in here with me.'

Josie hugged the firm young body to her but was unable to suppress a sob.

'What's the matter, Mam?'

Josie had bottled up the awful news about Eric Rimmer all day. She hadn't dared breathe a word to Gertie, though Gertie knew she was upset and had invited her confidence. It was so horrible and Josie felt she'd caused it herself. If only she hadn't taken Luke to live in the house in Upper Parliament Street.

'What is it?'

Suzy would have to know sooner or later. In a voice just above a whisper, and holding her in a tight hug, Josie began to tell her: that Luke was a bigamist, that she never had been his wife, what he'd done to Frankie and his father, everything. She couldn't stop her tears wetting Suzy's cheeks too.

And the worst thing of all was that Luke was on the run, and the police couldn't find him. 'If Frankie's told him where we are—'

'He won't have, Mam. He won't.'

'But if . . .?' Josie was beside herself with worry.

'I know he won't, don't worry about that. Let me read those newspaper cuttings, Mam.' Suzy got out of bed to switch on the light.

'I put them in my drawer, there.' She watched Suzy get them out to study them. She was standing on one foot on the cold lino, looking a waif in her crumpled flannelette nightdress.

'They'll tell you nothing new.' Josie had reread them several times, extracted every ounce of meaning.

Suzy asked: 'What are we going to do?' Josie heard the catch in her voice. 'Not run away from here? Not just when we're settling in? Oh no!'

'It's what we should do. Then I'd be sure he wouldn't find us.'

Suzy's face was creased with worry. 'I know Frankie won't have told him.'

'It was right to take you away from those rooms. If I hadn't, he'd have attacked you again and really hurt you.'

'And you, Mam.'

'Yes, he'll be looking for us,' Josie quaked. 'I feel hunted.' Fear was the most awful thing. She couldn't think of anything else. This was in her head the whole time, but not just her head; she couldn't stop shaking and her mouth was dry. She'd been in a state of panic since she'd found out.

'Mam, we ought to go to see Frankie and Auntie Olga.'

'We can't go back there!'

'Yes we can. Nosey isn't there. Everybody knows him and they'd tell the police. It stands to reason. He'd be arrested if he went back.'

Why hadn't she thought of that?

'It'll be quite safe.'

'The trams ... they go everywhere over there, and you can't see who's driving, not from any distance.'

'He can't go near the depot either. He'd be picked up there if he was. He's not working, Mam.'

'Neither is my head. You're right. I ought to go and see Olga, if only to say how sorry I am.'

'We can find out definitely whether Frankie told him or not. You'll feel safer here when you've spoken to him.'

Josie sighed. Somehow, when terror gripped her, it was no longer possible to reason. She could taste terror, see it all round her.

'It's an awful thing to have happened.' Suzy scrambled back into her bed and clung to her. She was cold now. 'We should go to see them.'

'It's Sunday tomorrow. I've got a half-day. We'll go then.'

Josie felt somewhat comforted that she'd told Suzy and taken some decision.

Chapter Fifteen

Josie felt bad again the next morning. She told herself she was lucky she'd worked as a cook for so much of her life because she could do it with only half her mind on the job.

After breakfast, when she went to get her instructions, Mrs Smallwood told her: 'There'll be just my parents and Louise for supper tonight. Both Christobel and I will be out.'

'In that case,' the colonel said, 'I'll have a small curry.'

'Do you think that's wise?'

'Don't be silly, Hebe.'

'Not too hot, Josephine,' Mrs Smallwood cautioned. 'Father, don't forget spicy food gives you indigestion. Especially when taken at night.'

'I want a bit of flavour in it. A curry's no good unless it's got a bit of bite.'

Mrs Smallwood decided her mother could have eggs mornay with Louise, and the Sunday roast lunch was to be beef.

Josie went back to the kitchen and cut a slice off the roast to make the curry, and in order to give it a bit more flavour, she marinated it in some of the speciality curry paste she'd seen in the cupboard. She'd always used curry powder before, but this was a product from India.

She got the lunch started and made a cheese sauce so that Gertie, who would be on her own this evening, would only have to warm it up and add the hard-boiled eggs to make eggs mornay.

Josie still felt agitated. Now that she'd had time to think about it, she was afraid of coming face to face with Olga. What could she say to her? Her husband had been murdered and they both knew Luke Palmer would never have gone near him if Josie hadn't asked him to live in the flat below. That had had the most awful consequences. Olga might not want to speak to her. Perhaps she'd shut the door in her face.

Josie started to make the curry. Her mind wasn't wholly on what she was doing and she was in haste to prepare as much of the supper as she could for Gertie. Suddenly she realised she was stirring in a second lot of curry paste and stopped. She tasted a little on the end of a spoon and her tongue was instantly in flames. She had a drink of water and thought about it.

She couldn't take it out. Should she throw the whole thing out and start again? She could take the joint out of the oven and take another slice off it. She doubted if even Brutus could eat this.

But time was getting short. Was there anything else she could do? Yes, add more vegetables, tomatoes and courgettes and long cooking would help – perhaps a bit of milk too. All the same, she wouldn't want to eat a curry as hot as this. She prided herself on being a good cook, and a mistake like this made her feel even more depressed.

After lunch had been served and eaten, Josie cut a couple of slices off the joint to take to Olga. She took some cake too because their cake tin was so full the lid wouldn't shut tight. She was still worrying as she changed out of her uniform. The colonel would probably be doubled up with pain all night. She'd been asked to make it mild for him and it was red hot.

* * *

It seemed strange to be walking up Upper Parliament Street. She hadn't thought she'd see it again. Her heart was hammering in her throat, panic taking her over.

'You're hurting me, Mam.' Suzy was trying to shake her hand free. 'You've got a grip like a grizzly bear.'

'Sorry, love.'

Josie took a deep breath. They were on the doorstep. It was Suzy who rang the bell. Mr Maynard opened the door and Josie saw his expression change. He didn't seem pleased to see her.

'Mrs Palmer!'

Her tongue wouldn't move to form words.

Suzy said: 'Good afternoon, Mr Maynard. We've come to see Frankie and Auntie Olga.'

The door opened wider. Josie knew it must be all right.

'I'm sorry,' she choked. 'So sorry . . . Luke Palmer must have caused you a lot of trouble.'

'He has that.'

'I felt I had to come and apologise.' She was fighting back the tears.

'It isn't you I blame, though he ruined my ceiling and paid no rent after you left.'

'I'll pay the rent he owes now,' Josie said quickly. She'd guessed he'd leave without paying if he could, and she'd had her wages for the month.

'No, you've troubles enough of your own. But come and see the mess he made on my ceiling.'

They were taken into his living room to see the huge brown stain.

'What caused that?'

'He threw a bottle of whisky at his grate. I couldn't believe he'd do such a thing. It still smells like a distillery in there, though we've had the window open since he left.'

Mrs Maynard was giving Suzy some boiled sweets. 'It's Mrs Rimmer and Frankie we're sorry for.'

'I must pay the rent that's owing,' Josie insisted, getting out her purse.

'You were always a good tenant. You and your first husband. It was the second one who was a bad lot.'

Josie said in a little rush: 'I had to get away from him to keep Suzy safe. I was afraid for her.'

Frankie had heard them and was coming downstairs. Suzy went out to the hall to meet him. Josie watched them fall on each other with cries of delight, but when she looked again they were both in tears and hugging each other for comfort. This was taking a heavy emotional toll on them all.

She climbed the stairs slowly; she'd never noticed how steep they were before. Olga was out on her landing weeping too, but she opened her arms to Josie, then drew them all into her familiar living room.

'Frankie!' Josie exclaimed. 'Your arm's in plaster! Is that . . .?'

'Yep, Nosey went for me and broke my arm.' Frankie also had scars on his face that were still red and noticeable.

'I'm sorry . . .'

'I'm OK now. I'm going back to school tomorrow. Come on, Suzy, autograph my plaster for me.'

'How much longer does it have to stay on?'

'Ages yet.'

Josie felt overwhelmed by her welcome. 'I was so shocked to read about Eric in the paper. I can't get what happened out of my mind. I'm so sorry.'

'We miss him, don't we, Frankie? So sudden and so violent . . .'

'I blame him for my dad's death too,' Suzy said.

'I never dreamed he'd harm Eric. I blame myself,' Josie told her friend.

'Don't,' Olga said. 'You suffered just as much at his hands. I don't blame you.'

'You really mean that? I was worried stiff you'd shut the door in my face.'

'Why would I do that?'

'I brought him here, didn't I?'

'We were good friends, Josie. I need my friends now I've lost Eric.'

Josie said vehemently: 'I wish I'd never set eyes on Luke Palmer. If he and Ted hadn't been put together to work the same tram route, none of this would have happened.'

'I wish they'd catch him,' Suzy sighed.

'So do I,' Frankie agreed wholeheartedly.

Olga said: 'At first, I thought they would catch him straight away, but the days are going on and I don't think they're any nearer to it.'

Josie shivered. 'They've got to catch him. Got to.'

'He killed my husband and did this to my son, and it looks as though he's going to get off scot-free. I can't rest, I know I won't until he's charged with murder and gets what he deserves.'

'He's dangerous.'

'It wasn't just our Eric he killed. There was . . .' Olga stopped, her big eyes larger than ever.

'Yes, he tried to kill his wife.' Josie had to say it for her.

Olga had her hand to her mouth. 'I read that in the paper.'

'Oh God, Olga, I didn't know he was married.' Josie was almost in tears again. 'He's a bigamist too.'

'We all gathered that. I was appalled – the way he treated you.'

'At least we're still alive, Mam,' Suzy said, bringing everything to a full stop. They sat looking at each other,

271

while Josie struggled to keep her tears at bay.

'I'll put the kettle on,' Frankie said, taking Suzy out of the room with him.

'Is he all right?' Josie asked his mother.

Olga nodded. 'He was very upset, losing his father like that. He said: "Dad should never have tried to help me. I was doing all right." '

Josie whispered, 'The young don't realise it's second nature to protect one's children.'

Olga was trying to smile: 'But he's all right. The young get over things like that more quickly.'

Josie said: 'A child doesn't lose quite so much as a wife.'

Olga was up from her chair, poking with great vigour the fire which didn't need poking. Josie couldn't hold back her tears any longer.

'Luke blames me for walking out on him. He said I was causing all the trouble. I couldn't take any more. He was always blowing up at Suzy, hurting her. Now, he's out there looking for me, I'm sure he is. Nobody wants to see him caught more than I do. I pray for it every night.'

'They'll get him,' Olga comforted. 'I keep telling myself they will. Where could he be hiding?'

Josie shook her head. 'I've been asking myself that over and over. He must have a job, Olga, otherwise he wouldn't be able to exist.'

'Driving a tram?'

'I don't know. Probably not. He was bone idle, but when he wanted to, he could turn his hand to almost anything.'

'All the time he was living with you, it never occurred to us that he was dangerous. Not even when I guessed he was thumping Suzy. We were all taken in by him. If he's got away from Liverpool to a place where nobody knows him, nobody will think he's a killer.'

'I wish to God they'd catch him,' Josie breathed. 'It's driving me up the wall. My nerves won't stand much more. I feel like a mouse in a trap who can see the cat coming to get her.'

'Ah, Josie, love, it must be dreadful for you.' Olga's plump face was harrowed with grief.

'Life's a lot harder on your own, isn't it?'

'Yes, but I've been lucky to get a job straight away to make ends meet. It'll be such a change, working with a crowd of girls. It's in a jam factory. I start tomorrow. It'll take me out of myself and leave me no time to mope.'

'Probably the best thing for you.'

'Yes, I suppose so. I thought Frankie was going to make some tea.'

Josie followed her to the kitchen. Frankie and Suzy were there deep in conversation. Suzy looked up.

'Frankie didn't tell old Nosey, Mam. He doesn't know where we've moved to.'

Olga's plump face crumpled in compassion. 'I'm sorry, Josie. It was me that let out you had a live-in job in Birkenhead. Luke was knocking hell out of Frankie. I'd have said anything to get him to stop.'

Frankie laughed. 'I told him you were working in a house in Waterford Road called Oakhurst. I made up the name of the house, but when I followed you, I heard somebody on the bus ask if it went near Waterford Road. I hope it's a long way away.'

'I don't know,' Suzy said. 'I've never heard of it.'

'Frankie kept his wits about him,' Olga said proudly. 'He's better at that than I am.'

Josie felt deeply grateful. 'Thank you, Frankie. Thank you.'

Olga made tea, and together they made sandwiches with the beef Josie had brought. Then they all sat talking over again where Luke could be hiding. Josie and Suzy stayed quite late.

'It was a bit like old times,' Suzy said as they made their way back to the tram stop.

Josie was filled with relief. 'I feel so much better now I know Luke doesn't have our address.'

When they got back to The Lawns, Gertie and Edna were drinking cocoa.

'That curry you made,' Gertie smiled, 'the colonel was mightily pleased with it. He said it was the best he'd tasted in years and asked me not to let the staff finish off what was left. He wants it kept for his lunch tomorrow.'

Josie smiled. That was another weight off her mind.

Edna said: 'We tasted it and we both said it set our mouths on fire. We didn't want to eat it.'

'Let's hope he doesn't get indigestion tonight.'

Josie went to bed feeling better than she had for some time.

Luke lay on his bed looking out on the soot-blackened brick wall, watching the sun cross the sky to shine into his frowsty room in the late afternoon.

After his picture had appeared in the *Echo*, he knew he was much more likely to be recognised and arrested if he went out. He was also worried about his new landlord – what if he'd seen the picture in the papers? Luke immediately tore everything incriminating into tiny pieces and put them down the lavatory in the yard. He'd never felt so scared in all his life. He had food and three bottles of whisky and he made them last two full days.

On the morning of the third day he had to go out for more supplies. He craved news of what the police were doing to find him, wanting to know if they were on his track.

He made a quick trip to the shops and rushed straight back to the safety of his room. He bought all the local newspapers but found only a small paragraph in one saying Mrs Flora Maud Palmer had been discharged from hospital and the police were still searching for her assailant.

He'd paid a week's rent on this room and thought the best thing would be to stay until the landlord started to worry him about paying again. He had very little money left now, and he'd done nothing about getting himself a job or another room. He spent an hour looking through his papers for a room on the other side of the river.

There were four advertised. He had no idea how to find them and they were all more expensive than this one. He'd need money to rent any of them. It occurred to him now that landlords who took the trouble to advertise in newspapers or put their property with an agent would also ask for references.

What Luke felt he needed was a room that was being advertised on a card in a front window. The sort you went in, looked round, and took it or decided it wasn't good enough. The sort of thing he had here. There'd be fewer people involved, fewer then who would see him. He needed it to be cheap – it would have to be very cheap. He counted up his money and found he had less than a pound left. It scared him even more when he discovered that.

As he cooked himself egg and sausage, he decided to cross the river by ferry today and see if he could get a room on the other side. Then he could see what jobs were available. He had to get on and do something, or he'd lie here and starve.

He cut himself a jam butty, wrapped it in a page of clean newspaper and put it in his pocket. He had to have food; he was the sort who drooped and lost all his energy when he was hungry and in need of a meal. He pulled his trilby low on his forehead to hide his face and set off for Birkenhead.

He had to walk quite a distance to a bus stop. Nothing must tempt him anywhere near a tram. After he'd spent two fine days cooped up in his room, today was cold and wet. On the almost empty ferry boat, he went straight up on top deck and hung over the rail where nobody could see his face.

He felt better once he was in Birkenhead. People huddled under umbrellas and no longer seemed to look at him. He had to remind himself that the *Echo* had good sales on this side of the water too.

Frankie had said he took the number 39 bus when he'd followed Josie. Luke did the same, sitting up on the top deck with his face turned towards the window and the wet streets.

He didn't know where Josie had got off this bus. Quite a distance, according to Frankie. It went through the town and was soon in a wide leafy road. Luke got off. This wouldn't do for him. His present purpose was to find himself a room, and he couldn't afford anything round here.

He headed back towards the river. He knew there were docks all along the bank, so there would be mean houses for the dockers to live in. There always were.

Luke found he was right. Soon he saw a front window with a notice against the glass offering a furnished room to let for three shillings and sixpence a week. There was another for four shillings on the next corner. This was the right place for him, but which one to choose?

He started with the cheaper one. A timid-looking woman answered his knock and showed him the room. It looked all right – if anything, better than the one he had at the moment.

'I'll take it,' he told her. 'I'll pay a week's rent now, and move in at the weekend.'

She pursed her lips doubtfully. 'You'll have to come back when my husband's at home. He sees to all that sort of thing. After six tonight.'

'Right,' he said, knowing he couldn't afford to hang about all day.

'Are you working?'

'Yes.'

'What d'you do?'

'I'm a clerk in a bank.' She was asking too many questions; he had to get away. 'I'll come back tonight.'

He needed to put some distance between himself and that street. He knocked on another door, which was answered by a burly man. Luke guessed that here a deal could be done on the spot. The room wasn't as good as the last, certainly not as clean, and he was asking five bob a week for it. Luke tried to drive the rent down but the man wouldn't go. The kitchen was shared by three other families and so was the lavatory in the yard. But it was urgent he got himself a different room, and this would have to do.

'I'll take it.'

The rent book was brought out quickly. 'I want two weeks' rent, that's ten bob. I keep a week's rent in advance.'

Luke tried to get him to accept one week's but he wouldn't budge. He had to part with his last ten-bob note.

'I'm moving here from Chester,' he told him. 'I won't be moving in until tomorrow or even the next day.'

'OK, but you pay again a week today, all right?'

Luke scribbled down the address in his pocket book. It would be a calamity if he couldn't find his way back here again. As he walked off, his pleasure in achieving another address was fading.

He went to a park and sat down on a bench to count up the change left in his pockets. He had only coppers, just about enough to get home to Liverpool and return here again. He was skint. He unwrapped his jam butty and bit into it. Thank goodness he'd had the forethought to bring that. He couldn't buy a meal now. He hated having no money to rattle in his pocket. It scared him, made him feel vulnerable. Everybody needed money. It was impossible to exist without it.

Even if he got a job today, he'd have to last out a whole week before they'd pay him. Some employers kept a week in hand, which meant working for a fortnight until he was paid. There was no way he could do that. He'd have to buy food. Luke knew he was in dire straits. He'd been telling himself he was doing well, but now without money he felt depressed. It cut his confidence and robbed him of the energy to do anything else.

He needed a job and he wanted to find Josie, but he sat on in the park doing nothing. Two young boys came past his bench kicking a ball.

'Can you tell me where Waterford Road is?' he asked them.

They pointed obligingly and told him which bus to catch. It seemed it was quite some way off. Luke counted his money again: he might be able to run to a bus back but not in both directions. He set off on foot. He might as well see if he could find Josie. That was business he'd very much like to finish.

He found the road at last, having asked for directions several times. It seemed likely that domestic staff would be employed in these big houses. He looked for the house called Oakhurst, walking up and down twice. He couldn't find it. He could feel anger and frustration knotting in his stomach. He'd been afraid all along that Frankie had not been telling him the truth. Now he was sure of it.

Luke decided to go home. He'd find it easier to job hunt when he was here on the spot. He was running out of energy and he needed a drink. He had whisky in his room.

Too tired to walk back to the ferry, he took the bus. The wind was getting up and he felt better after having a blow on the boat. He started to walk when he reached the Pier Head.

He hadn't far to go and it would save the twopence fare and allow him to buy ten Woodbines and an *Echo*. He'd left the centre of the city behind and was walking up the backstreets, already regretting his decision, when he saw a rundown newsagent's on the corner.

It was dark inside the shop and it was empty. As the sound of the doorbell faded, he saw the pile of *Echo*es and took one. Nobody was coming to serve him. He had his coins poised ready to drum on the counter with them when he wondered should he just walk out with the paper? He could get Woodbines somewhere else. At that moment he heard the shuffle of slippered feet, and a very old woman came behind the counter.

He pocketed the Woodbines as she slid them across to him and he watched as she rang up the till. It opened and he could see lots of coins and some notes held together with a paperclip. Luke was moving the moment the thought came into his head. He heaved himself round the open boxes of sweets displayed on the counter and gave the woman a sharp push. She grabbed out, trying to save herself, but went down, making a soft moan as she hit the floor. A box of bull's-eyes rained down on her.

Luke snatched the notes from the till. She was old, and had gone down very easily. She couldn't have been steady on her feet. He allowed himself another moment to scoop up some of the silver, then filled his pockets with Players Navy Cut.

He was out of the shop within seconds and walking more briskly now with his trilby pulled well down on his forehead. It was a longer walk than he'd thought but he felt euphoric and that put new bounce into his step. He'd solved his problem very quickly and cleverly. If the police were trying to pin charges of grievous bodily harm and murder on him, then what did another of shoplifting matter? There'd been no one about. It had been a brilliant spur-of-the-moment decision and it had come off.

Luke let himself into his room and looked round with distaste. It really was awful, but he needn't stay much longer. He sat at the rickety table and counted up how much he'd got. It totalled six pounds four shillings. He was ecstatic.

By way of celebration, he lit one of the Navy Cut cigarettes he'd picked up. He enjoyed it – far superior to his usual Woodbine. When he settled back for a rest and opened up his *Echo*, he saw it carried the same photograph of himself as before, but this time it gave a detailed description of him too.

His elation went as he read on. It said he was above normal height and of good bearing. It gave his exact age of fifty-five. Dark-haired, with a moustache, strong features and a Roman nose. He dressed smartly and was last seen wearing a brown trilby and fawn raincoat. That put the wind up him again.

He'd need to get some different clothes, perhaps shave his moustache. He didn't really want to do that because it suited him, but it would be safer if he did. He'd do it tomorrow, and he ought to move to the Birkenhead room as soon as he could.

Again, he was described as dangerous. Luke thought that was a bit over the top. He thought of himself as gentle and easily hurt.

He was worried about moving all his possessions in white bolster cases in broad daylight. It drew attention to him. Damn Josie for stealing his suitcases. Perhaps he should try and find something else to transport his possessions?

The next morning, he walked down to St John's market and bought himself some shabby second-hand clothes, a jacket in heavy grey tweed and a flat cloth cap such as workmen wear. He also managed to get an ancient Gladstone bag and a large battered suitcase. He could roll his eiderdown and pillow, and tie them to the case.

His moustache had already gone. He found he was able to mingle in the crowds and nobody took a second look at him, but he was nervous after what he'd seen in the paper and knew he'd be safer out of Liverpool. It would only take someone from the Tramways or one of Josie's friends and he'd be in big trouble.

He spent the afternoon and evening shut up in that room, only going out after dark to ram his trilby and raincoat into a dustbin a few streets away. He'd decided he'd move to Birkenhead the next day. He needed to find work if he could. He wasn't a thief, it was just that he'd been driven to it. It had been a question of survival.

Jobs were no longer easy to come by. More and more men were being thrown out of work as the economic position worsened. He opened every local newspaper he bought at the job adverts and hoped he'd find something.

Today, Birkenhead Corporation were wanting men for their dustcarts. Refuse collectors. Luke could see why that wasn't the most popular of jobs, and the wages offered were pathetic. He thought it over carefully. It might suit him. He'd be going round the neighbourhoods, street by street, week after week. Wasn't that what he wanted? He could keep an eye open for Josie and Suzy that way, and who looked twice at the men who emptied the dustbins?

The pay would give him something to subsist on; it wasn't as though he was wanting to make a career of it. He'd find Josie, pay her back for all the trouble she'd caused him and then move on. Go to London perhaps. Get right away from here. Get himself a new life.

* * *

The months passed quickly. Suzy was taking one day at a time and trying not to think of the past. She was pushing the spectre of Luke Palmer to the back of her mind, but she knew her mother couldn't do this.

Several times over the following months Suzy had been woken in the night and found her mother sweating and in a state of panic. Her nightmares about Luke Palmer finding them were not going away, nor fading in intensity. Suzy was spending more and more time with Louise. Usually, when she came home from school and had had her tea, she ran upstairs to find her friend. She knew her way round the house now and was always sure of Louise's welcome.

If she met Mrs Smallwood or the colonel on the way, they knew who she was and where she was going. Mam had told her just to say good morning or good afternoon to them, but sometimes they told her where she'd find Louise.

When she'd gone up to see her yesterday afternoon, Louise had been flushed with excitement.

'Has something nice happened?'

'Yes. I had such a miserable morning doing sums with Miss Greenall,' she told her, 'that I went down to lunch feeling quite out of sorts. You know what Mummy's like? She said, "Whatever is the matter now, Louise?"'

'I told her I was bored and then said: "I wish Suzy was here. Mummy, when she's fourteen and leaves school, could she be employed as my companion?" '

'Companion?' Suzy was puzzled.

' "Then she could be with me all the time," I said. "She cheers me up and you're always telling me I need help."'

'Christobel always takes my part and said: "Louise needs company, Mother. Suzy's very good with her."'

'Even Gramps said: "The girl needs some stimulation, Hebe."'

' "Suzy will be leaving school next summer. I won't like it if she goes somewhere else to work and I hardly see her," I told them.

'And Mummy said: "Perhaps yes, companion and personal maid. We'll have to see."

'I wailed at her: "Not *have to see*. Say yes, Mummy. Please say yes, before she gets herself a job somewhere else."

'And you know what? She said all right.'

Suzy threw her arms round her friend. 'That's wonderful! Much better than having to go to school. I'll love spending all day with you.'

Today, Suzy could hear ragtime music coming from the playroom. Louise was using it quite a lot now, and this afternoon Christobel was with her and was dancing alone with great energy. Enthralled, Suzy crept in and sat beside Louise to watch. Christobel's skimpy skirt lifted and fell as she gyrated and her silk-covered legs seemed to be flying everywhere.

Mam had told Suzy she'd heard the colonel complain he could see Christobel's knees when she was going out and that it was indecent. He'd called her a flapper. Christobel writhed and twirled as the record came to an end, then collapsed breathless on a chair.

Louise clapped and laughed. 'Chrissie, that was marvellous. I wish I could dance like that.'

'I'm going to teach you, that's why I've brought my gramophone in here.'

'Could I learn?'

Suzy thought even she would have problems keeping up with music with so fast a beat. She couldn't believe Lou would ever manage.

'Not the charleston or the black bottom, not yet. We'll start with something less energetic.'

283

Christobel put on another record. 'A slow waltz. Come on, Lou, let's try. This is what you do to the count of three. That's right. Over again, you're doing fine.'

Suzy knew the praise was meant as encouragement. Lou's left foot dragged and wouldn't move as fast as the right; she couldn't keep in step with the music but she was up and moving.

'Now we'll do it together. You go backwards like this.' Christobel had great patience with her little sister.

Suzy knew from Lou's frown of concentration and the way she was biting her lip that she was finding it hard. Christobel showed them both how to wind the gramophone up and start the record over again. It went on until Lou was exhausted.

Chrissie smiled at Suzy. 'Come on, it's your turn. I'm going to teach you so you can practise with Lou. You'll have to do the man's steps, like this.' Suzy thought it was lots of fun.

'If you practise every day, you'll learn. Then you'll both be able to go to dances and balls and nightclubs when you're grown up.'

'We'll do it,' Louise assured her. 'One day I'll be able to dance like you. Are you going? Leave us the gramophone.'

They started looking through the pile of records Chrissie had brought. Louise found one called 'Yes We Have No Bananas' and they played it over and over to learn the lyrics, singing along together to the bouncy tune and collapsing in a fit of giggles when it ended.

Mrs Smallwood burst in. 'I can't stand any more of this rubbish,' she said irritably. 'It's getting on my nerves. Christobel has no taste. I'll have to get you some better records.' She took the gramophone away with her.

Louise whispered: 'She's mad at Chrissie.'

'I know.'

'Alec and Chrissie are in love, but Mummy refuses to have anything to do with him. Chrissie told Mummy it was wrong to condemn him without even talking to him, and he ought to be invited for dinner.'

'Will your mother like him?'

'I like him, so I don't see why not. They took me to tea at the Kardoma.'

'What's that?'

'A café. Chrissie says they've waited long enough. Her plan is, Alec's going to ask Mummy if he can marry her. They're both going to be on their best behaviour and be very polite and hope she agrees.'

'She won't.' Suzy was awestruck. 'I'm sure she won't.'

'So am I. Even Chrissie doesn't really think she will. Alec says they've got to try and do things properly.'

'But what if . . .?'

'She says she'll be gone as soon as she's twenty-one whether Mother agrees or not. She's going to run away – what's it called?'

'Elope?'

'That's it. That's why she's teaching me to do things now. I'll have to manage without her after that.'

'I'll still be here. I'll help you.'

'That's what Chrissie said. That's why she pressed Mummy to let you play with me.'

'Did she? Where will she live if she runs away from here?'

'Alec's got a house in Rock Park already. Chrissie goes there sometimes, but I'm not supposed to tell anybody that. Mummy knows, but she doesn't want anybody else to find out.'

'I won't tell a soul. I promise.'

Christobel put her head round the door. 'It's time to get ready for dinner, Lou. Get Suzy to help you dress.'

There was nothing Suzy wanted to do more. She couldn't believe the dresses hanging in Louise's wardrobe.

'They're all so beautiful,' she breathed. 'Which one are you going to wear?'

'The blue wool. It's long and hides my leg iron.'

The preparations were long drawn out by Suzy's standards. 'You look beautiful,' she told Louise as she brushed her flaxen hair. 'Do you do all this washing and dressing before dinner every night?'

'Yes, don't you?'

'No. We just sit down and eat.'

The gong boomed through the house. Suzy knew her mother banged it every night before she dished up the meal for Gertie to take to the dining-room table.

Suzy had to hold Lou's dress up out of the way as they went down the stairs. Then she had some real news to take back to the kitchen.

Edna was almost overcome when she heard Christobel's plans, and Gertie had to take the soup tureen to the dining room in her place.

'You'd think it was her about to elope,' Mam whispered to Suzy. She knew they were all exceedingly interested.

Chapter Sixteen

One bright winter afternoon, Josie walked down to the school to meet Suzy and took her into town to buy her a new coat while the January sales were on. They were almost back at The Lawns when a little sports car came down the road and turned into the drive just ahead of them. The car sparkled, all chrome and new scarlet paint.

'That was Christobel,' Suzy said excitedly. 'Her boyfriend was teaching her. I've never seen her drive on her own before.'

'She's learned how to do it,' Josie murmured.

'I'd love to drive when I'm grown up.'

Christobel had opened up one of the garages when they drew level.

'Is this your own car?' Suzy asked her. 'It's new, isn't it? Not the one you learned on.'

Christobel giggled. 'Let's say I've borrowed it. It's an MG Midget, very sporty. Isn't it lovely?' Her blue eyes sparkled with delight.

Behind them, Harold was nosing the sedate Lagonda into the drive. Josie could see Mrs Smallwood on the back seat. She took Suzy's hand and hurried her away to the kitchen.

Within five minutes, a bell jangled furiously, indicating that Mrs Smallwood was impatient for her tea.

Edna propped open the kitchen door before running back and forth between there and the dining room with plates of cake and bread and butter, tea and hot water.

'I can't believe you'd do such a thing, Christobel. Borrow a car! And from a man I've forbidden you to see.'

Josie sat down quietly and pulled Suzy down beside her. Gertie rolled her eyes to the ceiling as she toasted the teacakes.

'I'm horrified that you continue to see him. Against my express wishes, and still without a chaperone.'

'Not that old chestnut again? Nobody bothers with chaperones these days.' Christobel's voice was full of disgust.

'Clearly the man has no thought for your reputation. He's quite unsuitable.'

'He's too old for you.' The colonel's voice reverberated round the house. 'How old did you say?'

'Thirty-seven, Gramps. He thinks he's in his prime.'

'It's the fact that he's been married twice before,' her mother declared, 'and has no thought for social niceties. He ought to be very careful of a young girl like you.'

'He's been widowed twice, but that's respectable. It's not as though he's been divorced.'

'I don't suppose it would stop you, even if he had.'

'No,' Christobel agreed.

'Two wives and they both died young?' barked the colonel. 'What did they die of? That's what I want to know.'

'Don't you go for me too, Gramps. One drowned in a boating accident and one killed herself trying to fly her own aeroplane like Amelia Earhart.'

'I'm appalled,' her mother said, 'accepting a loan of a sports car like that. Aren't you afraid of killing yourself? It's dangerous. Give it him back. Harold can drive you.'

'Harold's always out with you or Gramps when I want to go anywhere. Besides, it's more fun to drive myself.'

'You'd be far better off with Claude Ingleby-Jones. Far safer. Such a nice boy. He's our class, Christobel.'

'Don't harp on that again either. I don't like him.'

Edna came back. 'The colonel wants Gentleman's Relish. Have we got any? I didn't put it out.'

'Shush!' Gertie sped silently to the cupboard and pushed the relish into Edna's hand, together with the plate of teacakes. 'Here.'

'You cannot borrow a car from that man. It puts you under an obligation. You must drop him.'

Christobel screamed: 'I'm not going to drop him. You're all dead against him but you don't know him. Mother, the only time you've come face to face is when you got that fool of a vicar to appeal to our morals. That was disgusting, making out Alec was some sort of a satyr.'

Into the heavy silence that followed, Mrs Smallwood said: 'Thank you, Edna. Close that door behind you when you go.'

She came quietly back into the kitchen. 'A row and a half going on in there,' she giggled.

Raised voices could still be heard but they were muffled now and it was no longer possible to follow the conversation.

'We'd better have our tea,' Gertie sighed. 'I'll toast some of those teacakes for us, shall I?'

Five minutes later the dining-room door was snatched open, then slammed. Christobel was heard to rush upstairs.

The next morning at nine fifteen sharp, when Josie took her pad and pencil to the dining room, Mrs Smallwood said: 'We're expecting a guest for dinner tonight. We want a decent meal, mustn't disgrace ourselves. What do you suggest for the first course, Josephine?'

'What about smoked salmon?'

Josie watched her nose wrinkle up. 'A bit too fancy for the colonel's stomach.'

'It wouldn't be. I quite fancy smoked salmon.'

Mrs Smallwood said: 'No, Father. Onion soup, I think.'

'Yes, ma'am.'

'And a roast to follow. No, perhaps a chicken to follow.'

'Duck would be nice.'

'No, Father. Chicken is lighter.'

Christobel put in: 'Alec likes duck. He's very fond of it.'

'Chicken,' her mother said decisively.

Josie waited while the silence lengthened. 'Roast chicken?' she asked. 'With sage and onion stuffing and bread sauce?'

Christobel pushed her chair back and stood up. 'Cherry pie with cream for pud, Mother.'

'Your grandfather would prefer jam roly-poly.'

'I thought you said a special dinner,' her daughter retorted. 'It sounds like Sunday lunch to me.'

Josie was able to tell Gertie and Edna that Christobel's boyfriend was coming to dinner.

'Something must have softened Mrs Smallwood up,' Edna smiled. 'She swore she wouldn't have him in the house.'

That evening, while the first course was being consumed, Josie was setting the chicken out on the carving dish. She and Suzy were listening intently to sounds from the dining room. Edna was listening in the hall in order to be sure she didn't miss anything.

The conversation was not that exciting. The visitor was talking about a skiing trip he'd made last year and had very much enjoyed. The topic changed to the economic situation. That went on all the time the soup plates were coming out and the next course was taken in.

When the family settled down to eat again the conversation was of more interest to Josie. She saw Suzy straighten up to listen too. Alec was being questioned about his own business interests.

'I'm constructing an open-air swimming pool. The work's been going on all winter. It'll be ready to open this spring.'

'Not a good time to start a new business,' the colonel said.

'A swimming pool? Open air?' Mrs Smallwood asked. 'What a strange idea.'

'It was my idea,' Christobel said quickly. 'I'd love to have somewhere nice to swim.'

'If that's what you want,' her grandfather spluttered. 'It doesn't make sense to make it a commercial venture.'

Louise asked: 'You mean a sort of lido?'

'Yes, I'm going to provide grassy areas for sunbathing and a cafeteria as well.'

Josie could hear the enthusiasm in Alec's voice.

'It's going to be gorgeous,' Christobel breathed. 'I'll teach you to swim there, Lou. You'll love it.'

'Where are you building this?'

'In New Ferry. I've bought quite a big plot of land over-looking the Mersey at Shorefields. I shall build a pumphouse to draw the water from the river. It's going to hold a million gallons.'

'It won't be clean enough. The river always looks muddy and murky, and all that flotsam off the boats. They throw all their rubbish over the side. Nobody will want to swim in that.'

Alec laughed. 'It can be made a clear blue by having filter beds and it'll be treated chemically too.'

'You won't make any money out of that,' the Colonel boomed.

'He will. It'll be the coming thing in the nineteen thirties,' Christobel protested. 'Everybody now knows that fresh air and exercise keep us healthy. People will want to get out and swim in the future. Alec's pool will be in right at the beginning.'

'Nonsense.'

'It isn't, Gramps. Just think of all the cycling clubs that are being formed, and the Women's League of Health and Beauty.'

'Those are for cranks,' said her grandfather. 'Gives girls like you the chance to go round half naked.'

'I don't!'

'When you go to that Health and Beauty thing you wear a fancy white satin blouse and black satin shorts that show too much leg.'

Alec said calmly: 'Then the cranks will come to the swimming pool too.'

'Not if it's open air. The climate's against it, young man. I wouldn't waste my money if I were you. You'll collect the crowds on the few hot days in the summer and it'll be empty for most of the year.'

'I don't know, sir. As Chrissie says, everybody is getting out into the fresh air these days. Even hospitals—'

'If you expect a swimming pool to earn a profit, you must do one of two things.'

'What are those?'

'Put a roof over it and heat it well. Or build it in India or somewhere where the climate is suitable for outdoor swimming.'

Josie heard Christobel's tinkling laugh. 'That's too far away for Alec, Gramps.'

The staff listened carefully all through the time it took to eat the pudding.

'Is it going well?' Josie asked Gertie when she came for the cheese board. 'The colonel reckons his business venture won't get off the ground, but they seem friendly, don't they?'

'Alec hasn't asked Mrs Smallwood yet,' Suzy said.

But now the family were moving to the drawing room and Gertie took the coffee tray there.

Mrs Smallwood said: 'Shut the door, Gertrude. There's quite a draught tonight.'

292

'That's it,' she said when she returned to the kitchen. 'We'll not hear anything else.'

Josie carved up what was left on the chicken for their own supper.

Gertie said: 'The boyfriend seems to have plenty of money. An open-air baths!'

Edna was starting on the washing up. 'His father made a fortune from betting; he was a bookie in a big way, a self-made man who really lived it up. He died of heart trouble when he was sixty and left it all to Alec. The family don't approve of betting or of his father. That's why they don't like him.'

They ate a leisurely supper in the kitchen, discussing the pros and cons of the affair and coming to the conclusion that the family was mad to disapprove of a rich husband for Christobel. Gertie said he seemed a likeable fellow.

Josie said: 'I wish my job had taken me up to the dining room to see this young man.'

It so happened that she went up later to bring down the biscuit barrel to refill, together with other odds and ends that had been left on the table. It was almost ten o'clock and Edna and Gertie were still washing up and putting the best dinner service away.

Mrs Smallwood came out of the drawing room and crossed the hall to the colonel's study. Josie just caught a glimpse of the young man's back view as he followed her. Then the door closed behind them with a secure click.

In order to help Edna, Josie removed the cloth from the table and started to reset it ready for breakfast. She'd kept the door wide open so she wouldn't miss anything but it happened so fast, she almost did. Alec Landis slammed out of the study and headed straight for the front door.

Josie had not been the only one anticipating a result from

the study. Christobel came rushing out of the drawing room.
'He hasn't gone?'

'Yes.'

'Mother? What have you said to him?'

'I told him to get out, that you wouldn't be having any
more to do with him. The nerve of him! He asked if he could
marry you. I told him never. You're a naughty girl to put him
up to this.'

Christobel let out a wail of grief, and rushed outside after
him.

'Come back, Christobel, this instant. I forbid you to have
anything more to do with that man.'

Josie held her breath as the front door crashed shut for the
second time. Mrs Smallwood gave a grunt of disapproval and
swept back to the drawing room, slamming that door behind
her.

Within moments, Christobel came rushing back. She flung
the drawing-room door back on its hinges and it stayed wide
open.

'He's gone.' Josie could hear the fury in her voice.

'I told him to.'

'He didn't say good night to me. You must have upset
him.'

'He upset me. We don't want anyone like him in the family.'

'What's the matter with him?'

'He's not our sort, Christobel. Not a gentleman . . .'

'I don't know what you mean. He was very quiet and
polite. Anyway, he's my sort.'

'He has loud taste, the way he dresses—'

'He wore his dinner jacket. I told him you'd expect that.'

'Satin lapels, dear,' her mother said disparagingly. 'And
his tie. One of those clip-on things that saxophone players
wear.'

'I don't criticise that slob Haydn Ingleby-Jones,' Christobel burst out. 'But I could say worse things about him.'

'Neither of them officer material,' sighed her grandfather. 'Wouldn't have made temporary officer in the Great War, when we were glad of almost anybody.'

'You're wrong. Alec fought in the war, Gramps, and he was an officer. But I don't suppose Ingleby-Jones did.'

'I do wish you two wouldn't keep on so.'

'Gramps! Do you realise what Mother's just done?'

Josie had to strain her ears to hear what Mrs Ingram said.

'Your mother thinks his table manners aren't up to it. Did you notice how he drank his soup?'

'He didn't spill any, Gran, and he said it was excellent.'

Mrs Smallwood said in her loud and carrying voice: 'His father used to go round race courses taking bets.'

'You don't have to worry about Alec doing that, he doesn't need to,' Christobel retorted. 'He employs clerks to take bets at every race meeting.'

'There was a case, a few years back – I read it in the papers – Alec's father was accused of doing one of his punters down. Not honest, and I'm not sure Alec is.'

'Of course he's honest, Mother. What a horrible thing to say about anyone.'

'It's frightening. I couldn't trust him. I shudder at the thought. A man as experienced as Alec Landis is bound to be up to no good with you. You're too young and innocent. He'll take advantage.'

'Probably already has.'

'Gramps!'

Her mother was well into her stride. 'He's had too much money from an early age; too much for his own good. He can live on what his father left him, he's never had to think of

295

earning a living. That gives him too much time to prey on young girls like you.'

'He works hard, Mother. He enjoys setting up new businesses and building them up to earn a profit.'

'I expect he sells them off when he gets bored with managing them. He's the sort that would get easily bored. No idea of duty.'

'He sells them at a profit. That's Alec's way of making a living. You don't expect him to sit in an office every day from nine till five?'

'I see you still have his car. I won't tell you about that again. It goes back to him tomorrow, d'you understand?'

'I understand all right, but I'm enjoying it. Driving myself round, it gives me freedom.'

Mrs Smallwood seemed to explode. 'He's given it to you, hasn't he? An expensive gift like that.'

'What if he has?'

'It's quite improper for you to accept it. It reflects on your reputation.'

'You're so old-fashioned!'

'Go to bed, Christobel. I can't stand any more of this. I should never have given in to you and asked him here. He's worse than we thought. Drop him, and let's have an end to this.'

'I'm not going to drop him, Mother. I'm going to keep his car. I think he's a lovely, generous person, and I'm going to marry him.'

'Don't be so silly. I've said I won't allow it,' her mother boomed.

'You won't be able to stop me. I'll be twenty-one in a few months and I'll do what I like then.'

Christobel flounced off upstairs, leaving the door open.

There was a stunned silence. Then her grandmother said:

'The girl's out of control, Hebe. I've been telling you she needs a stronger hand on the reins.'

Josie had been holding her breath. She'd long since done all she could to get the table ready for breakfast. She crept back to the kitchen to regale Gertie and Edna with what she'd heard, but found they'd heard most of it already.

'Lou was right,' Suzy breathed. 'Christobel's going to elope.'

The next day when Suzy had come home from school and eaten her tea, she went up to see her friend as usual.

Louise now had some colour in her cheeks and her violet eyes shone with excitement.

'Mummy's making big plans. She's thinking of taking me and Christobel abroad on a long holiday. A continental tour, she called it. We're going to France and Switzerland and Italy, and we'll be away for months and months.'

Suzy said: 'That sounds wonderful.' Well, for Lou it would be, but for herself, left behind, she wouldn't like it. 'But I'll miss you.'

'Chrissie told Mummy she should take you too. She said you'd be useful.'

For Suzy, that opened up a very different vista. 'That would be marvellous. I'd make myself useful. Packing and unpacking and pressing clothes . . .'

'But Mummy didn't say whether she would or not. I do hope so.' Lou's face screwed up in thought. 'In fact, Chrissie suggested Mummy should take you instead of her. She doesn't want to go.'

'Why ever not?' Suzy couldn't imagine anyone not jumping at the chance.

'She and Mummy had another row. She believes this is Mummy's way of forcing a break between her and Alec.'

'It is, isn't it?'

'I think so. Mummy lost her temper and shouted at her: "I insist you come. It will do you good. You'll see something of the world and you'll love it. You really are being very silly about this."

'And Christobel said, "It's you who's being silly, Mother. First of all you say we'll have a party to celebrate my coming of age, but your fuddy-duddy friends are to be invited and Alec is barred. Now, you're trying to tempt me to go abroad. You think a long break from Alec will make me forget him. Well, it won't, and no thank you. I wouldn't enjoy it. You go, and take Louise." '

When Suzy related these facts in the kitchen, Mam and Gertie agreed that there would be no party and no trip.

'If Christobel won't go, nobody will. The whole point of it will be gone. So don't build your hopes up just yet, Suzy.'

'How could anyone not want to go abroad like that? Switzerland and Italy . . . And she'd stay in lovely hotels . . .'

Gertie said: 'No matter how good the hotels, it wouldn't stop mother and daughter having rows. It would be one long tussle.'

'You enjoy the tussles, Gertie.'

'Only other people's tussles. I'm nosy, and want to know what's going on. I wouldn't enjoy having Mrs Smallwood's bad temper directed at me the whole time. That would make anybody miserable.'

The next tussle came at dinner-time, sooner than anybody expected it. Christobel had said she would be out for dinner.

The rest of the family were at the table eating the first course. Suzy was chopping parsley to put in a white sauce while Mam was mashing potatoes. They heard Christobel come downstairs and go out. Moments later she came rushing back to the dining room.

'Mother!' She was outraged. 'You've put a lock on the garage. I want to get my car out.'

'I asked Harold to do it, dear . . .'

In a louder voice, Christobel repeated: 'I want my car out.'

'I intend to put a stop to that. You think you can do just what you like. I'm not prepared to have you driving that man's car round as though you own it.'

'I do, it was a present. I told you.'

'And I told you, you must not accept presents from him. Not expensive presents like that.'

'I'm meeting Alec . . . He'll wonder what's happened to me.'

'Good!'

'Christobel,' it was her grandmother's gentler voice, 'you must learn to behave yourself. A young girl like you defying your mother . . .'

Gertie, who had found it difficult to get out of the dining room with the dirty plates and the remains of the pâté they'd eaten for their first course, told them she'd never seen Christobel so furious. Her mother was exultant.

They all heard Christobel using the telephone in the hall.

'Alec, my mother's locked my car up. I can't get to it.' A pause during which they all strained their ears. 'Will you? Yes, thank you.'

Mrs Smallwood came to the dining-room door. 'If you want your dinner here, there's plenty of fish.'

Christobel gave what sounded like a snort of disgust, but she also said coldly, 'No, thank you, Mother,' before going up to her room. Ten minutes later she was down again.

'Don't be late,' her mother called as she crossed the hall. She didn't answer. The front door slammed violently behind her.

There'd been tension in the air all afternoon. Now it was worse than ever. The family were restless and quarrelsome all evening, their tempers frayed.

When Gertie took the tea trays up to the bedrooms early the next morning, she came racing back to the kitchen with the news that Christobel wasn't in her room and her bed hadn't been slept in.

Josie was shocked, Edna quite upset.

'Should I tell her mother?' Gertie worried. 'I don't want her to have a go at me because I haven't.'

But it seemed she didn't need to: Mrs Smallwood had found out. The whole household was swept into crisis. Little food was eaten at breakfast but they sent down first for extra tea and then extra coffee. Mrs Smallwood was showing no interest in menus when Josie went up for her instructions for the day. The family sat on round the table for another hour and kept the door firmly closed throughout.

It happened that Mrs Smallwood was going out for lunch that day, and no sooner had she gone than Christobel came home.

The colonel met her in the hall.

'Your mother's almost out of her mind with worry,' he barked. 'Staying out all night, disgraceful behaviour.'

'You can't put me on a charge, Gramps.'

'I hope you haven't been with that fellow?'

'Of course I have. Be sure to tell Mother I have.'

'What's that suitcase for?'

'Alec's lent it to me. I've come to get some of my clothes and things. I'm not staying here, Gramps. Tell Mother that in this day and age she can't dictate who I see or what I do.'

'You can't go off again, not just like that. Stay and tell her yourself. You owe her that.'

'No fear, it'll be the same arguments as before. We'll just go over the same ground. There's no point. I'm going to marry Alec. She's got to accept that I'm going to choose my own husband. I'm not having her do it for me.'

'Christobel, I'm shocked! Your mother knows best. You'll regret it. In my day, girls would never have dared defy a parent like this. It's your welfare she has at heart, believe me.'

'Let me into my room, Gramps. I want to get packed.'

The colonel came down muttering that he didn't know what the world was coming to, but the additional problem didn't rob him of his appetite. Josie had made another curry for his lunch, and he told her he hadn't tasted such good curries since he'd left India. It made Josie feel she'd found her feet, and was making a success of her job.

When Harold came to the kitchen for his lunch later, he said: 'Miss Christobel's driven her car away. The boyfriend cut the padlock off the garage. Missus sent me to buy the biggest padlock I could get, but the clasp to fix it on was pretty flimsy. Reckon it didn't take much strength to cut that off.'

Edna's hand flew to her mouth. 'She's eloped then! I don't know how she dares.'

'I do hope she'll be happy,' Josie said, 'and that she'll not regret it.'

'Hold on,' Gertie helped herself to more salad, 'she isn't twenty-one until the twelfth of October. That's months off.'

Harold sniggered. 'So she'll have to live in sin for a while. Or say she's older than she is.'

'No wonder the family's in a flap,' Gertie smiled. 'They should be worried. I'd be worried if she was my daughter.'

'Her mother drove her out,' Edna maintained. 'All that fuss about Alec not being good enough for her – they should just have accepted him.'

'He seemed a nice enough chap,' Harold agreed. 'They didn't treat him right. She used to bring him here to play on the tennis court but never took him into the house, and they wouldn't come out to speak to him. A rum do, that.'

'Perhaps they're sorry now.'

'Perhaps Christobel will be sorry later,' Gertie said sharply. 'Depends which one's right.'

'Mrs Smallwood's convinced she'll be killed in his swimming pool or his car or something. He's already lost two wives in strange accidents.'

'More like he'll get her in the family way,' Harold said, beaming round the table at them all. 'How's the missus going to feel about that? Such a disgrace!'

Josie felt her cheeks run with heat. Without marriage, there could be no worse fate for any girl than that, it didn't matter how much money she had.

Chapter Seventeen

A few days later, when Suzy went as usual up to the playroom to see Louise, she said: 'Guess what?'

There was such an air of suppressed excitement about her friend, Suzy knew immediately something had happened. Lou waved a letter at her. 'It's from Chrissie.'

'Where is she? Is she all right?'

'Yes, she's with her boyfriend. Living with him! Mummy's furious.'

'You told her?'

'She recognised Chrissie's writing on the envelope when it came. She brought it to me and insisted on seeing it.'

'Oh, gosh!'

'Mummy's shocked. She said it was what she suspected but she hoped she was wrong. This letter confirmed her worst fears. She had to go and lie down afterwards.'

'What does Chrissie say?'

'I'm to be sure to tell Mummy she's living in sin in great luxury in Alec's house. That they'll be getting married on her birthday . . .' Louise opened the pages and began to read:

'Alec wants us to be married immediately, but since Mummy's refused her permission we have to wait and my birthday will be the earliest we can do it.

Alec thinks she'll relent and let us do it sooner, but you know how obstinate Mother can be: once she digs her heels in, nothing will make her change her mind. So I'm going ahead with my plans for October. It's to be in the register office in the town hall at two o'clock.

I'm enclosing invitations for you and all the family. Give them out for me, Lou, and say I hope they'll all come. Georgina and Penelope have both agreed and they're bringing their families.'

Lou beamed up at her. 'I've got two nieces and a nephew, you know? They'll be going and there's to be a reception afterwards in Alec's house.'

'It'll be a lovely big party.'

'No, it's to be quiet, just for the family and a few friends. I'm thrilled.' She read again from the letter:

'I know I promised you could be my bridesmaid, Lou, and wear a gown of pink satin, but I'm not going to have the kind of wedding I envisaged. No white dress, veil or orange blossom. No bridesmaids in pink satin either. I've bought myself a smart scarlet suit because it'll be quite cold by then. Be sure to tell Mother that I'll be very suitably dressed. I'm sure she thinks I'm a scarlet woman already.

You can still stand behind me and be my attendant if you want. I think it's all going to be quite informal, so I won't call it being bridesmaid. Just wear your best blue hat and coat. I'd like you to. I want as many of my family round me on my wedding day as I can get, and I'm afraid Mother won't come.'

'Are you going to?' Suzy asked. 'How exciting!'

'Mummy was very cross and said I couldn't. She said I couldn't even go – that nobody is to go from here. I'm also forbidden to answer Chrissie's letter, but I'm going to do that.

You could post it for me on your way to school, couldn't you?'

'Of course.'

'Can I tell her to address it to you, when she writes again?'

'Yes, but your mother will still recognise her writing.'

'I'll tell her to get Alec to write the envelope and then she won't.'

'I've had two letters since I've been here from my friend Frankie. She won't suspect . . . Or will she? You could have it addressed to my mam. She wouldn't think that was really for you.'

'I don't want to miss the whole thing. Hang on, there's more.'

'If you're to be the only one from The Lawns, I could arrange for a car to pick you up at the front gate on the day. If this is the case, you'd better bring Suzy with you to make sure you're looked after because my mind will be on other things. Write back and let me know, won't you? Be sure to tell me too what Mother said about my defection and whether she and Gramps will come.

Love from your Big Sis.'

Lou's violet eyes shone with excitement. 'I'm going to write to Chrissie and tell her I want to be her attendant.'

'But your mother's said she won't let you.'

'I won't tell her.'

Suzy giggled. 'She'll say you're following in Chrissie's footsteps. That she's put you up to it.'

'I can't miss her wedding. It isn't fair to expect me to.'

'You'll be in trouble when your mother finds out. She's bound to know if you go.'

'I don't care. Mummy doesn't want me to do anything or go anywhere. She thinks I'm not strong enough and need more rest, but it makes life so dull. Chrissie was right, I'm better since I started getting up and walking about. Even Mummy admits that now.'

'Perhaps she'll come round, perhaps even before Chrissie's birthday. Then she could get married sooner and wouldn't be living in sin.'

'Let's write to her now, and then you can post it tomorrow.'

Josie and the rest of the staff guessed that the family crisis had deepened. Round the kitchen table at lunch-time they'd speculated as to what could have happened. Mrs Smallwood was particularly irritable and held repeated discussions with her parents behind closed doors. The atmosphere was growing more tense. Gertie and Edna had kept their eyes and ears open all day but had not been able to pick up a hint of what was afoot.

Now, at the supper table, Suzy was full of herself, regaling them with all the details of Christobel's letter and answering their questions. Josie could see she was enjoying being able to tell them what Christobel was planning to do.

When Edna started the washing up, and Gertie went to reset the table for breakfast, Suzy whispered to her mother: 'Lou's answered Chrissie's letter. She's told her to address her replies to you, so her mother won't know. Lou says she asks to see any letters that go straight to her. If she thought one had come from Chrissie, there'd be no way she could avoid showing it to her.'

That frightened Josie. 'Suzy! Mrs Smallwood will be furious if she finds out we've done that! It's bad enough you posting Louise's letters . . .'

'But I could say I didn't realise she was forbidden to write to her sister.'

'But to have Louise's letters addressed to me? You and I are helping her children to defy her. Mrs Smallwood could give me the sack.'

Suzy was contrite. 'I didn't think—'

'You must. It's a very dangerous thing for us. We don't want to be put out of here, not now we've settled in and got used to it.'

The worry gave Josie another restless night. In the morning, she told Suzy she must explain to Louise why Chrissie mustn't do it more than once.

A week later, when Josie went to the dining room for her daily instructions, Mrs Smallwood was sorting through the morning post. She pushed two letters towards her. 'For you.'

Josie felt her heart turn over. Her eyes went to Louise before she could stop herself. She was biting into her toast, but her big violet eyes were fixed on the envelopes.

'Thank you,' Josie tucked them quickly between the pages of her notebook, but the lady of the house seemed neither curious nor suspicious.

'Guests for both lunch and dinner today, Josephine,' she announced. 'We need something special.'

Louise smiled up at Josie. 'Penny and Gina, my two older sisters, are coming for the day, and Penny's bringing two of her children.'

'So we'll need something suitable for the very young, and a light tea for them too before they go home. Two extra for dinner this evening. Georgina and her husband will be staying.'

As soon as she'd returned to the kitchen, Josie looked at the letters. One was addressed to her in a hand she didn't recognise, and had a Rock Ferry postmark. The other was addressed to Suzy, and was, Josie thought, from Frankie. Suzy could deal with both of them when she returned from school.

It meant a busy morning for her and she tried not to think of that letter. As she whisked egg whites, she asked Gertie: 'What are the older sisters like?'

'Nice girls. Not quite as pretty and not as fair as the two younger ones, but still very attractive. They're both a quieter version of Christobel, but Georgina was a handful when she was younger too. Penelope, the eldest, lives quite close. She's the one with the three children. Her eldest, Bobby, has started school. Georgina lives in London and doesn't come home all that often.'

'The little girls are lovely,' Edna told her. 'They look like little angels with their blonde curls.'

After she'd served lunch, Gertie reported: 'The daughters are trying to talk their mother round. They want her to give her permission so Christobel can be married straight away. I think that's why they've both come together. I heard Penelope say it was nonsense to make her wait until her birthday in October.'

'It is,' Edna agreed wholeheartedly.

'Are they going to succeed?'

'No. She says it's Christobel's way of forcing her to do what she doesn't believe in. It's a sort of blackmail and she isn't going to give in to it.'

Josie said: 'Mrs Smallwood would lose face, wouldn't she?'

'Christobel has invited all the family to her wedding in October, but her mother is forbidding them to have anything to do with her. She says Christobel's a disgrace to them all.'

* * *

Suzy came in from school with glowing cheeks. Josie said: 'There's a letter for you, upstairs beside your bed.'

She didn't mention the other letter, which she'd put out of sight beneath it. She listened to Suzy's footsteps racing upstairs. She was back in moments waving one letter.

'It's from Frankie.'

Josie thought her daughter was growing more attractive with the years. She'd be fourteen in May and seemed suddenly taller and slimmer. Today, her eyes were sparkling with pleasure.

'I thought so.' Josie felt uneasy about what she'd done with the second letter, but she knew better than to mention it in front of Edna and Gertie.

'You've heard Frankie talk about his Auntie Maisie who lives in Lunar Street in Rock Ferry?'

'Yes, she's Olga's aunt really.'

'Well, she isn't very well and he's coming to stay with her once the Easter holidays start. It's to be a little holiday before he starts work. He's fourteen now and his mam's going to get him a job in the same jam factory.'

'He was fourteen on St Valentine's Day.'

'Yes, but she wanted him to stay at school until the end of term. He wants to know if he can come and see us.'

Josie sighed. 'We can't ask him here. Mrs Smallwood wouldn't like it. Perhaps we can arrange to meet him somewhere.'

'We must,' Suzy insisted. 'Can't miss seeing Frankie.'

'Is Olga coming too?'

'Only over Easter itself, because she has to work. Can I have that piece of fruit cake before I go up and see Louise?'

'She's got company,' Edna told her. 'Her sisters are here and Penelope's brought her little girls.'

'She'll still want me,' Suzy grinned at her.

'There's a lot going on today. Keep your ears open.'

Two hours later when she came back down for her supper they were all waiting to hear her news.

'We looked after the little girls in the playroom and kept them amused. Lou told them stories, and they were ever so good. Their mother, Penny, came up when Edna brought their supper and Lou asked her about Chrissie. She said: "She's done a very risky thing but she seems happy. Alec Landis is a nice chap, though he is a bit old for her. It's not him that's leading her astray, this is all Chrissie's doing. She fell out with Mother but it was wrong of her to walk out on her the way she did. And to go and live with him, well . . . I'd never have dared do that, and I hope you won't."

' "Of course I won't," Lou said. "But it's not just that. Mummy's afraid Alec will kill her."

' "She isn't really. That's just her way. She has to find something to object to."

' "Mummy's sure that's why Alec gave her that dangerous car. She's afraid Chrissie will be killed like his other wives."

' "That's nonsense. The car's new. It isn't dangerous," Penelope said. "It wasn't his fault his wives were killed. They were two terrible accidents."

' "Mummy says she's psychic and she can see it happening over again. She says everything goes in threes so it's bound to."

' "That's just folklore. According to Chrissie, Alec can hardly bear to talk about them even now. He was dreadfully upset, especially the second time. You'll like him. He's full of enthusiasm." '

At Edna's prompting, Suzy recalled the other things that Penny had said to her sister.

'You've heard about the open-air swimming pool he's building at New Ferry?'

'Is it finished?'

'Almost. He wants it to open in time for Easter.'

'Have you seen it?'

'Yes,' Penny said. 'Chrissie took me. It's a really gigantic pool, three hundred and thirty feet long and ninety feet wide. There are going to be grassy areas for sunbathing and a cafeteria as well. The shallow end is for children, and at its deepest, it'll be sixteen feet.'

'Before she ran away, Chrissie said she'd teach me to swim. But now . . .'

'Lou, once it's open, I'll take you on the first warm day we get.'

'I don't know whether Mummy will let me go.'

'Anyone can go, Lou. It's for the public. Alec says it's what the masses in Birkenhead need.'

'That won't help!' Lou wailed. 'Mummy doesn't want me to go where the masses go. She thinks I'll catch some dread disease from them.'

'I'll take you. You leave it to me.'

Easter Sunday turned out to be a cool overcast day, but Josie had promised Suzy that she'd invite Olga and Frankie to go with them on the bus to New Brighton. She'd packed a picnic tea which they ate on the beach in the teeth of a more-than-bracing breeze.

The youngsters paddled in the Mersey estuary and said the water was freezing cold, but she could hear them laughing together, so she knew they were happy enough.

Josie had a long heart-to-heart chat with Olga over a flask of tea, but Olga wanted to talk about Eric and though she tried to offer comfort and sympathy, Josie knew that comfort was impossible while Luke Palmer was still at large. Olga's grief and horror served to heighten Josie's fears and make her feel more nerve-wracked than ever.

Frankie and Suzy managed to arrange a visit to the pictures later in the week.

It happened that Easter was late that year, and no sooner was it over than the weather turned suddenly warmer. The following Saturday, the Reverend Haydn Ingleby-Jones and Nurse Silk had arranged a charabanc trip to New Brighton beach for the congregation.

One of his flock owned three charabancs and had agreed to take them. Another owned numerous donkeys and ran a prosperous business. Some of them collected cockles and mussels from Hoylake sands and hawked them about the streets of town, and others gave rides along the sands throughout the summer. That afternoon, the cockles and mussels would be sold to holiday-makers and the proceeds together with the money earned from the donkey rides would be given to the church fund.

Mrs Smallwood had organised the other ladies in Ingleby-Jones's flock to provide cakes and sandwiches and lemonade. She was planning to set up a stand on the promenade to sell them, the proceeds going to the same fund. Also, the man who operated the Punch and Judy show had promised to give that afternoon's takings to the same good cause.

These activities would be followed by early evening hymn singing and a short service.

Penelope telephoned Louise and told her that Saturday would be a good day to go to Alec's baths.

'We'd better take Suzy too, if she'll come. You might need somebody to help you in and out and it takes me all my time to watch my own babies.'

'She'll jump at the chance,' Lou laughed. 'But I haven't got a bathing costume.'

'I'd better take you out tomorrow to get one. What about Suzy? Will she need one too?'

'I'll ask her, but I think she said she had one.'

Suzy had been proud to tell Lou she already had a bathing suit when Lou did not.

'You'd better try it on,' Mam warned her. 'You might have grown out of it by now.'

Suzy found she was still able to get into it. It was backless and had straps that crossed on her back, then threaded through slots at waist level to tie in a bow.

Mam was triumphant. 'I chose that style for you because I knew you'd grow. It adjusts over several sizes.'

It was very eye-catching with its broad stripes, and Suzy liked it better than the plain blue one that Lou's sister had bought for her.

Penny had also bought two swimming rings, a blue one for Louise and a red one for Suzy, and a big beach ball. They blew them all up and could talk of nothing but their proposed trip to the baths.

'Can you swim?' Lou wanted to know.

Suzy said: 'A bit.'

'I wish I could. I've never tried.'

'I can take my foot off the bottom for a few strokes, but that's all. I went to the baths with Frankie a few times last summer, but he was better at it than me. I did a bit in the sea once when we went on holiday to Rhyl, but the sea's more scary.'

The next morning, the sun was shining from a cloudless sky at six thirty when Suzy woke up. She was in the garden with Lou at ten thirty when a car drew into the drive and

Penelope and her family got out. Suzy had seen her husband, Simon, when he'd come for dinner. Bobby had been at school that day. He had brown hair like his father.

'Are you both ready to go to the baths?' Penny asked.

'Yes, but I haven't said anything to Gramps about going. I'd better ask if I can.'

'Leave it to me,' her sister said. 'Take my brood up to the playroom for ten minutes.'

Her children were eager to play with toys that were new to them. Louise kept the door open and was continually putting her head out on the landing.

She said: 'What if Gramps won't let me go?'

She went to sit on the stairs and Suzy joined her. They moved closer a few steps at a time. The adults were having coffee in the drawing room when the colonel's voice boomed through the house.

'I don't think you should take Louise. Her mother won't like it.'

Penny's voice was calm and clear. 'It isn't fair to stop her. Lou will be so disappointed, if you do.'

'Your mother wouldn't allow it if she were here. You know that.'

'What's the harm? It's going to be a warm day, she'll love it. Lou's wrapped in cotton wool, Gramps, not allowed to do anything. What an existence for a child. She needs more to do, and swimming will be good for her.'

Penny came sweeping out and passed them as she shot upstairs to the airing cupboard to get some towels.

'You're coming. Get your things, girls.' They both had their costumes and swimming rings ready on their laps.

Within minutes, Suzy was sitting in the back of the big car with the other children and felt so lucky to be experiencing luxury like this. This was a different world, and Mam, Edna and Gertie could only see it from the outside.

Once through the turnstiles of the baths, Suzy looked round with anticipation. There were swimmers and paddlers splashing and calling to each other, and silent inert sunbathers stretched out on their towels. The Union Jack fluttered in the gentle breeze from the flag pole on top of the high diving board.

A man had climbed up and was poised with his toes on the edge. They all stood for a moment to watch his perfect dive into the sparkling water below before following Penny to the ladies' changing cubicles. Lou could get along quite well now by swinging her leg with the iron on it.

'I can get undressed by myself,' she said, closing the door of her cubicle. Suzy knew she wanted to be as independent as possible and used the next cubicle. She was changed in half the time and was stowing her clothes in one of the row of lockers provided before Lou was ready.

Penelope came out in an elegant black bathing suit having helped her little ones into theirs.

She said to Suzy: 'I'm relying on you to make sure Lou's all right. Don't, whatever you do, leave her side until Chrissie gets here. She's coming to give Lou a swimming lesson.'

'I won't, I promise.' Suzy knew only too well why they'd brought her.

'Stay in the shallow end, and if she's cold she's to come out straight away and get dressed, all right?'

Suzy waited for Louise, and when she came out in her bathing suit, Suzy saw her withered leg totally bare for the first time and was filled with pity. It was thin and misshapen, and she seemed to walk awkwardly on the ball of her foot rather than put it flat on the ground.

Lou was hanging on to Suzy's shoulder as they walked

slowly out to the pool to find Penny sitting in a deck chair with her youngest playing at her feet. The other two children were already in the baths with their father. Bobby waved to them from the other side of the pool and then swam over to show them how well he could do it.

'Doesn't it look lovely?' Suzy breathed. The water was somewhere between blue and green, and crystal clear.

Lou was thrilled. 'I want to go in,' she said, putting her arms through her swimming ring and pulling it down to her waist.

Suzy said, with a look at Penny: 'We'll go to the children's end where we can walk in.'

Bobby, dripping water at every step, came with them, holding Lou's hand. As they waded in, Suzy took a firm grip on Lou's other hand. The water felt cold, but Lou and Bobby were wading fearlessly out to deeper water and Suzy felt obliged to keep up. The water had crept up to her waist.

'What do I have to do to swim?' Lou demanded. Bobby showed her the arm movements for breaststroke, and within seconds she was down in the water trying them out. He lost interest quite soon and swam off.

Suzy did her best to stay close to Louise. She said: 'You're holding your head too high. Don't be afraid of getting your face wet.'

It was what Frankie had kept saying to her last year. Suzy didn't like putting her face under the water, but Lou took the advice. Suzy put an arm under her waist to lift her legs and she kicked out hard.

'Turn back to the side,' Suzy said, afraid Lou would get away from her. Lou stood up, all smiles, droplets of water running down her cheeks.

'I can move more easily in the water than out of it,' she

laughed aloud. 'It's lovely! Help me do that again.' She kicked out as hard as she could and stayed afloat for three strokes.

'You're better at this than I am.' Suzy had to laugh with her. Lou kept it up for some time until Chrissie came wading out to them.

'Hello, Lou. How are you getting on?'

'Am I doing it right? Watch me . . .'

'You're doing very well.'

'Better than I am,' Suzy chuckled. 'Lou will be looking after me soon.'

'She's a natural at this,' Chrissie said. 'We'll soon have you swimming on your own, Lou. Turn on to your back and let's see if you can float.'

Suzy did exactly what Chrissie was telling Lou to do. She wanted to improve her own swimming, but she was so pleased for her friend. Such rapid success didn't often come to Louise.

'I want to go down one of those chutes.' Lou was quite excited. 'I'd love to try it. Will you do it too, Suzy?'

She wasn't sure she wanted to, but didn't want to be thought a coward. She was behind Lou as she climbed the ladder; Lou looked pitifully awkward pulling herself up with her arms. Water was streaming down the chute itself and Suzy could see Chrissie treading water at the bottom. With a whoop of glee Lou went shooting down and Chrissie swooped to gather her into her arms. Then Chrissie looked up at Suzy.

'Come on, Suzy, your turn.'

She was already sitting at the top feeling a bit nervous. But if poor Lou could do it with such obvious enjoyment, she had to. She took a deep breath and pushed herself off.

When she hit the water it took her breath away. She could see it all green bubbles, as she went down until her feet touched the bottom and made her bounce back. Chrissie's hands caught at her waist and held her up.

'All right, Suzy?'

She was coughing and could barely see, but it had been wonderful.

Chrissie had brought a lunch basket. She spread a checked tablecloth on the grass. The adults sat in deck chairs and the children on rugs. Alec had come too and was wearing his swimming costume, which was striped in much the same way as Suzy's own.

A big fluffy towel had been brought for her use; she was offered the same brown bread sandwiches, fruit and lemonade. Later, when the other children had ice cream, the same sort was bought for her. Suzy was almost overcome; she felt she was being treated as an equal, and it gave her the wonderful feeling of being closer to Louise.

'Today has been absolute heaven,' she told Penny as she climbed back into the car to be taken home. 'Thank you for taking me.'

'It's been marvellous,' Louise agreed. 'I love swimming.'

'We'll be doing it again, quite often,' Penny told her from the front seat. 'You'll be a good swimmer soon if you go regularly.'

'I'd like to learn to dive too.'

'All in good time,' Penny laughed.

'I'm learning to dive now,' Bobby boasted.

Suzy noticed the taxi ahead of them turning into their drive. She shivered – was that Mrs Smallwood inside?

Beside her, Louise straightened up and said: 'Here's Mummy come home!'

The chatter stopped abruptly and the happy atmosphere cooled. The colonel was on the doorstep to meet them.

'Louise!' her mother thundered as they were getting out of the car. 'Where have you been?'

Suzy knew it must be obvious. Lou had her swimming ring on her arm and they all had wet hair.

'The baths, Mummy. It was lovely, pure heaven.'

'You mean those baths Alec Landis is constructing?'

'They're finished, open now.'

Mrs Smallwood let out a wail of distress. 'Penelope, how could you?'

'She insisted on taking her,' the colonel said. 'Wouldn't listen to me. I told her you wouldn't like it.'

'Poor child! You haven't even dried her hair properly.'

'Mine's still wet too,' one of the little angels piped up.

'Louise will catch her death of cold.'

'I don't feel cold, Mummy.'

'It was very pleasant there,' Simon put in. 'It's been a really warm day and swimming's very healthy.'

Penny said: 'Just look at her, she looks very well.'

'She could be running a temperature by bedtime.'

'Mother! She'll come to no harm.'

'If not tonight, then later. Goodness knows what germs there are in that water. The riffraff of Birkenhead are swimming in it.'

'There's a disinfectant in it to stop anything like that.'

'The water smelled lovely,' Lou breathed, 'I can still smell it on me.'

Her mother shook her head angrily. 'So can I; it's horrible. You need a bath. Go straight up, Louise, and take one.'

Obediently, she headed indoors. 'I love the water. I can move better in it than on dry land.'

Suzy wanted to get away. She whispered goodbye and moved off towards the back door. When she reached the kitchen, she could still hear Penny's voice. The family had moved into the hall.

'There's not much she can enjoy, Mother. It would be criminal to stop this now. She'll take to swimming, it'll make her leg stronger and Lou needs to be good at something.'

'I don't believe it will. You're putting your little sister at risk.' The drawing-room door clicked shut behind them.

Suzy knew Penny was right. Lou was looking healthier and growing stronger.

'We'll be going next weekend,' Lou told her later, 'either Saturday or Sunday. Penny's waiting to see what the weather will be like.' She laughed. 'She says she hopes I won't catch anything over the next week or Mummy will blame it on the baths.'

Suzy went upstairs to the bedroom she shared with her mother to write to Frankie. He'd still be with his great-aunt in Rock Ferry next weekend. He'd given her the address in Lunar Street so she wrote to him there, telling him about the new swimming baths and how much better they were than any they'd been to in Liverpool.

She wrote: 'Why don't you meet me there? It was great fun today. I'll drop you a postcard on Friday as to whether I'll be going on Saturday or Sunday.'

As it happened, the weather was set fair for the whole weekend. Penny decided they'd go on Saturday, and arrived mid-morning with her own family to take Louise and Suzy to the baths.

As soon as she was through the turnstiles, Suzy was looking for Frankie. But news of the new baths had gone round, and there were more swimmers and sunbathers on this hot day. Suzy followed Louise to the changing cubicles. When she and Louise came out, Frankie was waiting for her.

There was a wide smile on his face and his bright blue eyes shone with joy at seeing her again. Suzy knew she'd never have a closer friend than Frankie.

He looked more robust than he used to; he was taller than she was now, but still lightly built. His tight curly brown hair and swimsuit were dripping moisture.

'I got here early. I was watching out for you.'

'This is Lou,' Suzy said. Frankie put out a wet fist and she giggled.

'Suzy can't stop talking about you.'

'We're best friends.'

'Let's get in the water. I can't wait. It was lovely last week.'

'It's a smashing baths.'

'We go down to the shallow end to get in,' Suzy told him. Lou found it hard to walk without her leg iron. Frankie was attentive, helping her along. When she wanted to practise her swimming strokes he patiently held her up. Suzy was pleased to see her two friends hitting it off.

Louise introduced Frankie to her own family and when he said he could swim, and showed pride in his ability, Alec challenged him to a race over two lengths of the baths. They both did a fast crawl. Alec won by a yard and a half.

'I'm out of practice,' Frankie laughed. 'I'll race you again in a week or two. I reckon I might beat you then.'

Alec invited him to sit down with them and share their picnic lunch. Frankie never stopped talking – about his arm and his 'accident'; about the school he and Suzy had attended and the job he was going to have in the jam factory in a fortnight.

'I've been inside to see the place. My mam works there, you see. The whole building smells of boiling fruit, but it would be very hot and sticky on a day like this.'

Alec looked up from the pork pie he was cutting into slices. 'I need another life guard here, would you be interested?'

'You don't mean you pay people to stay here all day?'

Alec laughed. 'Yes, there's one of my life guards over there by the diving board. But you can't just swim up and down and enjoy yourself. You have to keep a constant watch for trouble; stay alert and make sure nobody is getting into difficulties.'

'And help them if they do?'

'Yes. Have you done any life-saving?'

Frankie shook his head.

'We run a course here, between seven and eight in the morning. You'd need to do that.'

'It sounds a wonderful job.' Frankie's grin told Suzy he couldn't believe his luck.

'You'll have to come now at the beginning of the season.'

'I could start right now,' he said. 'Except . . . I'll have to ask my aunt if I can lodge with her. I live in Liverpool, you see.'

'It's only temporary, mind,' Alec told him. 'As it's an open-air pool, it'll close at the end of September.'

'Yes . . .'

'But if you're keen and show willing, I'd be glad to have you back next summer. I'd want you to take some first-aid classes too.'

'I'll find something else by the autumn. I'll have time to look round, won't I?'

Frankie said to Suzy afterwards: 'To think of being paid to spend all day at a swimming pool.'

'We'll see you here every weekend,' Louise smiled, 'and you can be my friend as well as Suzy's.'

Frankie was thrilled to start work as a life guard. For some time, his mother had been coming over at weekends to help Aunt Maisie with her cleaning and shopping.

'It'll be good for her to have you living there,' she told Frankie. 'But don't expect to be waited on. You must look after yourself and help her.'

Olga continued to come over at the weekends. Occasionally on a Sunday afternoon, she and Josie would make their way to the baths too.

Chapter Eighteen

For Louise and Suzy, the trips to the baths went on every weekend, weather permitting, as summer progressed. Louise was very keen and was learning fast. Within two months she could swim two lengths of the baths in breaststroke, and Alec and Frankie were teaching her the fast crawl. Her leg was getting stronger.

'I think you should start leaving off your leg iron,' Christobel told her.

'What will Mother say?'

'Tell her that you're taking it off to swim, and not putting it back for an hour or so when you get dressed. Your knee is stiff because it's difficult for you to bend it with the leg iron on. So's your ankle because you wear those stiff and heavy boots.'

'Nurse Silk says my leg needs the support.'

'Forget her. It's years since she did any real nursing. The leg iron makes you rest your leg and you've done that long enough.'

'Yes, but what about Dr Howarth? He thinks support and rest—'

'Tell him too. Your muscles and joints need to be used. You need to start exercising, I know you do. Well – perhaps you'd better ask his opinion, it would be more diplomatic. When will you see him next?'

'This Wednesday.'

'Do it then, Lou. If he's agreeable Mother will be too. Leave that thing off for an hour or so today. See how you get on.'

'I haven't got any other shoes . . .'

'Bare feet will be fine here at the pool. Better than shoes.'

Louise walked round rather gingerly. She didn't find it easy to start with, but it felt lovely to be rid of the weight; she'd thought of the leg iron as an anchor. More than anything else, Louise longed to have two serviceable legs like everybody else. She started leaving her leg iron off for short periods at home and found she could manage without. Mother didn't notice what she was doing until she heard about it in Dr Howarth's surgery.

He was fairly noncommittal. 'A problem now is that your good leg has grown more than this one, Louise.'

'A quarter of an inch.' Christobel had been of the opinion that shouldn't make much difference.

He measured her. 'It's half an inch now, and you'll have to have your boot, and any other shoes you get, built up to that height. Leave your iron off only for short periods to start with. You must take it slowly and see how you get on. Be careful not to overtire yourself.'

Mother seemed pleased and took her straight to the shops to get some ordinary shoes. They were plain, flat-heeled laceups, but they were ordinary shoes like Suzy wore. The right one was left at the cobblers, to have the sole and heel built up.

Louise felt euphoric that day and despite Dr Howarth's advice, she danced with Suzy in the playroom for over an hour.

'It's less tiring without that heavy iron thing on,' she laughed. 'It feels wonderful without it.'

During the week, when Suzy was home from school, she spent almost all her time up in the playroom with Louise. They had become firm friends. They read a lot, played records on Chrissie's gramophone and danced to the music. They also played board and card games. Suzy tried to think of other ways to entertain Louise and fell back on what she and Frankie had done. She invented a series of fantastic adventures that would befall them when they were older. Louise was fascinated and took to turning what she was hearing into stories and writing them down. Her heroines were often cripples who were miraculously cured.

After several weeks, Lou said seriously: 'I can't make up my mind, whether to be an Olympic swimmer when I grow up, or a writer of books.'

Suzy laughed and thought how very like Frankie she was; neither seemed able to tell the difference between real life and fantasy.

Louise and Frankie were getting on famously together. At the pool, when they were tired of swimming, Louise got out her notebooks and they put their heads together and began creating a fictional world.

Their idea was that the world existed inside a giant; and inside every person was another world of tiny people, and inside each tiny person was yet another smaller world.

'Like a Russian doll,' Suzy said, when they explained it to her.

It sounded crazy to her, but they each strove to think up new adventures for the people inside them, and after a session with Frankie, Louise would go back to the playroom to sort out the notes she'd made. She told her mother she was writing a book for children which was to be called *The Inner World*.

It was a July afternoon and Josie could feel the sun hot on her back. She was wearing her bathing suit and lying prone on a towel on the grass at the New Ferry baths. She was beginning to feel soporific after getting up early and spending the morning cooking the traditional Sunday lunch at The Lawns.

Suzy and Frankie were swimming with Louise. Josie could hear shouts and splashes from the pool, but here in the garden she couldn't see it. Somewhere, not far away, were Louise's sisters. Josie tried to spread her towel some distance from theirs, where they couldn't see each other.

Beside her, Olga wiped her face on her towel. 'Isn't it hot today?' She was sunbathing too.

'Lovely. We'll have a swim later to cool down.' Not that either of them could swim, not properly. Josie hadn't had the chance to learn when she was young. There'd been no baths near where she'd lived, and there hadn't been any money for luxuries like swimming then.

Olga turned over on to her back with a sigh. 'I do wish they'd catch Luke Palmer. I'd feel so much better if I knew he was under lock and key and getting what he deserves.'

Josie knew they both felt that as an urgent need. Luke Palmer was a subject they couldn't stop discussing.

She said: 'It seems so unfair that he's still free after what he did.'

If only the police would catch Luke, she'd never have to worry about him finding them and taking revenge on Suzy. She was living in daily fear of that and felt she'd never be able to relax properly until he was caught. For both of them, it was an essential requirement, a prior condition for peace of mind and happiness.

She'd always been friendly with Olga but this pressing necessity they shared was drawing them closer. Though she was fond of Gertie and Edna, and they were great to work with, there were so many things she had to bottle up when she was with them. But with Olga she need have no secrets. Olga knew Luke and all the terrible things he'd done. Olga too had suffered at his hands.

'I do miss Eric. We were very happy together. Money was tight, but apart from that I hadn't a worry in the world. Everything went right for me until the night Luke Palmer came up to our flat.'

Josie whispered: 'I'm so grateful you don't hold it against me for bringing him . . . I wish I'd never set eyes on him.'

Olga said: 'I shouldn't go on about him like this. It was just the same for you, Josie. Until he killed your Ted, you had no worries either. He spoiled everything for us.'

Josie turned over. Her back was burning. 'Will you put some more cream on my shoulders, Olga?'

As she felt Olga's hand gently smoothing the cream in, she started to talk. 'I had my troubles even before . . .'

'Not with Ted?'

'No, he was a lovely person.'

Sitting with her back to her friend, looking into the middle distance across the bodies laid out in the sun, she began: 'I was very happy with Ted. It was before we were married – before we even met.'

There was something about Olga that invited confidences. 'I've never told anybody . . . Well, Ted knew . . .'

'What?'

'I had a baby, when I was eighteen.'

She couldn't stop it pouring out then. About giving up her baby son at six weeks of age; about meeting Nurse Silk again, the woman to whom she'd handed baby Robert over for adoption; of finding she was on good terms with her present employer. And the awful news that Christobel thought the woman was doing it for payment. Olga's hand covered hers in silent sympathy.

'I can't stop thinking about baby Robert. I'd love to know whether he had a happy upbringing and what he's doing now. Nurse Silk said he'd have a better life than I could give him, but if she was thinking more of the money she'd earn by placing him, rather than of his welfare . . .'

'You've had a very hard life, Josie.'

'I put it behind me when I married Ted. Well, partly. I still thought of the baby, wanting to know how he was, that sort of thing. Now, the whole time there are two things going round in my head. When I stop thinking about Luke Palmer I start thinking of my son. I'd rather think of the baby, except I feel so guilty about giving him away.'

'But you had no choice.'

'Sometimes I think I'll go mad.'

'You won't,' Olga soothed. 'You must try and think of Suzy.'

'I do that.'

'Frankie's been a great comfort to me.'

'I've kept all this bottled up for far too long. I'll feel better for having talked about him.'

'Of course you will.'

But Josie didn't. She felt overwhelmed again by the shame she'd felt as a girl. Olga was showing compassion; she was a friend who could be relied on. Olga didn't think she'd come from the gutter or that she was a slut. They lay down again and silently soaked up the sun for another half an hour.

Then Olga sat up and looked round. 'The children have come out of the pool. They're over there.'

Josie lifted her head. 'Louise is busy scribbling in her notebook.'

'That'll be the book Frankie's helping her to write. D'you think anything will come of it?'

'They've shown it to Christobel and Penny and they think it's quite good. The other sister, Georgina, lives in London and her husband works in publishing. When it's finished, he's going to read it. He'll know whether it's good enough.'

'I hope it is.'

'Christobel thinks he could help them improve it.'

'Frankie's very keen on it.'

'They both are.'

After two minutes' companionable silence, Olga said in worried tones: 'Luke must be somewhere.'

'He must have a job,' Josie added. 'He wouldn't be able to survive if he hadn't.'

It was what she and Olga did all the time: speculate as to where Luke Palmer could have gone after he'd killed Eric and attacked Frankie. But they had no way of finding out and it kept them both on edge.

Olga sighed heavily. 'My Auntie Maisie's worse. She's been in bed all this week. I'm glad Frankie's lodging with her. He called the doctor out to see her and he's making meals for her.'

'He's a good lad.'

'He is that. He's been lighting fires for her and carrying in the coals. She likes a bit of fire even on a warm day, and they cook on it, but Maisie's eighty-three and reaching the stage when she needs more help than that.

'I came over as soon as I finished work yesterday. I've changed her bed and done the washing, and I've been cooking all morning. We are her only relatives.' Olga sat up. Her plump face looked hot and worried, and her tight curls were damp with perspiration. 'I ought to help more, but ... it would mean giving up my job, and I'm settled and enjoying that, and she only has two bedrooms furnished. There is another boxroom that would do for Frankie, but it's full of things that belonged to her parents and we'd need to get a bed. I don't like to suggest clearing it out.'

'Is there anything I can do?' Josie offered. 'Most days I

can take a couple of hours off after lunch. I could go and see to things for you during the week.'

'Frankie's been taking a sandwich and not going back in the dinner hour. You've got your own job and Suzy to look after. It's asking an awful lot of you.'

'It isn't. I was very glad of what you did for me and Suzy in the past. I relied on you. I'd be glad to help.'

'Honest? Come back with me now then. We'll have a cup of tea together, so she'll know you. Thanks, Josie, you're the tops.'

When later Josie followed Olga into the terraced house in Lunar Street, Maisie was sitting by a small fire in the living room. She was white-haired, almost matchstick thin, and very frail.

'I've brought my friend Josie to see you, Auntie,' Olga told her. 'She'll look in on you next week while Frankie's at work.'

'I'm a trouble to everybody,' the old lady sighed.

'No you're not.'

Maisie had all her wits about her. 'I never got married, you see,' she told Josie. 'No children of my own. Olga's very good but she has to come over from Liverpool.'

'It's an easy journey. I told you, I take the underground. Rock Ferry station is just round the corner from here.'

Afterwards, Olga showed Josie round the house. Everything was old-fashioned but it sparkled with cleanliness after Olga's ministrations.

'I cooked a bit of beef this morning. There's enough food here for her and Frankie for the next couple of days.'

After lunch on Monday, Josie put some leftover soup in a jam jar and took the bus down to Lunar Street to see how Maisie was.

The front door of the terraced house was unlocked. She knocked and called and was eventually answered by a querulous voice from upstairs. Josie made her way to the front bedroom. Nothing seemed to have changed since she'd been here yesterday afternoon, except that the sandwich Frankie had left for her between two plates was still untouched and her false teeth were in a glass of water near her bed. Her hand was in front of her mouth as she reached for them and slid them in.

'Gone two o'clock? I've been asleep most of the morning. It's time I was up.'

'You can stay where you are if you like. I could bring you—'

'No, I can't spend the whole day here. I won't sleep tonight if I do.'

'I'll light the fire downstairs then, and get the kettle on. There's some chicken soup, do you fancy that if I heat it up?'

'Yes, I find sandwiches a bit dry.'

Josie went downstairs and found Frankie had laid the fire in the range. She had only to put a match to it. There seemed to be nowhere else she could boil the kettle. She filled it and set it to swing on the hook over the fire. It wasn't going to boil quickly: the flames were only just beginning to flicker round the coal.

There was no sound from upstairs. Josie went up to see if the old lady needed help. She was sitting on the side of the bed in her underwear.

'I'm such a nuisance to everybody,' she puffed breathlessly. 'I'd be better off dead.'

'Oh no! Olga would be very upset. She thinks a lot of you. She said she used to come here for holidays when she was a child.'

'Olga, yes. She's a good girl, and little Frankie tries so hard. But they've got their own lives to live now.'

Aunt Maisie needed a lot of help in dressing. She was shaky on her feet and the stairs were steep and narrow. Josie didn't think she'd be safe going down on her own.

The fire was blazing up nicely and the kettle singing. Josie found a pan and set the soup she'd brought to heat on a trivet. She found plenty to do: there was the old lady's bed to make and her slops to empty. Her only lavatory was outside in the yard.

Josie understood only too well now why Olga was so concerned about her aunt.

The next time Louise went to see Dr Howarth, she wore her new shoes. She was walking more easily and her limp was becoming less noticeable. He congratulated both her and her mother on the progress she was making, and, because of this, Mrs Smallwood became reconciled to Louise's swimming. Louise was so keen to practise that she wanted to go to the baths during the week too, and Suzy suggested she ask her mother if Harold could take her.

Hebe Smallwood barked out: 'You can't go alone.'

'But with Harold? And Frankie's always there. I know he's supposed to watch out for swimmers in trouble, but Alec doesn't mind if he talks to me. He says there aren't so many people there in the week.'

Her mother thundered: 'I don't like all these friends you're picking up. Who is this Frankie?'

Suzy had gone down to the drawing room with her. She said: 'He's a friend of mine and a very strong swimmer. He's a life-saver at the baths. He'd keep a special eye on Louise.'

'Certainly not. Not without a chaperone.'

But Mrs Smallwood was curious about the baths and wanted to see them. One warm afternoon, Louise managed to persuade her mother to take her, though she didn't swim, thinking it wasn't good for ladies of her age.

'You'll be able to sit on a deck chair and watch me, Mummy. It'll be nice there this afternoon.'

That evening Louise told Suzy about her visit to the baths.

'Frankie came over to speak to me before I'd even got in the water, so I introduced him to Mother. I could see she didn't like him. We got into the pool and swam a bit, then Frankie demonstrated some arm movements which he thought would improve my stroke.

'An instant later, Mummy was beckoning me to come out. She said: "That lad's far too familiar with you. He touched you."

' "He just curved my arms and moved them to show me."

' "Quite improper. I don't think you should allow him near you like that. Especially when you are both wearing such skimpy suits."

'You know how her voice carries, I saw Frankie pull himself out of the water on the other side of the baths and move away.

'Mummy said: "Just swim on your own, Louise." But then she grew nervous when she saw me swim right up to the deep end, and was on her feet again, waving to me to come out.

' "It's sixteen feet deep at that end and there's that high diving board above. Anybody could dive off on top of you."

'I hung on to the rail at the side of the bath near her chair and tried to explain: "I'm careful to stay out to the side, out of the way, and there's hardly anyone here, Mummy."

' "I don't think it's safe. It's too deep. You could drown. You really need someone in the water with you to make sure you don't get into difficulties. A woman."

'I just said: "I won't get into difficulties. I've swum up and down lots of times."

' "Just go across the width of the baths today. And you shouldn't stay in too long. Five more minutes should be more than enough."

' "Mummy! I'm perfectly safe."

'But there was nothing I could do about it. Mummy insisted I get out five minutes later, and neither was I allowed to sit around in my damp bathing suit. I was sent to get dressed straight away.

'It's much better at the weekend with you and Penny, but on the way home in the car, Mummy admitted that the baths were far better than she'd expected them to be.'

The summer holidays were approaching. Suzy's classmates were dreading the end of their school days and having to take up jobs as shop assistants or factory workers. Suzy was really looking forward to being employed as Louise's companion and spending more time with her.

Louise said she kept asking her mother and was sure it would happen, but Mrs Smallwood made no definite arrangement with her.

Suzy knew her mother was getting anxious and that ever since they'd come to The Lawns, she'd been dreading the time when Suzy would leave school. They'd both expected then that she'd have to seek work elsewhere and had hoped that if Suzy found a job in a shop or a factory she'd be allowed to sleep here with her mother. If not, her only other option would be to find a job as a live-in housemaid in a similar household.

Mam had thought it too good to be true when Suzy had first told her Mrs Smallwood would employ her, but now Mam was filled with anxiety again.

'She won't want to pay you to play with Louise. Not when you've been doing it for nothing.'

'Lou thinks she will. Ask her for me, Mam.'

During Suzy's last week at school, Josie screwed up her nerve to mention it during her daily audience.

That afternoon, Suzy was summoned to the dining room while the family were having their tea. She'd had nothing but a sandwich at dinner-time and the scent of freshly baked cakes was making her mouth water.

'I understand,' Mrs Smallwood was spreading strawberry jam on her scone, 'that you are leaving school and would like to be employed here?'

'Yes, please, Mrs Smallwood.'

'Louise wants you to be her personal maid and companion. You understand what your duties will be?'

'Yes, ma'am.' She said that just like Mam and Gertie did.

'Louise likes you and you've fitted into the household since you came. I know you help a little in the kitchen. Continue to make yourself useful where you can. Ten shillings a week then, and your keep.'

'Thank you, ma'am.'

Suzy was delighted to have it settled, and counted herself more fortunate than Edna, who had started as a scullery maid, and had to work hard.

Her last day at school came and the following day Suzy took up her duties. She hardly felt she had any. It was what she'd been doing in her leisure hours since she'd first come here. It was what she enjoyed most.

One Saturday, Louise persuaded Penny to talk to their mother about allowing Harold to run both girls to the baths on weekdays. Penny went into action that afternoon when she took the girls home. Louise and Suzy sat on the terrace just out of sight from the open French windows to listen.

'Suzy will be able to stay with Louise the whole time, both in the water and in the changing cubicles.'

'I didn't care for that boy . . .'

'Frankie Rimmer? He's writing this book with Louise.'

'What can a lad like that know about writing books?'

'Anyway, Alec says he's competent at life-saving.'

'Alec? I wouldn't trust anything he says, and that lad is far too familiar with Louise.'

'He seems pleasant and polite, Mother. It's perfectly safe. They're fourteen and Lou's a strong swimmer now.'

'I don't want her mixing with the likes of Alec.'

'He isn't there much in the week. He has work to do.'

'Even Christobel . . . She's a bad influence on her.'

'But swimming is doing Lou the world of good. Anybody can see it is. She's improved so much. She's healthier and stronger.'

Hebe Smallwood couldn't deny the truth of that. So Suzy and Louise were allowed to go alone during the week. Frankie had taught Louise to do backstroke and the fast crawl. With frequent practice she improved even more rapidly. She could swim faster than either of her two sisters and she'd left Suzy a long way behind.

Suzy said: 'And you're also moving more easily out of the water.'

'It's because you're using your leg more,' Frankie told her. 'You're walking well on your own.'

Suzy knew she was writing stories about that too, and was gaining in confidence. Other changes were being planned for Louise. Her mother had finally agreed that she'd outgrown Miss Greenall and Nurse Silk.

'If I'm going to write children's books I need to learn more about literature,' Louise told Suzy. 'And I also want to learn to type.'

It was arranged that when the school holidays were over, a retired schoolmaster would come on three mornings each week to teach her English language and literature, and on the other two days, both Louise and Suzy would go to a private secretarial class to learn to type. Then Suzy would be able to do some of the typing for her.

She was delighted with this. She was afraid a writing career for Louise was all pie in the sky, but if, later on, Mrs Smallwood decided Louise no longer needed her services, Suzy would be able to get a good job in an office.

She sat next to Lou at the playroom table and learned with her. She told her this was much better than going to school. The very latest Remington typewriter arrived on which they could type her stories.

Suzy was sorry to see the summer weather coming to an end. Alec reminded them he was planning to close the baths at the end of September. It was only the beginning of the month but they were having a wet spell, and, though it was her Sunday afternoon off, Mam decided it was already too cold for swimming.

Suzy didn't take regular time off duty. She enjoyed being with Louise – it wasn't like work to her – but today Lou and her mother had been invited to lunch at Penny's house and would spend the rest of the afternoon there.

Mam had been going regularly to Lunar Street to see to Auntie Maisie's needs.

'Are you going today?' Suzy wanted to know.

'Olga will be there herself but I might as well. We can have a gossip.'

'Frankie will be too.' Suzy had seen him yesterday when she and Louise had been swimming. 'I'll come with you.'

Olga let them in and led them back to the living room where Auntie Maisie was sleeping in the armchair by the fire.

'I'm glad you've come, Josie. I'm that worried. I'll make some tea.'

'Where's Frankie?' Suzy asked.

'Out in the yard, sweeping up.'

She found him in the wash house. Frankie jumped with surprise when she opened the door.

'Hello, Suzy. You haven't brought Lou?'

'I wouldn't bring her here. Not to your auntie's house.'

He propped the broom he'd been using against the wall and sat down on a bench.

'D'you realise it's the first time I've seen you on your own for months? You always have Lou with you.'

'I thought you liked her.'

'I do, very much, but sometimes I think it would be nice if it was just you and me. You know, like the old days.'

Suzy perched herself on a board over the washtub.

'There's no keeping you and Lou apart. Every time we go to the baths you've got your heads together.'

'It's this book we're writing. We sort of get engrossed. Wouldn't it be marvellous if . . . D'you think it could be published?'

'Chrissie thinks so, if it's good enough.'

'It's pretty good. The ideas are mine but she's putting it all into words. She does it well.'

'I know, I'm typing it. We'll have to see.'

'That's what Lou says. Let's go somewhere. I've been cooped up here all morning. There's a nice promenade over this side and it's not far away. The river looks different from this side.'

Suzy slid to her feet. 'We used to love the river when we were kids.'

Frankie was striding out, the brisk breeze off the river parting his curly hair. He looked down at her.

'Surely you're entitled to a night off from time to time?'

'Yes, but I haven't taken it because I'd rather stay with Louise than go out by myself.'

'You could come out with me. We could go to the pictures again. It was Easter when we last went. Or there's a dance at the church hall on Saturdays. How about it next week?'

Olga made a pot of tea and sat down at the living-room table with Josie. She kept her voice low so she wouldn't disturb her aunt.

'I'm going to have to do something soon,' she worried. 'Maisie's only coping because you keep coming in the afternoons and Frankie sleeps here at night. I've asked again at the jam factory and they've got a job for him there over the winter, but he's not looking forward to it, and if he isn't going to be here ... Well, I'm wondering whether the time has come ... I'd have to give up my job, and if I did that, I couldn't afford to keep the flat on.

'You've been a brick, Josie, bringing her calf's-foot jelly and custards and that. She tells me your food suits her and is easy to get down, but Maisie really needs someone living here with her all the time.'

Josie said: 'She fell in her bedroom the other day when I was getting her up. Didn't hurt herself, but . . .'

Olga nodded. 'It could happen on the stairs. I've got to make up my mind. I'll either have to take Maisie home with me, or me and Frankie will have to move over here.'

'I'm not leaving this house,' a querulous voice said from the armchair. 'I was born here and I've spent all my life here.'

'I just thought, Auntie, now you're needing a bit of help—'

'I'm staying till I'm carried out in my coffin. So don't ask me to move to Liverpool.'

341

'Right,' Olga said. 'Then Frankie and I had better move in here.'

'I'm an awful trouble to everyone, aren't I? I looked after my mam and dad when they got old, but there's no one to look after me.'

'There is,' Olga said. 'Do you want a cup of tea?'

Suzy and Louise wanted to keep on swimming but the weather was deteriorating and it was no longer much fun. The water seemed suddenly freezing, and it was far too cold to sit about in a swimsuit.

Christobel and Alec still went for a swim most days, but the family virtually had the pool to themselves. For the last week or so, Suzy had been jumping in and swimming about for ten minutes while Louise and Frankie did length after length at top speed. They would get dressed as soon as they got out, and go to the cafeteria for a cup of hot cocoa.

Louise was working hard on the book. She and Frankie always wanted to mull it over and discuss what should happen next. Frankie often had ideas worked out to show her, and Louise was afraid she'd see less of him than she had over the summer.

'Won't it be awful,' Lou lamented to everybody in turn, 'when I can't come to the baths and see Frankie? Our book will grind to a halt.'

'Nonsense,' her mother said. 'You and Suzy can carry on. You don't need him.'

'I do. He has such good ideas.'

The week the baths were closing, Alec asked Frankie if he'd like to work through the winter months as a general handyman and helper in his own house.

'Doing what?' Frankie was surprised.

'Washing cars, cleaning shoes, doing a bit of painting and

decorating. Helping the gardener, a bit of anything that's needed.'

Frankie was delighted. 'Nothing I'd like better. Thank you very much.'

'You'll have to wait until I've had a talk with Mother,' Chrissie told Louise. 'But once I'm married, there'll be no reason why you can't come here to see Frankie.'

Lou threw herself at Alec and hugged him. 'Thank you, thank you, thank you.'

'Thank your sister,' he laughed.

'I might have guessed. You asked Alec to arrange this. Oh, Chrissie, it's just what I need.'

The pile of typescript continued to grow.

Chapter Nineteen

The date of Christobel's birthday grew closer. Louise said: 'I don't know what to give her as a present. Grandma is giving her some pearls that have been in the family for a long time. Mummy says she doesn't deserve anything, but I heard her telling Grandma she has a diamond brooch she could give her. I must give her something but I haven't enough money for jewellery or anything like that.'

'As a wedding present?'

'Well, Alec already has a house and all the furniture for that. Chrissie's keen on handbags, I might get her one, but it's her birthday too. What do you give for birthday presents, Suzy?'

'Home-made sweets and chocolates usually. Mam helped me make some for Frankie's birthday.'

'That's it. Chrissie's always eating chocolates. She'd like that. Would your mother help me?'

'Yes, of course. But you'd need a box to put them in. When Mam worked in a hotel in Liverpool, she used to bring home chocolate boxes if the guests threw them out.'

'Perhaps I can buy one, or . . . I think Grandma's got one. Gramps bought her a huge box of chocs on their wedding anniversary a few weeks ago. She's very slow in eating them, but she might let me have the box if I ask her.'

Louise and Suzy spent several afternoons in the kitchen with Mam, who showed them how to make all manner of sweets from dried cherries in marzipan to fruit pastilles, chocolate creams and several sorts of toffee.

Mam provided little paper cases and Grandma gave Louise the box. Fortunately, it was a plain casket with a bow of pink ribbon on top and there was no mention of the original contents.

Penny talked to her mother about Chrissie's wedding every time she saw her. Louise was delighted when it was agreed she could go.

'You'll be coming with me,' she told Suzy. 'Mummy thinks I'll need you. She says weddings are very tiring and she's afraid none of the family will think about me.'

'I'd love that.'

'I was supposed to be Penny's bridesmaid, but I had to be carried down the aisle after her because I could hardly walk at all then. She gave me her bouquet to hold, though. At Georgina's wedding, I walked and held her train but she said I nearly pulled it off her head and Mummy was on tenterhooks because she thought I'd fall. I was hoping to do it properly for Chrissie, but now she's having this register office wedding. Mummy's against it – doesn't think it right.'

'Wouldn't she be against anything Chrissie does now?'

'That's what Penny said. She told Mummy she should be grateful that Alec's making an honest woman of her. Have you ever been a bridesmaid?'

'Yes, it was a register office wedding too. There was no bridal bouquet or anything like that.'

Suzy remembered that Mam had told her she mustn't say a word about Nosey to anyone, and shut up.

Louise was off again. 'I've never been to Alec's house either. Mummy made me promise never to go there until Chrissie was married. I'm dying to see it.'

Suzy would have been very disappointed if Louise had planned to leave her behind, but she was worried about what she could wear. She consulted her mother.

It was mid-September, and though the weather had turned cool and damp, Mam said: 'It would be all right to wear the straw hat I bought you for my—'

She was biting on her lip, and looking so down, Suzy was reminded that her marriage had not been the real thing.

She said: 'I can't get into that blue dress any more, I tried at the beginning of this summer. I've grown too much.'

'The only other possibility is that hat and coat I bought you in the sales last January. It still looks new. If it gets any colder I think that would be best.'

'It's a very ordinary hat, just a sort of tam,' Suzy protested.

'It's not going to be a dressy wedding,' Gertie said briskly, 'and you mustn't look smarter than Louise.'

'No danger of that. A dressmaker is making her a completely new outfit. It's to be of royal blue velvet.'

'I'll lend you the frock Chrissie gave me,' Edna offered. 'If you'd like it?'

'Will it fit her?' Mam wanted to know.

'It fits almost anyone because it has a dropped waist, but that's a bit old-fashioned now. Waists are back where they should be.'

Edna ran to fetch it straight away and Suzy tried it on in the kitchen. 'It fits, doesn't it?'

'Yes,' they agreed.

'It feels loose and floaty.'

'That style is supposed to be loose,' Mam told her. 'It looks quite nice on you, doesn't it, Edna? Why don't we say that you'll wear this with your straw hat if it's a warm day, and if it's cold, you can wear your coat over it, with your tam.'

Suzy was satisfied with that. She heard from Louise that she and Penny were doing their best to talk their mother and grandparents into accepting Chrissie's invitations.

'After all,' Louise pointed out, 'she'll only get married once and it'll be a shame to miss it.'

'I don't approve of that man. Letting her live with him like that. I'm shocked that any daughter of mine—'

'He's doing the right thing by marrying her now,' Penny pointed out. 'And on the first possible day he can, her twenty-first birthday. No harm's been done if they marry, Mother. He said he wasn't expecting any trouble, they've been following the advice of Marie Stopes—'

'Don't mention the name of that disgusting woman in my house. She's notorious. I won't have it. Where have you heard about her?'

'Mother, I'm a married woman and—'

'Not in front of Louise!'

'Well, you should be happy she's getting married, and put your quarrels behind you. Chrissie wants you to come.'

Chrissie's mother and grandparents came round sufficiently to say they'd attend the register office.

'Just to make sure it's all legal and above board,' Penny said up in the playroom. 'But Chrissie will be pleased they're coming.'

It turned out a cool, overcast day. Suzy wore her coat and tam. Gertie had given her a feathered brooch to pin in it to liven it up. Louise looked beautiful with her flaxen curls showing below her velvet bonnet.

Harold drove the family down to the town hall and Suzy went with them. Mam usually had an hour or so off, but this afternoon Gertie and Edna had been given time off too, and they were planning to go down to Hamilton Square and see if they too could get in to see the ceremony. Chrissie saw them on the steps as she arrived, and ushered them all inside ahead of her.

The ceremony was simple and over very quickly, there

being little of the tradition and pomp of a church marriage, but Suzy thought it a much more stylish occasion than Mam's wedding. There were several expensive cars lined up outside and quite a number of smartly dressed guests. Chrissie looked her beautiful best in her scarlet suit and a tiny matching hat mostly of veiling. She carried a small posy of cream roses.

They posed for photographs and after they'd watched Alec drive off to the wedding reception with Chrissie, old boots and tin cans jangling from the back bumper, the party from The Lawns headed back towards Harold and the limousine.

'You might as well come and inspect the house,' Penny told her mother. 'You haven't seen it so you must be curious, and it's Chrissie's home now. Well, it has been for some time, but it's official now.'

'Of course we're coming,' Gramps said. 'Come along, Hebe.'

'It's a lovely house,' Suzy whispered to Louise.

It was lighter and brighter than The Lawns, furnished with modern furniture and sumptuous carpets with masses of flowers everywhere.

Mrs Smallwood walked round all the rooms on the ground floor and, after one glass of champagne, prepared to leave half an hour later.

'Not yet,' Gramps told her irritably. 'Your mother's enjoying herself.'

'I'll send Harold back with the car for you. Louise, you're to come back with your grandparents.'

'Mother! No, I want to stay on.' Suzy knew she was expecting the party to go on until late.

Alec said: 'Of course she does. We've hardly started yet.'

'You mustn't get overtired. Suzy, you make sure she doesn't. And don't overstay your welcome here.'

'She'll never do that,' Chrissie laughed. 'It's a big occasion for me. I've a lot to celebrate, haven't I? Oh, and tomorrow morning, we're setting off to Paris and then going on to the South of France.' She sighed with delight. 'It'll be a fabulous honeymoon. Have you booked your grand tour, Mother?'

'Not yet,' she retorted.

Chrissie laughed again. 'Never mind, as Mrs Landis I'm respectable again.'

'That remains to be seen,' were her mother's last words as she headed down the front steps.

Alec announced that it was time to have the wedding breakfast. There was a magnificent buffet meal set out on the dining-room table to which the guests helped themselves. There were two cakes side by side, a wedding cake and a birthday cake. They were both the same size, but one was decorated with coloured fondant flowers and a silver key, while the other had silver horseshoes and swags of flowers in white icing and tiny figures of a bride and groom on top. Suzy ate a generous slice of birthday cake which was all cream and light sponge inside, and managed only a sliver of wedding cake, which was a traditional rich fruit cake.

She thought the bride and groom were both happy and excited, and Alec was looking at Christobel with such love in his eyes. She couldn't understand why Mrs Smallwood had taken against him. He took her and Louise, together with several other guests, upstairs to a room where the presents had all been set out.

Louise pointed to the casket which she'd filled with home-made sweets.

'That was Chrissie's birthday present.'

He smiled. 'She knows that.' He lifted the lid and Lou was delighted to see that half the top layer had already been eaten.

'Chrissie couldn't leave them alone,' he told her. 'She brought them here to remove temptation from the bedroom. She said there'd be so much other rich food today.'

'I love the house,' Louise breathed after he'd given them a whirlwind tour. 'It's not as big as The Lawns, but it's much smarter.'

'The views are lovely here,' Suzy breathed.

'Right across the river to Liverpool.'

Afterwards there was music and dancing and everybody congratulated Louise, who managed to keep up with the best of them.

Two weeks later, Louise and Suzy were in the back of the limousine having been picked up from their typing lesson by Harold.

Lou sighed: 'Do you really like learning to type?'

'Love it,' Suzy grinned at her, her pleasure in it obvious.

'You're better at it than I am.'

'Mam reckons I'm very lucky to be having lessons like this.'

'I need to learn, of course – a writer must be able to type – but I don't like it much. I make a lot of mistakes.'

'I'll be doing most of your typing for you.'

Louise stared out of the window as the car travelled its familiar route home.

'All the same, it's hard work. I hate figures. I told Miss Jones I didn't need to learn to type columns of figures, but she said I had to.'

'It's her job to turn us into typists, and she's going to do it whether we like it or not.'

'Suzy, you're always so happy with your lot. Content with what you get in life.'

At moments like this Louise felt ashamed. She knew she

was more fortunate than Suzy in many ways, but she was never satisfied and always wanted more. She said: 'I wish Chrissie and Alec were back.'

Suzy laughed. 'It won't be what they want. I bet they're having a lovely time.'

'I know. I'm being selfish. Alec said he thought physiotherapy might help my leg.'

'When did he mention that? At their wedding?'

'At the party afterwards. He said he injured his knee when he was skiing one year and found it helpful. He said he'd fix me up to have a few sessions when he got back.'

Louise no longer wore her leg iron. She could manage without it now, but though her leg was getting stronger she felt disappointed. She stretched both legs out in front of her in the car and pulled her skirt up. Compared with her good leg, the other still looked wasted and withered.

'It looks awful, doesn't it?'

'It's looking better than it did, and you don't get as tired as you used to. You're getting better, you just have to carry on with your exercises and be patient.'

'I'm glad longer skirts are fashionable now.' Lou knew she sounded grumpy. 'At least I can hide it.'

The date of Chrissie's return came and went.

The next morning, Louise went to her typing class, and when she returned and the family were having lunch, her mother said: 'Christobel's home again. She's been round to see us this morning.'

'And Alec?' Louise asked.

'No.' The chill was still there as far as Alec was concerned. 'They had an excellent holiday.'

Gramps said: 'She wants you to go down and see her. She thinks physiotherapy might help your leg. If you'd like to try it, she'll arrange it for you.'

Louise felt pleased that Alec hadn't forgotten. 'I'd love to. I'll try anything. Is it all right if I go this afternoon?'

'I suppose so,' her mother said. 'But I need the car. Harold can run you there if you send him straight back for me.'

When Louise left the table she went up to the playroom to wait for Suzy, feeling quite excited.

'Chrissie's home. She's been to see Mummy.'

'I know. Edna told me.'

'What else did she say?'

'Nothing much. The colonel left his wireless on, though he went to have coffee in the drawing room with Chrissie. Gertie thinks now she's married they've made it up and everything's back to normal.'

'Well, almost. I'm jolly glad, because I'm allowed to see her again. Get your hat and coat, Harold's going to drop us at her house now.'

Louise was delighted to find Alec had arranged twice-weekly sessions for her with the same physiotherapist that had treated him. Suzy went along with her the next day, and was shown how she could help by putting Louise through some basic movements each day.

Although Lou had seen Christobel throughout the summer at the baths, she felt she hadn't had as much of her company as she would have liked. She'd missed her.

Suzy found the atmosphere in Chrissie's house more relaxed than at The Lawns. She and her husband were out to enjoy life and they meant Louise to enjoy it too.

They were always suggesting trips out. Alec had a sailing boat so there were frequent trips upriver in that. There were picnic lunches on board, and visits to theatres and cinemas.

Suzy was usually included. Louise felt dismayed to see Suzy so clearly thrilled and telling everybody she was having the time of her life.

Of course she was glad that Suzy was happy, but for herself she felt she needed a lot more. There were two things she was obsessional about: getting her leg to a normal state, so she could walk and dance like everybody else, and writing her book. She was hoping against hope that one day it would be published.

As the weeks went by, Louise enjoyed her English lessons and felt her typing was improving. She was keen to learn all she could to help her make a career writing books.

She was now deemed old enough to have a pocket money allowance and she could get round the shops. She wasn't allowed a totally free hand when it came to choosing her own clothes, but if she saw a dress she liked, Mother could often be persuaded to buy it for her. She was allowed to get Harold to run her and Suzy into town, and if he was needed by another member of the family they took a taxi back.

One day, when they were in a bookshop, Louise picked up a book about a nurse called Agnes Hunt, who was herself a cripple. She bought it and settled down to read it as soon as she got home.

She was enthralled. 'Oh, Suzy, she offers such hope.'

'What for?' Suzy was retyping some of her manuscript.

'A cure. Agnes Hunt came from a rich family and had the same horrible disease I had when she was a child. She was treated by a Liverpool orthopaedic surgeon called Sir Robert Jones and could then walk well. But she felt so sorry for the poor crippled children she saw on the streets, she wanted to help them walk too.'

'I think I've heard about her before. When was this?'

'About the turn of the century.'

'That's history...'

'Let me tell you. This man Robert Jones was operating on crippled children and curing them, and she persuaded him to operate without payment on those whose parents couldn't afford it. She built a hospital at her own expense at Gobowen – well, not a hospital exactly. There's a picture of it here, look. She says it was just huts and corrugated iron shelters for her cots and beds; but that it helped the children to be nursed in the fresh air. She ran the hospital at her own expense too.' Louise pushed the book into Suzy's hands. 'You read it and tell me what you think. Perhaps they could cure me.'

'Is the hospital still there?'

'Yes. The huts and shelters formed the basis of an orthopaedic hospital and it's grown quite big. It's a voluntary hospital now, you know. They hold flag days and that to raise money for it.'

'But you're getting better, Lou. You can walk very well.'

'I get tired more quickly than you do, and I have to wear a shoe with a built-up sole. I'm not cured. Not completely. Read the book.'

Lou pushed it on her; she watched Suzy's eyes travelling across the pages and tried to be patient. Hours later, Suzy looked up, frowning. 'I don't know. It doesn't say he cured everybody, not gave them perfect limbs.'

'It offers hope, doesn't it? Strong hope.'

Louise could see the doubt on Suzy's face. She thought she was hoping for too much.

'It was a long time ago. I mean, is he still—'

'I do so want to have normal legs.'

With Suzy in tow, she went to find her mother and put the book into her hand. 'Read it, Mummy. It says this orthopaedic surgeon is specially interested in children, that he's cured hundreds of them. He operates on them and they can walk again. Perhaps he can cure me.'

'Louise, you've had two operations. Dr Howarth says in your case, nothing more can be done.'

'But it sounds as though Sir Robert Jones can do more.'

'I'm afraid he might not, dear. I know you dream of a complete cure but it isn't possible for everybody.'

'If you read the book, you'd see what I mean.'

Mrs Smallwood agreed to read it, but she gave it back to Louise the next day. Her opinion hadn't changed.

'I don't think any more can be done for you. Truly, dear, I wish it could. You've seen the best doctors in Liverpool.'

'This man is said to be the best in Britain, and I haven't seen him.'

Louise took the book to Christobel and even persuaded Alec to look at it.

He said: 'He may not be able to do anything for you, Lou, but there's no reason why you shouldn't see him if he's still working. That's the only way to find out definitely whether he can help you.'

She bit her lip. 'Surgeons are trying new treatments all the time, aren't they?'

'I don't know. He must be an old man by now, Lou.'

Christobel said: 'We'd better do it through Dr Howarth. He's organised things for you up to now. It'll look as though we're going behind his back if we don't. Mother will be cross if we upset him.'

She took her sister to see Dr Howarth and asked him to make the appointment for her with Robert Jones.

He looked dour. 'He can do nothing more for you, Louise.'

'Have you heard of this man?'

'Yes, he's a very eminent orthopaedic surgeon. Of the first order.'

'I've read about him – that he operates with great success

on children who've had the same disease I've had. On children with fractures that were never set and—'

'That's the whole point, Louise. These were poor children who'd received no prior treatment at all. They'd been left to lie on their beds, or pull themselves round as best they could. He operates on them as charity cases and the hospital looks after them for nothing.'

'Does he not take cases who would pay him?'

'Indeed he does, but you've already had the treatment he could provide. You've made great strides, Louise. You are so much better. Your leg is stronger and you can manage without your leg brace. I'm afraid there's nothing that can make it absolutely perfect.'

Louise turned pleading eyes at her sister, and was relieved when Christobel insisted on having the appointment made. Christobel understood just how much this meant to her.

'There's no need for you to go down to Gobowen. Mr Jones sees private patients at his house in Rodney Street, and he's had a consultancy at the Royal Southern Hospital in Liverpool for years.'

Christobel went back to The Lawns with Louise to break the news to their mother. Hebe Smallwood was not pleased.

'I don't know why you want to interfere, Christobel. This is none of your business. Everything possible has been done for Louise already. I've made sure of that.'

'Mother, new advances are being made—'

'It will do you no good, Louise. Dr Howarth assures me of that. So does Nurse Silk. You're wasting everybody's time.'

Louise felt deflated. She and Chrissie went up to the playroom afterwards to tell Suzy.

Louise said: 'I suppose I've just got to accept the way I am. That I'll always have to have one clodhopping shoe.'

Suzy rested her chin on her hands and looked at her. 'Even

if you do, who is going to notice your shoe when you have such a pretty face? And you've got sisters who love you and do their best to get you what you want. And you can swim like a fish.'

'And dive a bit,' Chrissie put in.

'Mummy went for you. I'm sorry.'

'I'm used to that.'

'I want you both to get on . . .'

'Suzy's right, you've got to look on the bright side, Lou. You're writing a book and you love doing that. And if, when it's finished it's good enough, Laurence will help you get it published.'

To Louise, hearing it said aloud like that made it seem possible. It would be absolutely wonderful, and if she could be a published writer she might be able to accept that her leg would never be perfect.

Suzy said: 'You've got a lot going for you.'

'You're right, I have.' A lot more than Suzy and her mother had.

'I'm never satisfied, am I? But I really would love to have two normal legs.'

Two weeks later, Alec and Christobel took Louise to keep the appointment with Robert Jones. The surgeon seemed a very old man, but Lou took to him straight away.

'I think I could help,' he said slowly. 'This poor leg here is now about three-quarters of an inch shorter than the other. I could try to make it the same length. I could certainly reduce the difference. That would help you to walk more normally and you wouldn't need your shoe built up.'

Lou felt hope mushrooming inside her. It was arranged that the operation should be done in a private nursing home in two weeks' time. She felt euphoric on the journey home.

* * *

On Sunday morning, a week later, when Josie was in the dining room getting her instructions for the day, Mrs Smallwood said: 'You've been with us for well over a year now, Josephine. You remember you're entitled to a week's paid holiday?'

That pleased her. 'Yes, ma'am.'

'I shall be going to London for a few days next week, so it would be convenient if you took it then. And since Louise will be going into hospital, Suzy might as well take her holiday with you. It's your half-day today, so you can start your holiday as soon as you've cooked lunch.'

Josie was so taken aback she said: 'It doesn't give me much time. To arrange holiday lodgings, I mean.' She would have liked more notice. Neither would she have chosen to take her holiday in November, given any choice.

'You can stay in your room here, Josephine, if that's what you want.'

Josie gasped: 'Thank you, ma'am.'

She had a little money saved. She and Suzy deserved a break, but where could they go now it was so cold?

'She's got a nerve.' Gertie was indignant when Josie told her. 'Jumping it on you without notice. It's because she's taking Mrs Ingram to stay with Georgina in London for a few days.'

'With only the colonel here, she thinks I'll be sitting around taking things easy.'

'I always ask for my week in July, to go and stay with my sister in Southport. I told you to ask for yours.'

'I did. I asked if I could have my holiday when Suzy left school. She said it wasn't convenient then and I could have it later.'

'You should have kept on at her, Josie.'

Suzy was very surprised. Nothing had been said directly to her. 'Where will we go, Mam?'

'Where would you like to go?'

'London. I've always wanted to go there.' Her eyes were wide with anticipation. 'There'd be lots to do, even in winter. I'd love to see Buckingham Palace and the Tower, and there're the theatres and big shops. Frankie's always talking about going.'

'Talk is what Frankie does best.' Josie smiled ruefully. 'Being with Louise all the time is giving you ideas above your station. London's a long way and it'll be expensive to get lodgings there. Perhaps Chester? Cheaper to get there, and there'd be theatres and shops and museums too.'

Suzy's disappointment was evident on her face. 'I've got some money.'

Josie said gently: 'What we've got won't go far in London.'

Suzy smiled. 'Anywhere would be a nice change, wouldn't it? You need a rest, Mam. It's different for me. I've only just started work, and it seems like one long holiday.'

Josie was so glad Suzy had found her niche. She was growing up into a lovely girl. Tall and graceful now, she was losing her baby fat. Her face was leaner and her features more finely drawn. She was becoming more attractive.

Josie felt very fortunate; having a daughter like Suzy was helping her accept the loss of her son. Talking about him to Olga was too. There were times when she still hankered to know Robert's present whereabouts but she knew she never would. She had to put him out of her mind and think only of Suzy.

As it was Josie's half-day, they both went down to Auntie Maisie's house in Lunar Street. It being a Sunday, they knew Olga and Frankie would be there.

A cosy fire burned in the living-room grate, but Olga and Frankie were alone. Maisie wasn't feeling well and had said she wanted to stay in bed.

'I'll get her up for an hour or so this evening. She can have her tea in front of the fire.'

Olga's cheeks were rosier than usual. 'I'm glad you've come. I wanted to tell you . . .' Tension showed in her overbright eyes. 'I've done it. I've given in my notice at work.'

'Olga!'

'Can't expect you and Frankie to do everything. Not for ever. I've had a long talk with Auntie. She wants me to clear out all her parents' stuff to make more space. She said she hadn't the energy to do it herself when they died, but now she says she wants me to come and live with her. Poor old Maisie, she's failing. I think she's afraid of being left on her own. She can't manage the stairs by herself.'

When Josie told them Mrs Smallwood had given her and Suzy a holiday, Frankie whooped.

'I wish you were staying here, Suzy. We could go out every night.'

'Next week?' Olga could hardly get her words out she was so excited. 'I hardly like to ask you, you've been so good all these months, but, Josie, I'd love you both to come and stay here. I couldn't see how I was going to do it, pack everything up in the flat and clear out all the stuff here to make room. I know I shouldn't ask . . . You need a rest.'

Josie smiled. 'Of course we'll help, won't we, Suzy? Mrs Smallwood only told me this morning, so we've not been able to make any plans.'

'Are you sure? Frankie and I, we'll both be out at work. We'll be leaving all the hard graft here to you two.'

'Of course I'm sure.'

In a way Josie was relieved. She wouldn't have to make any decisions nor spend the little money she'd managed to save. Planning a holiday was part of the enjoyment, and this one had been sprung on her.

'You'll have to tell us what you want us to do,' Suzy said.

'We'll have a cup of tea, and then we'll start sorting through the stuff in the third bedroom now.' Olga lowered the kettle on to the fire.

'You can sleep here tonight.' Frankie was all smiles. 'I'll move to the sofa in the parlour. There's a double bed, so there'll be room for both of you.'

Josie shook her head. 'We'll have to go home for our things, so we might as well stay overnight at The Lawns. We'll come back in the morning.'

Olga said: 'That'll give me time to put clean sheets on the bed.'

It was a very busy week for Josie. They cleared out the accumulated household bric-à-brac of decades, sorting it into what Olga might want to keep, what might be useful to others, and what was rubbish.

The room had not been used for years and was so dirty that Frankie and Suzy had to spend two evenings white-washing the walls and repainting the woodwork. Then they turned their attention to the parlour.

'Maisie never used this room much,' said Olga, who was coming over on some evenings after work. 'She said I could get rid of this horsehair sofa. I want to bring some of my own things over.'

By midweek, Josie went to stay in Olga's flat to help her pack up there. Frankie and Suzy went to the pictures on Wednesday night and on Thursday they went to see Louise in the nursing home. She looked a bit washed out but said her operation had been a success.

'My legs are both the same length. I'm thrilled.' She couldn't stop smiling. 'Totally thrilled.'

'It might take a bit of time to get back on your feet again,' Frankie cautioned.

'I know it will, but I'll work at it.'

Suzy said: 'You're very brave, facing an operation like that.'

'I welcomed it. I'd rather face that over again than a permanent limp.'

Frankie brought out some pages of manuscript he'd prepared. 'Here's something for you to work on when we've gone, Lou.'

'You've had time to do that too?' Suzy was amazed.

'Did it sitting in Alec's potting shed. He doesn't mind. Not if it's for Lou.'

On the train going back to Rock Ferry, Suzy said: 'You're very attentive to Louise.'

'Everybody is, you included.'

'I'm paid to be. I'm her personal maid and companion.'

'Even if you weren't paid, Suzy, you would be. You like her.'

'Yes,' she admitted readily. 'She's my friend.'

'I like her too,' Frankie said. 'But she's my working partner. You're my friend.'

By Friday evening, Olga had worked out her week's notice and a van had been hired for Saturday morning to take all her belongings over to Rock Ferry.

By Saturday evening, Frankie's bed had been erected in the third bedroom, and Olga's sofa installed in the parlour. They had time to indulge in their usual pastime over the special dinner Josie cooked for them.

'They've never found Luke Palmer,' Olga ruminated. 'Isn't that strange?'

'Mam,' Frankie said softly, 'don't remind them.'

Josie tried to smile. 'I can't get him out of my mind. I'm always wondering what he's doing and where he's living. When I'm out in the street or the shops, I find myself looking round half expecting to see him. I have this horrible feeling that he's near and watching me and I can't throw it off. I won't feel safe until I know he's under lock and key.'

'He should hang for it.' The colour had drained from Olga's cheeks. 'Attacking Frankie and killing Eric like that. I can't forgive . . .'

Suzy's mouth was set in a straight line. 'You'd think the police would find him. A murderer at large all this time.'

Olga shuddered. 'He could attack someone else. Kill someone else.'

'That's what I'm afraid of,' Josie said quietly.

Suzy said: 'You're afraid it's me he might come after, aren't you, Mam?'

'Or me. It makes my flesh creep every time I think of him.'

'I don't see how he can find you,' Frankie said firmly. 'And if he hasn't in all this time, he never will.'

Josie sighed. 'At least you're over it now, and looking very tanned and fit.'

'That's being beside the pool all summer.'

'Do come often to see us,' Olga said when they were packing their things to return to The Lawns. 'I don't know anybody else on this side of the water.'

Josie was pleased to have her friend living so much closer. 'It'll be lovely to come for a gossip when I have time off.'

Chapter Twenty

To be back at The Lawns and typing the book seemed like a rest-cure to Suzy.

Louise came home from hospital and her sisters came often to see her. She found she'd lost some of the strength she'd built up.

'You'll be fine in a few weeks,' Chrissie told her. 'You need time to get over the operation.'

She was working harder than ever on the book now it was almost finished. Mrs Smallwood even allowed Frankie to come to the playroom to finalise the last chapters.

They had a wonderful Christmas and New Year, and by January the book was finished.

Chrissie had been reading it chapter by chapter. Now Alec and Penny read it and thoroughly approved. Suzy parcelled it up and posted it off to Gina.

A week later, Gina's husband rang Louise and said he thought her book had possibilities. He explained that he didn't handle children's books but he knew somebody who did and had given it to him to read.

No sooner was January over, than Suzy and Louise were admiring the clothes and equipment Chrissie was buying for her first skiing holiday. Alec had made bookings for them to go to Klosters in Switzerland at the end of February.

'You'll have a wonderful time,' Lou said enviously.

'I won't be able to keep up with Alec. He's done a lot of skiing and he's good at it. I shall be in the beginners' class.'

'But you want to try?'

'Oh yes, of course, I'm thrilled. Alec has bought me some skates and a skating dress.'

'You're good at all sports, Chrissie. You'll soon catch him up and be as good as he is.'

'I hope so,' she smiled. 'I want to go high on the mountains with him. He says it's a marvellous feeling.'

Whenever Suzy went with Louise to see her these days, Christobel seemed to be doing exercises.

'I'm strengthening my muscles ready for skiing,' she told them. 'Legs and arms and shoulders. Come on, both of you. Do them with me.'

'I'll never be able to ski,' Lou mourned.

'And I'll never get the chance to try,' Suzy added. She didn't want Lou to feel she was the only one denied that pleasure.

'Maybe not, but it wouldn't hurt either of you to have stronger legs.'

Christobel was very keen on fresh air and exercise, and spent many hours each week walking, swimming, sailing and playing tennis. She also loved to dance.

Suzy thought it was her way of keeping fit and strong and that she was afraid of ill health because she'd seen what Louise had to put up with.

Suzy tried to imagine what a skiing holiday would be like. Alec's skis were brought down and oiled. Christobel brought out some photographs of Alec posing against a snowy mountain backdrop. Chrissie could think of nothing else, and her anticipation grew to fever heat so the others both felt it.

Then suddenly they were gone. The staff, including Frankie, were given a holiday at the same time. The Landises were expected to be away for three weeks. After a fortnight, Louise said she was mulling over ideas for another book and wanted to discuss them with Frankie.

'Try phoning him,' Suzy suggested. 'He's had his holiday.' She'd seen him twice. 'He should be back working at Chrissie's house now. Alec wanted a greenhouse built. He was to keep an eye on progress and do some gardening.'

Louise tried, but nobody picked up the receiver at the other end.

'He'll be outside. Probably can't hear it.'

'I feel at a loose end with no book to write. I need to talk to Frankie. We'll go this afternoon. You arrange with Harold to take us.'

The car drew up in the road outside Alec and Chrissie's house, and both the girls got out. The house was all locked up, but there were three men erecting a new greenhouse at the bottom of the garden. Suzy asked if they'd seen Frankie.

'You've just missed him. He's gone into Birkenhead on a message for us. We're short of glass – some pieces missing. He left only ten minutes ago.'

Lou was disappointed and turned to Suzy. 'What do we do now?'

'Leave a message to say we'll be back tomorrow. If he knows we're coming he'll be here.'

They walked slowly back to the car. 'Where now?' Harold asked.

'We could go to the pictures,' Lou suggested.

But by the time they'd been dropped in town, the matinée performance at the Scala was well advanced and the big picture had already started. Louise decided against going in and went shopping instead. They walked round Robb's, the big department store, but by then she was tired and not in the mood to buy anything.

Going home, Suzy squeezed her arm. 'Everything's falling a bit flat today.'

'It certainly is.'

When Louise let them both in with her key, her mother was using the telephone in the hall.

They heard her say: 'You need someone with you, dear, at a time like this.'

As soon as the front door closed behind them, Suzy felt a new and profound tension.

'Something's happened,' she whispered, catching at Louise's arm. 'Something terrible.'

Mrs Smallwood was weeping. 'You'll never manage, not alone. You need support. I'll try and arrange—'

'What's happened, Mummy?' Louise was ignored.

'You must be feeling dreadful, such a shock. I am myself.'

The colonel was at the drawing-room door, his voice booming through the house as usual, sounding very upset. 'I wish you'd calm down, Hebe. You're making such a fuss and it doesn't help. I thought you didn't like him. You were against the girl marrying him in the first place.

'What's that, Alma? Speak up. Of course I'm sorry for Christobel, but all this breast-beating and panic isn't helping.'

Louise's face creased with concern as she headed towards her grandparents. 'I'll find out what's happened, Suzy.'

Suzy hung back. When Lou joined her family, she couldn't barge in with her. Friend and companion she might be, but Mrs Smallwood had told her the family had to have some privacy. Neither could she stand here in the hall and listen to their conversation.

She heard Lou ask: 'Something's wrong. What's happened, Gramps?'

'It's Alec, he's been killed.'

Suzy felt rooted to the spot in horror. When she got herself to the kitchen, Mam and Edna were sitting at the table. All work had stopped. Edna was in tears, her sympathy for

Christobel overflowing as she whispered to Suzy: 'Alec's been killed in a skiing accident.'

Suzy's mouth was dry. She'd already gathered that much. 'What about Chrissie?'

'She's all right. She was having a lesson with the beginners. She's distraught. This is the second time she's phoned home.'

Suzy swallowed hard. 'I thought Alec was good at skiing.'

'He was, but this morning he went further up the mountain with two other expert skiers and they got caught in an avalanche.'

The phone had been put down but the family were all in the hall now.

Mrs Smallwood was weeping. 'I can't bear to think of this happening. I know what I went through when my husband died. I was bereft. The poor child, all alone in a foreign country, miles away from family and friends.'

'She's forgiven her, you see,' Edna whispered. 'She's in quite a state. Agitated.'

'So would you be. Put the kettle on. She'll ask for tea in a minute,' Josie answered. 'I feel agitated myself.'

'So do I,' Edna agreed. 'Such a shock.'

The colonel was heard to blow his nose. 'If Christobel needs help, I'll go to her.'

'What could you do?' His daughter's tone was withering. 'She needs looking after. You'd be more of a liability. You're an old man.'

'Go yourself then, Hebe. You're a woman in her prime.'

'Oh! I couldn't possibly! I daren't think of it – all those foreigners. It would make me really ill. He'd no business to take her off to the other side of the world.'

'It's not the other side of the world, don't be silly. I do wish you'd calm down.'

'I wish you'd stop telling me to calm down and *do* something.'

Louise was doubling up with shock and grief. 'Alec was lovely. To think of him dead . . .'

The phone was ringing again. Her mother leaped to lift it up.

'Yes, yes. It's the international operator again, Father. Yes, yes, put her through.'

'Hello, dear. . . . Yes, I know you're upset. Such a shock. You need somebody to help you. I'll ask Haydn. . . . The vicar dear, Haydn Ingleby-Jones. He'll be more than willing if I ask him. . . . No, listen. . . . He'd be ideal, a great comfort to you at a time like this. Really, dear he would. It's what you need. . . . Talk to Gramps? Yes, of course, but he'll advise the same.'

Louise saw her mother gulp with distress and wipe away a tear. 'She wants you, Father.'

The shock had stiffened poor Colonel Ingram. It was an effort for him to pull himself to his feet. 'Is she asking for me? She knows I don't like telephones. Can't hear properly . . . All right.

'Christobel dear, I'm so sorry, terribly upsetting. . . . Speak up. . . . Yes, that's right, get yourself home as soon as you can. . . . Tomorrow evening? What's that? . . . I can't get. . . . Let me put Louise on. She'll tell me what you want. What was that? . . . Write it down? All right.'

Louise felt rigid as she took the receiver. 'Hello, Chrissie,' she said. A pencil and pad was pushed in front of her. She began to write.

'Get Gramps to book an undertaker to meet your train, yes I've got that. . . . You're bringing Alec home with you, yes. . . . You're coming over on the boat train, and can catch a connection that'll be due at Woodside at six twenty tomorrow evening. . . . Yes, I'll ask him to do it right away and ring you back to confirm. Tell me your number again.' Louise gasped. 'Oh, Chrissie, what a terrible thing to happen.'

'What's she saying?' her mother demanded.

Louise covered her other ear in order to concentrate on what her sister was saying.

'I'm too upset,' Christobel told her. 'I can't cope with Mother at the moment. Don't let her come fussing to the station, for God's sake. I couldn't stand it. And I don't want Haydn Ingleby-Jones anywhere near me. I want the funeral to be at St Peter's. That was Alec's church, anyway.'

'I'll bring Harold to meet the train tomorrow.'

'Gramps too, if he wants to come. Don't forget to ring me back to let me know you've got an undertaker to meet the train with a hearse.'

'I won't.'

'Thank goodness you keep your wits about you, Lou. It's impossible to talk to Mother.'

'See you tomorrow,' Louise choked.

She wiped away a tear as she put the phone down. She'd been fond of Alec. Whatever Mother's opinion, he'd been ever thoughtful for her, and Chrissie had loved him. Poor, poor Chrissie, a widow after less than six months of marriage and still only twenty-one years old.

Gramps went to the telephone. Louise took her mother to the drawing room.

'Christobel will have to come and stay here,' Mrs Smallwood fussed. 'She's closed up her house and given the staff three weeks' holiday. I knew that would be too much. She should have kept them there to give the place a spring clean in her absence. Ring for Gertrude, dear. I must get her to make Christobel's room ready for her.'

'Let's have a cup of tea first, Mummy. We could all do with it.'

'Oh dear, dear, dear. Christobel doesn't know what she's doing. The poor girl can't think straight.'

'She seems to have everything organised at her end, Mummy.'

For Louise, the next day was a grim one, waiting for her sister to come home. Now she was here, Louise couldn't take her eyes from her. She'd never seen Christobel look so listless. She was white-faced and had eaten almost nothing at dinner. Louise felt desperately sorry for her.

'I knew there'd be another accident.' Mother couldn't stop twittering, and Louise could see she was getting on Chrissie's nerves. 'Everything comes in threes. Your grandfather said I was fatalistic but I was right. There's been another accident.'

Chrissie roused herself from her torpor. 'Not to me, Mother.'

'No, thank goodness. I'll take you shopping tomorrow to choose your mourning.'

'No!'

'What? Surely you'll need help to choose your clothes? At a time like this, you can't be in the right frame of mind, not to make decisions like that.'

'I'm not.'

'Have you got black? You'll need to outfit yourself for a year. I've never seen you wear—'

'It would depress me more to wear black. I won't. What's the point? It won't bring Alec back.'

Louise knew their mother was shocked. 'But what will the neighbours think?'

'Your neighbours won't see much of me. I think I'll go home.'

'Stay here for a week or two. Let's get the funeral over. There's one good thing, you'll be left a rich widow.'

The colonel tutted. 'We don't know what's in Alec's will, Hebe, or even if he left one.'

'He's no one else to leave it to.'

'We don't even know that.'

'Do you know, Christobel? As his wife you'll get a substantial amount even if he left no will. I mean, his parents are deceased already.'

'I'd rather go home now, Mother, if you don't mind.'

'All those roadhouses – public houses, really. We couldn't possibly keep them in our family. You'll have to sell them, and those baths too.'

'Could Harold drive me home? I feel I need some peace.'

'He's gone for the night, dear. You know he always does unless we tell him. At least stay until tomorrow.'

'I'll ring for a taxi.'

'You can't be alone at a time like this. And what about help at home? You've given your staff far too much time off.'

Christobel sighed. 'Edith, the housekeeper, was going to spend a fortnight with her sister, but she's due back tomorrow.'

'But tonight, you'll be going back to a cold empty house. Where's the sense in that? You'll be more comfortable here.'

'We have electric fires.'

Louise had never seen her sister look so exhausted and emotionally drained. Her heart went out to her. 'Will you come with me, Lou? And bring Suzy, of course. She could see to making up the beds if they aren't ready, and get us a bit of breakfast in the morning.'

'Of course.' Louise was pleased to be asked; it made her feel grown up. 'Suzy will be glad to come. We'll need to put a few things in a case. Ten minutes, all right?'

The colonel stood up. 'Hebe, you fuss too much. Do calm

down. What the girl needs is a stiff brandy. Then if she wants to go home, let her. I'll call a taxi.'

Louise was shocked to find Chrissie weeping openly during the taxi ride. 'It's been awful, Lou. I had to bottle it all up and stay in control, there was so much to arrange. I kept telling myself, once I get home I'll be able to let go.'

'Mother did go on a bit.'

'About his will! It's Alec I want. I don't care about his money.'

The house was cold and dark when they arrived. Chrissie turned on all the lights and the electric fires, while Suzy lit a fire in the sitting-room grate. She boiled water for hot-water bottles and made a pot of tea.

Chrissie shivered. 'I feel better now I'm here. I had to get away from Mother.'

She sipped her tea and talked on and on about Alec, about how much he'd meant to her, about how happy they'd been at the start of their holiday . . .

It was very late when they went up to bed.

The following day, Edith returned and the house ran with comfortable smoothness again. But over the following few days, Louise felt very down. Alec's sudden death had cast a blight over them all. Her sister went to bed early and got up late. She hadn't the energy to put her and Suzy through their exercises, nor do any herself. Her blonde hair lost its shine, she sat alone looking unkempt, staring into the fire for long periods.

Their mother came down every day to ask how they were, and to try to manage things in her way.

She said: 'Louise had better come home. Her tutor is due tomorrow. You don't want her to miss her English lessons.'

'Ask her tutor to come here,' Christobel said. 'I need the girls near me just now.'

Louise felt her sister was clinging to her. She was glad to give all the support she could. Chrissie and Alec had done so much for her in the past.

The day of the funeral came and St Peter's church was packed. Christobel had insisted it was held there.

She told Louise: 'Alec didn't go to church much but we live in this parish. Mother wanted it at St Buddolph's but that would mean the Reverend Haydn Ingleby-Jones officiating, and I couldn't put up with him.'

It was a very cold day. Louise thought Christobel, for once, looked almost plain. Her face was pinched and drawn, her pearl-grey hat and coat made her look washed out. She insisted on Lou wearing the dark blue velvet outfit she'd had for her wedding.

'No point in wearing black. We'd all look like crows.'

The family turned out in strength: Penelope and her husband, though not her children; and Georgina and her husband came up from London. Christobel's mother and grandparents wore traditional black. Chrissie asked the mourners back to her house for refreshments afterwards.

Her mother said: 'You should have let me do this at The Lawns, dear – take some of the work off your shoulders at this difficult time.'

'Edith has arranged everything, Mother. It hasn't meant work for me.'

'Who is Edith? You have so many new friends . . .'

'She's our housekeeper, I keep telling you. She wanted to do it. This was Alec's home. It's not only more fitting, but it's near to the church.'

A buffet was set out on the dining table in readiness for them. Afterwards, when all the guests and Alec's employees had gone, and Georgina and her husband had gone to catch a train home, Louise felt the family relax a little. What she'd been dreading was over and Chrissie had come through it with dignity.

The family settled into comfortable chairs in the sitting room and Louise sat down beside Chrissie on a sofa, while their mother poured tea from the fresh pot Edith made for them.

Mrs Smallwood said with earnest intent: 'We need to talk to you about the will, Christobel.'

Lou felt her sister flinch. 'Not today, Mother. I'm not in the mood.'

'You need to find out—'

'There's nothing I need to find out. Don't worry yourself.'

'But you need to know what you'll inherit—'

'I do know, it's no secret. Alec made a new will when I went to live with him.'

'Christobel! Don't say such things! He did make an honest woman of you in the eyes of the law, even if it wasn't blessed in—'

'Mother,' Louise could see her sister was making an effort not to offend her, 'I'm trying to explain to you . . . What you're dying to know. He left a small bequest to Edith. She's looked after him for fifteen years. Apart from that, he willed everything else to me.'

Nobody could miss the relief on Hebe's plump face. 'Well, that's one thing we can all be grateful for.'

Christobel let her prickliness show at that. 'Why don't you say it?'

'Say what?'

'At least some good has come from all the trouble you caused. That's how you think of it, isn't it?'

'At least Alec did the decent thing over making a will. Haydn will help you sort your finances out. He's got a good head for figures.'

'Mother, Alec looked after his finances, they don't need sorting out. And I don't want that man anywhere near me. I wouldn't trust him with money.'

Hebe Smallwood was affronted. 'That's not the right attitude to take. There's a good deal to think about when a husband dies. I know, I've been through it myself.'

Chrissie's lips pursed in distress. Louise felt for her hand and gave it a comforting squeeze.

'The trouble, darling, is that you're upset. You don't know who to trust in your present frame of mind. You'll need to sell those pubs. Not nice things for a young girl like you to own.'

'I have no intention of selling them! My money has nothing to do with you.'

'I only want to help you, dear.'

'I wish you wouldn't. I'm perfectly capable of looking after my own affairs.'

'I wouldn't want you to lose money. How much has he left you?'

'I don't know yet. Alec died very suddenly.'

'You'll need professional help—'

'Mother! I'll decide what I need. Alec showed me his accounts and how he ran his business. I'm going to carry it on.'

'I don't think, darling, it's a very suitable thing for—'

'Your opinion is the very last one I'd ever ask. And I don't need the opinions of your cronies Nurse Silk and Haydn Ingleby-Jones either. Gramps, I want you to keep Mother off my back in future.'

'My nerves . . . Oh dear . . .' Her mother let out a wail of protest.

The colonel said, 'Alma, have you got your sal volatile with you? What is the matter with you, Hebe?'

* * *

Suzy thought it was a miserable time for them all. Christobel threw herself into running Alec's business. She was determined to make a success of it. She talked at length to Penny's husband Simon. He was an accountant and she knew she could rely on him for advice.

He said: 'Alec didn't want to fill his day with routine work – he delegated all that. Each pub's making a profit. The publicans he appointed have run them well over the last few years. Just keep an eye on everything, Chrissie, especially the accounts. Alec's got everything set up well and it's all audited by a very reliable firm. Alec didn't talk of having difficulties?'

'No, he thought everything ran smoothly.'

'You should be able to manage all right. If you're worried, I'll always help.'

Mrs Smallwood kept coming down to Christobel's house and, after another week, insisted on taking Louise home. That meant Suzy went back too.

'You must come, Louise. I'm afraid Christobel will be a bad influence on you. She's wild in her ways and won't listen to reason. You'll be safer at home with me.'

'But Chrissie needs me now.' Louise added diplomatically: 'And the rest of the family. Without Alec, there's a gap in her life.'

'Then she can come home. I'll be glad to see her, you can tell her that, but I wouldn't want you to turn out as she's done.'

Suzy knew there was nothing Louise wanted more than to be exactly like her sister. For her own part she had to admire Christobel. She was clearly missing her husband but she was doing her best to pick up the pieces of her life.

She spoke of playing golf with Alec's cousin, Monica, and she was visiting Penelope's house more. She came home to The Lawns to eat Sunday lunch with her family every week and occasionally came for dinner in the evening. Louise and Suzy often went to her house in Rock Park, where they saw Frankie, though Louise said she was too upset to think about another book with him just yet.

One evening several weeks after Alec had been killed, the colonel was in his study at six o'clock, when Hebe threw open the door and burst in. She was smiling and there was about her an air of pent-up excitement. For once she didn't complain that Brutus smelled and ought not to be allowed inside the house. There was even something of a glow about her cheeks.

The colonel knew why, of course, and his spirits sank. The Reverend Haydn Ingleby-Jones and Nurse Silk had been invited for dinner yet again.

'Time for you to get dressed, Father. You haven't forgotten we're having guests tonight?'

'Haven't forgotten,' he assured her. 'But I want to hear the six o'clock news first.' He switched on his wireless.

'Don't leave it too late; you take a long time changing these days. Haydn will be here at a quarter to seven. Do be ready so we can have a nice glass of sherry together first.'

She knew he never drank anything but whisky before dinner and he preferred to have it here in peace. He grunted: 'You can have your nice glass of sherry without me,' and knew he sounded churlish.

'No, Father, we can't. Not tonight. I want us all together before dinner.'

Theo changed into his dinner jacket and was down in his study before the guests arrived. Gertrude let them in and took their coats. Hebe greeted them as though she hadn't seen them for years.

379

Theo sighed, picked up his glass of whisky and went to join them. It would only lead to trouble if he gave Hebe cause to complain about his manners. Alma was hunched silently in the corner, clutching the stem of her glass.

'What's going on, Theo?' she'd asked while she'd been changing into the black dinner dress she'd worn on all Hebe's formal occasions for the last six years. 'Hebe's up to something, I'm sure.'

Hebe beamed at him when he went in. She looked positively radiant as she drew him forward. She'd bought herself a new dress of plum-coloured silk, high-necked and long-sleeved, with a lot of glistened beads on the bodice. She'd put on more weight and the material was straining on the buttons across her immense bosom.

'No need for introductions,' she purred. 'We've all known each other a very long time and we're the closest of friends.'

Theo sighed again but knew it wasn't the moment to disagree with that.

'Evening, vicar,' he said, and nodded towards Nurse Silk. She wore a dress in a similar colour to Hebe's, which didn't flatter her either. She too was very overweight and had a puff of white hair on top of her head and another at each temple. 'I hope you're both keeping well.'

'Indeed, the Lord looks after His own.'

Haydn Ingleby-Jones was inclined to giggle after what he considered an apt reply. Louise said he had a very girlish giggle that didn't seem to fit his stout build. She giggled at him and then coughed to hide it.

Hebe was charging the glasses. Louise was given orange juice but Hebe was determined to make her father drink sherry. A glass of it was put in his hand. She would have taken his whisky from him but he swilled the last of it down in one big mouthful just in time.

'Mother, Father – Haydn and I have something to announce.'

Theo stiffened. Oh God! It was going to happen. Since he'd seen them together at the Harvest Festival last year, he'd been afraid that the vicar, a widower of three years, had designs on his daughter. He'd been more attentive to her than good manners required and she'd been smiling up at him all prim and coy. Hebe was too old to be acting like a love-struck maiden. He couldn't believe she was looking for another husband. He had to add up the years; yes, she'd be fifty-two.

Haydn hauled himself out of the easy chair and raised his glass.

'I just want to tell you that Hebe has done me the honour . . . the very great honour of agreeing to be my wife.'

Theo gasped. Alma's eyes met his across the room, registering shock.

He pulled himself together, shook the vicar's hand and kissed Hebe's cheek, then put one supporting arm round Alma's shaking shoulders and the other round Louise. They drank to the happy couple's future. Hebe showed off a modest sapphire and diamond ring.

In Theo's opinion, having reached middle age, she would be wise to stay single. Her deceased husband, Osbert, had left her well provided for, and since he and Alma had lost their two sons in the war, she was their only surviving child. Hebe could expect more from them before very much longer. She didn't need another man in her life. She could employ herself here looking after them. He wished she'd order some drier sherry if he was to be forced to drink it.

Hebe had elbowed poor gentle Alma out of her house-keeping duties six years ago when she had first come home. Should Hebe now move in with a new husband, Alma, poor dear, at eighty-two was past taking on the responsibility again.

She never had taken much interest in household matters, anyway – not like Hebe, who had to control everything in her tight grasp.

The food had greatly improved since Josephine had come, and Theo felt he ought to have enjoyed his dinner more. Hebe had served out the soup and then asked the vicar to say grace. It was understandable that he should want to, but he'd been so long-winded, the soup had gone cold.

Theo didn't dare ask when the marriage was to take place, or what their plans were afterwards. He didn't want the man here every night, and he didn't want Hebe to go and leave them in the lurch. The vicar invited them to call him Haydn.

'After all, I shall soon be your son-in-law.'

The thought ruined Theo's appetite, but Haydn ate heartily. Theo wished he could eat so well of rich food and good wine.

'A delightful meal,' Haydn complimented Hebe, as he helped himself to a large piece of cheese with his port. 'The Lord will provide.'

Theo couldn't stand any more. Haydn had made that fatuous remark every time he came for a meal. He boomed out as loudly as he could: 'Indeed the Lord does provide, vicar, but the meal you've just eaten was provided by a mere mortal. In other words, by me.'

In the stunned silence that followed, Theo stood up and left, taking refuge as usual in his study.

Still fuming at the man, Theo flung himself into his armchair and picked up his copy of *The Times*. He'd already read that through, as he had the *Evening Echo*. He tossed them aside and switched on his wireless but the programme didn't hold his attention. He felt decidedly put out and knew he'd been very rude.

He had to ask himself what attracted the man to Hebe. She was no longer handsome and was very self-opinionated –

bossy, even. Not an easy person to live with. Theo was afraid her only attraction could be her money – from Hebe's point of view, the worst possible reason to be sought out by a mate. And what on earth did she see in him, a complete bumbling oaf? Full of his own importance and with a talent for getting on Theo's nerves.

He poured himself more whisky and busied himself with a cigar, going painstakingly through the traditional rigmarole of cutting off the end and making the hole.

What could he do about it? He'd asked Christobel to find out more about this Adoption Society with which she said he was involved, but she was so wrapped up in her own affairs, she'd probably done nothing about it.

He felt so useless! Hebe needed protecting from herself; love was certainly blind. She was right about one thing, though: he was an irritable old man, made so by the irrational behaviour of his womenfolk, and the general aches and pains of old age.

He pulled on his cigar and sighed, regretting his lost youth. Once, he'd been at the centre of things, making decisions, giving orders, getting things done for Queen and country. Life had been invigorating; he'd had a wonderful time in India. Those tiger hunts in the Punjab when he'd been in his prime . . .

His eyes went to the tiger skin hanging on the wall. The single shot through the head could be clearly seen. He'd told everybody, including Alma, that he'd killed it with just one bullet. But the truth was some fool's shot gun had sprayed it with lead pellets and mortally wounded it first. He'd had to use his army Colt to put it out of its agony. Back in those days, he really had been an excellent shot – enjoyed it too.

He surveyed his three firearms hanging now one below the other over the mantelpiece, then took down his Winchester and put the stock against his shoulder to squint along the barrel. He'd bought it for shooting big game, but it wasn't all that good; the army Lee-Enfield was streets ahead.

Guns had always interested him. He took down the middle one and looked through the breech. This was his favourite, a twelve-bore double-barrelled shotgun. It suited him very well, and he'd used it for game and rough shooting.

Theo remembered the time when rabbits had got into the vegetable patch and the zest with which he'd shot three with this gun. The cook had made them into a good rabbit stew. The other guns had not been used for years. He opened a drawer in his mahogany roll-top pedestal desk. Yes, he still had some ammunition, but where could he go to use it today?

When he'd first come home to England he'd enjoyed a little shooting, mainly pheasant and partridge and, of course, wood pigeon. He'd tried clay pigeon shooting when he found walking over rough moorland difficult, but he hadn't taken to that. Old age was hell; he'd had to give up so much.

Theo's cigar had gone out. As he put it down on the ashtray he'd had made from an elephant's foot – another animal he'd shot on a big-game outing – it came to him that he could check whether Haydn Ingleby-Jones was in line to inherit a baronetcy. Tomorrow he'd do that.

Chapter Twenty-One

Theo didn't sleep well. In the bed beside him, Alma was snoring. Bless her, she gave him moments of irritation like this, but never any real worry. Not like the other two.

He was late getting down for breakfast but Hebe was still on cloud nine and didn't moan at him. She talked of meeting Haydn for lunch with such joy in her eyes that it made Theo more determined to look into his background. He asked Hebe for his full name and date of birth. He meant business.

Edna had let Brutus in as usual. The dog's sorrowful eyes wouldn't leave his master's when he took him back to the kitchen.

'Edna, tell Harold to get the car out. I want to go down to the library. And you'd better put Brutus outside. Explain to him that I won't be taking him for a walk this morning.'

Theo put on his hat and coat, and was on his way to the front door when he thought of taking pen and paper. He might want to take some notes. He stopped in the garden to break off a daffodil and pin it in his buttonhole.

He always felt better if there was some purpose to what he was doing. The reference room at the library was busy. He sat down at a table and the directories he asked for were brought to him. He started leafing through *Burke's Peerage*. As he'd suspected, the name Ingleby-Jones did not appear on the Roll of Baronets. He'd always thought it sounded a bit theatrical.

He learned a lot about the complications of hereditary baronetcies, even that they can change their name, but in this case it seemed far more likely that the man was lying. Just to make sure he consulted *Debrett's Peerage and Baronetage* too, but with the same result. Hebe stood no chance of becoming Lady Ingleby-Jones. But worse, what did that tell him about the man who claimed she would?

Theo turned to *Crockford's Clerical Dictionary*. It shocked him to find nothing there either. He hadn't doubted that Ingleby-Jones was an ordained priest. He caused a lot of trouble in the reference room by asking for directories showing the names of ministers of every nonconformist sect. The name of Haydn Albert Ingleby-Jones, born 1871, did not appear anywhere. Had he been defrocked and cast out? Possibly. Or his ordination was just a figment of his imagination, like inheriting a baronetcy?

Theo sat back and thought about him. It seemed he'd been right when he'd told Hebe that Haydn Ingleby-Jones had set up his own breakaway sect at St Buddolph's, and though she thought it was founded on faith, that now seemed unlikely.

Could it be for money? There'd be the Sunday collections, but even if his congregation was generous, it would hardly be generous enough, he thought, to make it worthwhile.

Marriage to Hebe would provide a meal ticket in his old age. And hadn't Christobel said something about how the Silk woman was his sister and had run a home for fallen women, and he'd arranged adoptions of the babies for cash?

Haydn Ingleby-Jones had attracted a large flock of middle-class parishioners, but mainly ladies of advanced years. There wouldn't be many amongst them of the right age to adopt. His style of preaching was rather flat but he had come to life when he'd spoken of the delights of family life and the joy of bringing up a child. He'd gone a bit over the top on that, painting the rosiest of pictures. Could it be that he was trying to instil a desire for children in the hearts of the young marrieds?

Theo decided he must see Christobel immediately to find out if she'd made any enquiries about this. He went back to his car and told Harold to drive him down to her house in Rock Park.

A maid answered his knock and showed him into a sitting room that looked like a Hollywood film set. Christobel was upstairs and came running down to see him. She looked better than she had for some time. There was a bit of colour in her cheeks and her blonde hair had recently received attention from a hairdresser.

'Gramps! Such a surprise, lovely of you to come. I was just going out. Some coffee first? What brings you?'

'Last night, your mother announced her engagement.'

Christobel's hand flew to cover her mouth. 'Not to . . .?'

'The Reverend Haydn Ingleby-Jones. I thought you ought to know.'

Her face was a picture. 'She's going to marry *him* when she refused permission for me to marry Alec? D'you know, Gramps, she had the nerve to say Alec wasn't good enough and here she is planning to marry that old rogue. I don't believe it.'

'You should. She's got a new ring on her finger.'

'Oh gosh, he was horrible to me and Alec, talked about Alec's lack of moral fibre and all that. Made him cringe.'

For once, he was seeing eye to eye with his granddaughter. 'He is a bit of a bounder. Got to stop this for your mother's sake, if I can.'

Theo told her then what he'd found out in the library. 'That should be enough to put your mother off, but you were going to find out about this Adoption Society. Did you ever get round to it?'

'Yes, some time ago, before . . .' he saw her lip quiver.

'All right?'

She took a steadying breath. 'I had a long talk with Monica. She was going to see what she could find out. I'll phone her now and see if she knows any more. She'll be at work . . .'

The phone was in the same room. Theo sat watching her. Christobel squealed with joy and smiled up at him.

'Tonight? . . . Yes, come and have supper with me . . . . No trouble, I'm much in need of company. Seven o'clock.' Theo understood Alec's cousin had been successful.

'She was just going to ring me, Gramps. She's written an article that'll be in tomorrow's *Liverpool Mercury*. Monica answered an advert for the Adoption Society and wrote to Nurse Silk, pretending she wanted to adopt a baby. She was invited to visit the mother-and-baby home and she saw Ingleby-Jones too. They quoted her a price and asked which sex she wanted, then took her round the nursery to choose one. They implied that if she didn't fancy any of the ones they had, there would soon be more to choose from.

'There was no research into her background to see if she'd make a suitable parent. Monica isn't married but she had to pretend she was. She was afraid they'd want to interview the husband she said she had, but all they asked was what work did he do.'

Theo rubbed his chin thoughtfully. 'And this is all going to be printed in a newspaper?'

'Yes, be sure to get the *Mercury* tomorrow. And there's more. Ingleby-Jones has served a prison sentence, for fraud and theft. He's a conman.'

Theo sat back in the chair and chortled. 'That should put Hebe off.'

Christobel felt strongly about it. 'I want to see him shamed, and that sister of his too. Because she was a nurse, Mother followed all her advice. She did Lou a lot of harm. How could Mother be so blind?'

'Love is said to be blind, Christobel.'

'You'd think she'd have more sense at her age. She gets everything wrong; she was so wrong about Alec. She's never apologised, you know.'

Theo made up his mind. 'I'm going to wait until I get the paper tomorrow, and then I'll—'

'Count me in, Gramps,' Christobel said quickly. 'I'm not missing this.'

'You'll come home?'

She flashed him a wicked smile. 'I want to be there when Mother finds out what her friends are really like. Monica says she's got more to tell me. She's coming to see me tonight.'

The next morning, Theo walked Brutus through Birkenhead Park to the newsagent's near the underground station. He bought *The Times* as well as the *Mercury*, and opened the latter on the doorstep to see if the article they were expecting had been published.

There was a two-page spread and a big headline: 'Self-styled Clergyman Shamed'.

Theo folded up the newspaper and strode briskly home to the privacy of his own room where he could study it in peace. It exceeded his highest hopes.

Christobel arrived and he said: 'I'll get your mother to come down. Perhaps I'd better bring some brandy in. She might need it.'

Alma wandered in to his study, and when she saw Christobel she asked: 'What's going on?'

Theo pushed the article in front of her. 'Read that,' he said. 'Christobel, can you organise a pot of coffee for us and bring another chair in?'

He found Hebe in her bedroom. 'Christobel's here.'

'Now?' She turned on him, irritation on her face. 'I hope she isn't staying to lunch. I told her dinner tonight.'

'There's something we'd both like to talk to you about,' he said, and she followed him down.

As soon as she caught sight of Christobel, she snapped. 'Haydn thinks I should try and get you to change your mind. All those pubs—'

'Roadhouses, Mother.'

'He thinks you should sell them. The devil does his work there. Not suitable for a young girl like you to own. He'd be happy to help you.'

'I bet he would. He'd diddle me out of a large slice of their value.'

'Christobel! Owning pubs brings such disgrace on our family, I hardly dare lift my head in church.'

'Mother, it's your church we want to talk to you about . . .'

Hebe caught sight Brutus. 'That dog smells, Father, he'll have to be put out. I can't sit in there with him.' A lace handkerchief fluttered to her nose.

Theo nodded to Christobel, who put down the coffee pot and pushed Brutus out into the hall. Then he handed Hebe a copy of the *Mercury*. 'Read that,' he said.

'Whatever is it?' she asked impatiently. 'I've a lot to do, I can't waste . . .'

Theo made sure the door was firmly shut. The kitchen girls were always hanging about listening if something was going on. A nosy lot, really.

Christobel said with rich enjoyment, 'An article about your friend Haydn Ingleby-Jones, setting out some home truths.'

The colour in Hebe's cheeks was draining away. After a few minutes, she looked up, shocked.

'It can't be true? A conman?'

Theo said: 'We thought you'd believe the printed word. Isn't it what Christobel's been trying to tell you? Haydn Ingleby-Jones and Henrietta Silk found a calling that seemed at first sight to be both legal and have the blessing of the Church. They exploited young unmarried girls and sold their illegitimate babies for their own private gain.'

Alma said gently: 'Hebe, do you see what it says about Henrietta Silk?'

'I haven't read it all yet.'

Christobel read it out: 'Trained as a midwife and for thirty years was in charge of a mother-and-baby home. Married John Silk, a dock labourer, and since she retired, their daughter has run the same home. Henrietta is still involved in the sale of babies but has now set herself up in a fine house in Oxton where she spends her time working to help her brother's other interests. She is a vigorous fund-raiser for his church.'

Christobel's head was thrown back, her eyes glinted. 'Gramps thinks he never was ordained.'

'Of course he was,' Hebe thundered, but he could see the doubt in his daughter's eyes.

Chrissie said: 'He's a conman and a good one. Knows the benefits of a dog collar if he wants women to trust him.'

Theo could see his granddaughter was having a field day.

'You did your best to push me into their clutches too. Kept going on about how eligible Haydn's son was and how he'd inherit a baronetcy one day. Thank goodness I wasn't tempted. Claude was a pain in the neck, but Haydn knew you'd be dazzled by a title.'

'An effective lure for a silly woman,' her father said.

'You've been conned, Mother. You fell for his story hook, line and sinker. Didn't we keep telling you? And all you could think of was that Alec didn't come up to your standards.'

Hebe looked dazed but her chin lifted. 'I can't speak ill of the dead, Christobel.'

'Alec was a loving and honest man.'

'You've been very silly, Hebe. Fancy being taken in by people like that.'

'But why . . .?' Hebe's shocked eyes went round them all. 'Why did they do it?'

'Power and money,' Christobel shrugged. 'It allowed them to become gentrified. They had a large congregation fund-raising as hard as they could go.'

'It was for a church building, one we could be proud of.'

'Where's the guarantee it would ever be built?' Alma was shaking her white head.

Christobel said: 'What's happened to all the money you collected? Who was looking after the account?'

Hebe's lips hardly moved. 'He was.'

Theo smiled to himself. 'As Haydn would say: The Lord helps those who help themselves. They took it too literally.'

Hebe tugged the engagement ring from her finger and flung it across the room, spitting out: 'You're all being very hurtful. Have you no thought for my feelings?' She snatched up the newspaper and ran for the stairs, but not before they all saw the tears on her cheeks.

Theo sat through the stunned silence. He was sorry now he'd plotted with Christobel to turn the tables on Hebe like this. They should have broken it to her more gently, have been kinder . . .

'Oh, Gramps!' Christobel was looking as contrite as he felt. 'She must have loved him. It must have been a terrible shock.'

Then her wicked smile flashed up at him. 'But I only treated her in the way she treated me.'

Alma got up. 'I'd better go to her. She's very upset, poor dear.'

* * *

The days were lengthening. Christobel spoke of opening up the baths for the summer season. She sent Frankie to join the gang there who were cleaning and painting and cutting the grass in readiness. She was going to open in time for Easter. Suzy got out her bathing suit. She could still get into it, but only just.

'You're going to need another one,' Mam told her.

'Louise says she wants to get a new one. I'll get one too at the same time.' Now that Suzy was in paid employment, she could buy clothes for herself.

Easter was late but the weather remained disappointingly cool and cloudy. Christobel suggested a swim on Easter Monday, and Louise and Suzy went to the baths with her. Frankie was on life-saving duty. They all swam vigorously up and down the pool, which they had almost to themselves because of the offputting weather.

Two weeks on, and Sunday was a warm sunny day and the baths were well patronised. Mam and Olga came too. After their swim they lay on the grass to sunbathe. Frankie and Louise were discussing their book. Laurence had found them an agent who was willing to handle it, but he'd suggested it needed some rewriting. Louise was throwing herself into the job. Suzy had a lot of retyping to do.

'Lovely to think of summer stretching ahead of us,' Olga said. 'I hope we'll have as good a time as we did last summer, but I do wish they'd catch Luke Palmer.'

'I would never have believed,' Josie agreed, 'that he could have evaded capture for so long. I live in dread of him finding us.'

When they returned to The Lawns, Suzy rinsed out the three bathing suits and pegged them out in a row on the clothesline in the walled garden. She leaned against the back

door for a moment, to catch the last of the evening sunshine
on her face. Mother and daughter swimsuits in eye-catching
black, red and white stripes, together with Louise's pale blue
one, fluttered over the dustbins.

Luke Palmer, who now called himself Bill Smith, found
working on the bins a poor substitute for tram driving. It was
a job that had no status. Everybody looked down on him and
despised him for doing it. It was impossible to keep himself
clean. He got no respect; a bin man was not in the same
league as a tram driver.

It was tiring too. The bins were heavy and he was expected
to carry them out on to the pavement and then tip them into
the truck. God knew what people put in them. Some weighed
over a hundred pounds, and he had to lift a couple of hundred
bins every day. By the time he got home from work, he'd had
it. Too tired even to think of going to a pub. More often than
not he fell asleep in his clothes before he'd even read his
paper.

It was a rotten existence. Nothing to look forward to, except
once in a while the truck would pull into an alley and they'd
take five minutes for a smoke.

Being outside in all weathers was a further trial. Every
bin contained grey ash and cinders from the fire grates, and
a bit of wind meant it blew round and got in his eyes when
he tipped the bin into the dustcart. In winter, he saw fewer
people out and about; anybody with any sense stayed at
home by the fire. The whole reason for doing the job was
going stale on him; he'd never seen sight nor sound of Josie
or Suzy.

Spring had come round again and, when summer followed,
crowds would throng the park once more. Luke scrutinised
faces whenever he could. It was pleasanter to be out in the

sunshine but the bins stank more on hot days and made his clothes stink too.

Luke began to feel disheartened. He was bored with the job and began to think of giving up and moving on. His was a miserable existence; he needed to better his standard of living. The only thing that pleased him was that the police had never managed to catch up with him.

Then one Monday morning, he was collecting refuse on his usual route, the big mansions around Manor Hill and Grosvenor Road. He liked doing the big houses though most of his colleagues did not. The bins had to be carried further when the houses were set in private grounds.

Many of them had two bins outside their kitchen doors, and the bin men collected in pairs. There was always a lot of ash in them – the rich kept fires burning in every room. Walking up their drives, Luke was fascinated by the scale of the houses and the general air of opulence. Life would be different if he could call one of these his home. How could he not be envious? They'd have servants in houses like these. Josie could be working in any one of them. He always kept his eyes open for her or the kid.

Luke swung one of the bins up on his shoulder – no light weight, but he'd developed muscles in the last year or so. He turned round to retrace his steps when his eye caught the washing fluttering on a clothesline.

Two bathing suits in black, red and white stripes: one for an adult and one for a twelve-year-old. He felt a surge of hope, of triumph even. He'd bought two just like that for Josie and Suzy. Were these they? He'd even bought himself one, but he'd long since left his behind. There was no swimming in his life now. There was another blue bathing suit swinging beside them of a sort he'd never seen, but that didn't mean anything.

He took a long and careful look round. He knew he had an inane grin on his face and he wanted to laugh out loud. He thought he might have found them at last. He made a mental note that the house was called The Lawns. He'd keep an eye on the place in future. Josie and her kid could be here. It had taken him a long time, but he felt he was getting closer. He'd give Josie what for when he caught up with her.

If they were here, then that little devil Frankie had told him a deliberate lie. He'd cheated him, made this long search necessary. Luke felt himself flush with anger. Frankie deserved everything he'd given him. He'd like to give him more.

These days, Josie felt she had more confidence about cooking for the family. She'd expected to be a bit rushed today because it was Edna's day off and that meant she and Gertie had to do her work too. But it had all gone smoothly. Suzy was a great support now she was growing up and as usual she'd come down to the kitchen in time to help her dish up.

The treacle pudding with custard had gone to the dining room and the coffee was perking away on the stove and would be ready when it was wanted. Gertie came back.

'The colonel praised your steak-and-kidney pie, and had a second helping.'

Josie was reheating what remained for their own meal, and when they sat down to eat she was pleased with her pastry, which was still crisp and tasty. She felt settled here and would be content with her life, if only Luke was not still out there evading capture. She tried to tell herself that if he hadn't found them in all this time, it was likely he never would, but the fear that he might wouldn't quite go.

An hour or so later, they'd eaten and done the washing up.

Gertie and Suzy had almost finished clearing up and the kitchen was clean and tidy again. Josie was making their bedtime cocoa when they heard the garden door slam shut and footsteps pound up the flagged path. The back door burst open and Edna flung herself across the kitchen, to collapse on the armchair by the stove.

Suzy came to the scullery door and was drying her hands. 'Gracious, what's the matter?'

Edna was panting. 'There was a man. Lurking in the bushes. I didn't see him until I got really close. Gosh, did he make me jump.'

'In our grounds, you mean?' Gertie asked.

Josie pulled the milk off the stove. The hairs on the back of her neck were standing up, her confidence and contentment shattered in an instant. Edna's round girlish face seemed to eddy round her. A man lurking in the bushes? Had Luke Palmer found them? Her head was swimming. She knew she'd been expecting this with every fibre of her body since the night she'd arrived.

She glanced at Suzy and she knew she understood. Her blue eyes were wide with fright.

'What was he like, this man?' Suzy asked the question that was foremost in Josie's mind.

'Tall and broad, a real bruiser. Scared the living daylights out of me, he did. Stepped out of the bushes as I came up the back drive. He shouted that he wouldn't hurt me, he just wanted to talk to me, but I took to my heels.'

Oh God! It sounded like him!

Suzy's eyes met her mother's. 'Shall I take Brutus down to chase him off?'

'No,' she said with such vehemence that both Edna and Gertie turned to look at her.

'No, Suzy. That wouldn't be safe.' Josie was afraid he'd

hurt her. It had been Suzy he'd been looking for. Suzy or her, not Edna.

Edna was recovering. 'I had a lovely day off. I was so happy when I came through the gate.'

'You went home to see your mam?'

'Yes, this morning we went round the shops, and after dinner I took my sister's little girl to feed the ducks in the park, and . . . Guess what? I met this lad I used to go to school with. Fred, his name is. He stayed talking to me for an hour. He's really nice. His mother knows mine and he called round for me after tea and we went for another walk round the park.'

'Pity he wasn't with you. When the man jumped out at you, I mean.'

'He'd said goodbye to me at the gate not two minutes before. I was thinking of him and it was dark. It was the shock that scared me, that's all. Is that cocoa for me? Thanks, Josie.'

Suzy reached for her cup. 'Two men in one day.'

Edna laughed. 'A real change for me. I tell you what, Suzy, you can have the second one, he wasn't my type.' She laughed again. 'Probably not yours either. He was old enough to be your father.'

Josie cringed back in her seat, appalled. If Edna knew how close she was!

'But I really like Fred. He wants to see me again.' She smiled happily round at them all.

Josie asked carefully: 'Are you going to report this to Mrs Smallwood?' She wanted Luke frightened off. She wanted him as far away as possible.

Edna shrugged. She might have found herself a boyfriend but she still looked like an overgrown child. 'Why bother? He's probably gone by now.'

Josie was glad to be going upstairs to her bed, though she was miles away from sleep.

'Don't put the light on for a minute,' she whispered to Suzy, and went straight to the window. She threw it open, hung out and strained her eyes into the night. Suzy pushed close and craned out too.

'We won't see him from here.'

Their room looked out over the back garden. They couldn't see the drive or the garages, and he wasn't on the lawns.

'He can't get near the kitchen unless he comes inside the walled garden.' The bean and pea poles cast dark shadows but there was definitely nobody there.

'How did he find us after all this time?' Josie wondered. 'I don't go out much; he can't have followed me back. I always look back up the road, anyway, before I turn in at the gate. I'm sure I've never been followed.'

'Mam, we don't know it is him.'

'You go out much more.'

'In the car with Lou mostly. He won't be watching cars if he's looking for us. I could understand it if I was still at school. He'd know I'd be coming out at four in the afternoon. If he'd found us then, I could understand it, but not now. I don't think it can be him, Mam. You're worrying for nothing. Come on, let's close these curtains and put the light on. It's time we went to bed.'

Chapter Twenty-Two

The following night, Christobel was going to have dinner at The Lawns and was driving herself there in the little red MG sports car that Alec had given her.

Alec's death had left a gaping hole in her life, and she couldn't stop thinking about him. She was doing her best to fill it, seeing much more of her family, but in truth it was all very dull. Only one step better than staying home alone.

She had to fill the gap with something, and Lou was always glad to see her. She felt closer to all her sisters than she used to – closer to all her family really. They'd made it clear she must fall back on their company now she no longer had Alec, and they did their best to entertain her. These days, she was rotten company for anybody.

Why, oh why, did it have to happen to Alec? If only they hadn't gone skiing, he'd still be with her. It had only been a holiday; it wouldn't have hurt to have gone without that.

Darkness had fallen earlier than usual tonight. The day had been rainy and overcast despite her prayers for sunshine. If the baths were to show a profit she needed the sun. She slowed down and glanced at the house as she drove past. It looked welcoming, the lights all on downstairs.

The gate at the bottom of the drive was latched back as it usually was. She turned the nose of the little car through it. Nothing changed here, never had in all the years she'd known it. The bushes grew higher and thicker, and the headlights were unable to penetrate. It was like driving through a cavern with the headlamps lighting up the road ahead. She was passing the garage when she saw a man, heavily built, with an uncouth face.

She braked hard and skidded to a halt, then slapped the gear into reverse and backed up, to make the beam of the headlights return to the place where she'd seen him. She caught a flash of movement, and then the bushes hung dark and silent. She got out but stood leaning on the car door.

'Who's there?' she called, but the only sound was the wind rattling at the bushes. There should be nobody here, unless it was Harold?

'Harold, is that you?'

It wouldn't be, he couldn't see to do anything in the garden now it was dark. He'd have gone home long ago. She shivered as she got back in her car and drove it up to the front door. She found her mother and grandmother in the drawing room.

'A man in the grounds?' Her mother was horrified, and immediately put down her glass of sherry. 'No business to be there. It's private property. We must keep that gate closed in future. Where's Father?'

'In his study, I think. His wireless is on.'

She watched her mother march across the hall, throw open the study door and switch off the wireless.

Gramps sounded irritable. 'What is it now, Hebe? What's the matter?'

'There's a trespasser in the grounds. Christobel's just seen someone watching the house.'

'Hello, Gramps – a man by the garages.'

'Are you sure?'

'Absolutely certain.'

'Really, Father, I don't know why you keep that animal shut in here.' Brutus opened soulful eyes and stared at her. 'How can he guard anything if he's in your study?'

Theo levered himself out of his armchair. 'Perhaps I'd better have a look round outside. Come on, Brutus.' The dog lifted his head, had a stretch, and put it down on the carpet again.

'The lazy thing,' Hebe said scornfully. 'He's no good as a guard dog. He's always asleep.'

'He's old like me. Come on, time for a walk. Have we got a torch, Hebe?'

'I'll come too.' Christobel took his arm. His body felt frail beside her own. In the porch, they armed themselves with walking sticks from the umbrella stand, and Theo picked up a torch. Their feet crunched on the gravel. The dog padded quietly ahead of them.

'We should have picked up umbrellas, not sticks,' Theo said in another flash of ill temper. 'It's starting to rain.'

'Brutus would be rushing about and barking if there was a stranger anywhere near. Gramps, why would anybody want to stand about in the drive on a night like this?'

'Hoping to steal something?'

They walked all the way round the building that had once been a stable and was now a garage. Christobel opened it up to make sure nobody was hiding inside. They walked round the garden and flashed the torch through the shrubbery. Brutus was taking little interest.

'I saw a man here, Gramps. I know I did. He hid himself from me.'

'He doesn't seem to be here now. You probably frightened him more than he frightened you.'

'No point in closing the gate, I'd only have to get out to open it when I go home.'

'Let's go in. I could do with a whisky. Come on, Brutus, you can stay out here and keep watch for prowlers. Hebe won't like you going in again now you're wet.'

'I don't think Mother likes him going in at all,' Christobel giggled.

They went in the back way, through the walled garden, the colonel carefully propping the door in the wall open behind them.

'So Brutus can get out to chase off intruders,' he said.

'If he feels up to it.'

She paused beside the huge kennel. 'Has he had his dinner, Gramps?'

'No, I'll get Edna to feed him tonight. Good night, Brutus.'

Josie was lifting a haunch of mutton out of the oven as they went into the warm kitchen. Christobel was hungry.

'Smells lovely,' she told her. 'We've been round the garden. It's given me an appetite.'

'Me too,' the colonel grunted. 'Chasing a prowler. You haven't had a follower here this evening, have you, Edna? Nice girl like you, bound to get boyfriends.'

'No, sir, not a follower, but I saw a man there last night when I came in from my day off. Big burly fellow, quite old.'

'That's him,' Christobel agreed. 'The same one. I saw him tonight when I came.'

'Not a follower? You're sure?'

'No, not a follower,' Gertie agreed. 'Edna was quite scared when she came in.'

'Better let the police know,' the colonel said. 'Two nights on the run, somebody watching the house? It seems very suspicious.'

'I'll ring them now,' Christobel said. 'Better do it before you have a break-in.'

'Will you girls be sure to lock all the doors before you go to bed?'

'We always do, sir. And close the downstairs windows.'

* * *

Josie felt faint. She'd really got the creeps now. Suzy was hovering at her elbow, trying to be twice as helpful as usual, making it obvious she was expecting her to make ghastly mistakes. The intruder had been seen by both Edna and Christobel. It had to be Luke.

She was glad the police had been called in. She only hoped they'd catch up with Luke before he caught up with her or Suzy. An officer came to the house and, after he'd talked to the family in the drawing room, Christobel brought him to the kitchen.

It was Edna he wanted to talk to, but they all sat round the table with him. Gertie was determined to miss none of the excitement. Suzy made them all cups of cocoa. The intruder had tried to talk to Edna. Luke must have recognised her as the kitchen help. To Josie, it seemed to prove that it was him.

She was torn in two: trying to decide whether she should tell the officer about her suspicions or keep quiet. Would it help them catch him more quickly if she did? Reason said they'd try harder, much harder, if they knew the intruder was a hardened criminal who'd been evading capture all these months. Suzy was sitting opposite, and every time Josie looked up, her eyes were urging her to tell all.

But Luke was notorious. He'd attracted a sensational press when he'd killed Eric Rimmer. She'd come here on false pretences and been accepted and befriended on those false terms. Josie couldn't bring herself to confess to the police she'd told a pack of lies to get the job, not with Gertie listening to every word. There was the stigma too: she'd lived with Luke as his wife, but she hadn't been married to him.

The stress was making her head spin. She couldn't decide on anything. Action of any sort was beyond her. The officer was closing his notebook. Getting to his feet. The opportunity had gone.

Josie felt a coward. She knew she was in a state of terror and had to calm down. Luke was having a terrible effect on her without ever making contact. Perhaps it wasn't Luke the girls had seen, just an ordinary burglar? She sighed; if only she could believe that.

Josie found the days that followed very hard. She'd wanted to vanish without trace and she'd failed. She went about her work in a state of dread. She felt relatively safe indoors or in the walled garden, but didn't dare go to town. She wouldn't even walk out into the road. She hadn't been to see Olga recently, and had a letter from her suggesting that if the weather was halfway reasonable, they should meet at the baths on Sunday afternoon. Josie had a half-day, but she was too scared to go. She was scared for Suzy too.

'I have to go out if Louise wants me to,' she told her.

'If Luke's watching the place, he'll recognise you. Don't walk out of here.'

'I won't, Mam. Louise can't walk far. We always set out by car.'

But Josie knew they spent a lot of time in the garden; in the summerhouse or on the lawn in front of it. Louise was starting to play tennis and Suzy was a patient partner. Luke had been seen near the garage, so it was possible he might see Suzy in the garden.

'He wouldn't come in broad daylight, Mam. Besides, he must know he's been seen about the place. He wouldn't risk coming in after that.'

'He would, but it might make him more careful.'

'It's making you overcareful, Mam. I think you should

come to the baths. Louise wouldn't mind if you came with us in the car.'

But Josie couldn't bring herself to go to such a public place.

Suzy said: 'Mam, you should have told the police about Luke Palmer when you had the chance. The officer did ask if we could add anything else.'

Josie had no answer to that. Sunday was a warm and sunny day. She spent the afternoon sitting in a deck chair between the dog kennel and the dustbins, with the door in the wall firmly shut. Gertie expressed surprise that she wasn't going to the baths.

'Don't you feel well?' she asked. 'Even if it's the wrong time of the month it would be nicer to sit in the sun there and see your friend.'

Only then did Josie realise she and Suzy must have said too much in her hearing. Josie liked Gertie very much, but she made other people's business her main interest in life.

Monday was the colonel and Mrs Ingram's wedding anniversary and a goose had been ordered from the farm that delivered their milk and eggs. During the morning, Josie plucked and cleaned it ready for dinner that evening. Mrs Smallwood liked the soft feathers kept to make new pillows, and Josie needed the neck, gizzard and heart to make giblet gravy, but there was still the head and unwanted entrails. She wrapped them in newspaper and looked outside. It was another warm day. Brutus was half asleep in the sun near the bins. He opened an eye when he heard her.

Although the goose entrails were somewhat unsavoury, Brutus considered anything like that a delicacy. She'd learned from past experience that if she put the entrails of any fowl in the dustbin, he'd push the lid off to get at them and spread gore over the path.

'Keep an eye open for the bin men,' she told Edna, who was washing the scullery floor and back steps. 'We don't want to miss them. This will be high before next week.' She put the parcel on the scullery windowsill.

Josie was chopping onions when she heard the clatter of bin lids being tossed on the flagstones. Edna had finished washing the floors and had gone upstairs to clean the servants' bathroom. Josie rushed out with the newspaper parcel of goose entrails, her eyes bleary with tears from the onions. One dustbin was going off down the path on the shoulders of a bin man.

'Hang on a sec,' she said to the giant of a man who was about to heave their other bin up on his shoulder. He was turning round as she tossed her parcel in.

Josie found herself looking up into Luke Palmer's vaguely lop-sided face. She gave a little shriek of alarm and dived for the safety of the kitchen, slamming the door behind her. She was in a panic and couldn't get her breath. The scuffle woke Brutus up and he was barking; she wasn't sure whether she heard Luke call her name. She had to get further away and made straight for her bedroom; standing well back from the window so as not to be seen, she peered out. Had that really been Luke Palmer? He'd grown a beard.

She was just in time to see the bin being lowered to pass through the door in the walled garden. It slammed shut in Brutus's face. She could see the bin moving along on the other side of the wall but the man was out of sight.

She stood still waiting, her heart in her mouth, sweat cold on her forehead. The bins were always brought back; she'd see him again. Had she really seen Luke? She wasn't sure now. A beard made him look quite different. Was it just her mind playing tricks? Was she worrying about him so much that she was now imagining she saw him?

The window was open a little and she heard the man returning behind the wall. The door was pushed open and the empty bins rattled. The man with the beard was carrying a bin on each arm.

From here, she could see that his dark hair was getting thinner and needed cutting, and so did the beard he'd grown. This was a rough and uncouth version of the Luke Palmer she'd known. He used to be fussy about his clothes but working on the bins, he couldn't be.

Even now she wasn't sure it really was Luke – his face seemed more swarthy ... But his eyes ... They hadn't changed – just heavily hooded slits.

She was expecting to see him round every corner, that was her trouble. It was all in her head, which was swimming round. When she tried to move, her legs were like jelly. She went to the bathroom and rinsed her face. In the mirror, she looked as though she'd seen a ghost, but she had to go back to the kitchen and cook. Today, she had more than usual to do. She took a few sips of water and went downstairs slowly, holding on to the banister. Her insides were still churning and she felt slightly sick.

Lunch had come and gone before she had a chance to speak to Suzy. She made an excuse to get her up to their bedroom.

'I think I've seen Luke Palmer,' she told her. 'He's working on the bins.'

Suzy's eyes fastened on her. They were round with shock, her mouth was open. Josie could see her face working. 'Did he see you?'

'I don't know.'

'Mam, you must know.'

Suzy's hand gripped her arm. Josie pushed a strand of hair under her cap and tried to explain. Her first fleeting glimpse had so terrified her she'd fled. He hadn't said anything, but she hadn't given him a chance.

Suzy said seriously: 'But don't you see? If you tell the police, they can pick him up. Just tell them you think he's working for the Corporation on the bins.'

'But I've got so much to do today. Visitors coming for tea and dinner, special food . . .'

'Gertie was setting the table for tea before we came up. You've got everything ready for that?'

'Yes, but the dinner—'

'The goose is stuffed ready to go in the oven, I've seen it. Look, if you're rushed, I'll help you when we come back.'

'Suzy, I'm not sure . . . Whether it was really him, I mean. Was it all in my mind? I think this is driving me crazy.' Josie sank down on her bed and covered her face with her hands.

'Sure or not, you must tell the police. Honest, Mam, you've got to. You have an hour or so off now. Go down to the police station. They'll be delighted if they can catch Luke Palmer after all this time.'

'But I'm not certain it was him.'

'Just tell them what you think. They'll check him out. You're always saying how much you want him caught. This is your chance.'

'But what if—'

'Even if you're wrong, you'll have done something about it. If you do nothing, you'll be scared out of your mind every Monday when the bin men come. You'll stay indoors for the rest of the summer in case you happen to meet him in the street. You can't go on like that. Mam, you've got to go to the police.'

Josie felt Suzy's arm go round her shoulders and pull her close. 'I'll come with you, if you want. Louise won't mind . . . Oh, she's going to the dentist this afternoon.'

Josie shivered. She felt punch-drunk and past doing anything; she no longer had the strength. Suzy was turning her round so she had to look at her daughter's face. She could see new determination there.

'If you don't go, Mam, I will. But it stands to reason, the police would rather talk to you than me. Mrs Smallwood would know if they came here to question you. Much better if we go together to the police station now.'

Josie wailed: 'I don't know where it is.'

'Neither do I, but I'll find out. What time is it? I think Lou's appointment is at three. Stay here, until I come back.'

Josie lay back on her bed and closed her eyes. Oh God, what a state she'd got herself into. Of course Luke Palmer had to be caught. It was the only way to protect Suzy from him.

Suzy was coming back. Josie could hear her pelting up the attic stairs. 'Get yourself ready, Mam. We're going into town with Harold.'

That panicked her: 'You haven't told anyone?'

'No. He's taking Lou to the dentist in Hamilton Square. I said you wanted to go shopping. I've picked up an A to Z from the hall stand. That will tell us . . .' She sat down on her bed to study it. 'Yes, here's the police station in Brandon Street. That's close to Hamilton Square.'

Suzy was kicking off her shoes. 'I'll be able to find it.' She was running a comb through her hair. 'Come on, we mustn't keep them waiting.'

Suzy couldn't believe the change in her mother. She used to be so keen to get everything organised and done as efficiently as possible. Now it was as though she'd had the stuffing knocked out of her. Suzy was used to Mam being in charge; used to Mam taking her by the hand and telling her what she

411

must do. Now, Suzy had to make the decisions and galvanise Mam to do anything.

When they got downstairs, Suzy slid the A to Z back on the hall stand. Harold had brought the car to the door but there was no sign of Lou.

Suzy said: 'Wait here, Mam, I'm going to fetch her.'

She found Louise cleaning her teeth in the bathroom. 'I am ready. Oh dear, I'm not looking forward to this.'

When she got Lou down into the hall, she thought her mother had panicked and run back to the bedroom, but then she saw her behind the car. Poor Mam, she was too nervous to wait in the hall and too nervous to get into the car in case Mrs Smallwood saw her and asked questions.

Suzy sat between them, feeling uneasy. Mam was a nervous wreck. She was ashen-faced and hadn't put her hat on straight, but she had to tell the police she thought she'd seen Nosey. Suzy knew she was right to insist on that. She wanted him caught. He was a murderer and he deserved all he got. Olga and Frankie would feel better if they knew he hadn't got off scot-free, and it was the only way Mam would get any peace. The car stopped outside the dentist's surgery.

'Shall I come in with you?' Suzy asked Lou.

'No, I'll be all right.'

'Harold will be waiting here to take you home.'

Lou's violet eyes looked into hers. 'Do you want him to take you to the shops?'

'No thanks, the market's just up here.'

'What are you going to buy?'

Suzy shook her head.

Mam said, always stiffly polite: 'Thank you, Louise, for the lift.'

Once they'd all got out, Harold put his head back and closed his eyes. Good, Suzy thought, he won't see in which direction we go. She took Mam's arm and they set off towards the market, but at the bottom of Brandon Street, she looked back. Louise had disappeared inside the building and the car was facing away from them. She could see Harold's cap against the back of his seat. He'd have his eyes closed. It was what he always did.

'We go up here, Mam. You see, nobody will know where we're going.'

Outside the police station, Mam hesitated again and had to be persuaded inside. Suzy had to explain why they'd come to the constable on reception duty. She found it a fearsome experience herself and Mam was giving every sign that she was finding it terrifying.

They had to wait then in a dark, stone-flagged room which Suzy knew would do nothing to calm Mam's nerves. The sergeant, when at last he came, was scary too. As he led them to another room, she thought he might just as easily be nicknamed Nosey. He had the same powerful build, glossy moustache and large nose, but his nose was not aquiline. It was fat and rounded, and the skin covering it was pitted like orange peel.

Mam had first to explain her connection with Luke Palmer, and then tell how she thought she'd seen him emptying bins in Oxton. Her voice stopped and started, she stuttered a little. Suzy wasn't sure he believed they were talking about the man who'd attacked his wife in a Liverpool tram and then killed his neighbour. His dark eyes were forbidding.

Then the sergeant made her go through it all again while a constable wrote down what she said. To Suzy, it seemed to go on for ever.

'Read it through,' the constable told her, 'and sign it if you agree with what I've written.'

Mam signed it and at last they were free to go.

'Thank you,' the sergeant said. 'If this man is Luke Palmer, the Corporation will have his name on their list.'

'Perhaps a different name,' Suzy suggested. Surely they wouldn't have employed a man of that name without asking questions?

'They'll know who emptied the bins in that area on Monday.'

Suzy was relieved it was over. Mam was oozing relief at every pore. She seemed to be thinking more clearly already. Just talking about Nosey had got some of the paralysing fear out of her system, and she might just have put the police on his track.

'We're over the worst,' Suzy told her. 'We've done all we can.'

When they turned into Hamilton Square again, Harold and the car had gone. Suzy led the way to the bus stop.

Colonel Ingram looked across the tea table to where his wife was cutting the celebration cake. It was their fifty-fifth wedding anniversary. Alma gave him the special smile she always kept for him.

'Josie's made a splendid cake.' It was iced all over and had 'Happy Anniversary' written across it.

'Where did all those years go?'

They seemed to flash past more quickly than they'd ever done when they were young. It seemed only yesterday that Alma had walked up the aisle towards him in her wedding gown, a young and pretty girl.

'Let me help you, Mother.'

Now, even Hebe's flesh was sagging and her hair was more grey than fair. She was making something of an occasion of this anniversary, inviting all the family to tea and dinner.

Georgina had come up from London and was staying with Christobel for a few days while her husband was away on business. She was in her prime, her blonde tresses bobbed and permed or whatever girls did with their hair these days. Very stylishly dressed too.

Penelope, Hebe's eldest, was most like Alma, but she was beginning to look a little matronly now. She'd kept her hair long. The girls all had beautiful hair – such a pity to cut it short and have it crimped into waves. Penny wore hers drawn back into what Louise had told him was a French pleat, and very sophisticated. It was probably her glasses that made her look older, because she was not much over thirty. She'd brought her two toddlers with her and a noisy pair they were. Fortunately, she'd also brought their nursemaid, who would take them out of Alma's way when she showed signs of tiring. Alma loved her great-grandchildren, but the very young could be wearing.

'Cake for you, Gramps?' Hebe had cut it into neat slices and her daughters were passing them round the table.

'Absolutely gorgeous.' Louise had cream round her lips. 'I love this raspberry jelly stuff in it.'

Theo knew Alma was enjoying all the fuss and having the children round her. She took a nap after her lunch these days, and the family had known not to arrive much before four o'clock.

Georgina and Christobel had arrived earlier and had come to his study. Brutus had made a great fuss of Gina and licked her all over.

She'd said: 'After tea, we'll do our special walk, Gramps.'

'It's too far for me these days,' he admitted. 'Brutus and I walk down to Birkenhead Park Station every morning to get the newspaper.' That was far enough for him.

'I'll drive you to Vyner Road North. Not too far from there.'

Georgina had apparently driven herself up from London in her Ford. He thought that very brave of her. He didn't like her open sports car, which looked much the same as Christobel's. Silly cars, really.

They wanted to take Brutus too. He sat in the dickey with Christobel and it all seemed a bit of a squash. Like Christobel, Gina drove too fast, and Theo felt too close to the road.

At one time, he and Gina used to walk Brutus up here regularly. It was magnificent up on Bidston Hill and they always enjoyed it. The rain clouds of the morning had cleared. It was a pleasant afternoon and clear enough to see right to the mouth of the Mersey and most of Liverpool set out on the opposite bank.

They walked past the windmill to Bidston Observatory and back. With the breeze on his face and a granddaughter supporting each arm, their girlish chatter made him feel quite in his prime again.

When they returned home, Penny told them that Harold had taken the nanny and the babies home and Simon, Penny's husband, had rung to say he'd felt unwell in the office. He'd gone home early and wanted to go straight to bed. He was sorry but he wouldn't be coming for dinner.

Hebe provided champagne to drink before the meal. Theo wasn't fond of it himself but Alma and the girls liked it. Fifty-five years really was something to celebrate. He was looking forward to the goose; the walk had sharpened his appetite.

It was cooked to a turn, absolutely delectable, two sorts of stuffing just as he liked it. Alma sang the praises of the sherry trifle.

'Our compliments to the cook,' Theo said to Gertrude. 'She's a lot better than the last one, isn't she?' he beamed round the table.

When they went back to the drawing room for their coffee, Gina started strumming on Hebe's piano and Christobel and Louise sang at the tops of their voices. He was really too old to appreciate all that jazz stuff and he knew Alma was relieved too when their mother, who couldn't stand anyone else playing her piano, pushed Gina aside.

Hebe gave them Shostakovich's Romance from *The Gadfly*, which was one of Alma's favourites. She was a very pretty pianist and it brought back some tranquillity. She'd just started on the Moonlight Sonata when Brutus started barking outside. It was hard to appreciate Beethoven with the dog booming on and on, deep and throaty, louder than a foghorn. It put Alma on edge.

Hebe had banned him from the drawing and dining rooms. When the gong had sounded for dinner, Theo had put him out and fed him by his kennel as usual.

Louise said: 'Something's disturbed him.'

Hebe stopped playing. 'I hope it isn't that trespasser again.' They were all listening.

'Let's go and see.' Gina and Christobel raced to the kitchen, Theo and his other two granddaughters following more slowly. They all moved to look through the scullery window because the maids were at the table eating their supper.

It was dark now but Brutus could be seen barking his head off and racing up and down the flagged path to jump up at the door in the wall. It was closed.

'There's somebody in the grounds,' Louise shivered.

'He sounds like the hound from hell,' Christobel giggled. 'Shall I open the door? He'll chase whoever it is away.'

She'd gone with her two older sisters before Theo had time to decide one way or the other. They saw Brutus bound through and go barking off into the garden. Beside him, Louise whispered: 'There is somebody there.'

Edna was behind them, a half-eaten piece of celebration cake in her hand. 'I bet it's that man spying on us again. Do you think he's going to break in and steal the silver?'

Theo felt a twinge of unease. He was the only man in a house full of women. 'I suppose Harold's gone home?'

'Yes.' Edna's mouth was full. 'He went before six.'

Theo turned back to the window. The dog came back to the door still barking, as though inviting the girls to follow him. He looked a fearsome beast but really he was a fool of a dog. He wouldn't hurt anybody.

Theo marched purposefully to his study and surveyed his firearms hanging on the chimney breast. A shotgun or his trusty rifle? A shotgun should be adequate. He took the better one down and found some cartridges in his desk drawer. He pushed a few spares in his pocket and was loading it when Hebe came to the door.

'I'm going to ring the police. They should be here keeping watch. Why do they think we complained about intruders?'

In the hall, Theo put on his hat and coat and found a torch.

'I'll see him off,' he said. He'd repelled attacks by Indian tribesmen and by Boers in his time. He could deal with a single intruder.

'No, Father.' Hebe held the telephone away from her face. 'Don't go out there by yourself. It's dark, you'll trip and fall.'

He ignored that and let himself out through the front door, slamming it shut behind him. He couldn't see a thing after the electric lights inside, but he knew his way round the house blindfold. He'd bought it as a home for Alma when they'd first married. No need to put on the torch to advertise his presence. If the fellow was still here, he was going to get him.

He walked down to the front gates. He'd told Harold to shut them both before he went home, but they wouldn't keep anybody out. They were easy enough to open or even climb over. The dog was silent now but the girls were calling to each other round the back somewhere. He headed in that direction.

Theo felt the shiver of anticipation as he'd used to feel before a battle. The blood was coursing through his veins and he felt young again. He'd never felt better. His eyes were getting used to the gloom. Gina and another were scampering noisily towards him. Yes, it was Christobel with her, he'd know her giggle anywhere.

'We're going indoors, Gramps,' Gina said. 'This is a waste of time.'

'It's cold now.'

'We should have put our coats on.'

He said: 'You're making too much noise. Any trespasser would just move away from you and keep out of sight. You have to be silent and listen for him.'

'He won't be able to get into the house to steal anything,' Penny laughed. 'Not tonight, there's too many of us here.'

'But you'll all be going home soon.'

There'd be only Hebe and Louise left with Alma and himself, and they'd all be going to bed. Any burglar with his wits about him would lie low for an hour or so and break in later on. 'All of you go in . . .'

'Penny's already on her way.'

'I'll take a quiet look round by myself. Nobody has any business to be here. This is private property.'

He headed on towards the garages, keeping to the verge of the drive, so that his footsteps didn't crunch on the gravel and he was in the shadow of the bushes. All was silent now.

He stopped. Something was lolloping towards him. It was Brutus and another slighter figure was catching up with the dog. It was Louise. The only one with the sense to keep quiet. He heard a click. She was bending to put a lead on Brutus's collar.

Suddenly, he saw another, heavier figure step out from the blackness round the garages and grab at Louise.

Theo had been carrying his gun with the barrel pointing forward and towards the ground. He raised it slowly, pushing the safety catch off.

He distinctly heard the intruder hiss: 'Got you this time, Suzy. You won't get away so easily again.'

Louise gave a little scream of surprise and the man's arm thumped down against her shoulder. She was struggling frantically to free herself and yelling: 'Who are you? What d'you want?'

Brutus growled, a ferocious rumbling growl. Theo saw the man jump back, startled.

Theo tucked the stock into the hollow between his collar and shoulder bones and, with his cheek pressed firmly along the comb of the stock, his right eye was in perfect alignment with the rib of the gun.

The dog was bounding towards him instead of going for the prowler. Louise, free and shrieking with terror now, followed as best she could. He waited a second until she'd almost reached him.

When Theo fired, the heavier figure was scrambling back into the shelter of the garage. The colonel discharged the left-hand barrel too for good measure. The rebound was greater than he remembered and it sent him a little off balance.

Chapter Twenty-Three

Brutus was barking and leaping round. Louise went on screaming, her terror and agitation going through Theo, making him shake. He tossed his gun into the shrubbery, ignoring all safety rules for firearms, and felt for his grand-daughter.

'Lou? What did he do to you?'

She was shaking too; her slight frame felt fragile and vulnerable. He put his arms round her, pulling her closer. He shouldn't have let this happen.

'Has he hurt you?'

'I didn't see him, until . . . He came at me and grabbed me.' Her teeth were chattering. 'He wrenched my arm and punched my shoulder.' Louise was sobbing. 'He called me Suzy.'

'Come on, let's get you indoors and see what damage he's caused.'

But within seconds he and Louise were surrounded by the family, who came rushing out to see what had happened. The maids came too, and everybody was talking at once.

Theo said into the clamour: 'Ring the police, Hebe.'

'I already have. You were there when I did it, you silly man. What have you done?'

'I've shot the prowler.'

'Shot him! Good God! Father, you've no business . . .' She peered into the darkness. 'Where is he?'

'Take care of your daughter, Hebe. I'm going to see if I can find him. I think he's behind the garage.'

'Father, no. Wait till the police get here. It isn't safe . . .'

'He attacked me, Mummy. Gramps saved me.'

'Louise? You ought not to have been out here on your own. It wasn't safe to go. Christobel, you shouldn't have left her.'

'I didn't know you'd come, Lou.'

'I was with Brutus.'

Brutus's stentorian bark continued.

'I wish you'd shut that damn dog up,' Hebe said irritably. 'He nearly knocked me over, rushing about like that.'

'He's excited.'

'Christobel, take him back to his kennel and chain him up,' her mother commanded. 'And close the garden door.'

Theo had the torch out of his pocket. The thin sliver of light picked up the empty drive ahead. Everybody was ignoring Hebe's commands. They were following him.

He heard a moan from the shadows around the garage and breathed a sigh of relief. He hadn't killed the fellow.

'Help me, help me,' grunted the dark mound lying half under a bush.

Theo shone the torch straight into his face. It was heavily bearded and contorting with pain. He'd never seen the man before. The cook was pressing forward to see him too. She let out a little cry and a gasp of distress.

Theo asked: 'D'you recognise him, Josephine?' But she'd melted back into the darkness.

Headlights of a car could be seen at the gate to the drive. Edna was running down to open it.

'Thank goodness! That'll be the police.'

'We'll leave this fellow to them. Come on, let's go inside.'

Josie was crying with relief to see Luke Palmer being stretchered into the ambulance. She hung back, scared to go too close; just near enough to make sure it was him. It was

definitely Luke Palmer, and he was in police custody at last!
She needn't fear him ever again.

'It's all right. They've got him now.' Suzy's hand gripped
her wrist and her shoulder was comfortingly close. They
turned and went slowly back to the house together. That was
wonderful, totally uplifting, but . . .

The unthinkable had happened: the household was in
turmoil and it was on account of her.

One of the policemen was herding them all into the
drawing room, saying: 'Please wait in here. You'll be inter-
viewed one at a time.'

Josie went reluctantly. How could she possibly feel at ease
in such a fine room with Mrs Smallwood's grand piano taking
up a third of the space? Gertie and Edna had been pushed in
too. The family were settling themselves into comfortable
chairs; the staff stood apart, in a line with their backs to the
wall.

'Good job we went to the police station this afternoon,'
Suzy whispered. Josie felt for her arm. She needed comfort.

Louise was distressed. Her mother was peeling off her
coat, inspecting her wounds. 'Up to bed, dear. That's the best
for you.'

'No, Mother, I'm all right. It was just the shock of . . .
Suzy?'

Josie felt her pull away. 'I'm here.'

'He thought I was you! He called me Suzy. He knows
you!'

Josie felt numb as she listened first to Suzy trying to soothe
Louise, and then to Mrs Smallwood, who'd swept out to the
hall to use the telephone. She was asking Dr Howarth to make
an immediate visit.

'Louise has been attacked by a prowler in our own
grounds. . . . What's that? The hospital? . . . No, definitely

not. She needs to be kept quiet, not rushed off into town. . . .
Bruises, I'm sure. Threw her to the ground, wrenched her
arm. . . . A sedative perhaps to help her sleep? She was
frightened, almost hysterical, poor girl.'

Hebe turned to her daughter. 'Up to your room, darling.
You need rest.'

'I don't want to miss this.' Louise was back in the room,
pulling Suzy to the couch.

Josie took a deep shuddering breath. She craved a cup of
tea. The colonel had shot Luke Palmer, and very soon she'd
have to admit she could identify him, and that she was the
reason he'd come to The Lawns – that he wasn't a burglar at
all. Somehow he'd found out where they were living and he'd
come to exact his revenge.

Among the police was the sergeant with the bulbous
orange-peel nose. He recognised Josie.

'Did you see the man who's been shot? Did you recognise
him?'

Her lips were clamped together in agony. She had to nod.

The colonel's voice boomed out: 'Somebody had to get
Louise out of his clutches; had to protect the ladies. I was the
only man in the house. He could have raped the lot of them.
Gave the man a dose of lead shot in his backside. No business
to be on my property.'

He marched out to his study, and Josie could hear him
pouring himself a restorative brandy.

'Alma? Will you have one? It'll settle your nerves.'

Alma declined. She'd been sitting quietly alone in the
drawing room all the time.

'I will,' Penelope said. 'I can't believe you actually shot
the fellow.'

'And me,' Christobel added.

'You girls are too young for brandy.'

424

'Shall I open another bottle of wine then?'

The colonel turned on his granddaughters. 'It's not a party, for heaven's sake!'

'Edna?' Mrs Smallwood took charge, pushing the maid past the police officer on the door. 'Make a cup of tea for everyone.'

Josie was grateful they were going to be questioned one at a time and she wouldn't have to admit what Luke Palmer had been to her in front of Mrs Smallwood. But she was asking questions of the police, and had already got the gist of what had taken place and why.

'Luke Palmer? Wasn't he that murderer?'

'Yes, we've been looking for him for the last two years.'

'A dangerous man like that! Was he hiding in our grounds? What made him choose our house?'

Josie closed her eyes as it was explained to the whole room. She could feel herself swaying. She leaned back against the wall to steady herself.

Hebe was indignant. 'You mean all this trouble has been brought on us because of our cook? Josephine! It's your fault! All this worry over Louise, and Father going round shooting people?'

She whispered: 'I'm sorry, Mrs Smallwood.'

'It's given me the most dreadful headache. Pack your things, and you too, Suzy. I want you both out of here tonight.'

'No!' Louise squealed and clung to Suzy. 'I want her to stay. She can't go.'

'Hold on a minute, Hebe.' The colonel was looking straight at Josie. 'Don't let's be hasty. We've never had anybody who could make a decent curry before.'

The sergeant held up his hand. 'Nobody is to leave until we've finished taking statements. We'll see you one at a time.'

Josie was ready to faint when Gertie pressed a cup of tea into her hands.

'Tell us about that man. What happened? I don't understand how you came to be mixed up in this.'

Since Edna too was waiting open-mouthed and all the others were gathering round her, Josie started telling how she'd first met Luke Palmer when he persuaded her husband to help prevent strike-breaking in the General Strike. Even Mrs Smallwood gasped when she told how her husband, Ted, had been killed; how Luke Palmer had wormed his way into her home and bigamously married her; how he'd battened on her and abused both her and Suzy until she'd had to leave her home and her job to escape from his clutches.

'How exciting!' Edna's eyes were shining.

'It was awful,' Suzy told her. 'Not exciting at all.'

'You are brave,' Gertie told her. 'And you never said a word to us all this time. You just got on with your work here.'

They sat round talking about every aspect of the affair, while one by one, they were summoned to the study to tell their own stories to the police. Josie was asked again if she was sure the man was Luke Palmer. Suzy whispered that she'd been asked the same thing.

At last, the sergeant with the orange-peel nose came and told them he'd finished with them.

'We are much indebted to your cook, who came forward with valuable information. As a result of what Mrs Lunt told us, we were watching Luke Palmer's lodgings and would have arrested him when he went back there. I'm very pleased to say that the Birkenhead police have succeeded in arresting a dangerous criminal who has been evading the Liverpool police for two years.'

Josie felt as though a great weight was being lifted off her shoulders as she listened. The police sergeant no longer looked forbidding.

He went on: 'I'd also like to thank Colonel Ingram, who did a very brave thing in protecting his granddaughter and preventing another tragedy. He is to be congratulated.'

Christobel saw the police out and came back to say: 'I'm going home, Mother. Good night, everyone.'

'Hang on,' Penny said. 'I'm coming with you.'

The colonel got slowly to his feet and yawned. 'It's after midnight. I think we should all go to bed. We can talk about this again tomorrow.'

His eye came to rest on Josie. 'I do hope you and Suzy will stay on here,' he said. 'I doubt if either Louise or I could manage without you.'

Over the following days the newspapers were full of the story. Because Luke Palmer had at last been captured, it made the headlines again. He was transferred to a prison hospital after having 141 pellets of lead shot removed.

Reporters tried to speak to Josie and the colonel, but without success. Josie opened the papers in trepidation each morning and squirmed as she found something of her story on the printed page.

'They're full of sympathy for you and Suzy,' Gertie assured her. 'And they say Luke Palmer battened on you, so that he could share your comfortable home.'

'They praise you for going to the police and telling them you'd seen him,' Edna said. 'You and Suzy coped marvellously, really you did. You've nothing to be ashamed of.'

'It's put me off men for life,' Josie said. 'I'm having nothing to do with men ever again. Marriage is a lucky dip. You never know what you're getting, not until it's too late.'

The newspapers treated the elderly colonel as a hero,

congratulating him for preventing another tragedy.

Josie felt she was coming back to life. She really had been afraid that one day she'd meet the same fate as Eric Rimmer. She no longer need worry about Suzy's safety, and the sickening dread in the pit of her stomach had gone at last.

She went down to see Olga the day after Luke's capture, but she'd already read the news. They sat round Maisie's fire, drinking tea and talking nonstop. They'd both been desperate to see Luke Palmer caught. It was such sweet relief to know it had happened at last. It forged another bond between them.

They arranged to meet again at the baths on the following Sunday because Frankie would be on duty there, and they expected Suzy and Louise to go.

The weather turned out wet and chilly. Olga and Josie had a quick dip and were in the cafeteria drinking tea when Christobel came in to check the stock. She invited them to her house to see Suzy.

'Lou and Suzy are going to stay with me. It's all agreed with Mother and Gramps. Their tutor will come to my place from now on. Gramps thinks it will be better for both of us. Mother isn't going to change; she's always going to fuss over Lou, and if she lived at home there'd be no escape for her. She'll have a more normal life with me, and, goodness knows, I need her.

'I'll tell Frankie he can leave early and come with us. There were so few people wanting to swim today that one person on life-saving duty will be enough.'

They spent the rest of the afternoon in Christobel's conservatory, drinking tea.

Frankie said: 'I didn't think old Nosey would come back and have another go at me, but I was afraid for Suzy and Josie. I'm glad it's all over and he's going to get his comeuppance.'

But in the following weeks they all found it was anything but over. Luke Palmer was charged with murder and two counts of grievous bodily harm. Josie spent long sessions in the witness box. Also, Suzy, Frankie and Olga, Mr Maynard and Colonel Ingram were asked to take the witness stand for the prosecution. The case dragged on and the papers were full of it yet again.

Josie felt a bag of nerves and everybody was wound up. Yet it horrified them all when Luke was found guilty and given the death sentence.

Olga had been in court day after day to hear most of the case.

'It's what he deserves,' she said, her lips in a straight line. 'I wanted this for Eric's sake. I hated to think Luke was getting off scot-free. Justice has been done, but it's turned my stomach.'

Epilogue

1936

Suzy, her hand on her new husband's wrist, helped to lever the knife into the wedding cake Mam had made for them. Frankie smiled down at her, his face lighting up with pleasure and happiness. She felt moved almost to tears. Their wedding was the culmination of all her hopes and many years of a friendship that had turned to love. Everything had come right for her and Frankie.

Christobel said from across the table: 'Both of you, hold that for a moment.' Suzy smiled for her Leica and two Box Brownies.

'Right.' Mam was at Frankie's elbow. 'Tradition has been observed. I'll cut the cake into slices for you.'

The reception was being held in the house in Rock Park that had once belonged to Christobel. She'd married again three years ago and now had a baby daughter of her own. Her husband worked in Chester.

'He thinks Rock Park is too far away from his office to travel in daily,' she'd told Louise, 'and he's not keen on coming to live in a house that belonged to my first husband.'

'I love it,' Louise had sighed, looking round. 'I don't want to move. But anyway, I don't suppose you'd want me and Suzy living with you?'

Chrissie had laughed. 'Not to start with; not with a new husband, not now you're grown up. It was different when you were young and had a gammy leg. Alec felt sorry for

431

you. He thought we should help if we could.'

'He did help. You both did. I don't want to go back to live with Mummy. I need a bolt hole, something of my own.'

'You and Suzy can stay here. Lou ... I've just had a thought. D'you want to buy this house off me? I'd give you a good price and you're earning a bit of money now.'

Louise pondered for a moment. 'And there's what Daddy left me . . . Yes, that's the answer. I'd love to buy it, Chrissie.'

Suzy and Frankie had planned to hold their wedding reception in the house that had once belonged to Auntie Maisie in Rock Ferry. She'd died peacefully five years ago and Olga had inherited her house. She'd asked Josie to share it with her shortly afterwards. Now, although Josie was still working at The Lawns, she lived out.

Suzy had wanted the reception held there because she was afraid her mother wouldn't be able to relax anywhere else, not in Mrs Smallwood's company. Louise had drawn both her and Frankie into her circle of sisters, and they spent time in their company. Suzy and Frankie wanted to invite them and their families to their wedding.

'Your mother's house is too small,' Louise had said to Frankie.

'Much too small,' Christobel had agreed. 'Besides, if you're inviting Mother . . .'

Suzy said: 'We did plan to.'

Josie had insisted an invitation was necessary but said she wasn't expecting her to accept.

'Then far better to have the reception here,' Louise insisted. 'More room for everybody.'

These days, Louise was walking smoothly, with no noticeable limp. She was now writing her tenth children's book. Seven were already in print. The first four had been written with Frankie as co-author, but some three years ago they'd split up. It had been by mutual agreement. Both felt they'd learned a great deal from the other but in future they wanted to be free to write different things.

Louise had said: 'I've found my niche. I love writing children's books but one day I might try my hand at writing for women.'

All three of her sisters were trying to improve her social life. They were inviting her to stay with them; inviting her out to theatres and dinners and introducing her to eligible young men. But Louise laughed at them and said she was happiest when she was at home at her desk, writing.

Louise counted Suzy and Frankie as her closest friends and was thrilled when Frankie had started to produce adult fiction and had found a publisher for it. Suzy thought his books were still bordering on fantasy, but it was of a very different sort. He was writing what she called *Boys' Own* stuff: tales of high adventure taking place on trains and planes in distant parts of the world. Frankie's second book had been published last month. Suzy had been doing a lot of typing for both writers.

Edna was refilling glasses with the champagne that Christobel had insisted on providing. Edna had come here today in her black dress and frilly cap and apron, to help wait on table. She'd left The Lawns to marry Fred and had two children now. She was living a short bus ride away and Josie popped in for a chat and a cup of tea from time to time. Occasionally, when there were guests at The Lawns, Edna went back to help. Gertie had retired and gone to live with her sister in Southport.

Mrs Smallwood had found it impossible to replace them and it had meant big changes. Josie now cooked lunch and dinner and took the food to the dining room where the family helped themselves. They had to get their own breakfasts too.

Two charwomen were employed to clean, and they came on alternate mornings. The laundry was sent out. Josie was very satisfied with her present life.

She arrived at The Lawns at mid-morning, in time to cook lunch, and left as soon as she'd put dinner on the table. She felt this gave her great freedom and that she had a life of her own. She still enjoyed cooking curries for the colonel, but Mrs Smallwood no longer wielded the same power over her.

With hindsight, Josie knew she'd made two bad mistakes in her life: becoming involved with Luke Palmer, and giving her baby Robert up for adoption. Both had seemed to be right at the time but she would always regret them. There was no way she could right them; what she'd done could not be undone, she had to accept them. It was some comfort that Mrs Smallwood had also been taken in by Nurse Silk and the Reverend Haydn Ingleby-Jones. She thought others might have been taken in by Luke Palmer too.

The cake distributed, Josie turned to help Edna open more champagne. All she'd ever wanted was for Suzy to be happy. In her smart blue suit, cut in the very latest fluid style, she was a beautiful bride, and looked as though she couldn't be happier. Today, she was wearing her long brown hair twisted into a sophisticated chignon, but usually she wore it loose about her shoulders. She and Frankie had always gravitated together. Josie caught Olga's eye, and knew her friend approved wholeheartedly of this wedding too. It was another bond between them.

After the loss of her son, Josie had been determined to hang on to Suzy, but time had shown her that nobody could hold on to their children for ever. They grew up and wanted lives of their own, and it was only right that they should have them. She and Suzy had always been good friends and she hoped the separation wouldn't alter that.

With all the glasses refilled, the colonel stood up.

'Every happiness to Suzy and Frankie,' he boomed, from the bottom of the table, encouraging the guests to raise their glasses. 'Health and happiness to the bride and groom.'

To Suzy, the colonel didn't seem to grow any older. He still held himself erect with military bearing. Alma was a little quieter and a little more bent.

Following the revelations in the *Liverpool Mercury*, St Buddolph's church and vicarage had been abandoned. The police were said to be looking for the Reverend Haydn Ingleby-Jones and his sister following the disappearance of the money in the church building fund. It was rumoured they'd fled to France.

Mrs Smallwood had not been much changed by her disappointment though she no longer attended any church.

Her father had said: 'You were always a silly woman, Hebe; never able to judge a man's worth. You're still full of damn fool ideas and still convinced you're always right.'

These days, Hebe was more concerned with family matters and made regular visits to her daughters' homes. Suzy had worked out that she spent more time with Louise and her than with the other sisters, though the others had time to entertain her, while Louise wanted to spend her time writing.

'Louise needs me,' Hebe told her father. 'Poor child, she's on her own.'

Hebe had decided she must oversee this reception since it was being held in Louise's home. She couldn't forgo an opportunity to organise something. 'To save Louise the time and trouble,' she said.

But Josie and Olga had done all the cooking and baking between them, and had found her interference quite difficult to cope with. Olga had been determined to arrange things as

Suzy and Frankie wanted them, and they'd managed not to upset Hebe too much.

'It's time we went,' Frankie whispered in Suzy's ear. They were catching the four twenty-three train to London, and Harold was to drive them to Woodside Station in the colonel's limousine.

Suzy raced upstairs to the bedroom that had been hers for the last three years. Her suitcase was open on the bed. She closed the lid and clicked the clasps. She meant to travel in the blue suit in which she'd been married. Frankie had brought his case round this morning and it was waiting in the hall. Everybody crowded out into the front garden to see them off.

'Good luck.'

'All the best.'

'Hope you'll be happy.'

'The world's your oyster,' Mam breathed as she kissed Suzy goodbye. 'Have a good time.'

'We will.' Suzy waved as the car moved slowly out into the road.

Frankie sank back into the seat and sighed with satisfaction. 'Years ago we promised ourselves this.'

'When we were ten,' Suzy nodded. 'You said you'd take me to London to see Buckingham Palace when we were grown up.'

'We'll do better than that,' Frankie grinned down at her. 'We're going to start married life by seeing something of the world. Better to do that before we settle down in a home of our own.'

With a flourish, Frankie drew a wad of tickets from his pocket. 'After we've had a couple of weeks in London, we're going by ship from Tilbury to see South Africa.'

'Frankie!' Suzy threw her arms round him in a delighted hug. 'That sounds marvellous!'

'And after that, we'll go on to Australia.'

She giggled. 'This isn't another of your daydreams?'

'No, I promise you,' he laughed. 'Daydreams are a thing of the past. This time we're really going.'

Suzy was tingling with anticipation and joy as his arms tightened round her.

A Glimpse of the Mersey

Anne Baker

Daisy Corkill has spent all her life living above Sampsons – the local fishmongers and greengrocers in Market Street. But she's never discovered who her parents were – nor why they left her to be brought up by the couple she now calls 'Uncle' Ern and 'Auntie' Glad. Daisy yearns for a family of her own, despite the close relationship she has with Brenda, her very beautiful, older 'sister'.

It's Brenda, however, who, in 1919, gets married first – to local businessman Gil Fox. But Gil is not quite the man he appears to be. While happiness continues to elude Brenda, Daisy hopes her dreams are about to come true. Ellis – Gil's upright, kind and dependable brother, a survivor of WWI – falls in love with her. Will marriage, and a family of her own, really give her true happiness? And are they enough to get her through some stormy times ahead?

Don't miss Anne Baker's previous Merseyside sagas, also published by Headline:

'A heartwarming saga' *Woman's Weekly*

'A stirring tale of romance and passion, poverty and ambition' *Liverpool Echo*

'Truly compelling . . . rich in language and descriptive prose' *Newcastle Upon Tyne Evening Chronicle*

0 7472 6777 4

headline

A Mersey Duet

Anne Baker

When Elsa Gripper dies in childbirth on Christmas Eve, 1912, her grief-stricken husband is unable to cope with his two newborn daughters, Lucy and Patsy, so the twins are separated.

Elsa's parents, who run a highly successful business, Mersey Antiques, take Lucy home and she grows up spoiled and pampered with no interest in the family firm. Patsy has a more down-to-earth upbringing, living with their father and other grandmother above the Railway Hotel. And through further tragedy she learns to be responsible from an early age. Then Patsy is invited to work at Mersey Antiques, which she hopes will bring her closer to Lucy. But it is to take a series of dramatic events before they are drawn together . . .

'A stirring tale of romance and passion, poverty and ambition . . . everything from seduction to murder, from forbidden love to revenge' *Liverpool Echo*

'Highly observant writing style . . . a compelling book that you just don't want to put down' *Southport Visitor*

0 7472 5320 X

headline

Merseyside Girls

Anne Baker

Nancy, Amy and Katie Siddons are three of the prettiest nurses south of the Mersey. They've been brought up to respect their elders and uphold family honour at all times. Then sweet, naïve Katie falls pregnant, bringing shame upon the family's name.

Alec Siddons, a local police constable, cannot and will not forgive his daughter for her immoral behaviour. But Katie isn't the only one with troubles ahead. Amy is in love with her cousin Paul, but owing to a family feud the mere mention of his name is forbidden in her father's presence; and Nancy is eager to wed her fiancé Stan before the Second World War takes him away.

With the outbreak of war, the three sisters offer each other comfort and support. Their mother, meanwhile, is battling with painful memories of the past, and their father lives in dread that his own dark secrets will be revealed. As the war takes its toll on the Merseyside girls they learn that few things in life are more precious than honesty, love and forgiveness.

0 7472 5040 5

headline

Now you can buy any of these other bestselling
books by **Anne Baker** from your bookshop
or *direct from her publisher*.

FREE P&P AND UK DELIVERY
(Overseas and Ireland £3.50 per book)

Nobody's Child	£5.99
Legacy of Sins	£5.99
Liverpool Lies	£5.99
The Price of Love	£5.99
With a Little Luck	£5.99
A Liverpool Lullaby	£6.99
Mersey Maids	£5.99
A Mersey Duet	£6.99
Moonlight on the Mersey	£6.99
Merseyside Girls	£5.99
Paradise Parade	£5.99
Like Father Like Daughter	£5.99

TO ORDER SIMPLY CALL THIS NUMBER

01235 400 414

or e-mail <u>orders@bookpoint.co.uk</u>

Prices and availability subject to change without notice.